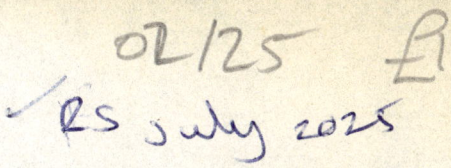

Anthony Hope (Sir Anthony Hope Hawkins) was born in London and educated at Marlborough and at Balliol College, Oxford. He became a lawyer in 1887, and dabbled in Liberal politics, but the immediate success of *The Prisoner of Zenda* (1894), his fourth work, turned him entirely to writing. This work and its sequel, *Rupert of Hentzau* (1898), describe the perilous adventures of the Englishman Rudolf Rassendyll in the mythical kingdom of Ruritania. The adventure, intrigue and romance of these novels are typical of the literature popular before World War I. Anthony Hope successfully published many other novels and plays. He was knighted in 1918 for his services in the British Ministry of Information during World War I. He died in 1933.

BY THE SAME AUTHOR
ALL PUBLISHED BY HOUSE OF STRATUS

HELENA'S PATH
THE PRISONER OF ZENDA
RUPERT OF HENTZAU
SIMON DALE
SOPHY OF KRAVONIA

Anthony Hope

Phroso

First published in 1899

Copyright by John Hope-Hawkins

All rights reserved. No part of this publication may be reproduced, stored in a retrieval system, or transmitted, in any form, or by any means (electronic, mechanical, photocopying, recording, or otherwise), without the prior permission of the publisher. Any person who does any unauthorised act in relation to this publication may be liable to criminal prosecution and civil claims for damages.

The right of Anthony Hope to be identified as the author of this work has been asserted.

This edition published in 2002 by House of Stratus, an imprint of House of Stratus Ltd, Thirsk Industrial Park, York Road, Thirsk, North Yorkshire, YO7 3BX, UK.
Also at: House of Stratus Inc., 2 Neptune Road, Poughkeepsie, NY 12601, USA.

www.houseofstratus.com

Typeset, printed and bound by House of Stratus.

A catalogue record for this book is available from the British Library and the Library of Congress.

ISBN 0-7551-0708-X

This book is sold subject to the condition that it shall not be lent, resold, hired out, or otherwise circulated without the publisher's express prior consent in any form of binding, or cover, other than the original as herein published and without a similar condition being imposed on any subsequent purchaser, or bona fide possessor.

This is a fictional work and all characters are drawn from the author's imagination. Any resemblance or similarities to persons either living or dead are entirely coincidental.

Contents

1	A Long Thing Ending in *'Poulos'*	1
2	A Conservative Country	13
3	The Fever of Neopalia	27
4	A Raid and a Raider	39
5	The Cottage on the Hill	51
6	The Poem of One-eyed Alexander	63
7	The Secret of the Stefanopouloi	76
8	A Knife at a Rope	88
9	Hats off to St Tryphon!	100
10	The Justice of the Island	114
11	The Last Card	127
12	Law and Order	139
13	The Smiles of Mouraki Pasha	152
14	A Stroke in the Game	166
15	A Strange Escape	179
16	An Unfinished Letter	192
17	In the Jaws of the Trap	206
18	The Unknown Friend	220
19	The Armenian Dog!	231
20	A Public Promise	244
21	A Word of Various Meanings	257
22	One More Run	271
23	The Island in a Calm	284

1

A Long Thing Ending in 'Poulos'

'*Quot homines tot sententiae;*' so many men, so many fancies. My fancy was for an island. Perhaps boyhood's glamour hung yet round sea-girt rocks, and 'faery lands forlorn,' still beckoned me; perhaps I felt that London was too full, the Highlands rather fuller, the Swiss mountains most insufferably crowded of them all. Money can buy company, and it can buy retirement. The latter service I asked now of the moderate wealth with which my poor cousin Tom's death had endowed me. Everybody was good enough to suppose that I rejoiced at Tom's death, whereas I was particularly sorry for it, and was not consoled even by the prospect of the island. My friends understood this wish for an island as little as they appreciated my feelings about poor Tom. Beatrice was most emphatic in declaring that 'a horrid little island' had no charms for her, and that she would never set foot in it. This declaration was rather annoying, because I had imagined myself spending my honeymoon with Beatrice on the island; but life is not all honeymoon, and I decided to have the island nonetheless. Besides I was not to be married for a year. Mrs Kennett Hipgrave had insisted on this delay in order that we might be sure that we knew our own hearts. And as I may say without unfairness that Mrs Hipgrave was to a considerable degree responsible for the engagement – she asserted the fact herself with much pride – I thought that she had a right to some voice in the date of the marriage. Moreover the postponement just gave me the time to go over and settle affairs in the island.

For I had bought it. It cost me seven thousand five hundred and fifty pounds, rather a fancy price but I could not haggle with the old lord – half to be paid to the lord's bankers in London, and the second half to him in Neopalia, when he delivered possession to me. The Turkish Government had sanctioned the sale, and I had agreed to pay a hundred pounds yearly as tribute. This sum I was entitled, in my turn, to levy on the inhabitants.

'In fact, my dear lord,' said old Mason to me when I called on him in Lincoln's Inn Fields, 'the whole affair is settled. I congratulate you on having got just what was your whim. You are over a hundred miles from the nearest land – Rhodes, you see.' (He laid a map before me.) 'You are off the steamship tracks; the Austrian Lloyds to Alexandria leave you far to the north-east. You are equally remote from any submarine cable; here on the south-west, from Alexandria to Candia, is the nearest. You will have to fetch your letters.'

'I shouldn't think of doing such a thing,' said I indignantly.

'Then you'll only get them once in three months. Neopalia is extremely rugged and picturesque. It is nine miles long and five broad. It grows cotton, wine, oil and a little corn. The people are quite unsophisticated, but very good hearted.'

'And,' said I, 'there are only three hundred and seventy of them, all told. I really think I shall do very well there.'

'I've no doubt you will. By the way, treat the old gentleman kindly. He's terribly cut up at having to sell. "My dear island," he writes, "is second to my dead son's honour, and to nothing else." His son, you know, Lord Wheatley, was a bad lot, a very bad lot indeed.'

'He left a heap of unpaid debts, didn't he?'

'Yes, gambling debts. He spent his time knocking about Paris and London with his cousin Constantine – by no means an improving companion, if report speaks truly. And your money is to pay the debts, you know.'

'Poor old chap,' said I. I sympathised with him in the loss of his island.

'Here's the house, you see,' said Mason, turning to the map and dismissing the sorrows of the old lord of Neopalia. 'About the middle of the island, nearly a thousand feet above the sea. I'm afraid it's a tumble-down old place, and will swallow a lot of money without looking much better for the dose. To put it into repair for the reception of the future Lady Wheatley would cost – '

'The future Lady Wheatley says she won't go there on any account,' I interrupted.

'But, my very dear lord,' cried he, aghast, 'if she won't – '

'She won't, and there's an end of it, Mr Mason. Well, good day. I'm to have possession in a month?'

'In a month to the very day – on the 7th of May.'

'All right; I shall be there to take it.'

Escaping from the legal quarter, I made my way to my sister's house in Cavendish Square.

She had a party, and I was bound to go by brotherly duty. As luck would have it, however, I was rewarded for my virtue (and if that's not luck in this huddle-muddle world I don't know what is); the Turkish Ambassador dropped in, and presently James came and took me up to him. My brother-in-law, James Cardew, is always anxious that I should know the right people. The Pasha received me with great kindness.

'You are the purchaser of Neopalia, aren't you?' he asked, after a little conversation 'The matter came before me officially.'

'I'm much obliged,' said I, 'for your ready consent to the transfer.'

'Oh, it's nothing to us. In fact our tribute, such as it is, will be safer. Well, I'm sure I hope you'll settle in comfortably.'

'Oh, I shall be all right. I know the Greeks very well, you see – been there a lot, and, of course, I talk the tongue, because I spent two years hunting antiquities in the Morea and some of the islands.'

The Pasha stroked his beard, as he observed in a calm tone:

'The last time a Stefanopoulos tried to sell Neopalia, the people killed him, and turned the purchaser – he was a Frenchman, a Baron d'Ezonville – adrift in an open boat, with nothing on but his shirt.'

'Good heavens! Was that recently?'

'No; two hundred years ago. But it's a conservative part of the world, you know.' And his Excellency smiled.

'They were described to me as good-hearted folk,' said I; 'unsophisticated, of course, but good hearted.'

'They think that the island is theirs, you see,' he explained, 'and that the lord has no business to sell it. They may be good hearted, Lord Wheatley, but they are tenacious of their rights.'

'But they can't have any rights,' I expostulated.

'None at all,' he assented. 'But a man is never so tenacious of his rights as when he hasn't any. However, *autres temps autres moeurs*; I don't suppose you'll have any trouble of that kind. Certainly I hope not, my dear lord.'

'Surely your Government will see to that?' I suggested.

His Excellency looked at me; then, although by nature a grave man, he gave a low humorous chuckle and regarded me with visible amusement.

'Oh, of course, you can rely on that, Lord Wheatley,' said he.

'That is a diplomatic assurance, your Excellency?' I ventured to suggest, with a smile.

'It is unofficial,' said he, 'but as binding as if it were official. Our Governor in that district of the empire is a very active man – yes, a decidedly active man.'

The only result of this conversation was that when I was buying my sporting guns in St James's Street the next day I purchased a couple of pairs of revolvers at the same time. It is well to be on the safe side, and, although I attached little importance to the bygone outrage of which the Ambassador spoke, I did not suppose that the police service would be very efficient. In fact I thought it prudent to be ready for any trouble that the old-world notions of the Neopalians might occasion. But in my heart I meant to be very popular with them. For I cherished the generous design of paying the whole tribute out of my own pocket, and of disestablishing in Neopalia what seems to be the only institution in no danger of such treatment here – the tax-gatherer. If they understood that intention of mine, they would hardly be so short-sighted as to set me adrift in my shirt like a second Baron d'Ezonville, or so unjust as to kill poor old Stefanopoulos as they had killed his ancestor. Besides, as I comforted myself by repeating, they were a good-hearted race; unsophisticated, of course, but thoroughly good hearted.

My cousin, young Denny Swinton, was to dine with me that evening at the Optimum. Denny (a familiar form of Dennis) was the only member of the family who sympathised thoroughly with me about Neopalia. He was wild with interest in the island, and I looked forward to telling him all I had heard about it. I knew he would listen, for he was to go with me and help me to take possession. The boy had almost wept on my neck when I asked him to come; he had just left Woolwich, and was not to join his battalion for six months; he was thus, as he put it, 'at a loose end,' and succeeded in persuading his parents that he ought to learn modern Greek. General Swinton was rather cold about the project; he said that Denny had spent ten years on ancient Greek, and knew nothing about it, and probably would not learn much of the newer sort in three months; but his wife thought it would be a nice trip for Denny. Well, it turned out to be a very nice trip for Denny; but if Mrs Swinton had known – however, if it comes to that, I might just as well exclaim, 'If I had known myself!'

Denny had taken a table next but one to the west end of the room, and was drumming his fingers impatiently on the cloth when I entered. He wanted both his dinner and the latest news about Neopalia; so I sat down and made haste to satisfy him in both respects. Travelling with equal steps through the two matters, we had reached the first entrée and the fate of the murdered Stefanopoulos (which Denny, for some reason, declared was 'a lark'), when two people came in and sat down at the table beyond ours and next to the wall, where two chairs had been tilted up in token of pre-engagement. The man – for the pair were man and woman – was tall and powerfully built; his complexion was dark, and he had good regular features; he looked also as if he had a bit of a temper somewhere about him. I was conscious of having seen him before, and suddenly recollected that by a curious chance I had run up against him twice in St James's Street that very day. The lady was handsome; she had an Italian cast of face, and moved with much grace; her manner was rather elaborate, and, when she spoke to the waiter, I detected a pronounced foreign accent. Taken together, they were a remarkable couple and presented a distinguished appearance. I believe I am not a conceited man, but I could not help wondering whether their thoughts paid me a similar compliment. For I certainly detected both of them casting more than one curious glance towards our table; and when the man whispered once to a waiter, I was sure that I formed the subject of his question; perhaps he also remembered our two encounters.

'I wonder if there's any chance of a row!' said Denny in a tone that sounded wistful. 'Going to take anybody with you, Charley?'

'Only Watkins; I must have him; he always knows where everything is; and I've told Hogvardt, my old dragoman, to meet us in Rhodes. He'll talk their own language to the beggars, you know.'

'But he's a German, isn't he?'

'He thinks so,' I answered. 'He's not certain, you know. Anyhow, he chatters Greek like a parrot. He's a pretty good man in a row, too. But there won't be a row, you know.'

'I suppose there won't,' admitted Denny ruefully.

'For my own part,' said I meekly, 'as I'm going for the sake of quiet, I hope there won't.'

In the interest of conversation I had forgotten our neighbours; but now, a lull occurring in Denny's questions and surmises, I heard the lady's voice. She began a sentence – and began it in Greek! That was a little unexpected; but it was more strange that her companion cut her short, saying very peremptorily, 'Don't talk Greek: talk Italian.' This he said in Italian, and I, though no great hand at that language, understood so much. Now why shouldn't the lady talk Greek, if Greek were the language that came naturally to her tongue? It would be as good a shield against eavesdroppers as most languages; unless indeed I, who was known to be an amateur of Greece and Greek things, were looked upon as a possible listener. Recollecting the glances which I had detected, recollecting again those chance meetings, I ventured on a covert gaze at the lady. Her handsome face expressed a mixture of anger, alarm, and entreaty. The man was speaking to her now in low urgent tones; he raised his hand once, and brought it down on the table as though to emphasise some declaration – perhaps some promise – which he was making. She regarded him with half-angry distrustful eyes. He seemed to repeat his words, and she flung at him in a tone that grew suddenly louder, and in words that I could translate:

'Enough! I'll see to that. I shall come too.'

Her heat stirred no answering fire in him. He dropped his emphatic manner, shrugged a tolerant 'As you will,' with eloquent shoulders, smiled at her, and, reaching across the table, patted her hand. She held it up before his eyes, and with the other hand pointed at a ring on her finger.

'Yes, yes, my dearest,' said he, and he was about to say more, when, glancing round, he caught my gaze retreating in hasty confusion to my plate. I dared not look up again, but I felt his scowl on me. I suppose that I deserved punishment for my eavesdropping.

'And when can we get off, Charley?' asked Denny in his clear young voice. My thoughts had wandered from him, and I paused for a moment as a man does when a question takes him unawares. There was silence at the next table also, The fancy seemed absurd, but it occurred to me that there too my answer was being waited for. Well, they could know if they liked; it was no secret,

'In a fortnight,' said I. 'We'll travel easily, and get there on the 7th of next month; – that's the day on which I'm entitled to take over my kingdom. We shall go to Rhodes. Hogvardt will have got me a little yacht, and then – goodbye to all this!' And a great longing for solitude and a natural life came over me as I looked round on the gilded cornices, the gilded mirrors, the gilded flower-vases, and the highly gilded company of the Optimum.

I was roused from my pleasant dreams by a high vivacious voice, which I knew very well. Looking up, I saw Miss Hipgrave, her mother, and young Bennett Hamlyn standing before me. I disliked young Hamlyn, but he was always very civil to me.

'Why, how early you two have dined!' cried Beatrice. 'You're at the savoury, aren't you? We've only just come.'

'Are you going to dine?' I asked, rising. 'Take this table, we're just off.'

'Well, we may as well, mayn't we?' said my fiancée. 'Sorry you're going, though. Oh, yes, we're going to dine with Mr Bennett Hamlyn. That's what you're for, isn't it, Mr Hamlyn? Why, he's not listening!'

He was not, strange to say, listening, although as a rule he listened to Beatrice with infinite attention and the most deferential of smiles. But just now he was engaged in returning a bow which our neighbour at the next table had bestowed on him. The lady there had risen already and was making for the door. The man lingered and looked at Hamlyn, seeming inclined to back up his bow with a few words of greeting. Hamlyn's air was not, however, encouraging, and the stranger contented himself with a nod and a careless 'How are you?' and, with that, followed his companion. Hamlyn turned round, conscious that he had neglected Beatrice's remark and full of penitence for his momentary rudeness.

'I beg your pardon?' said he, with an apologetic smile.

'Oh,' answered she, 'I was only saying that men like you were invented to give dinners; you're a sort of automatic feeding-machine. You ought to stand open all day. Really I often miss you at lunch time.'

'My dear Beatrice!' said Mrs Kennett Hipgrave, with that peculiar lift of her brows which meant, 'How naughty the dear child is – oh, but how clever!'

'It's all right,' said Hamlyn meekly. 'I'm awfully happy to give you a dinner anyhow, Miss Beatrice.'

Now I had nothing to say on this subject, but I thought I would just make this remark:

'Miss Hipgrave,' said I, 'is very fond of a dinner.' Beatrice laughed. She understood my little correction.

'He doesn't know any better, do you?' said she pleasantly to Hamlyn. 'We shall civilise him in time, though; then I believe he'll be nicer than you, Charley, I really do. You're – '

'I shall be uncivilised by then,' said I.

'Oh, that wretched island!' cried Beatrice. 'You're really going?'

'Most undoubtedly. By the way, Hamlyn, who's your friend?'

Surely this was an innocent enough question, but little Hamlyn went red from the edge of his clipped whisker on the right to the edge of his mathematically equal whisker on the left.

'Friend!' said he in an angry tone; 'he's not a friend of mine. I only met him on the Riviera.'

'That,' I admitted, 'does not, happily, in itself constitute a friendship.'

'And he won a hundred louis off me in the train between Cannes and Monte Carlo.'

'Not bad going that,' observed Denny in an approving tone.

'Is he then *un grec*?' asked Mrs Hipgrave, who loves a scrap of French.

'In both senses, I believe,' answered Hamlyn viciously.

'And what's his name?' said I.

'Really I don't recollect,' said Hamlyn rather petulantly.

'It doesn't matter,' observed Beatrice, attacking her oysters which had now made their appearance.

'My dear Beatrice,' I remonstrated, 'you're the most charming creature in the world, but not the only one. You mean that it doesn't matter to you.'

'Oh, don't be tiresome. It doesn't matter to you either, you know. Do go away and leave me to dine in peace.'

'Half a minute!' said Hamlyn. 'I thought I'd got it just now, but it's gone again. Look here, though, I believe it's one of those long things that end in *poulos*.'

'Oh, it ends in *poulos*, does it?' said I in a meditative tone.

'My dear Charley,' said Beatrice, 'I shall end in Bedlam if you're so very tedious. What in the world I shall do when I'm married, I don't know.'

'My dearest!' said Mrs Hipgrave, and a stage direction might add, *Business with brows as before*.

'*Poulos*,' I repeated thoughtfully.

'Could it be Constantinopoulos? asked Hamlyn, with a nervous deference to my Hellenic learning.

'It might conceivably,' I hazarded, 'be Constantine Stefanopoulos.'

'Then,' said Hamlyn, 'I shouldn't wonder if it was. Anyhow, the less you see of him, Wheatley, the better. Take my word for that.'

'But,' I objected – and I must admit that I have a habit of assuming that everybody follows my train of thought – 'it's such a small place, that, if he goes, I shall be almost bound to meet him.'

'What's such a small place?' cried Beatrice with emphasised despair.

'Why, Neopalia, of course,' said I.

'Why should anybody, except you, be so insane as to go there?' she asked.

'If he's the man I think, he comes from there,' I explained, as I rose for the last time; for I had been getting up to go and sitting down again several times.

'Then he'll think twice before he goes back,' pronounced Beatrice decisively; she was irreconcilable about my poor island.

Denny and I walked off together; as we went he observed:

'I suppose that chap's got no end of money?'

'Stefan – ?' I began.

'No, no. Hang it, you're as bad as Miss Hipgrave says. I mean Bennett Hamlyn.'

'Oh, yes, absolutely no end to it, I believe.'

Denny looked sagacious.

'He's very free with his dinners,' he observed.

'Don't let's worry about it,' I suggested, taking his arm. I was not worried about it myself. Indeed for the moment my island monopolised my mind, and my attachment to Beatrice was not of such a romantic character as to make me ready to be jealous on slight grounds. Mrs Hipgrave said the engagement was based on 'general suitability.' Now it is difficult to be very passionate over that.

'If you don't mind, I don't,' said Denny reasonably.

'That's right. It's only a little way Beatrice – ' I stopped abruptly. We were now on the steps outside the restaurant, and I had just perceived a scrap of paper lying on the mosaic pavement. I stooped down and picked it up. It proved to be a fragment torn from the menu card. I turned it over.

'Hullo, what's this?' said I, searching for my eye-glass, which was (as usual) somewhere in the small of my back,

Denny gave me the glass, and I read what was written on the back. It was in Greek, and it ran thus:

'By way of Rhodes – small yacht there – arrive seventh.'

I turned the piece of paper over in my hand. I drew a conclusion or two; one was that my tall neighbour was named Stefanopoulos; another that he had made good use of his ears – better than I had made of mine; for a third, I guessed that he would go to Neopalia; for a fourth, I fancied that Neopalia was the place to which the lady had declared she would accompany him. Then I fell to wondering why all these things should be so, why he wished to remember the route of my journey, the date of my arrival, and the fact that I meant to hire a yacht. Finally, those two chance encounters, taken with the rest, assumed a more interesting complexion.

'When you've done with that bit of paper,' observed Denny, in a tone expressive of exaggerated patience, 'we might as well go on, old fellow.'

'All right. I've done with it – for the present,' said I. But I took the liberty of slipping Mr Constantine Stefanopoulos' memorandum into my pocket.

The general result of the evening was to increase most distinctly my interest in Neopalia. I went to bed still thinking of my purchase, and I recollect that the last thing which came into my head before I went to sleep was, 'What did she mean by pointing to the ring?'

Well, I found an answer to that later on.

2

A Conservative Country

Until the moment of our parting came, I had no idea that Beatrice Hipgrave felt my going at all. She was not in the habit of displaying emotion, and I was much surprised at the reluctance with which she bade me goodbye. So far, however, was she from reproaching me that she took all the blame on herself, saying that if she had been kinder and nicer to me I should never have thought about my island. In this she was quite wrong; but when I told her so, and assured her that I had no fault to find with her behaviour, I was met with an almost passionate assertion of her unworthiness and an entreaty that I should not spend on her a love that she did not deserve. Her abasement and penitence compelled me to show, and indeed to feel, a good deal of tenderness for her. She was pathetic and pretty in her unusual earnestness and unexplained distress. I went the length of offering to put off my expedition until after our wedding; and although she besought me to do nothing of the kind, I believe that we might in the end have arranged matters on this footing had we been left to ourselves. But Mrs Hipgrave saw fit to intrude on our interview at this point, and she at once pooh-poohed the notion, declaring that I should be better out of the way for a few months. Beatrice did not resist her mother's conclusion; but when we were alone again, she became very agitated, begging me always to think well of her, and asking if I were really attached to her. I did not understand this mood, which was very unlike her ordinary manner; but I responded with a hearty and warm avowal of confidence in her; and I met her questions as to my own feelings by pledging my word very solemnly that absence should, so far as I was concerned, make no difference, and that she might rely implicitly on my faithful affection. This assurance seemed to give her very little comfort, although I repeated it more than once; and when I left her, I was in a state of some perplexity, for I could not follow the bent of her thoughts nor appreciate the feelings that moved her. I was however considerably touched, and upbraided myself for not having hitherto done justice to the depth and sincerity of nature which underlay her external frivolity. I expressed this self-condemnation to Denny Swinton, but he met it very coldly, and would not be drawn into any discussion of the subject. Denny was not wont to conceal his opinions and had never pretended to be enthusiastic about my engagement. This attitude of his had not troubled me before, but I was annoyed at it now, and I retaliated by asseverating my affection for Beatrice in terms of even exaggerated emphasis, and hers for me with no less vehemence.

 These troubles and perplexities vanished before the zest and interest which our preparations and start excited. Denny and I were like a pair of schoolboys off for a holiday, and spent hours in forecasting what we should do and how we should fare on the island. These speculations were extremely amusing, but in the long run they were proved to be, one and all, wide of the mark. Had I known Neopalia then as well as I came to know it afterwards, I should have recognised the futility of attempting to prophesy what would or would not happen there. As it was, we span our cobwebs merrily all the way to Rhodes, where we arrived without event and without accident. Here we picked up Hogvardt and embarked on the smart little steam yacht which he had procured for me. A day or two was spent in arranging our stores and buying what more we wanted, for we could not expect to be able to purchase any luxuries in Neopalia. I was rather surprised to find no letter for me from the old lord, but I had no thought of waiting for a formal invitation, and pressed on the hour of departure as much as I could. Here, also, I saw the first of my new subjects, Hogvardt having engaged a couple of men who had come to him saying that they were from Neopalia and were anxious to work their passage back. I was delighted to have them, and fell at once to studying them with immense attention. They were fine, tall, capable-looking fellows, and the two, with ourselves, made a crew more than large enough for our little boat; for both Denny and I could make ourselves useful on board, and Hogvardt could do something of everything on land or water, while Watkins acted as cook and steward. The Neopalians were, as they stated in answer to my questions, brothers; their names were Spiro and Demetri, and they informed us that their family had served the lords of Neopalia for many generations. Hearing this, I was less inclined to resent the undeniable reserve and even surliness with which they met my advances. I made allowance for their hereditary attachment to the outgoing family, and their natural want of cordiality towards the intruder did not prevent me from plying them with many questions concerning my predecessors on the throne of the island. My perseverance was ill-rewarded, but I succeeded in learning that the only member of the family on the island, besides the old lord was a girl whom they called 'the Lady Euphrosyne,' the daughter of the lord's brother who was dead. Next I asked after my friend of the Optimum Restaurant, Constantine. He was this lady's cousin once or twice removed – I did not make out the exact degree of kinship – but Demetri hastened to inform me that he came very seldom to the island, and had not been there for two years.

'And he is not expected there now?' I asked.

'He was not when we left, my lord,' answered Demetri, and it seemed to me that he threw an inquiring glance at his brother, who added hastily,

'But what should we poor men know of the Lord Constantine's doings?'

'Do you know where he is now?' I asked.

'No, my lord,' they answered together, and with great emphasis.

I cannot deny that something struck me as peculiar in their manner, but when I mentioned my impression to Denny he scoffed at me.

'You've been reading old Byron again,' he said scornfully. 'Do you think they're corsairs?'

Well, a man is not a fool simply because he reads Byron, and I maintained my opinion that the brothers were embarrassed at my questions. Moreover I caught Spiro, the more truculent looking of the pair, scowling at me more than once when he did not know I had my eye on him.

These little mysteries, however, did nothing but add sauce to my delight as we sprang over the blue waters; and my joy was complete when, on the morning of the day I had appointed, the seventh of May, Denny cried 'Land!' and looking over the starboard bow I saw the cloud on the sea that was Neopalia. Day came bright and glorious, and as we drew nearer to our enchanted isle we distinguished its features and conformation. The coast was rocky save where a small harbour opened to the sea, and the rocks ran up from the coast, rising higher and higher till they culminated in a quite respectable peak in the centre. The telescope showed cultivated ground and vineyards, mingled with woods, on the slopes of the mountain; and about half-way up, sheltered on three sides, backed by thick woods, and commanding a splendid sea-view, stood an old grey battlemented house.

'There's my house,' I cried in natural exultation, pointing with my finger. It was a moment in my life, a moment to mark.

'Hurrah!' cried Denny, throwing up his hat in sympathy.

Demetri was standing near and met this ebullition with a grim smile.

'I hope my lord will find the house comfortable,' said he.

'We shall soon make it comfortable,' said Hogvardt; 'I daresay it's half a ruin now.'

'It's good enough now for a Stefanopoulos,' said the fellow with a surly frown. The inference we were meant to draw was plain even to the point of incivility.

At five o'clock in the evening we entered the harbour of Neopalia, and brought up alongside a rather crazy wooden jetty which ran some fifty feet out from the shore. Our arrival appeared to create great excitement. Men, women, and children came running down the narrow steep street which climbed up the hill from the harbour. We heard shrill cries, and a hundred fingers were pointed at us. We landed; nobody came forward to greet us. I looked round, but saw no one who could be the old lord; but I perceived a stout man who wore an air of importance, and walking up to him I asked him very politely if he would be so good as to direct me to the inn; for I had discovered from Demetri that there was a modest house where we could lodge that night; I was too much in love with my island to think of sleeping on board the yacht. The stout man looked at Denny and me; then he looked at Demetri and Spiro, who stood near us, smiling their usual grim smiles. At last he answered my question by another, a rather abrupt one:

'What do you want, sir?' And he lifted his tasselled cap a few inches and replaced it on his head.

'I want to know the way to the inn,' I answered.

'You have come to visit Neopalia?' he asked. A number of people had gathered round us now, and all fixed their eyes on my face.

'Oh,' said I carelessly, 'I'm the purchaser of the island, you know. I have come to take possession.'

Nobody spoke. Perfect silence reigned for half a minute.

'I hope we shall get on well together,' I said, with my pleasantest smile.

Still no answer came. The people round still stared. But presently the stout man, altogether ignoring my friendly advances, said curtly,

'I keep the inn. Come. I will take you to it.'

He turned and led the way up the street. We followed, the people making a lane for us and still regarding us with stony stares. Denny gave expression to my feelings as well as his own;

'It can hardly be described as an ovation,' he observed.

'Surly brutes!' muttered Hogvardt.

'It is not the way to receive his lordship,' agreed Watkins, more in sorrow than in anger. Watkins had very high ideas of the deference due to his lordship.

The fat innkeeper walked ahead; I quickened my pace and overtook him.

'The people don't seem very pleased to see me,' I remarked.

He shook his head, but made no answer. Then he stopped before a substantial house. We followed him in, and he led us upstairs to a large room. It overlooked the street, but, somewhat to my surprise, the windows were heavily barred. The door also was massive and had large bolts inside and outside.

'You take good care of your houses, my friend,' said Denny with a laugh.

'We like to keep what we have, in Neopalia,' said he.

I asked him if he would provide us with a meal, and, assenting gruffly, he left us alone. The food was some time in coming, and we stood at the window, peering through our prison bars. Our high spirits were dashed by the unfriendly reception; my island should have been more gracious; it was so beautiful.

'However it's a better welcome than we should have got two hundred years ago,' I said with a laugh, trying to make the best of the matter.

Dinner, which the landlord himself brought in, cheered us again, and we lingered over it till dusk began to fall, discussing whether I ought to visit the lord, or whether, seeing that he had not come to receive me, my dignity did not demand that I should await his visit; and it was on this latter course that we finally decided.

'But he'll hardly come tonight,' said Denny, jumping up. 'I wonder if there are any decent beds here!'

Hogvardt and Watkins had, by my directions, sat down with us; the former was now smoking his pipe at the window, while Watkins was busy overhauling our luggage. We had brought light bags, the rods, guns, and other smaller articles. The rest was in the yacht. Hearing beds mentioned, Watkins shook his head in dismal presage, saying,

'We had better sleep on board, my lord.'

'Not I! What, leave the island now we've got here? No, Watkins!'

'Very good, my lord,' said Watkins impassively.

A sudden call came from Hogvardt, and I joined him at the window.

The scene outside was indeed remarkable. In the narrow paved street, gloomy now in the failing light, there must have been fifty or sixty men standing in a circle, surrounded by an outer fringe of women and children; and in the centre stood our landlord, his burly figure swaying to and fro as he poured out a low-voiced but vehement harangue. Sometimes he pointed towards us, oftener along the ascending road that led to the interior. I could not hear a word he said, but presently all his auditors raised their hands towards heaven. I saw that some of the hands held guns, some clubs, some knives; and all the men cried with furious energy, '*Nai, Nai.* Yes, yes!' Then the whole body – and the greater part of the grown men on the island must have been present – started off in compact array up the road, the innkeeper at their head. By his side walked another man whom I had not noticed before; he wore an ordinary suit of tweeds, but carried himself with an assumption of much dignity; his face I could not see.

'Well, what's the meaning of that?' I exclaimed, looking down on the street, empty again save for groups of white-clothed women, who talked eagerly to one another, gesticulating and pointing now towards our inn, now towards where the men had gone.

'Perhaps it's their Parliament,' suggested Denny; 'or perhaps they've repented of their rudeness and are going to erect a triumphal arch.'

These conjectures, being obviously ironical, did not assist the matter, although they amused their author.

'Anyhow,' said I, 'I should like to investigate the thing. Suppose we go for a stroll?'

The proposal was accepted at once. We put on our hats, took sticks, and prepared to go. Then I glanced at the luggage.

'Since I was so foolish as to waste my money on revolvers –?' said I, with an inquiring glance at Hogvardt.

'The evening air will not hurt them,' said he; and we each stowed a revolver in our pockets. We felt, I think, rather ashamed of our timidity, but the Neopalians certainly looked rough customers. Leading the way to the door I turned the handle; the door did not open. I pulled hard at it. Then I looked at my companions.

'Queer,' said Denny, and he began to whistle. Hogvardt got the little lantern, which he always had handy, and carefully inspected the door.

'Locked,' he announced, 'and bolted top and bottom. A solid door too!' and he struck it with his fist. Then he crossed to the window and looked at the bars; and finally he said to me, 'I don't think we can have our walk, my lord.'

Well, I burst out laughing. The thing was too absurd. Under cover of our animated talk the landlord must have bolted us in. The bars made the window no use. A skilled burglar might have beaten those bolts, and a battering ram would, no doubt, have smashed the door; we had neither burglar nor ram.

'We're caught, my boy,' said Denny, 'nicely caught! But what's the game?'

I had asked myself that question already, but had found no answer. To tell the truth, I was wondering whether Neopalia was going to turn out as conservative a country as the Turkish Ambassador had hinted. It was Watkins who suggested an answer,

'I imagine, my lord,' said he, 'that the natives' (Watkins always called the Neopalians 'natives') 'have gone to speak to the gentleman who sold the island to your lordship.'

'Gad,' said Denny, 'I hope it'll be a pleasant interview!'

Hogvardt's broad good-humoured face had assumed an anxious look. He knew something about the people of these islands; so did I.

'Trouble, is it?' I asked him.

'I'm afraid so,' he answered, and then we turned to the window again, except Denny, who wasted some energy and made a useless din by battering at the door till we beseeched him to let it alone.

There in the room we sat for nearly two hours. Darkness fell; the women had ceased their gossiping, but still stood about the street and in the doorways of their houses. It was nine o'clock before matters showed any progress. Then came shouts from the road above us, the flash of torches, the tread of men's feet in a quick triumphant march. Next the stalwart figures of the picturesque fellows, with their white kilts gleaming through the darkness, came again into sight, seeming wilder and more imposing in the alternating glare and gloom of the torches and the deepening night. The man in tweeds was no longer visible. Our innkeeper was alone in front. And all, as they marched, sang loudly a rude barbarous sort of chant, repeating it again and again; while the women and children, crowding out to meet the men, caught up the refrain in shrill voices, till the whole air seemed full of it. So martial and inspiring was the rude tune that our feet began to beat in time with it, and I felt the blood quicken in my veins. I have tried to put the words of it into English, in a shape as rough, I fear, as the rough original. Here it is:

> 'Ours is the land!
> Death to the hand
> That filches the land!
> Dead is that hand,
> Ours is the land!
>
> 'Forever we hold it,
> Dead's he that sold it!
> Ours is the land,
> Dead is the hand!'

Again and again they hurled forth the defiant words, until at last they stopped opposite the inn with one final long-drawn shout of savage triumph.

'Well, this is a go,' said Denny, drawing a long breath. 'What are the beggars up to?'

'What have they been up to?' I asked; for I could not doubt that the song we had heard had been chanted over a dead Stefanopoulos two hundred years before. At this age of the world the idea seemed absurd, preposterous, horrible. But there was no law nearer than Rhodes, and there only Turk's law. The sole law here was the law of the Stefanopouloi, and if that law lost its force by the crime of the hand which should wield it, why, strange things might happen even today in Neopalia. And we were caught in the inn like rats in a trap.

'I don't see,' remarked old Hogvardt, laying a hand on my shoulder, 'any harm in loading our revolvers, my lord!'

I did not see any harm in it either, and we all followed Hogvardt's advice, and also filled our pockets with cartridges. I was determined – I think we were all determined – not to be bullied by these islanders and their skull-and-crossbones ditty.

A quarter of an hour passed; then there came a knock at the door, while the bolts shot back.

'I shall go out,' said I, springing to my feet.

The door opened, and the face of a lad appeared.

'Vlacho the innkeeper bids you descend,' said he; and then, catching sight perhaps of our revolvers, he turned and ran downstairs again at his best speed. Following him we came to the door of the inn. It was ringed round with men, and directly opposite to us stood Vlacho. When he saw me he commanded silence with a gesture of his hand, and addressed me in the following surprising style.

'The Lady Euphrosyne, of her grace, bids you depart in peace. Go, then, to your boat and depart, thanking God for His mercy.'

'Wait a bit, my man,' said I; 'where is the lord of the island?'

'Did you not know that he died a week ago?' asked Vlacho, with apparent surprise.

'Died!' we exclaimed one and all.

'Yes, sir. The Lady Euphrosyne, Lady of Neopalia, bids you go.'

'What did he die of?'

'Of a fever,' said Vlacho gravely; and several of the men round him nodded their heads and murmured in no less grave assent, 'Yes, of a fever.'

'I am very sorry for it,' said I. 'But as he sold the island to me before he died, I don't see what the lady, with all respect to her, has got to do with it. Nor do I know what this rabble is doing about the door. Bid them disperse.'

This attempt at *hauteur* was most decidedly thrown away. Vlacho seemed not to hear what I said. He pointed with his finger towards the harbour.

'There lies your boat. Demetri and Spiro cannot go with you, but you will be able to manage her yourselves. Listen now! Till six in the morning you are free to go. If you are found in Neopalia one minute after, you will never go. Think and be wise.' And he and all the rest, as though one spring moved the whole body, wheeled round and marched off up the hill again, breaking out into the old chant when they had gone about a hundred yards. We were left alone in the doorway of the inn, looking, I must admit, rather blank.

Upstairs again we went, and I sat down by the window and gazed out on the night. It was very dark, and seemed darker now that the gleaming torches were gone. Not a soul was to be seen. The islanders, having put matters on a satisfactory footing, were off to bed. I sat thinking. Presently Denny came to me, and put his hand on my shoulder.

'Going to cave in, Charley?' he asked.

'My dear Denny,' said I, 'I wish you were at home with your mother.'

He smiled and repeated, 'Going to cave in, old chap?'

'No, by Jove, I'm not!' cried I, leaping up. 'They've had my money, and I'm going to have my island.'

'Take the yacht, my lord,' counselled Hogvardt, 'and come back with enough force from Rhodes.'

Well, here was sense; my impulse was nonsense. We four could not conquer the island. I swallowed my pride.

'So be it,' said I. 'But look here, it's only just twelve. We might have a look round before we go. I want to see the place, you know.' For I was very sorely vexed at being turned out of my island.

Hogvardt grumbled a little at my proposal, but here I overruled him. We took our revolvers again, left the inn, and struck straight up the road. We met nobody. For nearly a mile we mounted, the way becoming steeper with every step. Then there was a sharp turn off the main road.

'That will lead to the house,' said Hogvardt, who had studied the map of Neopalia very carefully.

'Then we'll have a look at the house. Show us a light, Hogvardt. It's precious dark.'

Hogvardt opened his lantern and cast its light on the way. But suddenly he extinguished it again, and drew us close into the rocks that edged the road. We saw coming towards us, in the darkness, two figures. They rode small horses. Their faces could not be seen; but as they passed our silent motionless forms, one said in a clear, sweet, girlish voice:

'Surely they will go?'

'Ay, they'll go or pay the penalty,' said the other voice. At the sound of it I started. For it was the voice of my neighbour in the restaurant, Constantine Stefanopoulos.

'I shall be near at hand, sleeping in the town,' said the girl's voice, 'and the people will listen to me.'

'The people will kill them if they don't go,' we heard Constantine answer, in tones that witnessed no great horror at the idea. Then the couple disappeared in the darkness.

'On to the house!' I cried in sudden excitement. For I was angry now, angry at the utter humbling scorn with which they treated me.

Another ten minutes' groping brought us in front of the old grey house which we had seen from the sea. We walked boldly up to it. The door stood open. We went in and found ourselves in a large hall. The wooden floor was carpeted here and there with mats and skins. A long table ran down the middle; the walls were decorated with medieval armour and weapons. The windows were but narrow slits, the walls massive and deep. The door was a ponderous iron-bound affair; it shamed even the stout doors of our inn. I called loudly, 'Is anyone here?' Nobody answered. The servants must have been drawn off to the town by the excitement of the procession and the singing; or, perhaps, there were no servants. I could not tell. I sat down in a large armchair by the table. I enjoyed the sense of proprietorship; I was in my own house. Denny sat on the table by me, dangling his legs. For a long while none of us spoke. Then I exclaimed suddenly:

'By Heaven, why shouldn't we see it through?' I rose, put my hands against the massive door, and closed and bolted it, saying, 'Let them open that at six o'clock in the morning.'

'Hurrah!' cried Denny, leaping down from his table, on fire with excitement in a moment.

I faced Hogvardt. He shook his head, but he smiled. Watkins stood by with his usual imperturbability. He wanted to know what his lordship decided – that was all; and when I said nothing more, he asked,

'Then your lordship will sleep here tonight?'

'I'll stay here tonight, anyhow, Watkins,' said I. 'I'm not going to be driven out of my own island by anybody.'

As I spoke, I brought my fist down on the table with a crash, And then to our amazement we heard, from somewhere in the dark recesses of the hall where the faint light of Hogvardt's lantern did not reach, a low but distinct groan, as of someone in pain. Watkins shuddered, Hogvardt looked rather uncomfortable; Denny and I listened eagerly. Again the groan came. I seized the lantern from Hogvardt's hand, and rushed in the direction of the sound. There, in the corner of the hall, on a couch covered with a rug, lay an old man in an uneasy attitude, groaning now and then and turning restlessly. By his side sat an old serving-woman in weary heavy slumber. In a moment I guessed the truth – part of the truth.

'He's not dead of that fever yet,' said I.

3

The Fever of Neopalia

I looked for a moment on the old man's pale, clean-cut, aristocratic face; then I shook his attendant by the arm vigorously. She awoke with a start.

'What does this mean?' I demanded. 'Who is he?'

'Heaven help us! Who are you?' she cried, leaping up in alarm. Indeed we four, with our eager fierce faces, must have looked disquieting enough.

'I am Lord Wheatley; these are my friends,' I answered in brisk sharp tones.

'What, it is you, then – ?' A wondering gaze ended her question.

'Yes, yes, it is I. I have bought the island. We came out for a walk and – '

'But he will kill you if he finds you here.'

'He? Who?'

'Ah, pardon, my lord! They will kill you, they – the people – the men of the island.'

I gazed at her sternly. She shrank back in confusion. And I spoke at a venture, yet in a well-grounded hazard:

'You mean that Constantine Stefanopoulos will kill me?'

'Ah, hush,' she cried. 'He may be here, he may be anywhere.'

'He may thank his stars he's not here,' said I grimly, for my blood was up. 'Attend, woman. Who is this?'

'It is the lord of the island, my lord,' she answered. 'Alas, he is wounded, I fear, to death. And yet I fell asleep. But I was so weary.'

'Wounded? By whom?'

Her face suddenly became vacant and expressionless.

'I do not know, my lord. It happened in the crowd. It was a mistake. My dear lord had yielded what they asked. Yet someone – no, by heaven, my lord, I do not know who – stabbed him. And he cannot live.'

'Tell me the whole thing,' I commanded.

'They came up here, my lord, all of them, Vlacho and all, and with them my Lord Constantine. The Lady Euphrosyne was away; she is often away, down on the rocks by the sea, watching the waves. They came and said that a man had landed who claimed our island as his – a man of your name, my lord. And when my dear lord said he had sold the island to save the honour of his house and race, they were furious; and Vlacho raised the death chant that One-eyed Alexander the Bard wrote on the death of Stefan Stefanopoulos long ago. Then they came near with knives, demanding that my dear lord should send away the stranger; for the men of Neopalia were not to be bought and sold like bullocks or like pigs. At first my lord would not yield, and they swore they would kill the stranger and my lord also. Then they pressed closer; Vlacho was hard on him with drawn knife, and the Lord Constantine stood by him, praying him to yield; and Constantine drew his own knife, saying to Vlacho that he must fight him also before he killed the old lord. But at that Vlacho smiled. And then – and then – ah, my dear lord!'

For a moment her voice broke, and sobs supplanted words. But she drew herself up, and after a glance at the old man whom her vehement speech had not availed to waken, she went on.

'And then those behind cried out that there was enough talk. Would he yield or would he die? And they rushed forward, pressing the nearest against him. And he, an old man, frail and feeble (yet once he was as brave a man as any), cried in his weak tones, "Enough, friends, I yield, I –" and they fell back But my lord stood for an instant, then he set his hand to his side, and swayed and tottered and fell; the blood was running from his side. The Lord Constantine fell on his knees beside him, crying, "Who stabbed him?" Vlacho smiled grimly, and the others looked at one another, But I, who had run out from the doorway whence I had seen it all, knelt by my lord and staunched the blood. Then Vlacho said, fixing his eyes straight and keen on the Lord Constantine, "It was not I, my lord." "Nor I by heaven," cried the Lord Constantine, and he rose to his feet, demanding, "Who struck the blow?" But none answered; and he went on, "Nay, if it were in error, if it were because he would not yield, speak. There shall be pardon." But Vlacho, hearing this, turned himself round and faced them all, saying, "Did he not sell us like oxen and like pigs?" and he broke into the death chant, and they all raised the chant, none caring any more who had struck the blow. And the Lord Constantine –' The impetuous flow of the old woman's story was frozen to sudden silence.

'Well, and the Lord Constantine?' said I, in low stern tones that quivered with excitement; and I felt Denny's hand, which was on my arm, jump up and down. 'And Constantine, woman?'

'Nay, he did nothing,' said she. 'He talked with Vlacho awhile, and then they went away, and he bade me tend my lord, and went himself to seek the Lady Euphrosyne. Presently he came back with her; her eyes were red, and she wept afresh when she saw my poor lord; for she loved him. She sat by him till Constantine came and told her that you would not go, and that you and your friends would be killed if you did not go. Then, weeping to leave my lord, she went, praying heaven she might find him alive when she returned. "I must go," she said to me, "for though it is a shameful thing that the island should have been sold, yet these men must be persuaded to go away and not meet death. Kiss him for me if he awakes." Thus she went and left me with my lord, and I fear he will die.' She ended in a burst of sobbing.

For a moment there was silence. Then I said again:

'Who struck the blow, woman? Who struck the blow?'

She shrank from me as though I had struck her.

'I do not know; I do not know,' she moaned.

But the question she dared not answer was to find an answer.

The stricken man opened his eyes, his lips moved, and he groaned, 'Constantine! You, Constantine!' The old woman's eyes met mine for a moment and fell to the ground again.

'Why, why, Constantine?' moaned the wounded man. 'I had yielded, I had yielded, Constantine. I would have sent them –'

His words ceased, his eyes closed, his lips met again, but met only to part. A moment later his jaw dropped. The old lord of Neopalia was dead.

Then I, carried away by anger and by hatred of the man who, for a reason I did not yet understand, had struck so foul a blow against his kinsman and an old man, did a thing so rash that it seems to me now, when I consider it in the cold light of memory, a mad deed. Yet then I could do nothing else; and Denny's face, ay, and the eyes of the others too told me that they were with me.

'Compose this old man's body,' I said, 'and we will watch it. But do you go and tell this Constantine Stefanopoulos that I know his crime, that I know who struck that blow, that what I know all men shall know, and that I will not rest day or night until he has paid the penalty of this murder. Tell him I swore this on the honour of an English gentleman.'

'And say I swore it too!' cried Denny; and Hogvardt and Watkins, not making bold to speak, ranged up close to me; I knew that they also meant what I meant.

The old woman looked at me with searching eyes.

'You are a bold man, my lord,' said she.

'I see nothing to be afraid of up to now,' said I. 'Such courage as is needed to tell a scoundrel what I think of him I believe I can claim.'

'But he will never let you go now. You would go to Rhodes, and tell his – tell what you say of him.'

'Yes, and further than Rhodes, if need be. He shall die for it as sure as I live.'

A thousand men might have tried in vain to persuade me; the treachery of Constantine had fired my heart and driven out all opposing motives.

'Do as I bid you,' said I sternly, 'and waste no time on it. We will watch here by the old man till you return.'

'My lord,' she replied, 'you run on your own death. And you are young; and the youth by you is yet younger.'

'We are not dead yet,' said Denny; I had never seen him look as he did then; for the gaiety was out of his face, and his lips had grown set and hard.

She raised her hands towards heaven, whether in prayer or in lamentation I do not know. We turned away and left her to her sad work; going back to our places, we waited there till dawn began to break and from the narrow windows we saw the grey crests of the waves dancing and frolicking in the early dawn. As I watched them, the old woman was by my elbow.

'It is done, my lord,' said she. 'Are you still of the same mind?'

'Still of the same,' said I.

'It is death, death for you all,' she said, and without more she went to the great door. Hogvardt opened it for her, and she walked away down the road, between the high rocks that bounded the path on either side. Then we went and carried the old man to a room that opened off the hall, and, returning, stood in the doorway, cooling our brows in the fresh early air. While we stood there, Hogvardt said suddenly,

'It is five o'clock.'

'Then we have only an hour to live,' said I, smiling, 'if we don't make for the yacht.'

'You're not going back to the yacht, my lord?'

'I'm puzzled,' I admitted. 'If we go this ruffian will escape. And if we don't go –'

'Why, we,' Hogvardt ended for me, 'may not escape.'

I saw that Hogvardt's sense of responsibility was heavy; he always regarded himself as the shepherd, his employers as the sheep. I believe this attitude of his confirmed my obstinacy, for I said, without further hesitation:

'Oh, we'll chance that. When they know what a villain the fellow is, they'll turn against him. Besides, we said we'd wait here.'

Denny seized on my last words with alacrity. When you are determined to do a rash thing, there is a great comfort in feeling that you are already committed to it by some previous act or promise.

'So we did,' he cried. 'Then that settles it Hogvardt.'

'His lordship certainly expressed that intention,' observed Watkins, appearing at this moment with a big loaf of bread and a great pitcher of milk. I eyed these viands.

'I bought the house and its contents,' said I; 'come along.'

Watkins' further researches produced a large lump of native cheese; when he had set this down he remarked:

'In a pen behind the house, close to the kitchen windows, there are two goats; and your lordship sees there, on the right of the front door, two cows tethered.'

I began to laugh, Watkins was so wise and solemn.

'We can stand a siege, you mean?' I asked. 'Well, I hope it won't come to that.'

Hogvardt rose and began to move round the hall, examining the weapons that decorated the walls. From time to time he grunted disapprovingly; the guns were useless, rusted, out of date; and there was no ammunition for them. But when he had almost completed his circuit, he gave an exclamation of satisfaction and came to me holding an excellent modern rifle and a large cartridge case.

'See!' he grunted in huge delight. ' "CS" on the stock. I expect you can guess whose it is, my lord.'

'This is very thoughtful of Constantine,' observed Denny, who was employing himself in cutting imaginary lemons in two with a fine damascened scimitar that he had taken from the wall.

'As for the cows,' said I, 'perhaps they will carry them off,'

'I think not,' said Hogvardt, taking an aim with the rifle through the window.

I looked at my watch. It was five minutes past six.

'Well, we can't go now,' said I. 'It's settled. What a comfort!' I wonder whether I had ever in my heart meant to go!

The next hour passed very quietly. We sat smoking pipes or cigars and talking in subdued tones. The recollection of the dead man in the adjoining room sobered the excitement to which our position might otherwise have given occasion. Indeed I suppose that I at least, who through my whim had led the rest into this quandary, should have been utterly overwhelmed by the burden on me. But I was not. Perhaps Hogvardt's assumption of responsibility relieved me; perhaps I was too full of anger against Constantine to think of the risks we ourselves ran; and I was more than half-persuaded that the revelation of what he had done would rob him of his power to hurt us. Moreover, if I might judge from the words I heard on the road, we had on our side an ally of uncertain, but probably considerable, power in the sweet-voiced girl whom the old woman called the Lady Euphrosyne; she would not support her uncle's murderer, even though he were her cousin.

Presently Watkins carried me off to view his pen of goats, and having passed through the lofty flagged kitchen, I found myself in a sort of compound formed by the rocks. The ground had been levelled for a few yards, and the rocks rose straight to the height of ten or twelve feet; from the top of this artificial bank they ran again in wooded slopes towards the peak of the mountain. I followed their course with my eye, and three hundred or more feet above us, just beneath the summit, I perceived a little wooden châlet or bungalow. Blue smoke issued from the chimneys; and, even while we looked, a figure came out of the door and stood still in front of it, apparently gazing down towards the house.

'It's a woman,' I pronounced.

'Yes, my lord. A peasant's wife, I suppose.'

'I daresay,' said I. But I soon doubted Watkins' opinion; in the first place, because the woman's dress did not look like that of a peasant woman; and secondly, because she went into the house, appeared again, and levelled at us what was, if I mistook not, a large pair of binocular glasses. Now such things were not likely to be in the possession of the peasants of Neopalia. Then she suddenly retreated, and through the silence of those still slopes we heard the door of the cottage closed with violence.

'She doesn't seem to like the looks of us,' said I.

'Possibly,' suggested Watkins with deference, 'she did not expect to see your lordship here.'

'I should think that's very likely, Watkins,' said I.

I was recalled from the survey of my new domains – my satisfaction in the thought that they were mine survived all the disturbing features of the situation – by a call from Denny. In response to it I hurried back to the hall and found him at the window, with Constantine's rifle rested on the sill.

'I could pick him off pat,' said Denny laughingly, and he pointed to a figure which was approaching the house. It was a man riding a stout pony; when he came within about two hundred yards of the house, he stopped, took a leisurely look, and then waved a white handkerchief.

'The laws of war must be observed,' said I, smiling. 'This is a flag of truce.' I opened the door, stepped out, and waved my handkerchief in return. The man, reassured, began to mop his brow with the flag of truce, and put his pony to a trot. I now perceived him to be the innkeeper Vlacho, and a moment later he reined up beside me, giving an angry jerk at his pony's bridle.

'I have searched the island for you,' he cried. 'I am weary and hot! How came you here?'

I explained to him briefly how I had chanced to take possession of my house and added significantly:

'But has no message come to you from me?'

He smiled with equal meaning, as he answered:

'No; an old woman came to speak to a gentleman who is in the village – '

'Yes, to Constantine Stefanopoulos,' said I with a nod.

'Well then, if you will, to the Lord Constantine,' he admitted with a careless shrug, 'but her message was for his ear only; he took her aside and they talked alone.'

'You know what she said, though?'

'That is between my Lord Constantine and me.'

'And the young lady knows it, I hope – the Lady Euphrosyne?'

Vlacho smiled broadly.

'We could not distress her with such a silly tale,' he answered; and he leant down towards me. 'Nobody has heard the message but the Lord Constantine and one man he told it to. And nobody will. If that old woman spoke, she – well, she knows and will not speak.'

'And you back up this murderer?' I cried.

'Murderer?' he repeated questioningly. 'Indeed, sir, it was an accident done in hot blood. It was the old man's fault, because he tried to sell the island.'

'He did sell the island,' I corrected; 'and a good many other people will hear of what happened to him.'

He looked at me again, smiling.

'If you shouted it in the hearing of every man in Neopalia, what would they do?' he asked scornfully.

'Well, I should hope,' I returned, 'that they'd hang Constantine to the tallest tree you've got here.'

'They would do this,' he said with a nod; and he began to sing softly the chant I had heard the night before.

I was disgusted at his savagery, but I said coolly:

'And the Lady?'

'The Lady believes what she is told, and will do as her cousin bids her. Is she not his affianced wife?'

'The deuce she is!' I cried in amazement, fixing a keen scrutiny on Vlacho's face. The face told me nothing.

'Certainly,' he said gently. 'And they will rule the island together.'

'Will they, though?' said I. I was becoming rather annoyed. 'There are one or two obstacles in the way of that. First, it's my island.'

He shrugged his shoulders again. 'That,' he seemed to say, 'is not worth answering.' But I had a second shot in the locker for him, and I let him have it for what it was worth. I knew it might be worth nothing, but I tried it.

'And secondly,' I went on, 'how many wives does Constantine propose to have?'

A hit! A hit! A palpable hit! I could have sung in glee. The fellow was dumbfounded. He turned red, bit his lip, scowled fiercely.

'What do you mean?' he blurted out, with an attempt at blustering defiance.

'Never mind what I mean. Something, perhaps, that the Lady Euphrosyne might care to know. And now, my man, what do you want of me?'

He recovered his composure, and stated his errand with his old cool assurance; but the cloud of vexation still hung heavy on his brow.

'On behalf of the Lady of the island –' he began.

'Or shall we say her cousin?' I interrupted.

'Which you will,' he answered, as though it were not worthwhile to wear the mask any longer. 'On behalf, then, of my Lord Constantine, I am to offer you safe passage to your boat, and a return of the money you have paid.'

'How's he going to pay that?'

'He will pay it in a year, and give you security meanwhile.'

'And the condition is that I give up the island?' I asked; I began to think that perhaps I owed it to my companions to acquiesce in this proposal however distasteful it might be to me.

'Yes,' said Vlacho, 'and there is one other small condition, which will not trouble you.'

'What's that? You're rich in conditions.'

'You're lucky to be offered any. It is that you mind your own business.'

'I came here for the purpose,' I observed.

'And that you undertake, for yourself and your companions, on your word of honour, to speak to nobody of what has passed on the island or of the affairs of the Lord Constantine.'

'And if I won't give this promise?'

'The yacht is in our hands; Demetri and Spiro are our men; there will be no ship here for two months.' The fellow paused, smiling at me. I took the liberty of ending his period for him.

'And there is,' I said, returning his smile, 'as we know by now, a particularly sudden and fatal form of fever in the island.'

'Certainly you may chance to find that out,' said he.

'But is there no antidote?' I asked, and I showed him the butt of my revolver in the pocket of my coat.

'It may keep it off for a day or two – not longer. You have the bottle there, but most of the drug is with your luggage at the inn.'

His parable was true enough; we had only two or three dozen cartridges apiece.

'But there's plenty of food for Constantine's rifle,' said I, pointing to the muzzle of it, which protruded from the window.

He suddenly became impatient.

'Your answer, sir?' he demanded peremptorily.

'Here it is,' said I. 'I'll keep the island and I'll see Constantine hanged.'

'So be it, so be it,' he cried. 'You are warned; so be it!' Without another word he turned his pony and trotted rapidly off down the road. And I went back to the house feeling, I must confess, not in the best of spirits. But when my friends heard all that had passed, they applauded me, and we made up our minds to 'see it through,' as Denny said.

The day passed quietly. At noon we carried the old lord out of his house, having wrapped him in a sheet; we dug for him as good a grave as we could in a little patch of ground that lay outside the windows of his own chapel, a small erection at the west end of the house. There he must lie for the present. This sad work done, we came back and – so swift are life's changes – killed a goat for dinner, and watched Watkins dress it. Thus the afternoon wore away, and when evening came we ate our goat-flesh and Hogvardt milked our cows; then we sat down to consider the position of the garrison.

But the evening was hot and we adjourned out of doors, grouping ourselves on the broad marble pavement in front of the door. Hogvardt had just begun to expound a very elaborate scheme of escape, depending, so far as I could make out, on our reaching the other side of the island and finding there a boat which we had no reason to suppose would be there, when Denny raised his hand, saying 'Hark!'

From the direction of the village and the harbour came the sound of a horn, blowing long and shrill and echoed back in strange protracted shrieks and groans from the hillside behind us. And following on the blast we heard, low in the distance and indistinct, yet rising and falling and rising again in savage defiance and exultation, the death-chant that One-Eyed Alexander the Bard had made on the death of Stefan Stefanopoulos two hundred years ago. For a few minutes we sat listening; I do not think that any of us felt very comfortable. Then I rose to my feet, saying:

'Hogvardt, old fellow, I fancy that scheme of yours must wait a little. Unless I'm very much mistaken, we're going to have a lively evening.'

Well, then we shook hands all round, and went in and bolted the door, and sat down to wait. We heard the death-chant through the walls now; it was coming nearer.

4

A Raid and a Raider

It was between eight and nine o'clock when the first of the enemy appeared on the road in the persons of two smart fellows in gleaming kilts and braided jackets. It was no more than just dusk, and I saw that they were strangers to me. One was tall and broad, the other shorter and of very slight build. They came on towards us confidently enough. I was looking over Denny's shoulder; he held Constantine's rifle, and I knew that he was impatient to try it. But, inasmuch as might was certainly not on our side, I was determined that right should abide with us, and was resolute not to begin hostilities. Constantine had at least one powerful motive for desiring our destruction; I would not furnish him with any plausible excuse for indulging his wish: so we stood, Denny and I at one window, Hogvardt and Watkins at the other, and quietly watched the approaching figures. No more appeared; the main body did not show itself, and the sound of the fierce chant had suddenly died away. But the next moment a third man came in sight, running rapidly after the first two. He caught the shorter by the arm, and seemed to argue or expostulate with him. For a while the three stood thus talking; then I saw the last comer make a gesture of protest as though he yielded his point unwillingly, and they all came on together.

'Push the barrel of that rifle a little farther out,' said I to Denny. 'It may be useful to them to know it's there.'

Denny obeyed; the result was a sudden pause in our friends' advance; but they were near enough now for me to distinguish the last comer and I discerned in him, although he had discarded his tweed suit and adopted the national dress, Constantine Stefanopoulos himself.

'Here's an exercise of self-control!' I groaned, laying a detaining hand on Denny's shoulder.

As I spoke, Constantine put a whistle to his lips and blew loudly. The blast was followed by the appearance of five more fellows; in three of them I recognised old acquaintances – Vlacho, Demetri and Spiro. These three all carried guns. The whole eight came forward again, till they were within a hundred yards of us. There they halted, and, with a sudden swift movement, three barrels were levelled straight at the window where Denny and I were stationed. Well, we ducked; there is no use in denying it; for we thought that the bombardment had really begun. Yet no shot followed, and after an instant, holding Denny down, I peered out cautiously myself. The three stood motionless, their aim full on us. The other five were advancing warily, well under the shelter of the rock, two on the left side of the road and three on the right. The slim boyish fellow was with Constantine on the left; a moment later the other three dashed across the road and joined them. In a moment what military men call 'the objective,' the aim of these manoeuvres, flashed across me. It was simple almost to ludicrousness; yet it was very serious, for it showed a reasoned plan of campaign with which we were very ill-prepared to cope. While the three held us in check, the five were going to carry off our cows. Without our cows we should soon be hard put to it for food. For the cows had formed in our plans a most important *piece de résistance*.

'This won't do,' said I. 'They're after the cows.' I took the rifle from Denny's hand, cautioning him not to show his face at the window. Then I stood in the shelter of the wall, so that I could not be hit by the three, and levelled the rifle, not at my human enemies, but at the unoffending cows.

'A dead cow,' I remarked, 'is a great deal harder to move than a live one.'

The five had now come quite near the pen of rude hurdles in which the cows were. As I spoke, Constantine appeared to give some order; and while he and the boy stood looking on, Constantine leaning on his gun, the boy's hand resting with jaunty elegance on the handle of the knife in his girdle, the others leapt over the hurdles. Crack! went the rifle, and a cow fell. I reloaded hastily. Crack! and the second cow fell. It was very fair shooting in such a bad light, for I hit both mortally; my skill was rewarded by a shout of anger from the robbers. (For robbers they were; I had bought the livestock.)

'Carry them off now!' I cried, carelessly showing myself at the window. But I did not stay there long, for three shots rang out, and the bullets pattered on the masonry above me. Luckily the covering party had aimed a trifle too high.

'No more milk, my lord,' observed Watkins in a regretful tone. He had seen the catastrophe from the other window.

The besiegers were checked. They leapt out of the pen with alacrity. I suppose they realised that they were exposed to my fire while at that particular angle I was protected from the attack of their friends. They withdrew to the middle of the road, selecting a spot at which I could not take aim without showing myself at the window. I dared not look out to see what they were doing. But presently Hogvardt risked a glance, and called out that they were in retreat and had rejoined the three, and that the whole body stood together in consultation and were no longer covering my window. So I looked out, and saw the boy standing in an easy graceful attitude, while Constantine and Vlacho talked a little way apart. It was growing considerably darker now, and the figures became dim and indistinct.

'I think the fun's over for tonight,' said I, glad to have it over so cheaply.

Indeed what I said seemed to be true, for the next moment the group turned and began to retreat along the road, moving briskly out of our sight. We were left in the thick gloom of a moonless evening and the peaceful silence of still air.

'They'll come back and fetch the cows,' said Hogvardt. 'Couldn't we drag one in, my lord, and put it where the goat is, behind the house?'

I approved of this suggestion; Watkins having found a rope, I armed Denny with the rifle took from the wall a large keen hunting-knife, opened the door and stole out, accompanied by Hogvardt and Watkins, who carried their revolvers. We reached the pen without interruption, tied our rope firmly round the horns of one of the dead beasts and set to work to drag it along. It was no child's play, and our progress was very slow, but the carcase moved, and I gave a shout of encouragement as we got it down on to the smoother ground of the road and hauled it along with a will. Alas, that shout was a great indiscretion! I had been too hasty in assuming that our enemy was quite gone. We heard suddenly the rush of feet; shots whistled over our heads. We had but just time to drop the rope and turn round, when Denny's rifle rang out, and then – somebody was at us! I really do not know exactly how many there were. I had two at me, but by great good luck I drove my big knife into one fellow's arm at the first hazard, and I think that was enough for him. In my other assailant I recognised Vlacho. The fat innkeeper had got rid of his gun and had a knife much like the one I carried myself. I knew him more by his voice as he cried fiercely, 'Come on!' than by his appearance, for the darkness was thick now. Parrying his fierce thrust – he was very active for so stout a man – I called out to our people to fall back as quickly as they could, for I was afraid that we might be taken in the rear also.

But discipline is hard to maintain in such a force as mine.

'Bosh!' cried Denny's voice.

'*Mein Gott*, no!' exclaimed Hogvardt. Watkins said nothing, but for once in his life he also disobeyed me.

Well, if they would not do as I said I must do as they did. The line advanced – the whole line, as at Waterloo. We pressed them hard. I heard a revolver fired, and a cry follow. Fat Vlacho slackened in his attack, wavered, halted, turned, and ran. A shout of triumph from Denny told me that the battle was going well there. Fired with victory, I set myself for a chase. But, alas, my pride was checked. Before I had gone two yards, I fell headlong over the body for which we had been fighting (as Greeks and Trojans fought for the body of Hector), and came to an abrupt stop, sprawling most ignominiously over the cow's broad back.

'Stop! Stop!' I cried. 'Wait a bit, Denny! I'm down over this infernal cow.' It was an inglorious ending to the exploits of the evening.

Prudence or my cry stopped them. The enemy was in full retreat; their steps pattered quick along the rocky road; and Denny observed in a tone of immense satisfaction:

'I think that's our trick, Charley.'

'Anybody hurt?' I asked, scrambling to my feet.

Watkins owned to a crack from the stock of a gun on his right shoulder, Hogvardt to a graze of a knife on the left arm. Denny was unhurt. We had reason to suppose that we had left our mark on at least two of the enemy. For so great a victory it was cheaply bought.

'We'll just drag in the cow,' said I – I like to stick to my point – 'and then we might see if there's anything in the cellar.'

We did drag in the cow; we dragged it through the house, and finally bestowed it in the compound behind. Hogvardt suggested that we should fetch the other also, but I had no mind for another surprise, which might not end so happily, and I decided to run the risk of leaving the second animal till the morning. So Watkins ran off to seek for some wine, for which we all felt very ready, and I went to the door with the intention of securing it. But before I shut it, I stood for a moment on the step, looking out on the night and sniffing the sweet, clear, pure air. It was in quiet moments like these, not in such a tumult as had just passed, that I had pictured my beautiful island; and the love of it came on me now and made me swear that these fellows and their arch-ruffian Constantine should not drive me out of it without some more, and more serious, blows than had been struck that night. If I could get away safely and return with enough force to keep them quiet, I would pursue that course. If not – well, I believe I had very bloodthirsty thoughts in my mind, as even the most peaceable man may, when he has been served as I had and his friends roughly handled on his account.

Having registered these determinations, I was about to proceed with my task of securing the door, when I heard a sound that startled me. There was nothing hostile or alarming about it; rather it was pathetic and appealing, and, in spite of my previous fierceness of mood, it caused me to exclaim, 'Hullo, is that one of those poor beggars we mauled?' For the sound was a faint distressed sigh, as of somebody in suffering; it seemed to come from out of the darkness about a dozen yards ahead of me. My first impulse was to go straight to the spot, but I had begun by now to doubt whether the Neopalians were not unsophisticated in quite as peculiar a sense as that in which they were good hearted, and I called to Denny and Hogvardt, bidding the latter to bring his lantern with him. Thus protected, I stepped out of the door in the direction from which the sigh had come. Apparently we were to crown our victory by the capture of a wounded enemy.

An exclamation from Hogvardt told me that he, aided by the lantern, had come on the quarry; but Hogvardt spoke in disgust rather than triumph.

'Oh, it's only the little one!' said he. 'What's wrong with him, I wonder.' He stooped down and examined the prostrate form. 'By heaven, I believe he's not touched – yes, there's a bump on his forehead, but not big enough for any of us to have given it.'

By this time Denny and I were with him, and we looked down on the boy's pale face, which seemed almost death-like in the glare of the lantern. The bump was not such a very small one, but it could hardly have been made by any of our weapons, for the flesh was not cut. A moment's further inspection showed that it must be the result of a fall on the hard rocky road.

'Perhaps he tripped on the cord, as you did on the cow,' suggested Denny with a grin.

It seemed likely enough, but I gave very little thought to the question, for I was busy studying the boy's face.

'No doubt,' said Hogvardt, 'he fell in running away and was stunned; and they didn't notice it in the dark, or were afraid to stop. But they'll be back, my lord, and soon.'

'Carry him inside,' said I. 'It won't hurt us to have a hostage.'

Denny lifted the lad in his long arms – Denny was a tall powerful fellow – and strode off with him. I followed, wondering who it was that we had got hold of: for the boy was strikingly handsome. I was last in and barred the door. Denny had set our prisoner down in an armchair, where he sat now, conscious again, but still with a dazed look in his large dark eyes as he glanced from me to the rest and back again to me, finally fixing a long gaze on my face.

'Well, young man,' said I, 'you've begun this sort of thing early. Lifting cattle and taking murder in the day's work is pretty good for a youngster like you. Who are you?'

'Where am I?' he cried, in that blurred indistinct kind of voice that comes with mental bewilderment.

'You're in my house,' said I, 'and the rest of your infernal gang's outside and going to stay there. So you must make the best of it.'

The boy turned his head away and closed his eyes. Suddenly I snatched the lantern from Hogvardt. But I paused before I brought it close to the boy's face, as I had meant to do, and I said:

'You fellows go and get something to eat, and a snooze if you like. I'll look after this youngster. I'll call you if anything happens outside.'

After a few unselfish protests they did as I bade them. I was left alone in the hall with the prisoner; soon merry voices from the kitchen told me that the battle was being fought again over the wine. I set the lantern close to the boy's face.

'H'm,' said I, after a prolonged scrutiny. Then I sat down on the table and began to hum softly that wretched chant of One-eyed Alexander's, which had a terrible trick of sticking in a man's head.

For a few minutes I hummed. The lad shivered, stirred uneasily, and opened his eyes. I had never seen such eyes; I could not conscientiously except even Beatrice Hipgrave's, which were in their way quite fine. I hummed away; and the boy said, still in a dreamy voice, but with an imploring gesture of his hand:

'Ah, no, not that! Not that, Constantine!'

'He's a tender-hearted youth,' said I, and I was smiling now. The whole episode was singularly unusual and interesting.

The boy's eyes were on mine again; I met his glance full and square. Then I poured out some water and gave it to him. He took it with a trembling hand – the hand did not escape my notice – and drank it eagerly, setting the glass down with a sigh.

'I am Lord Wheatley,' said I, nodding to him. 'You came to steal my cattle, and murder me, if it happened to be convenient, you know.'

The boy flashed out at me in a minute.

'I didn't. I thought you'd surrender if we got the cattle away.'

'You thought!' said I scornfully. 'I suppose you did as you were bid.'

'No; I told Constantine that they weren't to –' The boy stopped short, looked round him, and said in a surprised voice, 'Where are all the rest of my people?'

'The rest of your people,' said I, 'have run away, and you are in my hands. And I can do just as I please with you.'

His lips set in an obstinate curve, but he made no answer. I went on as sternly as I could.

'And when I think of what I saw here yesterday, of that poor old man stabbed by your bloodthirsty crew –'

'It was an accident,' he cried sharply; the voice had lost its dreaminess and sounded clear now.

'We'll see about that when we get Constantine and Vlacho before a judge,' I retorted grimly. 'Anyhow, he was foully stabbed in his own house for doing what he had a perfect right to do.'

'He had no right to sell the island,' cried the boy, and he rose for a moment to his feet with a proud air, only to sink back into the chair again and stretch out his hand for water.

Now at this moment Denny, refreshed by meat and drink and in the highest of spirits, bounded into the hall.

'How's the prisoner?' he cried.

'Oh, he's all right. There's nothing the matter with him,' I said, and as I spoke I moved the lantern, so that the boy's face and figure were again in shadow.

'That's all right,' observed Denny cheerfully. 'Because I thought, Charley, we might get a little information out of him.'

'Perhaps he won't speak,' I suggested, casting a glance at the captive who sat now motionless in the chair.

'Oh, I think he will,' said Denny confidently: and I observed for the first time that he held a very substantial-looking whip in his hand; he must have found it in the kitchen. 'We'll give the young ruffian a taste of this, if he's obstinate,' said Denny, and I cannot say that his tone witnessed any great desire that the boy should prove at once compliant.

I shifted my lantern so that I could see the proud young face, while Denny could not. The boy's eyes met mine defiantly.

'Do you see that whip?' I asked. 'Will you tell us all we want to know?'

The boy made no answer, but I saw trouble in his face, and his eyes did not meet mine so boldly now.

'We'll soon find a tongue for him,' said Denny, in cheerful barbarity; 'upon my word, he richly deserves a thrashing. Say the word, Charley!'

'We haven't asked him anything yet,' said I.

'Oh, I'll ask him something. Look here, who was the fellow with you and Vlacho?'

Denny spoke in English; I turned his question into Greek. But the prisoner's eyes told me that he had understood before I spoke. I smiled again.

The boy was silent; defiance and fear struggled in the dark eyes.

'You see he's an obstinate beggar,' said Denny, as though he had observed all necessary forms and could now get to business; and he drew the lash of the whip through his fingers. I am afraid Denny was rather looking forward to executing justice with his own hands.

The boy rose again and stood facing that heartless young ruffian Denny – it was thus that I thought of Denny at the moment; then once again he sank back into his chair and covered his face with his hands.

'Well, I wouldn't go out killing if I hadn't more pluck than that,' said Denny scornfully. 'You're not fit for the trade, my lad.'

I did not interpret this time; there was no need; the boy certainly understood. But he had no retort. His face was buried in those slim hands of his. For a moment he was quite still: then he moved a little; it was a movement that spoke of helpless pain, and I heard something very like a stifled sob.

'Just leave us alone a little, Denny,' said I. 'He may tell me what he won't tell you.'

'Are you going to let him off?' demanded Denny, suspiciously. 'You never can be stiff in the back, Charley.'

'I must see if he won't speak to me first,' I pleaded, meekly.

'But if he won't?' insisted Denny.

'If he won't,' said I, 'and you still wish it, you may do what you like.'

Denny sheered off to the kitchen, with an air that did not seek to conceal his opinion of my foolish tender-heartedness. Again I was alone with the boy.

'My friend is right,' said I gravely. 'You're not fit for the trade. How came you to be in it?'

My question brought a new look, as the boy's hands dropped from his face.

'How came you,' said I, 'who ought to restrain these rascals, to be at their head? How came you, who ought to shun the society of men like Constantine Stefanopoulos and his tool Vlacho, to be working with them?'

I got no answer; only a frightened look appealed to me in the white glare of Hogvardt's lantern. I came a step nearer and leant forward to ask my next question.

'Who are you? What's your name?'

'My name – my name?' stammered the prisoner. 'I won't tell my name.'

'You'll tell me nothing? You heard what I promised my friend?'

'Yes, I heard,' said the lad, with a face utterly pale, but with eyes that were again set in fierce determination.

I laughed a low laugh.

'I believe you are fit for the trade after all,' said I, and I looked at him with mingled distaste and admiration. But I had my last weapon still, my last question. I turned the lantern full on his face, I leant forward again, and I said in distinct slow tones – and the question sounded an absurd one to be spoken in such an impressive way:

'Do you generally wear – clothes like that?'

I had got home with that question. The pallor vanished, the haughty eyes sank. I saw long drooping lashes and a burning flush, and the boy's face once again sought his hands.

At that moment I heard chairs pushed back in the kitchen. In came Hogvardt with an amused smile on his broad face; in came Watkins with his impassive acquiescence in anything that his lordship might order; in came Master Denny brandishing his whip in jovial relentlessness.

'Well, has he told you anything?' cried Denny. It was plain that he hoped for the answer 'No.'

'I have asked him half a dozen questions,' said I, 'and he has not answered one.'

'All right,' said Denny, with wonderful emphasis.

Had I been wrong to extort this much punishment for my most inhospitable reception? Sometimes now I think that I was cruel. In that night much had occurred to breed viciousness in a man of the most equable temper. But the thing had now gone to the extreme limit to which it could go, and I said to Denny:

'It's a gross case of obstinacy, of course, Denny, but I don't see very well how we can horsewhip the lady.'

A sudden astounded cry, 'The lady!' rang from three pairs of lips, while the lady herself dropped her head on the table and fenced her face round about with her protecting arms.

'You see,' said I, 'this lad is the Lady Euphrosyne.'

For who else could it be that would give orders to Constantine Stefanopoulos, and ask where 'my people' were? Who else, I also asked myself, save the daughter of the noble house, would boast the air, the hands, the face, that graced our young prisoner? And who else would understand English? In all certainty here was the Lady Euphrosyne.

5

The Cottage on the Hill

The effect of my remark was curious. Denny flushed scarlet and flung his whip down on the table; the others stood for a moment motionless, then turned tail and slunk back to the kitchen. Euphrosyne's face remained invisible. On the other hand, I felt quite at my ease. I had a triumphant conviction of the importance of my capture, and a determination that no misplaced chivalry should rob me of it. Politeness is, no doubt, a duty, but only a relative duty; and, in plain English, men's lives were at stake here. Therefore I did not make my best bow, fling open the door, and tell the lady that she was free to go whither she would, but I said to her in a dry severe voice:

'You had better go, madam, to the room you usually occupy here, while we consider what to do with you. You know where the room is; I don't.'

She raised her head, and said in tones that sounded almost eager:

'My own room? May I go there?'

'Certainly,' said I. 'I shall accompany you as far as the door; and when you've gone in, I shall lock the door.'

This programme was duly carried out, Euphrosyne not favouring me with a word during its progress. Then I returned to the hall, and said to Denny:

'Rather a trump card, isn't she?'

'Yes, but they'll be back pretty soon to look for her, I expect.'

Denny accompanied this remark with such a yawn that I suggested he should go to bed.

'Aren't you going to bed?' he asked.

'I'll take first watch,' said I. 'It's nearly twelve now. I'll wake you at two, and you can wake Hogvardt at five; then Watkins will be fit and fresh at breakfast-time, and can give us roast cow.'

Thus I was again left alone; and I sat reviewing the position. Would the islanders fight for their lady? Or would they let us go? They would let us go, I felt sure, only if Constantine were outvoted, for he could not afford to see me leave Neopalia with a head on my shoulders and a tongue in my mouth. Then probably they would fight. Well, I calculated that so long as our provisions held out, we could not be stormed; our stone fortress was too strong. But we could be blockaded and starved out, and should be very soon unless the lady's influence could help us. I had just arrived at the conclusion that I would talk to her very seriously in the morning when I heard a remarkable sound.

'There never was such a place for queer noises,' said I, pricking up my ears.

This noise seemed to come directly from above my head; it sounded as though a light stealthy tread were passing over the roof of the hall in which I sat. The only person in the house besides ourselves was the prisoner: she had been securely locked in her room; how then could she be on the top of the hall? For her room was in the turret above the doorway. Yet the steps crept over my head, going towards the kitchen. I snatched up my revolver and trod, with a stealth equal to the stealth of the steps overhead, across the hall and into the kitchen beyond. My three companions slept the sleep of tired men, but I roused Denny ruthlessly.

'Go on guard in the hall,' said I. 'I want to have a look round.'

Denny was sleepy but obedient. I saw him start for the hall, and went on till I reached the compound behind the house.

Here I stood deep in the shadow of the wall; the steps were now over my head again. I glanced up cautiously, and above me, on the roof, three yards to the left, I saw the flutter of a white kilt.

'There are more ways out of this house than I know,' I thought to myself.

I heard next a noise as though of something being pushed cautiously along the flat roof. Then there protruded from between two of the battlements the end of a ladder. I crouched closer under the wall. The light flight of steps was let down; it reached the ground, the kilted figure stepped on it and began to descend. Here was the Lady Euphrosyne again. Her eagerness to go to her own room was fully explained: there was a way from it across the house and out on to the roof of the kitchen; the ladder shewed that the way was kept in use. I stood still. She reached the ground, and, as she touched it, she gave the softest possible little laugh of gleeful triumph; a pretty little laugh it was. Then she walked briskly across the compound, till she reached the rocks on the other side. I crept forward after her, for I was afraid of losing sight of her in the darkness, and yet did not desire to arrest her progress till I saw where she was going. On she went, skirting the perpendicular drop of rock. I was behind her now. At last she came to the angle formed by the rock running north and that which, turning to the east, enclosed the compound.

'How's she going to get up?' I asked myself.

But up she began to go, her right foot on the north rock, her left on the east. She ascended with such confidence that it was evident that steps were ready for her feet. She gained the top; I began to mount in the same fashion, finding the steps cut in the face of the cliff. I reached the top and saw her standing still, ten yards ahead of me. She went on; I followed; she stopped, looked, saw me, screamed. I rushed on her. Her arm dealt a blow at me; I caught her hand, and in her hand there was a little dagger. Seizing her other hand, I held her fast.

'Where are you going to?' I asked in a matter-of-fact tone, taking no notice of her hasty resort to the dagger. No doubt that was merely a national trait.

Seeing that she was caught, she made no attempt to struggle.

'I was trying to escape,' she said. 'Did you hear me?'

'Yes, I heard you. Where were you going to?'

'Why should I tell you? Shall you threaten me with the whip again?'

I loosed her hands. She gave a sudden glance up the hill. She seemed to measure the distance.

'Why do you want to go to the top of the hill?' I asked. 'Have you friends there?'

She denied the suggestion, as I thought she would.

'No, I have not. But anywhere is better than with you.'

'Yet there's someone in the cottage up there,' I observed. 'It belongs to Constantine, doesn't it?'

'Yes, it does,' she answered defiantly. 'Dare you go and seek him there? Or dare you only skulk behind the walls of the house?'

'As long as we are four against a hundred I dare only skulk,' I answered. She did not annoy me at all by her taunts. 'But do you think he's there?'

'There! No; he's in the town; and he'll come from the town to kill you tomorrow.'

'Then is nobody there?' I pursued.

'Nobody,' she answered.

'You're wrong,' said I. 'I saw somebody there today.'

'Oh, a peasant perhaps.'

'Well, the dress didn't look like it. Do you really want to go there now?'

'Haven't you mocked me enough?' she burst out. 'Take me back to my prison.'

Her tragedy-air was quite delightful. But I had been leading her up to something which I thought she ought to know.

'There's a woman in that cottage,' said I. 'Not a peasant; a woman in some dark-coloured dress, who uses opera-glasses.'

I saw her draw back with a start of surprise. 'It's false,' she cried, 'There's no one there. Constantine told me no one went there except Vlacho and sometimes Demetri.'

'Do you believe all Constantine tells you?' I asked.

'Why shouldn't I? He's my cousin, and – '

'And your suitor?'

She flung her head back proudly.

'I have no shame in that,' she answered.

'You would accept his offer?'

'Since you ask, I will answer. Yes. I had promised my uncle that I would.'

'Good God!' said I, for I was very sorry for her.

The emphasis of my exclamation seemed to startle her afresh. I felt her glance rest on me in puzzled questioning.

'Did Constantine let you see the old woman whom I sent to him?' I demanded.

'No,' she murmured. 'He told me what she said.'

'That I told him he was his uncle's murderer?'

'Did you tell her to say that?' she asked, with a sudden inclination of her body towards me.

'I did. Did he give you the message?'

She made no answer. I pressed my advantage. 'On my honour, I saw what I have told you at the cottage,' I said, 'I know what it means no more than you do. But before I came here I saw Constantine in London. And there I heard a lady say she would come with him. Did any lady come with him?'

'Are you mad?' she asked; but I could hear her breathing quickly, and I knew that her scorn was assumed. I drew suddenly away from her, and put my hands behind my back.

'Go to the cottage if you like,' said I. 'But I won't answer for what you'll find there.'

'You set me free?' she cried with eagerness.

'Free to go to the cottage; you must promise to come back. Or I'll go to the cottage, if you'll promise to go back to your room and wait till I return.'

She hesitated, looking towards where the cottage was; but I had stirred suspicion and disquietude in her. She dared not face what she might find in the cottage.

'I'll go back and wait for you,' she said. 'If I went to the cottage and – and all was well, I'm afraid I shouldn't come back.'

The tone sounded softer. I would have sworn that a smile or a half-smile accompanied the words, but it was too dark to be sure, and when I leant forward to look, Euphrosyne drew back.

'Then you mustn't go,' said I decisively; 'I can't afford to lose you.'

'But if you let me go I could let you go,' she cried.

'Could you? Without asking Constantine? Besides, it's my island you see.'

'It's not,' she cried, with a stamp of her foot. And without more she walked straight by me and disappeared over the ledge of rock. Two minutes later I saw her figure defined against the sky, a black shadow on a deep grey ground; then she disappeared. I set my face straight for the cottage under the summit of the hill. I knew that I had only to go straight and I must come to the little plateau scooped out of the hillside, on which the cottage stood. I found, not a path, but a sort of rough track that led in the desired direction, and along this I made my way very cautiously. At one point it was joined at right angles by another track, from the side of the hill where the main road across the island lay. This, of course, afforded an approach to the cottage without passing by my house. In twenty minutes the cottage loomed, a blurred mass, before me. I fell on my knees and peered at it.

There was a light in one of the windows. I crawled nearer. Now I was on the plateau, a moment later I was under the wooden verandah and beneath the window where the light glowed. My hand was on my revolver; if Constantine or Vlacho caught me here, neither side would be able to stand on trifles; even my desire for legality would fail under the strain. But for the minute everything was quiet, and I began to fear that I should have to return empty-handed; for it would be growing light in another hour or so, and I must be gone before the day began to appear. Ah, there was a sound, a sound that appealed to me after my climb, the sound of wine poured into a glass; then came a voice I knew.

'Probably they have caught her,' said Vlacho the innkeeper. 'What of that? They will not hurt her, and she'll be kept safe.'

'You mean she can't come spying about here?'

'Exactly. And that, my lord, is an advantage. If she came here –'

'Oh, the deuce!' laughed Constantine. 'But won't the men want me to free her by letting that infernal crew go?'

'Not if they think Wheatley will go to Rhodes and get soldiers and return. They love the island more than her. It will all go well, my lord. And this other here?'

I strained my ears to listen. No answer came, yet Vlacho went on as though he had received an answer.

'These cursed fellows make that difficult too,' he said. 'It would be an epidemic.' He laughed, seeming to see wit in his own remark.

'Curse them, yes. We must move cautiously,' said Constantine. 'What a nuisance women are, Vlacho.'

'Ay, too many of them,' laughed Vlacho.

'I had to swear my life out that no one was here, and then, "If no one's there, why mayn't I come?" You know the sort of thing.'

'Indeed, no, my lord. You wrong me,' protested Vlacho humorously, and Constantine joined in his laugh.

'You've made up your mind which, I gather?' asked Vlacho,

'Oh, this one, beyond doubt,' answered his master.

Now I thought that I understood most of this conversation, and I was very sorry that Euphrosyne was not by my side to listen to it. But I had heard about enough for my purposes, and I had turned to crawl away stealthily – it is not well to try fortune too far – when I heard the sound of a door opening in the house. Constantine's voice followed directly on the sound.

'Ah, my darling, my sweet wife,' he cried, 'not sleeping yet? Where will your beauty be? Vlacho and I must work and plan for your sake, but you need not spoil your eyes with sleeplessness.'

Constantine did it uncommonly well. His manner was a pattern for husbands. I was guilty of a quiet laugh all to myself in the verandah.

'For me? You're sure it's for me?' came in that Greek with a strange accent, which had first fallen on my ears in the Optimum Restaurant.

'She's jealous, she's most charmingly jealous!' cried Constantine in playful rapture. 'Does your wife pay you such compliments, Vlacho?'

'She has no cause, my lord. But my Lady Francesca thinks she has cause to be jealous of the Lady Euphrosyne.'

Constantine laughed scornfully at the suggestion. 'Where is she now?' came swift and sharp from the woman. 'Where is Euphrosyne?'

'Why, she's a prisoner to that Englishman,' answered Constantine.

I suppose explanations passed at this point, for the voices fell to a lower level, as is apt to happen in the telling of a long story, and I could not catch what was said till Constantine's tones rose again as he remarked:

'Oh, yes; we must have a try at getting her out, just to satisfy the people. For me, she might stay there as long as she likes, for I care for her just as little as, between ourselves, I believe she cares for me.'

Really this fellow was a very tidy villain; as a pair, Vlacho and he would be hard to beat – in England, at all events. About Neopalia I had learned to reserve my opinion. Such were my reflections as I turned to resume my interrupted crawl to safety.

But in an instant I was still again – still, and crouching close under the wall, motionless as an insect that feigns death, holding my breath, my hand on the trigger. For the door of the cottage was flung open, and Constantine and Vlacho appeared on the threshold.

'Ah,' said Vlacho, 'dawn is near. See, it grows lighter on the horizon.'

A more serious matter was that, owing to the open door and the lamp inside, it had grown lighter on the verandah, so light that I saw the three figures – for the woman had come also – in the doorway, so light that my huddled shape would be seen if any of the three turned an eye towards it. I could have picked off both men before they could move; but a civilised education has drawbacks; it makes a man scrupulous; I did not fire. I lay still, hoping that I should not be noticed. And I should not have been noticed but for one thing. Acting up to his part in the ghastly farce which these two ruffians were playing with the wife of one of them, Constantine turned to bestow kisses on the woman before he parted from her. Vlacho, in a mockery that was horrible to me who knew his heart, must needs be facetious. With a laugh he drew back; he drew back farther still; he was but a couple of feet from the wall of the house; and that couple of feet I filled. In a moment, with one step backwards, he would be upon me. Perhaps he would not have made that step; perhaps I should have gone, by grace of that narrow interval, undetected. But the temptation was too strong for me. The thought of the thing threatened to make me laugh. I had a penknife in my pocket. I opened it, and dug it hard into that portion of Vlacho's frame which came most conveniently and prominently to my hand. Then, leaving the penknife where it was, I leapt up, gave the howling ruffian a mighty shove, and with a loud laugh of triumph bolted for my life down the hill. But when I had gone twenty yards I dropped on my knees, for bullet after bullet whistled over my head. Constantine, the outraged Vlacho too, perhaps, carried a revolver! Their barrels were being emptied after me. I rose and turned one hasty glance behind me. Yes, I saw their dim shapes like moving trees. I fired once, twice, thrice, in my turn, and then went crashing and rushing down the path that I had ascended so cautiously. I cannoned against the tree trunks; I tripped over trailing branches; I stumbled over stones. Once I paused and fired the rest of my barrels. A yell told me I had hit – but Vlacho, alas, not Constantine; I knew the voice. At the same instant my fire was returned, and a bullet went through my hat. I was defenceless now, save for my heels, and to them I took again with all speed. But as I crashed along, one at least of them came crashing after me. Yes, it was only one! I had checked Vlacho's career. It was Constantine alone. I suppose one of your heroes of romance would have stopped and faced him, for with them it is not etiquette to run away from one man. Ah, well, I ran away. For all I knew, Constantine might still have a shot in the locker; I had none. And if Constantine killed me, he would kill the only man who knew all his secrets. So I ran. And just as I got within ten yards of the drop into my own territory, I heard a wild cry, 'Charley! Charley! Where the devil are you, Charley?'

'Why, here, of course,' said I, coming to the top of the bank and dropping over.

I have no doubt that it was the cry uttered by Denny which gave pause to Constantine's pursuit. He would not desire to face all four of us. At any rate the sound of his pursuing feet died away and ceased. I suppose he went back to look after Vlacho, and show himself safe and sound to that most unhappy woman, his wife. As for me, when I found myself safe and sound in the compound, I said, 'Thank God!' And I meant it too. Then I looked round. Certainly the sight that met my eyes had a touch of comedy in it.

Denny, Hogvardt and Watkins stood in the compound. Their backs were towards me, and they were all staring up at the roof of the kitchen, with expressions which the cold light of morning revealed in all their puzzled foolishness. And on the top of the roof, unassailable and out of reach – for no ladder ran from roof to ground now – stood Euphrosyne, in her usual attitude of easy grace. Euphrosyne was not taking the smallest notice of the helpless three below, but stood quite still with unmoved face, gazing up towards the cottage. The whole thing reminded me of nothing so much as of a pretty composed cat in a tree, with three infuriated helpless terriers barking round the trunk. I began to laugh.

'What's all the shindy?' called out Denny. 'Who's doing revolver practice in the wood? And how the dickens did she get there, Charley?'

But when the still figure on the roof saw me, the impassivity of it vanished. Euphrosyne leant forward, clasping her hands, and said to me:

'Have you killed him?'

The question vexed me. It would have been civil to accompany it, at all events, with an inquiry as to my own health.

'Killed him?' I answered gruffly. 'No, he's sound enough.'

'And –' she began; but now she glanced, seemingly for the first time, at my friends below. 'You must come and tell me,' she said, and with that she turned and disappeared from our gaze behind the battlements. I listened intently. No sound came from the wood that rose grey in the new light behind us.

'What have you been doing?' demanded Denny surlily; he had not enjoyed Euphrosyne's scornful attitude.

'I have been running for my life,' said I, 'from the biggest scoundrels unhanged. Denny, make a guess who lives in that cottage.'

'Constantine?'

'I don't mean him.'

'Not Vlacho – he's at the inn.'

'No, I don't mean Vlacho.'

'Who then, man?'

'Someone you've seen.'

'Oh, I give it up. It's not the time of day for riddles.'

'The lady who dined at the next table to ours at the Optimum,' said I.

Denny jumped back in amazement, with a long low whistle.

'What, the one who was with Constantine?' he cried.

'Yes,' said I, 'the one who was with Constantine.' They were all three round me now; and thinking that it would be better that they should know what I knew, and four lives instead of one stand between a ruffian and the impunity he hoped for, I raised my voice and went on in an emphatic tone,

'Yes. She's there, and she's his wife.'

A moment's astonished silence greeted my announcement. It was broken by none of our party. But there came from the battlemented roof above us a low, long, mournful moan that made its way straight to the heart, armed with its dart of outraged pride and trust betrayed. It was not thus, boldly and abruptly, that I should have told my news. But I did not know that Euphrosyne was still above us, hidden by the battlements. We all looked up. The moan was not repeated. Presently we heard slow steps retreating, with a faltering tread, across the roof; and we also went into the house in silence and sorrow. For a thing like that gets hold of a man; and when he has heard it, it is hard for him to sit down and be merry, until the fellow that caused it has paid his reckoning. I swore then and there that Constantine Stefanopoulos should pay his.

6

The Poem of One-eyed Alexander

There is a matter on my conscience which I cannot excuse but may as well confess. To deceive a maiden is a very sore thing, so sore that it had made us all hot against Constantine; but it may be doubted by a cool mind whether it is worse, nay, whether it is not more venial than to contrive the murder of a lawful wife. Poets have paid more attention to the first offence – maybe they know more about it – the law finds greater employment, on the whole, in respect to the second. For me, I admit that it was not till I found myself stretched on a mattress in the kitchen, with the idea of getting a few hours' sleep, that it struck me that Constantine's wife deserved a share of my concern and care. Her grievance against him was at least as great as Euphrosyne's; her peril was far greater. For Euphrosyne was his object; Francesca (for that appeared from Vlacho's mode of address to be her name) was an obstacle which prevented him attaining that object. For myself I should have welcomed a cut throat if it came as an alternative to Constantine's society; but probably his wife would not agree with me, and the conversation I had heard left me in little doubt that her life was not safe. They could not have an epidemic, Vlacho had prudently reminded his master; the island fever could not kill Constantine's wife and our party all in a day or two. Men suspect such an obliging malady, and the old lord had died of it, pat to the happy moment, already.

But if the thing could be done, if it could be so managed that London, Paris, and the Riviera would find nothing strange in the disappearance of one Madame Stefanopoulos and the appearance of another, why, to a certainty, done the thing would be, unless I could warn or save the woman in the cottage. But I did not see how to do either. So (as I set out to confess) I dropped the subject. And when I went to sleep I was thinking not how to save Francesca, but how to console Euphrosyne, a matter really of less urgency, as I should have seen had not the echo of that sad little cry still filled my ears.

The news which Hogvardt brought me when I rose in the morning, and was enjoying a slice of cow steak, by no means cleared my way. An actual attack did not seem imminent – I fancy these fierce islanders were not too fond of our revolvers – but the house was, if I may use the term, carefully picketed, and that both before and behind. Along the road which approached it in front there stood sentries at intervals. They were stationed just out of range of our only effective long-distance weapon, but it was evident that egress on that side was barred. And the same was the case on the other; Hogvardt had seen men moving in the wood, and had heard their challenges to one another repeated at regular intervals. We were shut off from the sea; we were shut off from the cottage. A blockade would reduce us as surely as an attack. I had nothing to offer except the release of Euphrosyne. And to release Euphrosyne would, in all likelihood, not save us, while it would leave Constantine free to play out his relentless game to its appointed end.

I finished my breakfast in some perplexity of spirit. Then I went and sat in the hall, expecting that Euphrosyne would appear from her room before long. I was alone, for the rest were engaged in various occupations, Hogvardt being particularly busy over a large handful of hunting knives which he had gleaned from the walls; I did not understand what he wanted with them, unless he meant to arm himself in porcupine fashion.

Presently Euphrosyne came, but it was a transformed Euphrosyne. The kilt, knee-breeches, and gaiters were gone; in their place was the white linen garment with flowing sleeves and the loose jacket over it, the national dress of the Greek woman; but Euphrosyne's was ornamented with a rare profusion of delicate embroidery, and of so fine a texture that it seemed rather some delicate, soft, yielding silk. The change of attire seemed reflected in her altered manner. Defiance was gone, and appeal glistened from her eyes as she stood before me. I sprang up, but she would not sit. She stood there, and, raising her glance to my face, asked simply:

'Is it true?'

In a business-like way I told her the whole story, starting from the everyday scene at home in the restaurant, ending with the villainous conversation and the wild chase of the night before. When I related how Constantine had called Francesca his wife, Euphrosyne started. While I sketched lightly my encounter with him and Vlacho, she eyed me with a sort of grave curiosity; and at the end she said:

'I'm glad you weren't killed.'

It was not an emotional speech, nor delivered with any *empressement*, but I took it for thanks and made the best of it. Then at last she sat down and rested her head on her hand; her absent reverie allowed me to study her closely, and I was struck by a new beauty which the fantastic boy's disguise had concealed. Moreover, with the doffing of that, she seemed to have put off her extreme hostility; but perhaps the revelation I had made to her, which showed her the victim of an unscrupulous schemer, had more to do with her softened air. Yet she had borne the story firmly, and a quivering lip was her extreme sign of grief or anger. And her first question was not of herself.

'Do you mean that they will kill this woman?' she asked.

'I'm afraid it's not unlikely that something will happen to her, unless, of course –' I paused, but her quick wit supplied the omission.

'Unless,' she said, 'he lets her live now, because I am out of his hands?'

'Will you stay out of his hands?' I asked. 'I mean, as long as I can keep you out of them.'

She looked round with a troubled expression.

'How can I stay here?' she said in a low tone.

'You will be as safe here now as you were in your uncle's care,' I answered.

She acknowledged my promise with a movement of her head; but a moment later she cried:

'But I am not with you – I am with the people! The island is theirs and mine. It's not yours. I'll have no part in giving it to you.'

'I wasn't proposing to take pay for my hospitality,' said I. 'It'll be hardly handsome enough for that, I'm afraid. But mightn't we leave the question for the moment?' And I described briefly to her our present position.

'So that,' I concluded, 'while I maintain my claim to the island, I am at present more interested in keeping a whole skin on myself and my friends.'

'If you will not give it up, I can do nothing,' said she. 'Though they knew Constantine to be all you say, yet they would follow him and not me if I yielded the island. Indeed they would most likely follow him in any case. For the Neopalians like a man to follow, and they like that man to be a Stefanopoulos; so they would shut their eyes to much, in order that Constantine might marry me and become lord.'

She stated all this in a matter-of-fact way, disclosing no great horror of her countrymen's moral standard. The straightforward barbarousness of it perhaps appealed to her a little; she loathed the man who would rule on those terms, but had some toleration for the people who set the true dynasty above all else.

And she spoke of her proposed marriage as though it were a natural arrangement.

'I shall have to marry him, I expect, in spite of everything,' she said.

I pushed my chair back violently. My English respectability was appalled.

'Marry him?' I cried. 'Why, he murdered the old lord!'

'That has happened before among the Stefanopouloi,' said Euphrosyne, with a calmness dangerously near to pride.

'And he proposes to murder his wife,' I added.

'Perhaps he will get rid of her without that.' She paused; then came the anger I had looked for before. 'Ah, but how dared he swear that he had thought of none but me, and loved me passionately? He shall pay for that!' Again it was injured pride which rang in her voice, as in her first cry. It did not sound like love; and for that I was glad. The courtship probably had been an affair of state rather than of affection. I did not ask how Constantine was to be made to pay, whether before or after marriage. I was struggling between horror and amusement at my guest's point of view. But I take leave to have a will of my own, even sometimes in matters which are not exactly my concern; and I said now, with a composure that rivalled Euphrosyne's:

'It's out of the question that you should marry him. I'm going to get him hanged; and, anyhow, it would be atrocious.'

She smiled at that; but then she leant forward and asked:

'How long have you provisions for?'

'That's a good retort,' I admitted. 'A few days, that's all. And we can't get out to procure any more; and we can't go shooting, because the wood's infested with these ruff – I beg pardon – with your countrymen.'

'Then it seems to me,' said Euphrosyne, 'that you and your friends are more likely to be hanged.'

Well, on a dispassionate consideration, it did seem more likely; but she need not have said so. She went on with an equally discouraging good sense:

'There will be a boat from Rhodes in about a month or six weeks. The officer will come then to take the tribute; perhaps the Governor will come. But till then nobody will visit the island, unless it be a few fishermen from Cyprus.'

'Fishermen? Where do they land? At the harbour?'

'No; my people do not like them; but the Governor threatens to send troops if we do not let them land. So they come to a little creek at the opposite end of the island, on the other side of the mountain. Ah, what are you thinking of?'

As Euphrosyne perceived, her words had put a new idea in my mind. If I could reach that creek and find the fishermen and persuade them to help me or to carry my party off, that hanging might happen to the right man after all.

'You're thinking you can reach them?' she cried.

'You don't seem sure that you want me to,' I observed.

'Oh, how can I tell what I want? If I help you I am betraying the island. If I do not –'

'You'll have a death or two at your door, and you'll marry the biggest scoundrel in Europe,' said I.

She hung her head and plucked fretfully at the embroidery on the front of her gown.

'But anyhow you couldn't reach them,' she said. 'You are close prisoners here.'

That, again, seemed true, so that it put me in a very bad temper. Therefore I rose and, leaving her without much ceremony, strolled into the kitchen. Here I found Watkins dressing the cow's head, Hogvardt surrounded by knives, and Denny lying on a rug on the floor with a small book which he seemed to be reading. He looked up with a smile that he considered knowing.

'Well, what does the Captive Queen say?' he asked with levity.

'She proposes to marry Constantine,' I answered, and added quickly to Hogvardt:

'What's the game with those knives, Hog?'

'Well, my lord,' said Hogvardt, surveying his dozen murderous instruments, 'I thought there was no harm in putting an edge on them, in case we should find a use for them,' and he fell to grinding one with great energy.

'I say, Charley, I wonder what this yarn's about. I can't construe half of it. It's in Greek, and it's something about Neopalia; and there's a lot about a Stefanopoulos.'

'Is there? Let's see,' and, taking the book, I sat down to look at it. It was a slim old book, bound in calfskin. The Greek was written in an old-fashioned style; it was verse. I turned to the title page. 'Hullo, this is rather interesting,' I exclaimed. 'It's about the death of old Stefanopoulos – the thing they sing that song about, you know.'

In fact I had got hold of the poem which One-eyed Alexander composed. Its length was about three hundred lines, exclusive of the refrain which the islanders had chanted, and which was inserted six times, occurring at the end of each fifty lines. The rest was written in rather barbarous iambics; and the sentiments were quite as barbarous as the verse. It told the whole story, and I ran rapidly over it, translating here and there for the benefit of my companions. The arrival of the Baron d'Ezonville recalled our own with curious exactness, except that he came with one servant only. He had been taken to the inn as I had, but he had never escaped from there, and had been turned adrift the morning after his arrival. I took more interest in Stefan, and followed eagerly the story of how the islanders had come to his house and demanded that he should revoke the sale. Stefan, however, was obstinate; it cost the lives of four of his assailants before his door was forced. Thus far I read, and expected to find next an account of a mêlée in the hall. But here the story took a turn unexpected by me, one that might make the reading of the old poem more than a mere pastime.

'But when they had broken in,' sang One-eyed Alexander, 'behold the hall was empty, and the house empty! And they stood amazed. But the two cousins of the Lord, who had been the hottest in seeking his death, put all the rest to the door, and were themselves alone in the house; for the secret was known to them who were of the blood of the Stefanopouloi. Unto me, the Bard, it is not known. Yet men say they went beneath the earth, and there in the earth found the lord. And certain it is they slew him, for in a space they came forth to the door, bearing his head; this they showed to the people, who answered with a great shout. But the cousins went back, barring the door again; and again, when but a few minutes had passed, they came forth, opening the door, and the elder of them, being now by the traitor's death become lord, bade the people in, and made a great feast for them. But the head of Stefan none saw again, nor did any see his body; but body and head were gone whither none know, saving the noble blood of the Stefanopouloi; for utterly they disappeared, and the secret was securely kept.'

I read this passage aloud, translating as I went. At the end Denny drew a breath.

'Well, if there aren't ghosts in this house there ought to be,' he remarked. 'What the deuce did those rascals do with the old gentleman, Charley?'

'It says they went beneath the earth.'

'The cellar,' suggested Hogvardt, who had a prosaic mind.

'But they wouldn't leave the body in the cellar,' I objected; 'and if, as this fellow says, they were only away a few minutes, they couldn't have dug a grave for it. And then it says that they "there in the earth found the lord."'

'It would have been more interesting,' said Denny, 'if they'd told Alexander a bit more about it. However I suppose he consoles himself with his chant again?'

'He does. It follows immediately on what I've read, and so the thing ends.' And I sat looking at the little yellow volume. 'Where did you find it, Denny?' I asked.

'Oh, on a shelf in the corner of the hall, between the *Iliad* and a *Life of Byron*. There's precious little to read in this house.'

I got up and walked back to the hall. I looked round. Euphrosyne was not there. I inspected the hall door; it was still locked on the inside. I mounted the stairs and called at the door of her room; when no answer came, I pushed it open and took the liberty of glancing round; she was not there. I called again, for I thought she might have passed along the way over the hall and reached the roof, as she had before. This time I called loudly. Silence followed for a moment. Then came an answer, in a hurried, rather apologetic tone, 'Here I am.' But then – the answer came not from the direction that I had expected, but from the hall! And, looking over the balustrade, I saw Euphrosyne sitting in the armchair.

'This,' said I, going downstairs, 'taken in conjunction with this' – and I patted One-eyed Alexander's book, which I held in my hand – 'is certainly curious and suggestive.'

'Here I am,' said Euphrosyne, with an air that added, 'I've not moved. What are you shouting for?'

'Yes, but you weren't there a minute ago,' I observed, reaching the hall and walking across to her.

She looked disturbed and embarrassed.

'Where have you been?' I asked.

'Must I give an account of every movement?' said she, trying to cover her confusion with a show of haughty offence.

The coincidence was really a remarkable one; it was as hard to account for Euphrosyne's disappearance and reappearance as for the vanished head and body of old Stefan. I had a conviction, based on a sudden intuition, that one explanation must lie at the root of both these curious things, that the secret of which Alexander spoke was a secret still hidden – hidden from my eyes, but known to the girl before me, the daughter of the Stefanopouloi.

'I won't ask you where you've been, if you don't wish to tell me,' said I carelessly.

She bowed her head in recognition of my indulgence.

'But there is one question I should like to ask you,' I pursued, 'if you'll be so kind as to answer it.'

'Well, what is it?' She was still on the defensive.

'Where was Stefan Stefanopoulos killed, and what became of his body?'

As I put the question I flung One-eyed Alexander's book open on the table beside her.

She started visibly, crying, 'Where did you get that?'

I told her how Denny had found it, and I added:

'Now, what does "beneath the earth" mean? You're one of the house and you must know.'

'Yes, I know, but I must not tell you. We are all bound by the most sacred oath to tell no one.'

'Who told you?'

'My uncle. The boys of our house are told when they are fifteen, the girls when they are sixteen. No one else knows.'

'Why is that?'

She hesitated, fearing, perhaps, that her answer itself would tend to betray the secret,

'I dare tell you nothing,' she said. 'The oath binds me; and it binds every one of my kindred to kill me if I break it.'

'But you've no kindred left except Constantine,' I objected.

'He is enough. He would kill me.'

'Sooner than marry you?' I suggested rather maliciously.

'Yes, if I broke the oath.'

'Hang the oath!' said I impatiently. 'The thing might help us. Did they bury Stefan somewhere under the house?'

'No, he was not buried,' she answered.

'Then they brought him up and got rid of his body when the islanders had gone?'

'You must think what you will.'

'I'll find it out,' said I. 'If I pull the house down, I'll find it. Is it a secret door or – ?'

She had coloured at the question. I put the latter part in a low eager voice, for hope had come to me.

'Is it a way out?' I asked, leaning over to her.

She sat mute, but irresolute, embarrassed and fretful.

'Heavens,' I cried impatiently, 'it may mean life or death to all of us, and you boggle over your oath!'

My rude impatience met with a rebuke that it perhaps deserved. With a glance of the utmost scorn, Euphrosyne asked coldly,

'What are the lives of all of you to me?'

'True, I forgot,' said I, with a bitter politeness. 'I beg your pardon. I did you all the service I could last night, and now – I and my friends may as well die as live! But, by God, I'll pull this place to ruins, but I'll find your secret.'

I was walking up and down now in a state of some excitement. My brain was fired with the thought of stealing a march on Constantine through the discovery of his own family secret.

Suddenly Euphrosyne gave a little soft clap with her hands. It was over in a minute, and she sat blushing, confused, trying to look as if she had not moved at all.

'What did you do that for?' I asked, stopping in front of her.

'Nothing,' said Euphrosyne.

'Oh, I don't believe that,' said I.

She looked at me. 'I didn't mean to do it,' she said. 'But can't you guess why?'

'There's too much guessing to be done here,' said I impatiently; and I started walking again. But presently I heard a voice say softly, and in a tone that seemed to address nobody in particular – me least of all:

'We Neopalians like a man who can be angry, and I began to think you never would.'

'I am not the least angry,' said I with great indignation. I hate being told that I am angry when I am merely showing firmness.

Now at this protest of mine Euphrosyne saw fit to laugh – the most hearty laugh she had given since I had known her. The mirthfulness of it undermined my wrath. I stood still opposite her, biting the end of my moustache.

'You may laugh,' said I, 'but I'm not angry; and I shall pull this house down, or dig it up, in cold blood, in perfectly cold blood.'

'You are angry,' said Euphrosyne, 'and you say you're not. You are like my father. He would stamp his foot furiously like that, and say, "I am not angry, I am not angry, Phroso."'

Phroso! I had forgotten that diminutive of my guest's classical name. It rather pleased me, and I repeated gently after her, 'Phroso, Phroso!' and I'm afraid I eyed the little foot that had stamped so bravely.

'He always called me Phroso. Oh, I wish he were alive! Then Constantine – '

'Since he isn't,' said I, sitting on the table by Phroso (I must write it, it's a deal shorter) – by Phroso's elbow – 'since he isn't, I'll look after Constantine. It would be a pity to spoil the house, wouldn't it?'

'I've sworn,' said Phroso.

'Circumstances alter oaths,' said I, bending till I was very near Phroso's ear.

'Ah,' said Phroso reproachfully, 'that's what lovers say when they find another more beautiful than their old love.'

I shot away from Phroso's ear with a sudden backward start. Her remark somehow came home to me with a very remarkable force. I got off the table, and stood opposite to her in an awkward and stiff attitude.

'I am compelled to ask you, for the last time, if you will tell me the secret?' said I, in the coldest of tones.

She looked up with surprise; my altered manner may well have amazed her. She did not know the reason of it.

'You asked me kindly and – and pleasantly, and I would not. Now you ask me as if you threatened,' she said, 'Is it likely I should tell you now?'

Well, I was angry with myself and with her because she had made me angry with myself; and, the next minute, I became furiously angry with Denny, whom I found standing in the doorway that led to the kitchen with a smile of intense amusement on his face.

'What are you grinning at?' I demanded fiercely.

'Oh, nothing,' said Denny, and his face strove to assume a prudent gravity.

'Bring a pickaxe,' said I.

Denny's eyes wandered towards Phroso. 'Is she as annoying as that?' he seemed to ask. 'A pickaxe?' he repeated in surprised tones.

'Yes, two pickaxes. I'm going to have this floor up, and see if I can find out the great Stefanopoulos secret.' I spoke with an accent of intense scorn.

Again Phroso laughed; her hands beat very softly against one another. Heavens, what did she do that for, when Denny was there, watching everything with those shrewd eyes of his?

'The pickaxes!' I roared.

Denny turned and fled; a moment elapsed. I did not know what to do, how to look at Phroso, or how not to look at her. I took refuge in flight. I rushed into the kitchen, on pretence of aiding or hastening Denny's search. I found him taking up an old pick that stood near the door leading to the compound. I seized it from his hand.

'Confound you!' I cried, for Denny laughed openly at me; and I rushed back to the hall. But on the threshold I paused, and said what I will not write.

For, though there came from somewhere the ripple of a mirthful laugh, the hall was empty! Phroso was gone! I flung the pickaxe down with a clatter on the boards, and exclaimed in my haste:

'I wish to heaven I'd never bought the island!'

But I did not really mean that.

7

The Secret of the Stefanopouloi

Was this a pantomime? For a moment I declared angrily that it was no better; but the next instant changed the current of my feelings, transforming irritation into alarm and perplexity into the strongest excitement. For Phroso's laugh ended – ended as a laugh ends that is suddenly cut short in its career of mirth – and there was a second of absolute stillness. Then from the front of the house, and from the back, came the sharp sound of shots – three in rapid succession in front, four behind. Denny rushed out from the kitchen, rifle in hand.

'They're at us on both sides!' he cried, leaping to his perch at the window and cautiously peering round. 'Hogvardt and Watkins are ready at the back; they're firing from the wood,' he went on. Then he fired. 'Missed, confound it!' he muttered. 'Well, they don't come any nearer, I'll see to that.'

Denny was a sure defence in front. I turned towards the kitchen, for more shots came from that direction, and although it was difficult to do worse than harass us from there, our perpendicular bank of rock being a difficult obstacle to pass in face of revolver fire, I wanted to see that all was well and to make the best disposition against this unexpected onset. Yet I did not reach the kitchen; half-way to the door which led to it I was arrested by a cry of distress. Phroso's laugh had gone, but the voice was still hers. 'Help!' she cried, 'help!' Then came a chuckle from Denny at the window, and a triumphant, 'Winged him, by Jove!' And then from Phroso again, 'Help!' – and at last an enlightening word, 'Help! Under the staircase! Help!'

At this summons I left my friends to sustain the attack or the feigned attack; for I began to suspect that it was no more than a diversion, and that the real centre of operations was 'under the staircase;' thither I ran. The stairs rose from the centre of the right side of the hall, and led up to the gallery; they rose steeply, and a man could stand upright up to within four feet of the spot where the staircase sprang from the level floor. I was there now; and under me I heard no longer voices, but a kind of scuffle. The pick was in my hand, and I struck savagely again and again at the boards; for I did not doubt now that there was a trap-door, and I was in no mind to spend my time seeking for its cunning machinery. And yet where knowledge failed, chance came to my help; at the fifth or sixth blow I must have happened on the spring, for the boards yawned, leaving a space of about three inches. Dropping the pick, I fell on my knees and seized the edge nearest me. With all my strength I tugged and pulled. My violence was of no avail, the boards moved no more. Impatient yet sobered I sought eagerly for the spring which my pick had found. Ah, here it was! It answered now to a touch light as Phroso's own. At the slightest pressure the boards rolled away, seeming to curl themselves up under the base of the staircase; and there was revealed to me an aperture four feet long by three broad; beneath lay a flight of stone steps. I seized my pick again, and took a step downwards. I heard nothing except the noise of retreating feet. I went on. Down six steps I went, then the steps ended, and I was on an incline. At that moment I heard again, only a few yards from me, 'Help!' I sprang forward. A loud curse rang out, and a shot whistled by me, The open trap-door gave a glimmer of light. I was in a narrow passage, and a man was coming at me. I did not know where Phroso was, but I took the risk. I fired straight at him, having shifted my pick to the left hand. The aim was true, he fell prone on his face before me. I jumped on and over his body, and ran along the dark passage; for I still heard retreating steps. But then came a voice I knew, the voice of Vlacho the innkeeper. 'Then stay where you are, curse you!' he cried savagely. There was a thud, as though someone fell heavily to the ground, a cry of pain, and then the rapid running of feet that fled now at full pace and unencumbered. Vlacho the innkeeper had heard my shot and had no stomach for fighting in that rat run, with a girl in his arms to boot! And I, pursuing, was brought up short by the body of Phroso, which lay, white and plain to see, across the narrow passage.

'Are you hurt?' I cried eagerly.

'He flung me down violently,' she answered. 'But I'm not hurt otherwise.'

'Then I'll go after him,' I cried.

'No, no, you mustn't. You don't know the way. You don't know the dangers; there may be more of them at the other end.'

'True,' said I. 'What happened?'

'Why, I came down to hide from you, you know. But directly I reached the foot of the steps Vlacho seized me. He was crouching there with Spiro – you know Spiro. And they said, "Ah, she has saved us the trouble!" and began to drag me away. But I would not go, and I called to you. I twisted my feet round Vlacho, so that he couldn't go fast; then he told Spiro to catch hold of me, and they were just carrying me off when you came. Vlacho kept hold of me while Spiro went to meet you and – '

'It seems,' I interrupted, 'that Constantine was less scrupulous about that oath than you were. Or how did Vlacho and Spiro come here?'

'Yes, he must have told them,' she admitted reluctantly.

'Well, come along, come back; I'm wanted,' said I; and (without asking leave, I fear) I caught her up in my arms and began to run back. I jumped again over Spiro – friend Spiro had not moved – and regained the hall.

'Stay there, under the stairs; you're sheltered there,' I said hastily to Phroso. Then I called to Denny, 'What cheer, Denny?'

Denny turned round with a radiant smile. I don't think he had even noticed my absence.

'Prime,' said he. 'This is a rare gun of old Constantine's; it carries a good thirty yards farther than any they've got, and I can pick 'em off before they get dangerous. I've got one and winged another, and the rest have retired a little way to talk it over.'

Seeing that things were all right in that quarter I ran into the kitchen. It was well that I did so. We were indeed in no danger; from that side, at all events, the attack was evidently no more than a feint. There was desultory firing from a safe distance in the wood. I reckoned there must be four or five men hidden behind trees and emerging every now and then to pay us a compliment. But they had not attempted a rush. The mischief was quite different, being just this, that Watkins, who was not well-instructed in the range of firearms, was cheerfully emptying his revolver into space, and wasting our precious cartridges at the rate of about two a minute. He was so magnificently happy that it went to my heart to stop him, but I was compelled to seize his arm and command him very peremptorily to wait till there was something to fire at.

'I thought I'd show them that we were ready for them, my lord,' said he apologetically.

I turned impatiently to Hogvardt.

'Why did you let him make a fool of himself like that?' I asked.

'He would miss, anyhow, wherever the men were,' observed Hogvardt philosophically. 'And,' he continued, 'I was busy myself.'

'What were you doing?' I asked in a scornful tone.

Hogvardt made no answer in words; but he pointed proudly to the table. There I saw a row of five long and strong saplings; to the head of each of these most serviceable lances there was bound strongly, with thick wire wound round again and again, a long, keen, bright knife.

'I think these may be useful,' said Hogvardt, rubbing his hands, and rising from his seat with the sigh of a man who had done a good morning's work.

'The cartridges would have been more useful still,' said I severely.

'Yes,' he admitted, 'if you would have taken them away from Watkins. But you know you wouldn't, my lord. You'd be afraid of hurting his feelings. So he might just as well amuse himself while I made the lances.'

I have known Hogvardt for a long while, and I never argue with him. The mischief was done; the cartridges were gone; we had the lances; it was no use wasting more words over it. I shrugged my shoulders.

'Your lordship will find the lances very useful,' said Hogvardt, fingering one of them most lovingly.

The attack was dying away now in both front and rear. My impression was amply confirmed. It had been no more than a device for occupying our attention while those two daring rascals, Vlacho and Spiro, armed with the knowledge of the secret way, made a sudden dash upon us, either in the hope of getting a shot at our backs and finding shelter again before we could retaliate, or with the design of carrying off Phroso. Her jest had forestalled the former idea, if it had been in their minds, and they had then endeavoured to carry out the latter. Indeed I found afterwards that it was the latter on which Constantine laid most stress; for a deputation of the islanders had come to him, proposing that he should make terms with me as a means of releasing their Lady. Now since last night Constantine, for reasons which he could not disclose to the deputation, was absolutely precluded from treating with me; he was therefore driven to make an attempt to get Phroso out of my hands in order to satisfy her people. This enterprise I had happily frustrated for the moment. But my mind was far from easy. Provisions would soon be gone; ammunition was scanty; against an attack by day our strong position, aided by Denny's coolness and marksmanship, seemed to protect us very effectually; but I could feel no confidence as to the result of a grand assault under the protecting shadow of night. And now that Constantine's hand was being forced by the islanders' anxiety for Phroso, I was afraid that he would not wait long before attempting a decisive stroke.

'I wish we were well out of it,' said I despondently, as I wiped my brow.

All was quiet. Watkins appeared with bread, cheese and wine.

'Your lordship would not wish to use the cow at luncheon?' he asked, as he passed me on his way to the hall.

'Certainly not, Watkins,' I answered, smiling. 'We must save the cow.'

'There is still a goat, but she is a poor thin creature, my lord.'

'We shall come to her in time, Watkins,' said I. But if I were depressed, the other three were very merry over their meal. Danger was an idea which found no hospitality in Denny's brain; Hogvardt was as cool a hand as the world held; Watkins could not believe that Providence would deal unkindly with a man of my rank. They toasted our recent success, and listened with engrossed interest to my account of the secret of the Stefanopouloi. Phroso sat a little apart, saying nothing, but at last I turned to her and asked, 'Where does the passage lead to?'

She answered readily enough; the secret was out through Constantine's fault, not hers, and the seal was removed from her lips.

'If you follow it to the end, it comes out in a little cave in the rocks on the seashore, near the creek where the Cypriote fishermen come,'

'Ah,' I cried, 'it might help us to get there!'

She shook her head, answering:

'Constantine is sure to have that end strongly guarded now, because he knows that you have the secret.'

'We might force our way.'

'There is no room for more than one man to go at a time; and besides – ' she paused.

'Well, what besides?' I asked.

'It would be certain death to try to go in the face of an enemy,' she answered.

Denny broke in at this point.

'By the way, what of the fellow you shot? Are we going to leave him there, or must we get him up?'

Spiro had been in my mind; and now I said to Phroso:

'What did they do with the body of Stefan Stefanopoulos? There was not time for them to have taken it to the end of the way, was there?'

'No, they didn't take it to the end of the way,' said she. 'I will show you if you like. Bring a torch; you must keep behind me, and right in the middle of the path.'

I accepted her invitation eagerly, telling Denny to keep guard. He was very anxious to accompany us, but another and more serious attack might be in store, and I would not trust the house to Hogvardt and Watkins alone. So I took a lantern in lieu of a torch and prepared to follow. At the last moment Hogvardt thrust into my hand one of his lances.

'It will very likely be useful,' said he. 'A thing like that is always useful.'

I would not disappoint him, and I took the lance. Phroso signed to me to give her the lantern and preceded me down the flight of stairs.

'We shall be in earshot of the hall?' I asked.

'Yes, for as far as we are going,' she answered, and she led the way into the passage. I prayed her to let me go first, for it was just possible that some of Constantine's ruffians might still be there.

'I don't think so,' she said. 'He would tell as few as possible. You see, we have always kept the secret from the islanders. I think that, if you had not killed Spiro, he would not have lived long after knowing it.'

'The deuce!' I exclaimed. 'And Vlacho?'

'Oh, I don't know. Constantine is very fond of Vlacho. Still, perhaps, some day –' The unfinished sentence was expressive enough.

'What use was the secret?' I asked, as we groped our way slowly along and edged by the body of Spiro which lay, six feet of dead clay, in the path.

'In the first place, we could escape by it,' she answered, 'if any tumult arose in the island. That was what Stefan tried to do, and would have done, had not his own kindred been against him and overtaken him here in the passage.'

'And in the second place?' I asked.

Phroso stopped, turned round, and faced me.

'In the second place,' she said, 'if any one of the islanders became very powerful – too powerful, you know – then the ruling lord would show him great favour; and, as a crowning mark of his confidence, he would bid him come by night and learn the great secret; and they two would come together down this passage. But the lord would return alone.'

'And the other?'

'The body of the other would be found two, three, four days, or a week later, tossing on the shores of the island,' answered Phroso. 'For look!' and she held the lantern high above her head so that its light was projected in front of us, and I could see fifteen or twenty yards ahead.

'When they reached here, Stefanopoulos and the other,' she went on, 'Stefanopoulos would stumble, and feign to twist his foot, and he would pray the other to let him lean a little on his shoulder. Thus they would go on, the other a pace in front, the lord leaning on his shoulder; and the lord would hold the torch, but he would not hold it up, as I hold the lantern, but down to the ground, so that it should light no more than a pace or two ahead. And when they came there – do you see, my lord – there?'

'I see,' said I, and I believe I shivered a bit.

'When they came there the torch would suddenly show the change, so suddenly that the other would start and be for an instant alarmed, and turn his head round to the lord to ask what it meant.'

Phroso paused in her recital of the savage, simple, sufficient old trick.

'Yes?' said I. 'And at that moment –'

'The lord's hand on his shoulder,' she answered, 'which had rested lightly before, would grow heavy as lead and with a great sudden impulse the other would be hurled forward, and the lord would be alone again with the secret, and alone the holder of power in Neopalia.'

This was certainly a pretty secret of empire, and nonetheless although the empire it protected was but nine miles long and five broad. I took the lantern from Phroso's hand, saying, 'Let's have a look.'

I stepped a pace or two forward, prodding the ground with Hogvardt's lance before I moved my feet: and thus I came to the spot where the Stefanopoulos used with a sudden great impulse to propel his enemy down. For here the rocks, which hitherto had narrowly edged and confined the path, bayed out on either side. The path ran on, a flat rock track about a couple of feet wide, forming the top of an upstanding cliff; but on either side there was an interval of seven or eight feet between the path and the walls of rock, and the path was unfenced. Even had the Stefanopoulos held his hand and given no treacherous impulse, it would have needed a cool-headed man to walk that path by the dim glimmer of a torch. For, kneeling down and peering over the side, I saw before me, some seventy feet down as I judged, the dark gleam of water, and I heard the low moan of its wash. And Phroso said:

'If the man escaped the sharp rocks he would fall into the water; and then, if he could not swim, he would sink at once; but if he could swim he would swim round, and round, and round, like a fish in a bowl, till he grew weary, unless he chanced to find the only opening; and if he found that and passed through, he would come to a rapid, where the water runs swiftly, and he would be dashed on the rocks. Only by a miracle could he escape death by one or other of these ways. So I was told when I was of age to know the secret. And it is certain that no man who fell into the water has escaped alive, although their bodies came out.'

'Did Stefan's body come out?' I asked, peering at the dark water with a fascinated gaze.

'No, because they tied weights to it before they threw it down, and so with the head. Stefan is there at the bottom. Perhaps another Stefanopoulos is there also; for his body was never found. He was caught by the man he threw down, and the two fell together.'

'Well, I'm glad of it,' said I with emphasis, as I rose to my feet, 'I wish the same thing had always happened.'

'Then,' remarked Phroso with a smile, 'I should not be here to tell you about it.'

'Hum,' said I. 'At all events I wish it had generally happened. For a more villainous contrivance I never heard of in all my life. We English are not accustomed to this sort of thing.'

Phroso looked at me for a moment with a strange expression of eagerness, hesitation and fear. Then she suddenly put out her hand, and laid it on my arm.

'I will not go back to my cousin who has wronged me, if – if I may stay with you,' she said.

'If you may stay!' I exclaimed with a nervous laugh.

'But will you protect me? Will you stand by me? Will you swear not to leave me here alone on the island? If you will, I will tell you another thing – a thing that would certainly bring me death if it were known I had told.'

'Whether you tell me or whether you don't,' said I, 'I'll do what you ask.'

'Then you are not the first Englishman who has been here. Seventy years ago there came an Englishman here, a daring man, a lover of our people, and a friend of the great Byron. Orestes Stefanopoulos, who ruled here then, loved him very much, and brought him here, and showed him the path and the water under it. And he, the Englishman, came next day with a rope, and fixed the rope at the top, and let himself down. Somehow, I do not know how, he came safe out to the sea, past the rocks and the rapids. But, alas, he boasted of it! Then, when the thing became known, all the family came to Orestes and asked him what he had done. And he said:

' "Sup with me this night, and I will tell you." For he saw that what he had done was known.

'So they all supped together, and Orestes told them what he had done, and how he did it for love of the Englishman. They said nothing, but looked sad; for they loved Orestes. But he did not wait for them to kill him, as they were bound to do; but he took a great flagon of wine, and poured into it the contents of a small flask. And his kindred said: "Well done, Lord Orestes!" And they all rose to their feet, and drank to him. And he drained the flagon to their good fortune, and went and lay down on his bed, and turned his face to the wall and died.'

I paid less attention to this new episode in the family history of the Stefanopouloi than it perhaps deserved: my thoughts were with the Englishman, not with his too generous friend. Yet the thing was handsomely done – on both sides handsomely done.

'If the Englishman got out!' I cried, gazing at Phroso's face.

'Yes, I mean that,' said she simply. 'But it must be dangerous.'

'It's not exactly safe where we are,' I said, smiling; 'and Constantine will be guarding the proper path. By Jove, we'll try it!'

'But I must come with you; for if you go that way and escape, Constantine will kill me.'

'You've just as good a right to kill Constantine.'

'Still he will kill me. You'll take me with you?'

'To be sure I will,' said I.

Now when a man pledges his word, he ought, to my thinking, to look straight and honestly in the eyes of the woman to whom he is promising. Yet I did not look into Phroso's eyes, but stared awkwardly over her head at the walls of rock. Then, without any more words, we turned back and went towards the secret door. But I stopped at Spiro's body, and said to Phroso:

'Will you send Denny to me?'

She went, and when Denny came we took Spiro's body and carried it to where the walls bayed, and we flung it down into the dark water below. And I told Denny of the Englishman who had come alive through the perils of the hidden chasm. He listened with eager attention, nodding his head at every point of the story.

'There lies our road, Denny,' said I, pointing with my finger. 'We'll go along it tonight.'

Denny looked down, shook his head and smiled.

'And the girl?' he asked suddenly.

'She comes too,' said I.

We walked back together, Denny being unusually silent and serious. I thought that even his audacious courage was a little dashed by the sight and the associations of that grim place, so I said:

'Cheer up. If that other fellow got through the rocks, we can.'

'Oh, hang the rocks!' said Denny scornfully. 'I wasn't thinking of them.'

'Then what are you so glum about?'

'I was wondering,' said Denny, freeing himself from my arm, 'how Beatrice Hipgrave would get on with Euphrosyne.'

I looked at Denny. I tried to feel angry, or even, if I failed in that, to appear angry. But it was no use. Denny was imperturbable. I took his arm again.

'Thanks, old man,' said I. 'I'll remember.'

For when I considered the very emphatic assertions which I had made to Denny before we left England, I could not honestly deny that he was justified in his little reminder.

8

A Knife at a Rope

Some modern thinkers, I believe – or perhaps, to be quite safe, I had better say some modern talkers – profess to estimate the value of life by reference to the number of distinct sensations which it enables them to experience. Judged by a similar standard, my island had been, up to the present time, a brilliant success; it was certainly fulfilling the function, which Mrs Kennett Hipgrave had appropriated to it, of whiling away the time that must elapse before my marriage with her daughter and providing occupation for my thoughts during this weary interval. The difficulty was that the island seemed disinclined to restrict itself to this modest sphere of usefulness; it threatened to monopolise me, and to leave very little of me or my friends, by the time that it had finished with us. For, although we maintained our cheerfulness, our position was not encouraging. Had matters been anything short of desperate above ground it would have been madness to plunge into that watery hole, whose egress was unknown to us, and to take such a step on the off-chance of finding at the other end the Cypriote fishermen, and of obtaining from them either an alliance, or, if that failed, the means of flight. Yet we none of us doubted that to take the plunge was the wiser course. I did not believe in the extreme peril of the passage, for, on further questioning, Phroso told us that the Englishman had come through, not only alive and well, but also dry. Therefore there was a path, and along a path that one man can go four men can go; and Phroso, again attired, at my suggestion, in her serviceable boy's suit, was the equal of any of us. So we left considering whether, and fell to the more profitable work of asking how, to go. Hogvardt and Watkins went off at once to the point of departure, armed with a pick, a mallet, some stout pegs, and a long length of rope. All save the last were ready on the premises, and that last formed always part of Hogvardt's own equipment; he wore it round his waist, and, I believe, slept in it, like a medieval ascetic. Meanwhile Denny and I kept watch, and Phroso, who seemed out of humour, disappeared into her own room.

Our idea was to reach the other end of the journey somewhere about eight or nine o'clock in the evening. Phroso told us that this hour was the most favourable for finding the fishermen; they would then be taking a meal before launching their boats for the fishing grounds. Three hours seemed ample time to allow for the journey, for the way could hardly, however rich it were in windings, be more than three or four miles long. We determined, therefore, to start at five. At four Hogvardt and Watkins returned from the underground passage; they had driven three stout pegs into excavations in the rocky path, and built them in securely with stones and earth. The rope was tied fast and firm round the pegs, and the moistness of its end showed the length to be sufficient. I wished to descend first, but I was at once overruled; Denny was to lead, Watkins was to follow; then came Hogvardt, then Phroso, and lastly myself. We arranged all this as we ate a good meal; then each man stowed away a portion of goat – the goat had died the death that morning – and tied a flask of wine about him. It was a quarter to five, and Denny rose to his feet, flinging away his cigarette.

'That's my last!' said he, regretfully regarding his empty case.

His words sounded ominous, but the spirit of action was on us, and we would not be discouraged. I went to the hall door and fired a shot, and then did the like at the back. Having thus spent two cartridges on advertising our presence to the pickets we made without delay for the passage. With my own hand I closed the door behind us. The secret of the Stefanopouloi would thus be hidden from profane eyes in the very likely event of the islanders finding their way into the house in the course of the next few hours.

I persuaded Phroso to sit down some little way from the chasm and wait till we were ready for her; we four went on. Denny was a delightful boy to deal with on such occasions. He wasted no time in preliminaries. He gave one hard pull at the rope; it stood the test; he cast a rapid eye over the wedges; they were strong and strongly imbedded in the rock. He laid hold of the rope.

'Don't come after me till I shout,' said he, and he was over the side. The lantern showed me his descending figure, while Hogvardt and Watkins held the rope ready to haul him up in case of need. There was one moment of suspense; then his voice came, distant and cavernous.

'All right! There's a broad ledge – a foot and a half broad – twenty feet above the water, and I can see a glimmer of light that looks like the way out.'

'This is almost disappointingly simple,' said I.

'Would your lordship desire me to go next?' asked Watkins.

'Yes, fire away, Watkins,' said I, now in high good humour.

'Stand from under, sir,' called Watkins to Denny, and over he went.

A shout announced his safe arrival. I laid down the lantern and took hold of the rope.

'I must hang on to you, Hog,' said I. 'You carry flesh, you see.'

Hogvardt was calm, smiling and leisurely.

'When I'm down, my lord,' he said, 'I'll stand ready to catch the young lady. Give me a call before you start her off.'

'All right,' I answered. 'I'll go and fetch her directly.'

Over went old Hogvardt. He groaned once; I suppose he grazed against the wall; but he descended with perfect safety. Denny called:

'Now we're ready for her, Charley. Lower away!' And I, turning, began to walk back to where I had left Phroso.

My island – I can hardly resist personifying it in the image of some charming girl, full of tricks and surprises, yet all the while enchanting – had now behaved well for two hours. The limit of its endurance seemed to be reached. In another five minutes Phroso and I would have been safely down the rope and the party reunited at the bottom, with a fair hope of carrying out prosperously at least the first part of the enterprise. But it was not to be. My eyes had grown accustomed to the gloom, and when I went back I left the lantern standing by the rope. Suddenly, when I was still a few yards from Phroso, I heard a curious noise, a sort of shuffling sound, rather like the noise made by a rug or carpet drawn along the floor. I stood still and listened, turning my head round to the chasm. The noise continued for a minute. I took a step in the direction of it. Then I seemed to see a curious thing. The lantern appeared to get up, raise itself a foot or so in the air, keeping its light towards me, and throw itself over the chasm. At the same instant there was a rasp. Heavens, it was a knife on the rope! A cry came from far down in the chasm. I darted forward. I rushed to where the walls bayed and the chasm opened. The shuffling sound had begun again; and in the middle of the isolated path I saw a dark object. It must be the figure of a man, a man who had watched our proceedings, unobserved by us, and seized this chance of separating our party. For a moment – a fatal moment – I stood aghast, doing nothing. Then I drew my revolver and fired once – twice – thrice. The bullets whistled along the path, but the dark figure was no longer to be seen there. But in an instant there came an answering shot from across the bridge of rock. Denny shouted wildly to me from below. I fired again; there was a groan, but two shots flashed at the very same moment. There were two men there, perhaps more. I stood again for a moment undecided; but I could do no good where I was. I turned and ran fairly and fast.

'Come, come,' I cried, when I had reached Phroso. 'Come back, come back! They've cut the rope and they'll be on us directly.'

In spite of her amazement she rose as I bade her. We heard feet running along the passage. They would be across the bridge now. Would they stop and fire down the chasm? No, they were coming on. We also went on; a touch of Phroso's practised fingers opened the door for us; I turned, and in wrath gave the pursuers one more shot. Then I ran up the stairs and shut the door behind us. We were in the hall again – but Phroso and I alone.

A hurried story told her all that had happened. Her breath came quick and her cheek flushed.

'The cowards!' she said. 'They dared not attack us when we were all together!'

'They will attack us before very long now,' said I, 'and we can't possibly hold the house against them. Why, they may open that trap-door any moment.'

Phroso stepped quickly towards it, and, stooping for a instant, examined it. 'Yes,' she said, 'they may. I can't fasten it. You spoilt the fastening with your pick.'

Hearing this, I stepped close up to the door, reloading my revolver as I went, and I called out, 'The first man who looks out is a dead man.'

No sound came from below. Either they were too hurt to attempt the attack, or, more probably, they preferred the safer and surer way of surrounding and overwhelming us by numbers from outside. Indeed we were at our last gasp now; I flung myself despondently into a chair; but I kept my finger on my weapon and my eye on the trap-door.

'They cannot get back – our friends – and we cannot get to them,' said Phroso.

'No,' said I. Her simple statement was terribly true.

'And we cannot stay here!' she pursued.

'They'll be at us in an hour or two at most, I'll warrant. Those fellows will carry back the news that we are alone here,'

'And if they come?' she said, fixing her eyes on me.

'They won't hurt you, will they?'

'I don't know what Constantine would do; but I don't think the people will let him hurt me, unless –'

'Well, unless what?'

She hesitated, looked at me, looked away again. I believe that my eyes were now guilty of neglecting the trap-door which I ought to have watched.

'Unless what?' I said again. But Phroso grew red and did not answer.

'Unless you're so foolish as to try to protect me, you mean?' I asked. 'Unless you refuse to give them back what Constantine offers to win for them – the island?'

'They will not let you have the island,' she said in a low voice. 'I dare not face them and tell them it is yours.'

'Do you admit it's mine?' I asked eagerly.

A slow smile dawned on Phroso's face, and she held out her hand to me. Ah, Denny, my conscience, why were you at the bottom of the chasm? I seized her hand and kissed it.

'Between friends,' she said softly, 'there is no thine nor mine.'

Ah, Denny, where were you? I kissed her hand again – and dropped it like a red-hot coal.

'But I can't say that to my islanders,' said Phroso, smiling.

Charming as it was, I wished she had not said it to me. I wished that she would not speak as she spoke, or look as she looked, or be what she was. I forgot all about the trap-door. The island was piling sensations on me.

At last I got up and went to the table. I found there a scrap of paper, on which Denny had drawn a fancy sketch of Constantine (to whom, by the way, he attributed hoofs and a tail). I turned the blank side uppermost, and took my pencil out of my pocket.

I was determined to put the thing on a business-like footing; so I began: 'Whereas' – which has a cold, legal, business-like sound:

'Whereas,' I wrote in English, 'this island of Neopalia is mine, I hereby fully, freely, and absolutely give it to the Lady Euphrosyne, niece of Stefan Georgios Stefanopoulos, lately Lord of the said island – Wheatley.' And I made a copy underneath in Greek, and, walking across to Phroso, handed the paper to her, remarking in a rather disagreeable tone, 'There you are; that'll put it all straight, I hope.' And I sat down again, feeling out of humour. I did not like giving up my island, even to Phroso. Moreover I had the strongest doubt whether my surrender would be of the least use in saving my skin.

I do not know that I need relate what Phroso did when I gave her back her island. These southern races have picturesque but extravagant ways. I did not know where to look while she was thanking me, and it was as much as I could do not to call out, 'Do stop!' However presently she did stop, but not because I asked her. She was stayed by a sudden thought which had been in my mind all the while, but now flashed suddenly into hers.

'But Constantine?' she said. 'You know his – his secrets. Won't he still try to kill you?'

Of course he would if he valued his own neck. For I had sworn to see him hanged for one murder, and I knew that he meditated another.

'Oh, don't you bother about that!' said I. 'I expect I can manage Constantine.'

'Do you think I'm going to desert you?' she asked in superb indignation.

'No, no; of course not,' I protested, rather in a fright. 'I shouldn't think of accusing you of such a thing.'

'You know that's what you meant,' said Phroso, a world of reproach in her voice.

'My dear lady,' said I, 'getting you into trouble won't get me out of it, and getting you out may get me out. Take that paper in your hand, and go back to your people. Say nothing about

Constantine just now; play with him. You know what I've told you, and you won't be deluded by him. Don't let him see that you know anything of the woman at the cottage. It won't help you, it may hurt me, and it will certainly bring her into greater danger; for, if nothing has happened to her already, yet something may if his suspicions are aroused.'

'I am to do all this. And what will you do, my lord?'

'I say, don't call me "my lord"; we say "Lord Wheatley." What am I going to do? I'm going to make a run for it.'

'But they'll kill you!'

'Then shall I stay here?'

'Yes, stay here.'

'But Constantine's fellows will be here before long.'

'You must give yourself up to them, and tell them to bring you to me. They couldn't hurt you then.'

Well, I wasn't sure of that, but I pretended to believe it. The truth is that I dared not tell Phroso what I had actually resolved to do. It was a risky job, but it was a chance; and it was more than a chance. It was very like an obligation that a man had no right to shrink from discharging. Here was I, planning to make Phroso comfortable; that was right enough. And here was I planning to keep my own skin whole; well, a man does no wrong in doing that. But what of that unlucky woman on the hill? I knew friend Constantine would take care that Phroso should not come within speaking distance of her. Was nobody to set her on her guard? Was I to leave her to her blind trust of the ruffian whom she was unfortunate enough to call husband, and of his tool Vlacho? Now I came to think of it, now that I was separated from my friends and had no lingering hope of being able to beat Constantine in fair fight, that seemed hardly the right thing, hardly a thing I should care to talk about or think about, if I did save my own precious skin. Would not Constantine teach his wife the secret of the Stefanopouloi? Urged by these reflections, I made up my mind to play a little trick on Phroso, and feigned to accept her suggestion that I should rely on her to save me.

Evidently she had great confidence in her influence now that she held that piece of paper. I had less confidence in it, for it was clear that Constantine wielded immense power over these unruly islanders, and I thought it likely enough that they would demand from Phroso a promise to marry him as the price of obeying her; then, whether Constantine did or did not promise me my life, I felt sure that he would do his best to rob me of it.

Well, time pressed. I rose and unbolted the door of the house. Phroso sat still. I looked along the road. I saw nobody, but I heard the blast of the horn which had fallen on my ears once before and had proved the forerunner of an attack. Phroso also heard it, for she sat up, saying, 'Hark, they are summoning all the men to the town! That means they are coming here.'

But it meant something else also to me; if the men were summoned to the town there would be fewer for me to elude in the wood.

'Will they all go?' I asked, as though in mere curiosity.

'All who are not on some duty,' she answered.

I had to hope for the best; but Phroso went on in distress

'It means that they are coming here – here, to take you.'

'Then you must lose no time in going,' said I, and I took her hand and gently raised her to her feet. She stood there for a moment, looking at me. I had let go her hand, but she took mine again now, and she said with a sudden vehemence, and a rush of rich deep red on her cheeks:

'If they kill you, they shall kill me too.'

The words gushed impetuously from her, but at the end there was a choke in her throat.

'No, no, nonsense,' said I. 'You've got the island now. You mustn't talk like that.'

'I don't care –' she began; and stopped short.

'Besides, I shall pull through,' said I.

She dropped my hand, but she kept her eyes on mine.

'And if you get away?' she asked. 'What will you do? If you get to Rhodes, what will you do?'

'All I shall do is to lay an information against your cousin and the innkeeper. The rest are ignorant fellows, and I bear them no malice. Besides, they are your men now.'

'And when you've done that?' she asked gravely.

'Well, that'll be all there is to do,' said I, with an attempt at playful gaiety. It was not a very happy attempt.

'Then you'll go home to your own people?'

'I shall go home; I've got no people in particular.'

'Shall you ever come to Neopalia again?'

'I don't know. Yes, if you invite me.'

She regarded me intently for a full minute. She seemed to have forgotten the blast of the horn that summoned the islanders. I also had forgotten it; I saw nothing but the perfect oval face, crowned with clustering hair and framing deep liquid eyes. Then she drew a ring from her finger.

'You have fought for me,' she said. 'You have risked your life for me. Will you take this ring from me? Once I tried to stab you. Do you remember, my lord?'

I bowed my head, and Phroso set the ring on my finger.

'Wear it till a woman you love gives you one to wear instead,' said Phroso with a little smile. 'Then go to the edge of your island – you are an islander too, are you not? so we are brethren – go to the edge of your island and throw it into the sea; and perhaps, my dear friend, the sea will bring it back, a message from you to me. For I think you will never again come to Neopalia.'

I made no answer: we walked together to the door of the house, and paused again for a moment on the threshold.

'See the blue sea!' said Phroso. 'Is it not – is not your island – a beautiful island? If God brings you safe to your own land, my lord, as I will pray Him to do on my knees, think kindly of your island, and of one who dwells there.'

The blast of the horn had died away. The setting sun was turning blue to gold on the quiet water. The evening was very still, as we stood looking from the threshold of the door, under the portal of the house that had seen such strange wild doings, and had so swiftly made for itself a place for ever in my life and memory.

I glanced at Phroso's face. Her eyes were set on the sea, her cheeks had turned pale again, and her lip was quivering. Suddenly came a loud sharp note on the horn.

'It is the signal for the start,' said she. 'I must go, or they will be here in heat and anger, and I shall not be able to stop them. And they will kill my lord. No, I will say "my lord."'

She moved to leave me. I had answered nothing to all she had said. What was there that an honourable man could say? Was there one thing? I told myself (too eager to tell myself) that I had no right to presume to say that. And anything else I would not say.

'God bless you,' I said, as she moved away; I caught her hand and again lightly kissed it. 'My homage to the Lady of the Island,' I whispered.

Her hand dwelt in mine a moment, briefer than our divisions of time can reckon, fuller than is often the longest of them. Then, with one last look, questioning, appealing, excusing, protesting, confessing, ay, and (for my sins) hoping, she left me, and stepped along the rocky road in the grace and glory of her youthful beauty. I stood watching her, forgetting the woman at the cottage, forgetting my own danger, forgetting even the peril she ran whom I watched, forgetting everything save the old that bound me and the new that called me. So I stood till she vanished from my sight; and still I stood, for she was there, though the road hid her. And I was roused at last only by a great cry of surprise, of fierce joy and triumph, that rent the still air of the evening, and echoed back in rumblings from the hill. The Neopalians were greeting their rescued Lady.

Then I turned, snatched up Hogvardt's lance again, and fled through the house to do my errand. For I would save that woman, if I could; and my own life was not mine to lose any more than it was mine to give to whom I would. And I recollect that, as I ran through the kitchen and across the compound, making for the steps in the bank of rocks, I said, 'God forgive me!'

9

Hats off to St Tryphon!

A man's mind can move on more than one line; even the most engrossing selfish care may fail entirely to occupy it or to shut out intruding rivals. Not only should I have been wise, but I should have chosen, in that risky walk of mine through the wood that covered the hill-slope, to think of nothing but its risk. Yet countless other things exacted a share of my thoughts and figured amongst my brain's images. Sometimes I was with Denny and his faithful followers, threading dark and devious ways in the bowels of the earth, avoiding deep waters on the one side, sheer falls on the other, losing the track, finding it again, deluded by deceptive glimmers of light, finding at last the true outlet; now received hospitably by the Cypriote fishermen, now fiercely assailed by them, again finding none of them; now making allies of them, now carried prisoners by them to Constantine, again scouring the sea with vain eagerness for a sight of their sails. Then I was off, far away, to England, to my friends there, to the gaiety of London now in its full rushing tide, to Mrs Hipgrave's exclusive receptions, to Beatrice's gay talk and pretty insolence, to Hamlyn's gilded dullness, in rapid survey of all the panorama that I knew so well. Then I would turn back to the scene I had left, and again bid my farewell under the quiet sky, in prospect of the sea that turned to gold. So I passed back and forward till I seemed myself hardly a thinking man, but rather a piece of blank glass, across which the myriad mites of the kaleidoscope chased one another, covering it with varying colours, but none of them imparting their hue to it. Yet all this time, by the strange division of mental activity of which I have spoken, I was crawling cautiously but quickly up the mountain side, with eyes keen to pierce the dusk that now fell, with ears apt to find an enemy in every rustling leaf and a hostile step in every woodland sound. Of real foes I had as yet seen none. Ah! Hush! I dropped on my knees. Away there on the right – what was it leaning against that tree trunk? It was a tall lean man ; his arms rested on a long gun, and his face was towards the old grey house. Would he see me? I crouched lower. Would he hear me? I was as still as dead Spiro had lain in the passage. But then I felt stealthily for the butt of my revolver, and a recollection so startling came to me that I nearly betrayed myself by some sudden movement. In the distribution of burdens for our proposed journey, Denny had taken the case containing the spare cartridges which remained after we had all reloaded. Now I had one barrel only loaded, one shot only left. That one shot and Hogvardt's lance were all my resources. I crouched yet lower. But the man was motionless, and presently I ventured to move on my hands and knees, sorely inconvenienced by the long lance, but determined not to leave it behind me. I passed another sentry a hundred yards or so away on the left; his head was sunk on his breast and he took no notice of me. I breathed a little more freely as I came within fifty feet of the cottage.

Immediately about the house nobody was in sight. This however, in Neopalia, did not always mean that nobody was near, and I abated none of my caution. But the last step had to be taken; I crawled out from the shelter of the trees, and crouched on one knee on the level space in front of the cottage. The cottage door was open. I listened but heard nothing. Well, I meant to go in; my entrance would be none the easier for waiting. A quick dart was safest; in a couple of bounds I was across, in the verandah, through the entrance, in the house. I closed the door noiselessly behind me, and stood there, Hogvardt's lance ready for the first man I saw; but I saw none. I was in a narrow passage; there were doors on either side of me. Listening again, I heard no sound from right or left. I opened the door to the right. I saw a small square room: the table was spread for a meal, three places being laid, but the room was empty. I turned to the other door and opened it. This room was darker, for heavy curtains, drawn, no doubt, earlier in the day to keep out the sun, had not been drawn back, and the light was very dim. For a while I could make out little, but, my eyes growing more accustomed to the darkness, I soon perceived that I was in a sitting-room, sparsely and rather meanly furnished. Then my eyes fell on a couch which stood against the wall opposite me. On the couch lay a figure. It was the figure of a woman. I heard now the slight but regular sound of her breath. She was asleep. This must be the woman I sought. But was she a sensible woman? Or would she scream when I waked her, and bring those tall fellows out of the wood? In hesitation I stood still and watched her. She slept like one who was weary, but not at peace: restless movements and, now and again, broken incoherent exclamations witnessed to her disquiet. Presently her broken sleep passed into half-wakeful consciousness, and she sat up, looking round her with a dazed glance.

'Is that you, Constantine?' she asked, rubbing her hands across her eyes. 'Or is it Vlacho?'

With a swift step I was by her.

'Neither. Not a word!' I said, laying my hand on her shoulder.

I was, I daresay, an alarming figure, with the butt of my revolver peeping out of my pocket and Hogvardt's lance in my right hand. But she did not cry out.

'I am Wheatley. I have escaped from the house there,' I went on; 'and I have come here because there's something I must tell you. You remember our last meeting?'

She looked at me still in amazed surprise, but with a gleam of recollection.

'Yes, yes. You were – we went to watch you – yes, at the restaurant.'

'You went to watch and to listen? Yes, I supposed so. But I've been near you since then. Do you remember the man who was on your verandah?'

'That was you?' she asked quickly.

'Yes, it was. And while I was there I heard –'

'But what are you doing here? This house is watched. Constantine may be here any moment, or Vlacho.'

'I'm as safe here as I was down the hill. Now listen. Are you this man's wife, as he called you that night?'

'Am I his wife? Of course I'm his wife. How else should I be here?' The indignation expressed in her answer was the best guarantee of its truth, and became her well. And she held her hand up to me, as she had to the man himself in the restaurant, adding, 'There is his ring.'

'Then listen to me, and don't interrupt,' said I brusquely. 'Time's valuable to me, and even more, I fear, to you.'

Her eyes were alarmed now, but she listened in silence as I bade her. I told her briefly what had happened to me, and then I set before her more fully the conversation between Constantine and Vlacho which I had overheard. She clutched the cushions of the sofa in her clenched hand; her breathing came quick and fast; her eyes gleamed at me even in the gloom of the curtained room. I do not believe that in her heart she was surprised at what she heard. She had mistrusted the man; her manner, even on our first encounter, had gone far to prove that. She received my story rather as a confirmation of her own suspicions than as a new or startling revelation. She was fearful, excited, strung to a high pitch; but astonished she was not, if I read her right. And when I ended, it was not astonishment that clenched her lips and brought to her eyes a look which I think Constantine himself would have shrunk from meeting. I had paused at the end of my narrative, but I recollected one thing more. I must warn her about the secret passage; for that offered her husband too ready and easy a way of relieving himself of his burden. But now she interrupted me.

'This girl?' she said. 'I have not seen her. What is she like?'

'She is very beautiful,' said I simply. 'She knows what I have told you, and she is on her guard. You need fear nothing from her. It is your husband whom you have to fear.'

'He would kill me?' she asked, with a questioning glance.

'You've heard what he said,' I returned. 'Put your own meaning on it.'

She sprang to her feet.

'I can't stay here; I can't stay here. Merciful heaven, they may come any moment! Where are you going? How are you going to escape? You are in as much danger as I am.'

'I believe in even greater,' said I. 'I was going straight from here down to the sea. If I can find my friends, we'll go through with the thing together. If I don't find them, I shall hunt for a boat. If I don't find a boat – well, I'm a good swimmer, and I shall live as long in the water as in Neopalia, and die easier, I fancy.'

She was standing now, facing me, and she laid her hand on my arm.

'You stand by women, you Englishmen,' she said. 'You won't leave me to be murdered?'

'You see I am here. Doesn't that answer your question?'

'My God, he's a fiend! Will you take me with you?'

What could I do? Her coming gave little chance to her and robbed me of almost all prospect of escape. But of course I could not leave her.

'You must come if you can see no other way,' said I.

'Why, what other is there? If I avoid him he will see I suspect him, If I appear to trust him, I must put myself in his power.'

'Then we must go,' said I. 'But it's a thousand to one that we don't get through.'

I had hardly spoken when a voice outside said, 'Is all well?' and a heavy step echoed in the verandah.

'Vlacho!' she hissed in a whisper. 'Vlacho! Are you armed?'

'In a way,' said I, with a shrug. 'But there are at least two besides him. I saw them in the wood.'

'Tis, yes, true. There are four generally. It would be death. Here, hide behind the curtains. I'll try to put him off for the moment. Quick, quick!'

She was hurried and eager, but I saw that her wits were clear. I stepped behind the curtains and she drew them close. I heard her fling herself again on the couch. Then came the innkeeper's voice, its roughness softened in deferential greeting.

At the same time a strong smell of eau de Cologne pervaded the room.

'Am I well?' said Madame Stefanopoulos fretfully. 'My good Vlacho, I am very ill. Should I sit in a dark room and bathe my head with this stuff if I were well?'

'My lady's sickness grieves me beyond expression,' said Vlacho politely. 'And the more so because I am come from my Lord Constantine with a message for you.'

'It is easier for him to send messages than to come himself,' she remarked, with an admirable pretence of resentment.

'Think how occupied he has been with this pestilent Englishman!' said the plausible Vlacho. 'We have had no peace. But at last I hope our troubles are over. The house is ours again.'

'Ah, you have driven them out?'

'They fled themselves,' said Vlacho. 'But they are separated and we shall catch them. Oh, yes, we know where to look for most of them.'

'Then you've not caught any of them yet? How stupid you are!'

'My lady is severe. No, we have caught none yet.'

'Not even Wheatley himself?' she asked. 'Has he shown you a clean pair of heels?'

Vlacho's voice betrayed irritation as he answered:

'We shall find him also in time, though heaven knows where the rascal has hidden himself.'

'You're really very stupid,' said Francesca. I heard her sniff her perfume. 'And the girl?' she went on.

'Oh, we have her safe and sound,' laughed Vlacho. 'She'll give no more trouble.'

'Why, what will you do with her?'

'You must ask my lord that,' said Vlacho. 'If she will give up the island, perhaps nothing.'

'Ah, well, I take very little interest in her. Isn't my husband coming to supper, Vlacho?'

'To supper here, my lady? Surely no. The great house is ready now. That is a more fitting place for my lady than this dog-hole. I am here to escort you there. There my lord will sup with you. Oh, it's a grand house!'

'A grand house!' she echoed scornfully. 'Why, what is there to see in it?'

'Oh, many things,' said Vlacho. 'Yes, secrets, my lady! And my lord bids me say that from love to you he will show you tonight the great secret of his house. He desires to show his love and trust in you, and will therefore reveal to you all his secrets.'

When I, behind the curtain, heard the ruffian say this, I laid firmer hold on my lance. But the lady was equal to Vlacho.

'You're very melodramatic with your secrets,' she said contemptuously. 'I am tired, and my head aches. Your secrets will wait; and if my husband will not come and sup with me, I'll sup alone here. Tell him I can't come, please, Vlacho.'

'But my lord was most urgent that you should come,' said Vlacho.

'I would come if I were well,' said she.

'But I could help you. If you would permit, I and my men would carry you down all the way on your couch.'

'My good Vlacho, you are very tedious, you and your men. And my husband is tedious also, if he sent all these long messages. I am ill and I will not come. Is that enough?'

'My lord will be very angry if I return alone,' pleaded Vlacho humbly.

'I'll write a certificate that you did your best to persuade me,' she said with a scornful laugh.

I heard the innkeeper's heavy feet move a step or two across the floor. He was coming nearer to where she lay on the couch.

'I daren't return without you,' said he.

'Then you must stay here and sup with me.'

'My lord does not love to be opposed.'

'Then, my good Vlacho, he should not have married me,' she retorted.

She played the game gallantly, fencing and parrying with admirable tact, and with a coolness wonderful for a woman in such peril. My heart went out to her, and I said to myself that she should not want any help that I could give.

She had raised her voice on the last words, and her defiant taunt rang out clear and loud. It seemed to alarm Vlacho.

'Hush, not so loud!' he said hastily. There was the hint of a threat in his voice.

'Not so loud!' she echoed. 'And why not so loud? Is there harm in what I say?'

I wondered at Vlacho's sudden fright. The idea shot into my head – and the idea was no pleasant one – that there must be people within earshot, perhaps people who had not been trusted with Constantine's secrets, and would, for that reason, do his bidding better.

'Harm! No, no harm; but no need to let everyone hear,' said Vlacho, confusedly and with evident embarrassment.

'Everyone? Who is here, then?'

'I have brought one or two men to escort my lady,' said he. 'With these cut-throat Englishmen about' (Bravo, bravo, Vlacho!) 'one must be careful.'

A scornful laugh proclaimed her opinion of his subterfuge, and she met him with a skilful thrust.

'But if they don't know – yes, and aren't to know that I am the wife of Constantine, how can I go to the house and stay with him?' she asked.

'Oh,' said he, ready again with his plausible half-truths, 'that is one of the secrets. Must I tell my lady part of it? There is an excellent hiding-place in the house, where my lord can bestow you most comfortably. You will want for nothing, and nobody will know that you are there, except the few faithful men who have guarded you here.'

'Indeed, if I am still to be a stowaway, I'll stay here,' said she. 'If my lord will announce me publicly to all the island as his wife, then I will come and take my place at the head of his house; but without that I will not come.'

'Surely you will be able to persuade him to that yourself,' said Vlacho. 'But dare I make conditions with my lord?'

'You will make them in my name,' she answered. 'Go and tell him what I say.'

A pause followed. Then Vlacho said in sullen obstinate tones:

'I'll not go without you. I was ordered to bring you, and I will. Come.'

I heard the sudden rustle of her dress as she drew back; then a little cry: 'You're hurting me.'

'You must come,' said Vlacho. 'I shall call my men and carry you.'

'I will not come,' she said in a low voice, resolute and fierce.

Vlacho laughed. 'We'll see about that,' said he, and his heavy steps sounded on the floor.

'What are you going to the window for?' she cried.

'To call Demetri and Kortes to help me,' said he; 'or will you come?'

I drew back a pace, resting against the window-sill. Hogvardt's lance was protruded before me. At that moment I asked nothing better than to bury its point in the fat innkeeper's flesh.

'You'll repent it if you do what you say,' said she.

'I shall repent it more if I don't obey my lord,' said Vlacho. 'See, my hand is on the curtains. Will you come, my lady?'

'I will not come,' said she.

There was one last short interval. I heard them both breathing, and I held my own breath. My revolver rested in my pocket; the noise of a shot would be fatal. With God's help I would drive the lance home with one silent sufficient thrust. There would be a rogue less in the world and another chance for her and me.

'As you will, then,' said the innkeeper.

The curtain-rings rattled along the rod; the heavy hangings gave back. The moon, which was newly risen, streamed full in Vlacho's eyes and on the pale strained face behind him. He saw me; he uttered one low exclamation:

'Christ!' His hand flew to his belt. He drew a pistol out and raised it; but I was too quick for him. I drove the great hunting-knife on the end of the sapling full and straight into his breast. With a groan he flung his arms over his head and fell sideways, half-supported by the curtain till the fabric was rent away from the rings and fell over his body, enveloping him in a thick pall. I drew my lance back. The force of the blow had overstrained Hogvardt's wire fastenings; the blade was bent to an angle with the shaft and shook loosely from side to side. Vlacho's blood began to curl in a meandering trickle from beneath the curtain. Madame Stefanopoulos glared at me, speechless. But my eyes fell from her to the floor; for there I saw two long black shadows. A sudden and desperate inspiration seized me. She was my ally, I hers. If both were held guilty of this act we could render no service to each other. If she were still unsuspected – and nobody except myself had heard her talk with Vlacho – she might yet help herself and me.

'Throw me over,' I whispered in English. 'Cry for help.'
'What?'
'Cry. The men are there. You may help me afterwards.'
'What, pretend –?'
'Yes. Quick.'
'But they'll – '
'No, no. Quick, for God's sake, quick!'

'God help us,' she whispered. Then she cried loudly, 'Help! help! help!'

I sprang towards her. There was the crash of a man leaping through the open window. I turned. Behind him I saw Demetri standing in the moonlight. Other figures hurried up; feet pattered on the hard ground. The man who had leaped in – a very tall, handsome and athletic fellow, whom I had not seen before – held to my head a long old-fashioned pistol. I let my hands drop to my side and faced him with a smile on my lips. It must be death to resist – death to me and death to my new friend; surrender might open a narrow way of safety.

'I yield,' said I.

'Who are you?' he cried.

'I am Lord Wheatley,' I answered.

'But did you not fly to the – ?' He stopped.

'To the passage?' said I. 'No, I came here. I was trying to escape. I came in while Madame here was asleep and hid behind the curtain.'

'Yes, yes,' said she. 'It is so, Kortes, it is as he says; and then Vlacho came – '

'And,' said I, 'when the lady had agreed to go with Vlacho, Vlacho came to the window to call you; and by misadventure, sir, he came on me behind the curtain. And – won't you see whether he's dead?'

'Kill him, Kortes, kill him!' cried Demetri, fiercely and suddenly, from the window.

Kortes turned round.

'Peace!' said he. 'The man has yielded. Do I kill men who have yielded? The Lady of the island and my Lord Constantine must decide his fate; it is not my office. Are you armed, sir?'

It went to my heart to give up that last treasured shot of mine. But he was treating me as an honourable man. I handed him my revolver with a bow, saying:

'I depend on you to protect me from that fellow and the rest till you deliver me to those you speak of.'

'In my charge you are safe,' said Kortes, and he stooped down and lifted the curtain from Vlacho's face. The innkeeper stirred and groaned. He was not dead yet. Kortes turned round to Demetri.

'Stay here and tend him. Do what you can for him. When I am able, I will send aid to him; but I don't think he will live.'

Demetri scowled. He seemed not to like the part assigned to him.

'Are you going to take this man to my Lord Constantine?' he asked. 'Leave another with Vlacho, and let me come with you to my lord.'

'Who should better stay with Vlacho than his nephew Demetri?' asked Kortes with a smile. (This relationship was a new light to me.) 'I am going to do what my duty is. Come, no questioning. Do not I command, now Vlacho is wounded?'

'And the lady here?' asked Demetri.

'I am not ordered to lay a finger on the lady,' answered Kortes. 'Indeed I don't know who she is.'

Francesca interposed with great dignity:

'I will come with you,' said she. 'I have my story to tell when this gentleman is put on his trial. Who I am you will know soon.'

Demetri had climbed in at the window. He passed me with a savage scowl, and I noticed that one side of his head was bound with a bloodstained bandage. He saw me looking at it.

'Aye,' he growled, 'I owe you the loss of half an ear.'

'In the passage?' I hazarded, much pleased.

'I shall pay the debt,' said he, 'or see it paid handsomely for me by my lord,'

'Come,' said Kortes, 'let us go.'

Fully believing that the fact of Kortes being in command instead of Demetri had saved me from instant death, I was not inclined to dispute his orders. I walked out of the house and took the place he indicated to me in the middle of a line of islanders, some ten or twelve in number. Kortes placed himself by my side, and Madame Stefanopoulos walked on his other hand. The islanders maintained absolute silence. I followed their example, but my heart (I must confess) beat as I waited to see in what direction our column was to march. We started down the hill towards the house. If we were going to the house I had perhaps twenty minutes to live, and the lady who was with us would not long survive me. In vain I scanned Kortes' comely grave features. He marched with the impassive regularity of a grenadier and displayed much the same expressionless steadiness of face. Nearer to the fatal house we came; but my heart gave a sudden leap of hope and excitement, for Kortes cried softly, 'To the right.' We turned down the path that led up from the town, leaving the house on the left. We were not going straight to death then, and every respite was pregnant with unforeseen chances of escape. I touched Kortes on the shoulder.

'Where are we going?' I asked.

'To the town,' he answered.

Again in silence we pursued our way down the hillside. The path broadened and the incline became less steep; a few lights twinkled from the sea, which now spread before us. Still we went on. Then I heard the bell of a church strike twelve. The strokes ended, but another bell began to ring. Our escort stopped with one accord. They took off their caps and signed the cross on their breasts. Kortes did the same as the rest. I looked at him in question, but he said nothing till the caps were replaced and we were on our way again. Then he said:

'Today is the feast of St Tryphon. Didn't you know?'

'No,' said I. 'St Tryphon I know, but his feast is not kept always on this day.'

'Always on this day in Neopalia,' he answered, and he seemed to look at me as though he were asking me some unspoken question.

The feast of St Tryphon might have interested me very much at any ordinary time, but just now my study of the customs of the islanders had been diverted into another channel, and I did not pursue the subject. Kortes walked in silence some little way farther. We had now reached the main road and were descending rapidly towards the town. I saw again the steep narrow street, empty and still in the moonlight. We held on our way till we came to a rather large square building, which stood back from the road and had thus escaped my notice when we passed it on the evening of our arrival. Before this Kortes halted. 'Here you must lodge with me,' said he. 'Concerning the lady I have no orders.'

Madame Stefanopoulos caught my arm.

'I must stay too,' said she. 'I can't go back to my house.'

'It is well,' said Kortes calmly. 'There are two rooms.'

The escort ranged themselves outside the building, which appeared to be either a sort of barrack or a place of confinement. We three entered. At a sign from Kortes, Madame Stefanopoulos passed into a large room on the right. I followed him into a smaller room, scantily furnished, and flung myself in exhaustion on a wooden bench that ran along the wall. For an instant Kortes stood regarding me. His face seemed to express hesitation, but the look in his eyes was not unfriendly. The bell, which had continued to ring till now, ceased. Then Kortes said to me in a low voice:

'Take courage, my lord. For a day you are safe. Nor even Constantine would dare to kill a man on the feast of St Tryphon.'

Before I could answer he was gone. I heard the bolt of the door run home. I was a prisoner.

Yet I took courage as he bade me. Four-and-twenty hours' life was more than I had been able to count on for some time past. So I also doffed my hat in honour of the holy St Tryphon. And presently I lifted my legs on to the bench, took off my coat and made a pillow of it, and went to sleep.

10

The Justice of the Island

Helplessness brings its own peculiar consolation. After a week's planning and scheming what you will do to the enemy, it is a kind of relief to sit with hands in pockets and wonder what the enemy may be pleased to do with you. This relaxation was vouchsafed to my brain when I awoke in the morning and found the sun streaming into the whitewashed cell-like room. It was the feast of St Tryphon, all praise to him! Kortes said that I could not be executed that day. I doubted Constantine's scruples; yet probably he would not venture to outrage the popular sentiment of Neopalia. But nothing forbade my execution tomorrow. Well, tomorrow is tomorrow, and today is today, and there will be that difference between them so long as the world lasts. I stretched myself and yawned luxuriously. I was, strangely enough, in a hopeful frame of mind. I made sure that Denny had found his way safely, and that the Cypriote fishermen had been benevolent. I proved to myself that with Constantine's exposure his power would end. I plumed myself on having put Vlacho *hors de combat*. I believe I said to myself that villainy would not triumph, that honest men would come by their own, and that unprotected beauty would find help from heaven: convictions which showed that relics of youth hung about me, and (I am afraid it depends on this rather) that I was feeling very well after my refreshing sleep.

Alas, my soothing reveries were rudely interrupted.

> 'At a touch sweet pleasure melteth,
> Like to bubbles when rain pelteth!'

And at the sound of a gruff voice outside, my dreams melted: harsh reality was pressing hard on me again, crushing hope into resignation, buoyancy into a grim resolve to take what came with courage.

'Bring him out,' cried the voice.

'It's that brute Demetri,' said I to myself, wondering what had become of my friendly gaoler, Kortes.

A moment later half a dozen men filed into the room, Demetri at their head. I asked him what he wanted. He answered only with a command that I should get up. 'Bring him along,' he added to his men; and we walked out into the street.

Evidently Neopalia was *en fête*. The houses were decked with flags; several windows exhibited pictures of the Saint. Women in their gay and spotlessly clean holiday attire strolled along the road, holding their children by the hand. Everybody made way for our procession, many whispers and pointed fingers proving the interest and curiosity which it was my unwilling privilege to arouse. For about a quarter of a mile we mounted the road, then we turned suddenly down to the left and began to descend again towards the sea. Soon now we arrived at the little church whose bell I had heard. Here we halted; and presently another procession appeared from the building. An old white-bearded man headed it, carrying a large picture of St Tryphon. The old man's dress was little different from that of the rest of the islanders, but he wore the gown and cap of a priest. He was followed by some attendants; the women and children fell in behind him, three or four cripples brought up the rear, praying as they went, and stretching out their hands towards the sacred picture which the old man carried. At a sign from Demetri we also put ourselves in motion again, and the whole body of us thus made for the seashore. But some three hundred yards short of the water I perceived a broad level space, covered with short rough turf and surrounded for about half its circuit by a crescent-shaped bank two or three feet high. On this bank sat some twenty people, and crowded in front of it was the same ragged picturesque company of armed peasants that I had seen gather in the street on the occasion of our arrival. The old man with the picture made his way to the centre of the level ground. Thrice he raised the picture towards the sky, everyone uncovering his head and kneeling down the while. He began to pray, but I did not listen to what he said; for by this time my attention had wandered from him and was fixed intently on a small group which occupied the centre of the raised bank. There, sitting side by side, with the space of a foot or so between them, were Phroso and her cousin Constantine. On a rude hurdle, covered with a rug, at Constantine's feet lay Vlacho, his face pale and his eyes closed. Behind Phroso stood my new acquaintance, Kortes, with one hand on the knife in his girdle and the other holding a long gun, which rested on the ground. One figure I missed. I looked round for Constantine's wife, but she was nowhere to be seen. Then I looked again at Phroso. She was dressed in rich fine garments of white, profusely embroidered, but her face was paler even than Vlacho's, and when I sought her eyes she would not meet mine, but kept her gaze persistently lowered. Constantine sat motionless, with a frown on his brow but a slight smile on his lips, as he waited with an obviously forced patience through the long rigmarole of the old man's prayer.

Evidently important business was to be transacted; yet nobody seemed to be in a hurry to arrive at it. When the old priest had finished his prayers the cripples came and prostrated themselves before the sacred picture. No miracle, however, followed; and the priest took up the tale again, pouring forth a copious harangue, in which I detected frequent references to 'the barbarians' – a term he used to denote my friends, myself, and all the world apparently, except the islanders of Neopalia. Then he seated himself between Phroso and Constantine, who made room for him. I was surprised to see him assume so much dignity, but I presumed that he was treated with exceptional honour on the feast day. When he had taken his place, about twenty of the men came into the middle of the ring and began to dance, arranging themselves in a semicircle, moving at first in slow rhythmical steps, and gradually quickening their motions till they ended with a wonderful display of activity. During this performance Phroso and Constantine sat still and impassive, while Vlacho's lifeless face was scorched by the growing heat of the sun. The men who had been told off to watch me leaned on their long guns, and I wondered wearily when my part in this strangely mixed ceremony was to begin.

At last it came. The dance ended, the performers flung themselves fatigued on the turf, there was a hush of expectation, and the surrounding crowd of women and children drew closer in towards where the rest of the men had taken up their position in ranks on either side of the central seats. 'Step forward,' said one of my guards, and I, obeying him, lifted my hat and bowed to Phroso. Then replacing my hat, I stood waiting the pleasure of the assembly. All eyes were fixed on Constantine, who remained seated and silent yet a little while longer. Then he rose slowly to his feet, bowed to Phroso, and pointed in a melodramatic fashion at Vlacho's body. But I was not in the least inclined to listen to an oration in the manner of Mark Antony over the body of Caesar, and just as Constantine was opening his mouth I observed loudly:

'Yes, I killed him, and the reason no man knows better than Constantine Stefanopoulos.'

Constantine glared at me, and, ignoring the bearing of my remark, launched out on an eulogium of the dead innkeeper. It was coldly received. Vlacho's virtues were not recognised by any outburst of grief or indignation; indeed there was a smothered laugh or two when Constantine called him 'a brave true man.'

The orator detected his failure and shifted his ground dexterously, passing on, in rapid transition, to ask in what quarrel Vlacho had died. Now he was gripping his audience. They drew closer; they became very still; angry and threatening glances were bent on me. Constantine lashed himself to fury as he cried, 'He died for our island, which this barbarian claims as his!'

'He died –' I began; but a heavy hand on my shoulder and the menace of a knife cut short my protest. Demetri had come and taken his stand by me, and I knew that Demetri would jump at the first excuse to make my silence perpetual. So I held my peace, and the men caught up Constantine's last point, crying angrily, 'Ay, he takes our island from us.'

'Yes,' said Constantine, 'he has taken our island, and he claims it for his. He has killed our brethren and put our Lady out of her inheritance. What shall he suffer? For although we may not kill on St Tryphon's day, we may judge on it, and the sentence may be performed at daybreak tomorrow. What shall this man suffer? Is he not worthy of death?'

It was what lawyers call a leading question, and it found its expected answer in a deep fierce growl, of 'Death, death!' Clearly the island was the thing, Vlacho's death merely an incidental affair of no great importance. I suppose that Phroso understood this as well as I, for now she rose suddenly. Constantine seemed disinclined to suffer the interruption; but she stood her ground firmly, though her face was very pale, and I saw her hands tremble. At last he sank back on to the bank.

'Why this turmoil?' she asked. 'The stranger did not know our customs. He thought that the island was his by right, and when he was attacked he defended himself. I pray you may all fight as bravely as he has fought.'

'But the island, the island!' they cried.

'Yes,' said she, 'I also love the island. Well, he has given back the island to me. Behold his writing!' She held up the paper which I had given to her and read the writing aloud in a clear voice. 'What have you against him now?' she asked. 'His people have loved the Hellenes. He has given back the island. Why shall he not depart in peace?'

The effect was great. The old priest seized the paper and scanned it eagerly: it was snatched from him and passed rapidly from hand to hand, greeted with surprised murmurs and intense excitement. Phroso stood watching its progress. Constantine sat with a heavy scowl on his face, and the frown grew yet deeper when I smiled at him with pleasant urbanity.

'It is true,' said the priest, with a sigh of relief. 'He has given back the island. He need not die.'

Phroso sat down; a sudden faintness seemed to follow on the strain, and I saw Kortes support her with his arm. But Constantine was not beaten yet. He sprang up and cried in bitterly scornful tones:

'Ay, let him go – let him go to Rhodes and tell the Governor that you sought to slay him and his friends, and that you extorted the paper from him by threat of death, and that he gave it in fear, but did not mean it, and that you are turbulent murderous men who deserve great punishment. How guileless you are, O Neopalians! But this man is not guileless. He can delude a girl. He can delude you also, it seems. Ay, let him go with his story to the Governor at Rhodes, and do you hide in the rocks when the Governor comes with his soldiers. Hide yourselves, and hide your women, when the soldiers come to set this man over your island and to punish you! Do you not remember when the Governor came before? Is not the mark of his anger branded on your hearts?'

Hesitation and suspicion were aroused again by this appeal. Phroso seemed bewildered at it and gazed at her cousin with parted lips. Angry glances were again fixed on me. But the old priest rose and stretched out his hand for silence.

'Let the man speak for himself,' he said. 'Let him tell us what he will do if we set him free. It may be that he will give us an oath not to harm us, but to go away peaceably to his own land and leave us our island. Speak, sir. We will listen.'

I was never much of a hand at a speech, and I did not enjoy being faced with the necessity of making one which might have such important results this way or that. But I was quite clear in my own mind what I wanted to say; so I took a step forward and began:

'I bear you Neopalians no malice,' said I. 'You've not succeeded in hurting me, and I suppose you've not caught my friends, or they would be here, prisoners as I am a prisoner. Now I have killed two good men of yours, Vlacho there, and Spiro. I am content with that. I'll cry you quits. I have given back the island to the Lady Euphrosyne; and what I give to a woman – ay, or to a man – I do not ask again either of a Governor or of anybody else. Therefore your island is safe, and I will swear to that by what oath you will. And, so far as I have power, no man or woman of all who stand round me shall come to any harm by reason of what has been done; and to that also I will swear.'

They had heard me intently, and they nodded in assent and approbation when the old priest, true to his part of peacemaker, looking round, said:

'He speaks well. He will not do what my lord feared. He will give us an oath. Why should he not depart in peace?'

Phroso's eyes sought mine, and she smiled sadly. Constantine was gnawing his finger nails and looking as sour as a man could look. It went to my heart to go on, for I knew that what I had to say next would give him another chance against me; but I preferred that risk to the only alternative.

'Wait,' said I. 'An oath is a sacred thing, and I swore an oath when I was there in the house of the Stefanopouloi. There is a man here who has done murder on an old man his kinsman, who has contrived murder against a woman, who has foully deceived a girl. With that man I'll not cry quits; for I swore that I would not rest till he paid the penalty of his crimes. By that oath I stand. Therefore, when I go from here, I shall, as

Constantine Stefanopoulos has said, go to Rhodes and to the Governor, and I shall pray him to send here to Neopalia, and take that one man and hang him on the highest tree in the island. And I will come with the Governor's men and see that thing done. Then I will go peaceably to my own land.'

There was a pause of surprise. Constantine lifted his lids and looked at me; I saw his hand move towards a pocket. I suspected what lay in that pocket. I heard low eager whisperings and questions. At last the old priest asked in a timid hesitating voice:

'Who is this man of whom you speak?'

'There he is,' said I. 'There – Constantine Stefanopoulos.'

The words were hardly out when Demetri clapped a large hairy hand across my mouth, whispering fiercely, 'Hold your tongue.' I drew back a step and struck him fairly between the eyes. He went down. A hoarse cry rose from the crowd; but in an instant Kortes had leapt from where he stood behind Phroso and was by my side. I had some adherents also among the bystanders; for I had been bidden to speak freely, and Demetri had no authority to silence me.

'Yes, Constantine Stefanopoulos,' I cried. 'Did he not stab the old man after he had yielded? Did he not –'

'The old man sold the island,' growled a dozen low fierce voices; but the priest's rose high above them.

'We are not here to judge my Lord Constantine,' said he, 'but this man here.'

'We all had a hand in the business of the old man,' said Demetri, who had picked himself up and was looking very vicious.

'You lie, and you know it,' said I hotly. 'He had yielded, and the rest had left off attacking him; but Constantine stabbed him. Why did he stab him?'

There came no answer, and Constantine caught at this advantage.

'Yes,' he cried. 'Why? Why should I stab him? He was stabbed by someone who did not know that he had yielded.' Then I saw his eye fall suddenly on Vlacho. Dead men tell no tales and deny no accusations.

'Since Vlacho is dead,' Constantine went on with wonderful readiness, 'my tongue is loosed. It was Vlacho who, in his hasty zeal, stabbed the old man.'

He had gained a point by this clever lie, and he made haste to press it to the full against me.

'This man,' he exclaimed, 'will go to Rhodes and denounce me! But did I kill the old man alone? Did I besiege the Englishman alone? Will the Governor be content with one victim? Is it not one head in ten when he comes to punish? Men of the island, it is your lives and my life against this man's life!'

They were with him again, and many shouted:

'Let him die! Let him die!'

Then suddenly, before I could speak, Phroso rose, and, stretching out her hands towards me, said:

'Promise what they ask, my lord. Save your own life, my lord. If my cousin be guilty, heaven will punish him.'

But I did not listen even to her. With a sudden leap I was free from those who held me; for, in the ranks of listening women, I saw that old woman whom we had found watching by the dying lord of the island. I seized her by the wrist and dragged her into the middle, crying to her:

'As God's above you, tell the truth. Who stabbed the old lord? Whose name did he utter in reproach when he lay dying?'

She stood shivering and trembling in the centre of the throng. The surprise of my sudden action held them all silent and motionless.

'Did he not say "Constantine! You, Constantine"?' I asked, 'just before he died?'

The old woman's lips moved, but no sound came; she was half-dead with fear and fastened fascinated eyes on Constantine. He surveyed her with a rigid smile on his pale face.

'Speak the truth, woman,' I cried. 'Speak the truth.'

'Yes, speak the truth,' said Constantine, his eyes gleaming in triumph as he turned a glance of hatred on me. 'Tell us truly who killed my uncle.'

My witness failed me. The terror of Constantine, which had locked her tongue when I questioned her at the house, lay on her still: the single word that came from her trembling lips was 'Vlacho.' Constantine gave a cry of triumph, Demetri a wild shout; the islanders drew together. My chance looked black. Even St Tryphon would hardly save me from immediate death. But I made another effort.

'Swear her on the sacred picture,' I cried. 'Swear her on the picture. If she swears by the picture, and then says it was Vlacho, I am content to die as a false accuser, and to die here and now.'

My bold challenge won me a respite: it appealed to their rude sense of justice and their strong leaven of superstition.

'Yes, let her swear on the sacred picture,' cried several. 'Then we shall know.'

The priest brought the picture to her and swore her on it with great solemnity. She shook her head feebly and fell to choked weeping. But the men round her were resolute, one of them menacing even Constantine himself when he began to ask whether her first testimony were not enough.

'Now you are sworn, speak,' said the priest solemnly.

A hush fell on us all. If she answered 'Constantine,' my life still hung by a thread; but by saying 'Vlacho' she would cut the thread. She looked at me, at Constantine, then up to the sky, while her lips moved in rapid whispered prayers.

'Speak,' said the priest to her gently.

Then she spoke in low fearful tones.

'Vlacho was there, and his knife was ready. But my lord yielded, and cried that he would not sell the island. When they heard that they drew back, Vlacho with the rest. But my Lord Constantine struck; and when my lord lay dying it was the name of Constantine that he uttered in reproach.' And the old woman reeled and would have fallen, and then flung herself on the ground at Constantine's feet, crying, 'Pardon, my lord, pardon! I could not swear falsely on the picture. Ah, my lord, mercy, mercy!'

But Constantine, though he had, as I do not doubt, a good memory for offences, could not afford to think of the old woman now. One instant he sat still, then he sprang to his feet, crying:

'Let my friends come round me! Yes, if you will, I killed the old man. Was not the deed done? Was not the island sold? Was he not bound to this man here? The half of the money had been paid! If he had lived, and if this man had lived, they would have brought soldiers and constrained us. So I slew him, and therefore I have sought to kill the stranger also. Who blames me? If there be any, let him stand now by the stranger, and let my friends stand by me. Have we not had enough talk? Is it not time to act? Who loves Neopalia? Who loves me?'

While he spoke many had been gathering round him. With every fresh appeal more flocked to him. There were but three or four left now, wavering between him and me, and Kortes alone stood by my side,

'Are you children, that you shrink from me because I struck a blow for our country? Was the old man to escape and live to help this man to take our island? Yes, I, Constantine Stefanopoulos, though I was blood of his blood – I killed him. Who blames me? Shall we not finish the work? There the stranger stands! Men of the island, shall we not finish the work?'

'Well, it's come at last,' thought I to myself. St Tryphon would not stop it now. 'It's no use,' I said to Kortes. 'Don't get yourself into trouble!' Then I folded my arms and waited. But I do not mean to say that I did not turn a little pale. Perhaps I did. At any rate I contrived to show no fear except in that.

The islanders looked at one another and then at Constantine. Friend Constantine had been ready with his stirring words, but he did not rush first to the attack. Besides myself there was Kortes, who had not left his place by me, in spite of my invitation to him. And Kortes looked as though he could give an account of one or two. But the hesitation among Constantine's followers did not last long. Demetri was no coward at all events, although he was as big a scoundrel as I have known. He carried a great sword which he must have got from the collection on the walls of the hall; he brandished it now over his head and rushed straight at me. It seemed to be all over, and I thought that the best I could do was to take it quietly; so I stood still. But on a sudden I was pulled back by a powerful arm. Kortes flung me behind him and stood between me and Demetri's rush. An instant later ten or more of them were round Kortes. He struck at them, but they dodged him. One cried, 'Don't hurt Kortes,' and another, running agilely round, caught his arms from behind, and, all gathering about him, they wrested his weapons from him. My last champion was disarmed; he had but protracted the bitterness of death for me by his gallant attempt. I fixed my eyes steadily on the horizon and waited. The time of my waiting must have been infinitesimal, yet I seemed to wait some little while. Then Demetri's great sword flashed suddenly between me and the sky. But it did not fall. Another flash came – the flash of white, darting across between me and the grim figure of my assailant – and Phroso, pale, breathless, trembling in every limb, yet holding her head bravely, and with anger gleaming in her dark eyes, cried:

'If you kill him you must kill me; I will not live if he dies.'

Even Demetri paused; the rest gave back. I saw Constantine's hatchet-face peering in gloomy wrath and trembling excitement from behind the protecting backs of his stout adherents. But Demetri, holding his sword poised for the stroke, growled angrily:

'What is his life to you, Lady?'

Phroso drew herself up. Her face was away from me, but as she spoke I saw a sudden rush of red spread over her neck; yet she spoke steadily and boldly in a voice that all could hear:

'His life is my life; for I love him as I love my life – ah, and God knows, more, more, more!'

11

The Last Card

In most families – at least among those that have any recorded history to boast of or to deplore – there is a point of family pride: with one it is grace of manner; with another, courage; with a third, statecraft; with a fourth, chivalrous loyalty to a lost cause or a fallen prince. Tradition adds new sanction to the cherished excellence; it becomes the heirloom of the house, the mark of the race – in the end, perhaps, a superstition before which greater things go down. If the men cling to it they are compensated by licence in other matters; the women are held in honour if they bear sons who do not fail in it. It becomes a new god, with its worship and its altar; and often the altar is laden with costly sacrifices. Wisdom has little part in the cult, and the virtues that are not hallowed by hereditary recognition are apt to go unhonoured and unpractised. I have heard it said, and seen it written, that we Wheatleys have, as a stock, few merits and many faults. I do not expect my career – if, indeed, I had such an ambitious thing as a career in my life's wallet – to reverse that verdict. But no man has said or written of us that we do not keep faith. Here is our pride and palladium. Promises we neither break nor ask back. We make them sometimes lightly; it is no matter: substance, happiness, life itself must be spent in keeping them. I had learnt this at my mother's knee. I myself had seen thousands and thousands poured forth to a rascally friend on the strength of a schoolboy pledge which my father made. 'Folly, folly!' cried the world. Whether it were right or not, who knows? We wrapped ourselves in the scanty mantle of our one virtue and went our way. We always – but a man grows tedious when he talks of his ancestors; he is like a doting old fellow, garrulous about his lusty youth. Enough of it. Yet not more than enough, for I carried this religion of mine to Neopalia, and built there an altar to it, and prepared for my altar the rarest sacrifice. Was I wrong? I do not care to ask.

'His life is my life. For I love him as my life.' The words rang in my ears, seeming to echo again through the silence that followed them: they were answered in my heart by beats of living blood. 'Was it true?' flashed through my brain. Was it truth or stratagem, a noble falsehood or a more splendid boldness? I did not know. The words were strange, yet to me they were not incredible. Had we not lived through ages together in those brief full hours in the old grey house? And the parting in the quiet evening had united while it feigned to sever. I believe I shut my eyes, not to see the slender stately form that stood between death and me. When I looked again, Demetri and his angry comrades had fallen back and stood staring in awkward bewilderment, but the women had crowded in upon us with eager excited faces; one broad-browed kindly creature had run to Phroso and caught her round the waist, and was looking in her eyes, and stroking her hand, and murmuring soft woman's comforting. Demetri took a step forward.

'Come, if you dare!' cried the woman, bold as a legion of men. 'Is a dog like you to come near my Lady Euphrosyne?' And Phroso turned her face away from the men and hid it in the woman's bosom.

Then came a cold rasping voice, charged with a bitter anger that masqueraded as amusement.

'What is this comedy, cousin?' asked Constantine. 'You love this man? You, the Lady of the island – you who have pledged your troth to me?' He turned to the people, spreading out his hands.

'You all know,' said he – 'you all know that we are plighted to one another.'

A murmuring assent greeted his words. 'Yes, they are betrothed,' I heard half a dozen mutter, as they directed curious glances at Phroso. 'Yes, while the old lord lived they were betrothed.'

Then I thought it time for me to take a hand in the game; so I stepped forward, in spite of Kortes' restraining arm.

'Be careful,' he whispered. 'Be careful.'

I looked at him. His face was drawn and pale, like the face of a man in pain, but he smiled still in his friendly open fashion.

'I must speak,' I said. I walked up to within two yards of Constantine, the islanders giving way before me, and I said loudly and distinctly:

'Was that same betrothal before you married your wife or afterwards?'

He sprang half-way up from his seat, as if to leap upon me, but he sank back again, his face convulsed with passion and his fingers picking furiously at the turf by his side. 'His wife!' went round the ring in amazed whisperings.

'Yes, his wife,' said I. 'The wife who was with him when I saw him in my country; the wife who came with him here, who was in the cottage on the hill, whom Vlacho would have dragged by force to her death, who lay last night yonder in the guard-house. Where is she, Constantine Stefanopoulos? Or is she dead now, and you free to wed the Lady Euphrosyne? Is she alive, or has she by now learnt the secret of the Stefanopouloi?'

I do not know which made more stir among the people, my talk of his wife or my hint about the secret. They crowded round me, hemming me in. I saw Phroso no more; but Kortes pushed his way to my side. Then the eyes of all turned on Constantine, where he sat with face working and nails fiercely plucking the turf.

'What is this lie?' he cried. 'I know nothing of a wife. True, there was a woman in the cottage.'

'Ay, there was a woman in the cottage,' said Kortes. 'And she was in the guard-house; but I did not know who she was, and I had no commands concerning her; and this morning she was gone.'

'That woman is his wife,' said I; 'but he and Vlacho had planned to kill her, in order that he might marry your Lady and have your island for himself.'

Demetri suddenly cried, with a great appearance of horror and disgust:

'Shall he live to speak such a slander against my lord?'

But Demetri gained no attention. I had made too much impression.

'Who was the woman, then,' said I, 'and where is she?'

Constantine, tricky and resourceful, looked again on the dead Vlacho.

'I may not tell my friend's secrets,' said he, with an admirable assumption of honour. 'And a foul blow has sealed Vlacho's lips.'

'Yes,' cried I. 'Vlacho killed the old lord, and Vlacho brought the woman! Indeed Vlacho serves my lord as well dead as when he lived! For now his lips are sealed. Come, then – Vlacho bought the island, and Vlacho slew Spiro, and now Vlacho has slain himself! Neither Constantine nor I have done anything; but it is all Vlacho – the useful Vlacho – Vlacho – Vlacho!'

Constantine's face was a sight to see, and he looked no pleasanter when my irony wrung smiles from some of the men round him, while others bit their lips to stop smiles that sought to come.

'Oh faithful servant!' I cried, apostrophising Vlacho, 'heavy are thy sins! May'st thou find mercy for them!'

I did not know what cards Constantine held. If he had succeeded in spiriting away his wife, by fair means or foul, he had the better chance; but if she were still free, alive and free, then he played a perilous hand and was liable to be utterly confounded. Yet he was forced to action; I had so moved the people that they looked for more than mere protests from him.

'The stranger who came to steal our island,' said he, skilfully prejudicing me by this description, 'asks me where the woman is. But I ask it of him – where is she? For it stands with him to put her before you that she may tell you whether I, Constantine Stefanopoulos, am lying to you. Yet how long is it since you doubted the words of the Stefanopouloi and believed strangers rather than them?'

His appeal won on them. They met it with murmured applause.

'You know me, you know my family,' he cried. 'Yet you hearken to the desperate words of a man who fights for his life with lies! How shall I satisfy you? For I have not the woman in my keeping. But have you not heard me when I swore my love for my cousin before you and the old lord who is dead? Am I a man to be forsworn? Shall I swear to you now?'

The current began to run strongly with him. He had called to his aid patriotism, and the old clan-loyalty which bound the Neopalians to his house, and they did not fail him. The islanders were ready to trust him if he would pledge himself to them.

'Swear then!' they cried. 'Swear to us on the sacred picture that what the stranger says is a lie.'

'On the sacred picture?' said he. 'Is it not too great and holy an oath for such a matter? Is not my word enough for you?'

But the old priest stepped forward.

'It is a great matter,' said he, 'for it touches closely the honour of your house, my lord, and on it hangs a man's life. Is any oath too great when honour and life lie in the balance? Let your life stand against his, for he who swears thus and falsely has no long life in Neopalia. Here we guard the honour of St Tryphon.'

'Yes, swear on the picture,' cried the people. 'It is enough if you swear on the picture!'

I could see that Constantine was not in love with the suggestion, but he accepted it with tolerable grace, acquiescing in the old priest's argument with a half-disdainful shrug. The people greeted his consent with obvious pleasure, save only Demetri, who regarded him with a doubtful expression. Demetri knew the truth, and, though he would cut a throat with a light heart, he would shrink from a denial of the deed when sworn on the holy picture. Truly conscience works sometimes in strange ways, making the lesser sin the greater, and dwarfing vile crimes to magnify their venial brethren. No, Demetri would not have sworn on the picture; and when he saw it brought to Constantine he shrank away from his leader, and I saw him privily and furtively cross himself. But Constantine, freed by the scepticism he had learnt in the West to practise the crimes the East had taught him, made little trouble about it. When the ceremonies that had attended the old woman's oath earlier in the day had been minutely, solemnly, and tediously repeated, he swore before them as bravely as you please and thereby bid fair to write my death-warrant in his lying words. For when the oath was done, the most awful names in heaven standing sanction to his perjury, and he ceased, saying, 'I have sworn,' the eyes of the men round him turned on me again and seemed to ask me silently what plea for mercy I could now advance. But I caught at my chance.

'Let Demetri swear,' said I coolly, 'that, so far as his knowledge goes, the truth is no other than what the Lord Constantine has sworn.'

'A subterfuge!' cried Constantine impatiently. 'What should Demetri know of it?'

'If he knows nothing it is easy for him to swear,' said I. 'Men of the island, a man should have every chance for his life. I have given you back your island. Do this for me. Make Demetri swear. Ah, look at the man! See, he shakes, his face goes pale, there is a sweat on his brow. Why, why? Make him swear!'

I should not have prevailed without the assisting evidence of the rascal's face. It was as I said he grew pale and sweated on the forehead; he cleared his throat hoarsely, but did not speak. Constantine's eyes said, 'Swear, fool, swear!'

'Let Demetri also swear,' cried some. 'Yes, it is easy, if he knows nothing.'

Suddenly Phroso sprang forward.

'Yes, let him swear,' she cried. 'Who is Chief here? Have I no power? Let him swear!' And she signed imperiously to the priest.

They brought the picture to Demetri. He shrank from it as though its touch would kill him.

'In the name of Almighty God, as you hope for mercy; in the name of our Lord the Saviour, as you pray for pity; in the name of the Most Blessed Spirit, whose Word is Truth; by the Most Holy Virgin, and by our Holy Saint – ' began the old man. But Demetri cried hoarsely:

'Take it away, take it away. I will not swear.'

'Let him swear,' said Phroso, and this time the whole throng caught up her command and echoed it in fierce urgency.

'Let him swear to tell the whole truth of what he knows, hiding nothing, according to the terms of the oath,' said the priest, pursuing his ritual.

'He shall not swear,' cried Constantine, speaking up. But he spoke to deaf ears and won only looks of new-born suspicion.

'It is the custom of the island,' they growled. 'It has been done in Neopalia time out of mind.'

'Yes,' said the priest. 'Time out of mind has a man been free to ask this oath of whomsoever he suspected. Swear, Demetri, as our Lady and our law bid.' And he ended the words of the oath.

Demetri looked round to right, to left, and to right again. He sought escape. There was none; his way was barred. His arms fell by his side.

'Will you let me go unharmed if I speak the truth?' he asked sullenly.

'Yes,' answered Phroso, 'if you speak the whole truth, you shall go unhurt.'

The excitement was intense now; for Demetri took the oath, Constantine watching, with pale strained face. Then followed a moment's utter silence, broken an instant later by an irresistible outbreak of wondering cries, for Demetri said, 'Follow me,' and turned and began to walk in the direction of the town. 'Follow me,' he said again. 'I will tell the truth. I have served my lord well, but a man's soul is his own. No master buys a man's soul. I will tell the truth.'

The change in feeling was witnessed by what happened. At a sign from the priest Kortes and another each took one of Constantine's arms and raised him. He was trembling now and hardly able to set one foot before the other. The dogs of justice were hard on his heels, and he was a craven at heart. Thus bearing him with us, in procession we followed Demetri from the place of assembly back to the steep narrow street that ran up from the sea. On the way none spoke. In the middle I walked; and in front of me went Phroso, the woman who had come to comfort her still holding her arm in hers.

On Demetri led us with quick decisive steps; but when he came to the door of the inn which had belonged to that Vlacho whose body lay now deserted on the level grass above the seashore, he halted abruptly, then turned and entered. We followed, Constantine's supporters bringing him also with us. We passed through the large lower room and out of the house again into an enclosed yard, bounded on the seaward side by a low stone wall, towards which the ground sloped rapidly. Here Demetri stopped.

'By my oath,' said he, 'and as God hears me! I knew not who this woman was; but last night Vlacho bade me come with him to the cottage on the hill, and, if he called me, I was to come and help him to carry her to the house of my Lord Constantine. He called, and I, coming with Kortes, found Vlacho dead. Kortes would not suffer me to touch the lady, but bade me stay with Vlacho. But when Kortes was gone and Vlacho dead, I ran and told my lord what had happened. My lord was greatly disturbed and bade me come with him; so we came together to the town and passed together by the guard-house.'

'Lies, foul lies,' cried Constantine; but they bade him be quiet, and Demetri continued in a composed voice:

'There Kortes watched. My lord asked him whom he held prisoner; and when he heard that it was the Englishman, he sought to prevail on Kortes to deliver him up; but Kortes would not without the command of the Lady Euphrosyne. Then my lord said, "Have you no other prisoner, Kortes?" Kortes answered, "There is a woman here whom we found in the cottage; but you gave me no orders concerning her, my lord, neither you, nor the Lady of the island." "I care nothing about her," said my lord with a shrug of his shoulders, and he and I turned away and walked some paces up the street. Then, at my lord's bidding, I crouched down with him in the shadow of a house and waited. Presently, when the clock had struck two, we saw Kortes come out from the guard-house; and the woman was with him. Now we were but fifty feet from them, and the wind was blowing from them to us, and I heard what the lady said.'

'It happened as he says,' interrupted Kortes in a grave tone. 'I promised secrecy, but I will speak now.'

' "I must go to the Lady Euphrosyne," said she to Kortes,' continued Demetri. ' "I have something to say to her." Kortes answered, "She is lodging at the house of the priest. It is the tenth house on the left hand as you mount the hill." She thanked him, and he turned back into the guard-house, and we saw no more of him. The lady came slowly and fearfully up the road; my lord beside me laughed gently, and twisted a silk scarf in his hand; there was nobody in the street except my lord, the lady and me; and as she went by my lord sprang out on her, and twisted the scarf across her mouth before she could cry out. Then he and I lifted her, and carried her swiftly down the street. We came here, to Vlacho's inn; the door was open, for Vlacho had gone out; it had not yet become known that he would never return. We carried her swiftly through the house and brought her where we stand now, and laid her on the ground. My lord tied her hands and her feet, so that she lay still her mouth was already gagged. Then my lord drew me aside and took five pieces of gold from his purse and said, looking into my eyes, "Is it enough?" I understood, and said, "It is enough, my lord," and he pressed my hand and left me, without going again near the woman. And I, having put the five pieces in my purse, drew my knife from its sheath and came and stood over the woman, looking how I might best strike the blow. She was gagged and tied and lay motionless. But the night was bright, and I saw her eyes fixed on mine. I stood long by her with my knife in my hand; then I knelt down by her to strike. But her eyes burned into my heart, and suddenly I seemed to hear Satan by my side, chuckling and whispering, "Strike, Demetri, strike! Art thou not damned already? Strike!" And I did not dare to look to the right or the left, for I felt the Fiend by me. So I shut my eyes and grasped my knife; but the lady's eyes drew mine open again, although I struggled to keep them shut. Now many devils seemed to be round me; and they were gleeful, saying, "Oh, he is ours! Yes, Demetri is ours. He will do this thing and then surely he is ours!" Suddenly I sobbed; and when my sob came, a gleam lighted the lady's eyes. Her eyes looked like the eyes of the Blessed Virgin in the church; I could not strike her. I flung down my knife and fell to sobbing. As I sobbed the noise of the devils ceased; and I seemed to hear instead a voice from above that said to me very softly, "Have I died to keep thy soul alive, and thou thyself wouldst kill it, Demetri?" I know not if anyone spoke; but the night was very still, and I was afraid, and I cried low, "Alas, I am a sinner!" But the voice said, "Sin no more;" and the eyes of the lady implored me. But then they closed, and I saw that she had fainted. And I raised her gently in my arms and carried her across this piece of ground where we stand.'

He ended, and stood for a moment silent and motionless. None of us spoke.

'I took her,' said he, 'there, where the wall ends; for I knew that Vlacho had his larder there. The door of the larder was locked, but I set the lady down and returned and took my knife from the ground, and I forced the lock and took her in, and laid her on the floor of the larder. Then I returned to the house, and called to Panayiota, Vlacho's daughter, with whom I am of kin. When she came I charged her to watch the lady till I returned, saying that Vlacho had bidden me bring her here; for I meant to return in a few hours and carry the lady to some place of safety, if I could find one. Panayiota, fearing Vlacho and having an affection for me, promised faithfully to keep the lady safe. Then I ran after my lord, and found him at the house, and told him that the deed was done, and that I had hidden the body here; and I craved leave to return and make a grave for the body or carry it to the sea. But he said, "It will be soon enough in the evening. We shall be quit of troubles by the evening. Does anyone know?" I answered rashly, "Panayiota knows." And he was enraged, fearing Panayiota would betray us; but when he heard that she and I were lovers, he was appeased; yet I could not find means to leave him and return to the lady.'

Demetri ended. Phroso, without a look at any one of us, stepped lightly to the spot he had described. There was a low hut there, with a stout wooden door. Phroso knocked on it, but there came no answer. She beckoned to Kortes, and he, coming, wrenched open the door, which seemed to have been fastened by some makeshift arrangement. Kortes disappeared for an instant then he came out again and motioned with his hand. We crowded round the door, I among the first. There, indeed, was a strange sight. For on the floor, propped against the side of the hut, sat a buxom girl; her eyes were closed, her lips parted, and she breathed in heavy regular breaths; Panayiota had watched faithfully all night, and now slept at her post. Yet her trust was not betrayed. On her lap rested the head of the lady whom Demetri had not found it in his heart to kill; the bonds with which she had been bound lay on the floor by her; and she also, pale and with shadowed rings about her eyes, slept the sleep of utter exhaustion and weariness. We stood looking at the strange sight – a sudden gleam of peace and homely kindness breaking across the dark cloud of angry passions.

'Hush,' said Phroso very softly. She stepped forward and fell on her knees by the sleeping woman, and she lightly kissed Constantine's wife on the brow. 'Praise be to God!' said Phroso softly, and kissed her again.

12

Law and Order

At last the whirligig seemed to have taken a turn in my favour, the revolutions of the wheel at last to have brought my fortune uppermost. For the sight of Francesca in Panayiota's arms came pat in confirmation of the story wrung from Demetri by the power of his oath, and his 'Behold!' was not needed to ensure acceptance for his testimony. From women rose compassionate murmurs, from men angry growlings which expressed, while they strove to hide, the shamefaced emotions that the helpless woman's narrow escape created. Her salvation must bring mine with it; for it was the ruin of her husband and my enemy.

Kortes and another dragged Constantine Stefanopoulos forward till he stood within two or three yards of his wife. None interposed on his behalf or resented the rough pressure of Kortes' compelling hand. And even as he was set there, opposite the women, they, roused by the subdued stir of the excited throng, awoke. First into one another's eyes, then round upon us, came their startled glances; then Francesca leapt with a cry to her feet, ran to me, and threw herself on her knees before me, crying, 'You'll save me, my lord, you'll save me?' Demetri hung his head in sullen half-contrition mingled with an unmistakable satisfaction in his religious piety; Constantine bit and licked his thin lips, his fists tight clenched, his eyes darting furtively about in search of friends or in terror of avengers. And Phroso said in her soft clear tones:

'There is no more need of fear, for the truth is known.'

Her eyes, though they would not meet mine, rested long in tender sympathy on the woman who still knelt at my feet. Here indeed she remained till Phroso came forward and raised her, while the old priest lifted his voice in brief thanks to heaven for the revelation wrought under the sanction of the Holy Saint. For myself I gave a long sigh of relief; the strain had been on me now for many hours, and it tires a man to be knocking all day long at the door of death. Yet almost in the instant that the concern for my own life left me (that is a thing terribly apt to fill a man's mind) my thoughts turned to other troubles: to my friends, who were – I knew not where; to Phroso, who had said – I scarcely knew what.

Suddenly, striking firm and loud across the murmurs and the threats that echoed round the ring in half-hushed voices, came Kortes' tones.

'And this man? What of him?' he asked, his hand on Constantine's shaking shoulder. 'For he has done all that the stranger declared of him: he has deceived our Lady Euphrosyne, he has sought to kill this lady here, we have it from his own mouth that he slew the old lord, though he knew well that the old lord had yielded.'

Constantine's wife turned swiftly to the speaker. 'Did he kill the old lord?' she asked. 'He told me that it was Spiro who struck him in the heat of the brawl.'

'Ay, Spiro or Vlacho, or whom you will,' said Kortes with a shrug. 'There was no poverty of lies in his mouth.'

But the old feeling was not dead, and one or two again murmured:

'The old lord sold the island.'

'Did he die for that?' cried Francesca scornfully; 'or was it not in truth I who brought him to death?'

There was a movement of surprised interest, and all bent their eyes on her.

'Yes,' she went on, 'I think I doomed him to that death when I went and told him my story, seeking his protection. Constantine found me with him, and heard him greet me as his nephew's wife, on the afternoon of the day that the deed was done. Can this man here deny it? Can he deny that the old lord was awaiting the return of the Lady Euphrosyne to tell her of the thing, when his mouth was shut for ever by the stroke?'

This disclosure, showing a new and vile motive for what Constantine had tried to play off as a pardonable excess of patriotism, robbed him of his last defenders. He seemed to recognise his plight; his eyes ceased to canvass possible favour, and dropped to the ground in dull despair. There was not a man now to raise a voice or a hand for him; their anger at having been made his dupes and his tools sharpened the edge of their hatred. To me his wife's words caused no wonder, for I had from the first believed that some secret motive had nerved Constantine's arm, and that he had taken advantage of the islanders' mad folly for his own purposes. What that motive was stood out now clear and obvious. It explained his act, and abundantly justified the distrust and fear of him which I had perceived in his wife's mind when first I talked with her on the hill. But she, having launched her fatal bolt, turned her eyes away again, and laying her hand in Phroso's stood silent.

Kortes, appearing to take the lead now by general consent – for Phroso made no sign – looked round on his fellow-countrymen, seeking to gather their decision from their faces. He found the guidance and agreement that he sought.

'We may not put any man to death on St Tryphon's day,' said he.

The sentence was easy to read, for all its indirectness. The islanders understood it, and approved in a deep stern murmur; the women followed it, and their faces grew pale and solemn. The criminal missed nothing of its implied doom and tottered under the strong hands that now rather supported than imprisoned him. 'Not on this day, but tomorrow at break of day.' The voice of the people had spoken by the mouth of Kortes, and none pleaded for mercy or delay.

'I will take him to the guard-house and keep him,' said Kortes; and the old priest murmured low, 'God have mercy on him!' Then, with a swift dart, Phroso sprang towards Kortes; her hands were clasped, her eyes prayed him to seek some ground of mercy, some pretext for a lighter sentence. She said not a word, but every one of us read her eloquent prayer. Kortes looked round again; the faces about him were touched with a tenderness that they had not worn before; but the tenderness was for the advocate, no part of it reached the criminal. Kortes shook his head gravely. Phroso turned to the woman who had comforted her before, and hid her face. Constantine, seeing the last hope gone, swayed and fell into the arms of the man who, with Kortes, held him, uttering a long low moan of fear and despair, terrible to listen to, even from lips guilty as his. Thus was Constantine Stefanopoulos tried for his life in the yard of Vlacho's inn in Neopalia. The trial ended, he was carried out into the street on his way to the prison, and we, one and all, in dead silence, followed. The yard was emptied, and the narrow street choked with the crowd which attended Kortes and his prisoner till the doors of the guard-house closed on them.

Then, for the first time that day, Phroso's eyes sought mine in a rapid glance, in which I read joy for my safety; but the glance fell as I answered it, and she turned away in confusion. Her avowal, forgotten for an instant in gladness, recurred to her mind and dyed her cheeks red. Averting my eyes from her, I looked down the slope of the street towards the sea. The thought of her and of nothing else was in my mind.

Ah, my island! My sweet capricious island!

A sudden uncontrollable exclamation burst from my lips and, raising my hand, I pointed to the harbour and the blue water beyond. Every head followed the direction of my outstretched finger; every pair of eyes was focused on the object that held mine. A short breathless silence – a momentary wonder – when, shrill or deep, low in fear or loud in excitement, broke forth the cry:

'The Governor! The Governor!'

For a gunboat was steaming slowly into the harbour of Neopalia, and the Turkish flag flew over her.

The sight wrought transformation. In a moment, as it seemed to me, the throng round me melted away. The street grew desolate, the houses on either side swallowed their eager occupants; Kortes alone, with his prisoner, knew nothing of the fresh event, only Phroso and Francesca stood their ground. Demetri was slinking hastily away. The old priest was making for his home. The shutters of dead Vlacho's inn came down, and girls bustled to and fro, preparing food. I stood unwatched, unheeded, apparently forgotten; festival, tumult, trial, condemnation seemed passed like visions; the flag that flew from the gunboat brought back modern days, the prose of life, and ended the wild poetic drama that we had played and a second One-eyed Alexander might worthily have sung. How had the Governor come before his time, and why?

'Denny!' I cried aloud in inspiration and hope, and I ran as though the foul fiends whom Demetri had heard were behind me. Down the steep street and on to the jetty I ran. As I arrived there the gunboat also reached it, and, a moment later, Denny was shaking my hand till it felt like falling off, while from the deck of the boat Hogvardt and Watkins were waving wild congratulations.

Denny had jumped straight from deck to jetty; but now a gangway was thrust out, and I passed with him on to the deck, and presented myself with a low bow, to a gentleman who stood there. He was a tall full-bodied man, apparently somewhat under fifty years old; his face was heavy and broad, in complexion dark and sallow; he wore a short black beard; his lips were full, his eyes acute and small. I did not like the look of him much; but he meant law and order and civilisation and an end to the wild ways of Neopalia. For this, as Denny whispered to me, was no less a man than the Governor himself Mouraki Pasha. I bowed again yet lower; for I stood before a man of whom report had much to tell – something good, much bad, all interesting.

He spoke to me in low, slow, suave tones, employing the Greek language, which he spoke fluently, although as a foreigner. For Mouraki was by birth an Armenian.

'You must have much to tell me, Lord Wheatley,' he said with a smile. 'But first I must assure you with what pleasure I find you alive and unhurt. Be confident that you shall not want redress for the wrongs which these turbulent rascals have inflicted on you. I know these men of Neopalia: they are hard men; but they also know me, and that I, in my turn, can be a hard man if need be.' His looks did not belie his words, as his sharp eye travelled with an ominous glance over the little town by the harbour. 'But you will wish to speak with your friends first,' he went on courteously. 'May I ask your attention in half an hour's time from now?'

I bowed obedience. The great man turned away, and Denny caught me by the arm, crying, 'Now, old man, tell us all about it.'

'Wait a bit,' said I rather indignantly. 'Just you tell me all about it.'

But Denny was firmer than I, and my adventures came before his. I told them all faithfully, save one incident; it may perhaps be guessed which. Denny and the other two listened with frequent exclamations of surprise, and danced with exultation at the final worsting of Constantine Stefanopoulos.

'It's all right,' said Denny reassuringly. 'Old Mouraki will hang him just the same.'

'Now it's your turn,' said I.

'Oh, our story's nothing. We just got through that old drain, and came out by the sea, and all the fishermen had gone off to the fishing grounds, except one old chap they left behind to look after their victuals. Well, we didn't know how to get back to you, and the old chap told us that the whole place was alive with armed ruffians, so – '

'Just tell the story properly, will you?' said I sternly.

At last, by pressing and much questioning, I got the story from them, and here it is; for it was by no means so ordinary a matter as Denny's modesty would have had me think. When the consternation caused by the cutting of our rope had passed away, a hurried council decided them to press on with all speed, and they took their way along a narrow, damp and slippery ledge of rock which encircled the basin. So perilous did the track seem that Hogvardt insisted on their being roped as though for a mountaineering ascent, and thus they continued the journey. The first opening from the basin they found without much difficulty. Now the rope proved useful, for Denny, passing through first, fell headlong into space and most certainly would have perished but for the support his companions gave him. The track turned at right angles to the left, and Denny had walked straight over the edge of the rock Sobered by this accident and awake to their peril (it must be remembered that they had no lantern), they groped their way slowly and cautiously, up and down, in and out. Hours passed. Watkins, less accustomed than the others to a physical strain, could hardly lift his feet. All this while the dim glimmer which Denny had seen retreated before them, appearing to grow no nearer for all their efforts. They walked, as they found afterwards – or walked, crawled, scrambled and jumped – for eleven hours, their haste and anxiety allowed no pause for rest. Then they seemed to see the end, for the winding tortuous track appeared at last to make up its mind. It took a straight downward line, and Denny's hard-learned caution vanishing, he started along it at a trot and with a hearty hurrah. He tempted fate. The slope became suddenly a drop. This time all three fell with a splash and a thud into a deep pool, one on the top of the other. Here they scrambled for some minutes, Watkins coming very near to finding an end of the troubles of his eventful service. But Denny and Hogvardt managed to get him out. The path began again. Content with its last freak, it pursued now a business-like way the glimmer grew to a gleam, the gleam spread into a glad blaze. 'The sea, the sea!' cried Denny. A last spurt landed them in a cave that bordered on the blue waters. What they did on that I could by no means persuade them to tell; but had I been there I should have thanked God and shaken hands; and thus, I dare say, did they. And besides that, they lay there, dog-tired and beaten, for an hour or more, in one of those despondent fits that assail even brave men, making sure that I was dead or taken, and that their own chances of escape were small, and, since I was dead or taken, hardly worth the seeking.

They were roused by an old man, who suddenly entered the cave, bearing a bundle of sticks in his arms. At sight of them he dropped his load and turned to fly; but they were on him in an instant, seizing him and crying to know who he was. He had as many questions for them; and when he learned who they were and how they had come, he raised his hands in wonder, and told Hogvardt, who alone could make him understand, that their fears were well grounded. He had met a Neopalian but an hour since, and the talk in all the island was of how the stranger had killed Vlacho and been taken by Kortes, and would die on the next day; for this was the early morning of the feast-day. Denny was for a dash; but a dash meant certain death. Watkins was ready for the venture, though the poor fellow could hardly crawl. Hogvardt held firm to the chance that more cautious measures gave. The old man's comrades were away at their fishing grounds, ten miles out at sea; but he had a boat down on the beach. Thither they went, and set out under the fisherman's guidance, pulling in desperate perseverance, with numb weary limbs, under the increasing heat of the sun. But their wills asked too much of their bodies. Watkins dropped his oar with a groan; Denny's moved weakly and uselessly through the water that hardly stirred under its blade; Hogvardt at last flung himself into the stern with one groan of despair. The old fisherman cast resigned eyes up to heaven, and the boat tossed motionlessly on the water. Thus they lay while I fought my duel with Constantine Stefanopoulos on the other side of Neopalia.

Then, while they were still four miles from the fishing-fleet, where lay their only known chance of succour for me or for themselves, there came suddenly to their incredulous eyes a shape on the sea and a column of smoke. Denny's spring forward went near to capsizing the boat. Oars were seized again, weariness fled before hope, the gunboat came in view, growing clear and definite. She moved quickly towards them, they slowly, yet eagerly, to her; the interval grew less and less. They shouted before they could be heard, and shouted still in needless caution long after they had been heard, A boat put out to them: they were taken on board, their story heard with shrugs of wonder. Mouraki could not be seen. 'I'll see him!' cried Denny, and Hogvardt plied the recalcitrant officer with smooth entreaties. The life of a man was at stake! But he could not be seen. The life of an Englishman! His Excellency slept through the heat of the day. The life of an English lord! His Excellency would be angry, but –! The contents of Denny's pocket, wild boasts of my power and position (I was a favourite at Court, and so forth), at last clinched the matter. His Excellency should be roused; heaven knew what he would say, but he should be roused. He went to Neopalia next week; now he was sailing past it, to inspect another island; perhaps he would alter the order of his voyage. He was fond of Englishmen. It was a great lord, was it not? So, at last, when Hogvardt was at his tongue's end, and Denny almost mad with rage, Mouraki was roused. He heard their story, and pondered on it, with leisurely strokings of his beard and keen long glances of his sharp eyes. At last came the word, 'To the island then!' and a cheer from the three, which Mouraki suffered with patient uplifted brows. Thus came Mouraki to Neopalia; thus came, as I hoped, an end to our troubles.

More than the half-hour which the Governor had given me passed swiftly in the narrative; then came Mouraki's summons and my story to him, heard with courteous impassivity, received at its end with plentiful assurances of redress for me and punishment for the islanders.

'The island shall be restored to you,' said he. 'You shall have every compensation, Lord Wheatley. These Neopalians shall learn their lesson.'

'I want nothing but justice on Constantine,' said I. 'The island I have given back.'

'That goes for nothing,' said he. 'It was under compulsion: we shall not acknowledge it. The island is certainly yours. Your title has been recognised: you could not transfer it without the consent of my Government.'

I did not pursue the argument. If Mouraki chose to hand the island back to me, I supposed that I could, after such more or less tedious forms as were necessary, restore it to Phroso. For the present the matter was of small moment; for Mouraki was there with his men, and the power of the Lord – or Lady – of Neopalia in abeyance. The island was at the feet of the Governor.

Indeed such was its attitude, and great was the change in the islanders when, in the cool of the evening, I walked up the street by Mouraki's side escorted by soldiers and protected by the great gun of the gunboat commanding the town. There were many women to watch us, few men, and these unarmed, with downcast eyes and studious meekness of bearing. Mouraki seemed to detect my surprise.

'They made a disturbance here three years ago,' said he, 'and I came. They have not forgotten.'

'What did you do to them?' I made bold to ask.

'What was necessary,' he said; and – 'They are not Armenians,' added the Armenian Governor with a smile which meant much; among other things, as I took it, that no tiresome English demanded fair trial for riotous Neopalians.

'And Constantine?' said I. I hope that I was not too vindictive.

'It is the feast of St Tryphon,' said his Excellency, with another smile.

We were passing the guard-house now. An officer and five men fell out from the ranks of our escort and took their stand by its doors. We passed on, leaving Constantine in this safe-keeping; and Mouraki, turning to me, said, 'I must ask you for hospitality. As Lord of the island, you enjoy the right of entertaining me.'

I bowed. We turned into the road that led to the old grey house; when we were a couple of hundred yards from it, I saw Phroso coming out of the door. She walked rapidly towards us, and paused a few paces from the Governor, making a deep obeisance to him and bidding him welcome to her poor house in stately phrases of deference and loyalty. Mouraki was silent, surveying her with a slight smile. She grew confused under his wordless smiling; her greetings died away. At last he spoke, in slow deliberate tones:

'Is this the lady,' said he, 'who raises a tumult and resists my master's will, and seeks to kill a lord who comes peaceably and by lawful right to take what is his?'

I believe I made a motion as though to spring forward. Mouraki's expressive face displayed a marvelling question; did I mean such insolence as lay in interrupting him? I fell back; a public remonstrance could earn only a public rebuff.

'Strange are the ways of Neopalia,' said he, his gaze again on Phroso.

'I am at your mercy, my lord,' she murmured. 'And what is this talk of your house? What house have you? I see here the house of this English lord, where he will receive me courteously. Where is your house?'

'The house belongs to whom you will, my lord,' she said. 'Yet I have dared to busy myself in making it ready for you.'

By this time I was nearly at boiling point, but still I controlled myself. I rejoiced that Denny was not there, he and the others having resumed possession of the yacht, and arranged to sleep there, in order to leave more room for Mouraki's accommodation. Phroso stood in patient submission; Mouraki's eyes travelled over her from head to foot.

'The other woman?' he asked abruptly. 'Your cousin's wife – where is she?'

'She is at the cottage on the hill, my lord, with a woman to attend on her.'

After another pause he motioned with his hand to Phroso to take her place by him, and thus we three walked up to the house. It was alive now with women and men, and there was a bustle of preparation for the great man.

Mouraki sat down in the armchair which I had been accustomed to use, and, addressing an officer who seemed to be his aide-de-camp, issued quick orders for his own comfort and entertainment; then he turned to me and said civilly enough:

'Since you seem reluctant to act as host, you shall be my guest while I am here.'

I murmured thanks. He glanced at Phroso and waved his hand in dismissal. She drew back, curtseying, and I saw her mount the stairs to her room. Mouraki bade me sit down, and his orderly brought him cigarettes. He gave me one and we began to smoke, Mouraki watching the coiling rings, I furtively studying his face. I was in a rage at his treatment of Phroso. But the man interested me. I thought that he was now considering great matters: the life of Constantine, perhaps, or the penalties that he should lay on the people of Neopalia. Yet even these would seem hardly great to him, who had moved in the world of truly great affairs, and was in his present post rather by a temporary loss of favour than because it was adequate to his known abilities. With such thoughts I studied him as he sat smoking silently.

Well, man is very human, and great men are often even more human than other men. For when Mouraki saw that we were alone, when he had finished his cigarette, flung it away and taken another, he observed to me, obviously summarising the result of those meditations to which my fancy had imparted such loftiness:

'Yes, I don't know that I ever saw a handsomer girl.'

There was nothing to say but one thing, and I said it.

'No more did I, your Excellency,' said I. But I was not pleased with the expression of Mouraki's eye; the contentment induced in me by the safety of my friends, by my own escape, and by the end of Constantine's ill-used power, was suddenly clouded as I sat and looked at the baffling face and subtle smile of the Governor. What was it to him whether Phroso were a handsome girl or not?

And I suppose I might just as well have added – What was it to me?

13

The Smiles of Mouraki Pasha

At the dinner-table Mouraki proved a charming companion. His official reserve and pride vanished; he called me by my name simply, and extorted a like mode of address from my modesty. He professed rapture at meeting a civilised and pleasant companion in such an out-of-the-way place; he postponed the troubles and problems of Neopalia in favour of a profusion of amusing reminiscences and pointed anecdotes. He gave me a delightful evening, and bade me the most cordial of good nights. I did not know whether his purpose had been to captivate or merely to analyse me; he had gone near to the former, and I did not doubt that he had succeeded entirely in the latter. Well, there was nothing I wanted to conceal – unless it might be something which I was still striving to conceal even from myself.

I rose very early the next morning. The Pasha was not expected to appear for two or three hours, and he had not requested my presence till ten o'clock breakfast. I hastened off to the harbour, boarded the yacht, enjoyed a merry cup of coffee and a glorious bathe with Denny. Denny was anxious to know my plans – whether I meant to return or to stay. The idea of departure was odious to me. I enlarged on the beauties of the island, but Denny's shrug insinuated a doubt of my candour. I declared that I saw no reason for going, but must be guided by the Pasha.

'Where's the girl?' asked Denny abruptly.

'She's up at the house,' I answered carelessly.

'Hum, Heard anything about Constantine being hanged?'

'Not a word; Mouraki has not touched on business.'

Denny had projected a sail, and was not turned from his purpose by my unwillingness to accompany him. Promising to meet him again in the evening, I took my way back up the street, where a day or two ago my life would have paid for my venturing, where now I was as safe as in Hyde Park. Women gave me civil greetings; the men did the like, or, at worst, ignored me. I saw the soldiers on guard at Constantine's prison, and pursued my path to the house with a complacent smile. My island was beautiful that morning, and the blood flowed merrily in my veins. I thought of Phroso. Where was the remorse which I vainly summoned?

Suddenly I saw Kortes before me, walking along slowly. He was relieved of his duty then, and Constantine was no longer in his hands. Overtaking him, I began to talk. He listened for a little, and then raised his calm honest eyes to mine.

'And the Lady Phroso?' he said gently. 'What of her?'

I told him what I knew, softening the story of Mouraki's harshness.

'You have not spoken to her yet?' he asked. Then, coming a step nearer, he said, 'She shuns you perhaps?'

'I don't know,' said I, feeling embarrassed under the man's direct gaze.

'It is natural, but it will last only till she has seen you once. I pray you not to linger, my lord. For she suffers shame at having told her love, even though it was to save you. It is hard for a maiden to speak unasked.'

I leaned my back against the rocky bank by the road.

'Lose no time in telling her your love, my lord,' he urged. 'It may be that she guesses, but her shame will trouble her till she hears it from your lips. Seek her, seek her without delay.'

I had forgotten my triumph over Constantine and the beauty of the island. I felt my eyes drop before Kortes' look; but I shrugged my shoulders, saying carelessly:

'It was only a friendly device the Lady Phroso played to save me. She doesn't really love me. It was a trick. But I'll thank her for it heartily; it was of great help to me, and a hard thing for her to do.'

'It was no trick. You know it was none. Wasn't the love in every tone of her voice? Isn't it in every glance of her eyes when she is with you – and most when she won't look at you?'

'How come you to read her looks so well?' I asked.

'From studying them deeply,' said he simply. 'I do not know if I love her, my lord; she is so much above me that my thoughts have not dared to fly to the height. But I would die for her, and I love no other. To me, you, my lord, should be the happiest, proudest man alive. Pray speak to her soon, my lord. My sister, whom you saw hold her in her arms, would have made me sure if I had doubted. The lady murmurs your name in her sleep.'

A sudden irresistible exultation took hold of me. I think it turned my face red, for Kortes smiled, saying, 'Ah, you believe now, my lord!'

'Believe!' I cried. 'No, I don't believe. A thousand times, no! I don't believe!' For I was crushing that exultation now as a man crushes the foulest temptings.

A puzzled look invaded Kortes' eyes. There was silence between us for some moments.

'It's absurd,' said I, in weak protest. 'She has known me only a few days – only a few hours rather – and there were other things to think of then than love-making.'

'Love,' said he, 'is made most readily when a man does not think of it, and a stout arm serves a suitor better than soft words. You fought against her and for her; you proved yourself a man before her eyes. Fear not, my lord; she loves you.'

'Fear not!' I exclaimed in a low bitter whisper.

'She said it herself' continued Kortes. 'As her life, and more.'

'Hold your tongue, man!' I cried fiercely. 'In the devil's name, what has it to do with you?'

A great wonder showed on his face, then a doubting fear; he came closer to me and whispered so low that I hardly heard:

'What ails you? Is it not well that she should love you?'

'Let me alone,' I cried; 'I'll not answer your questions.' Why was the fellow to cross-examine me? Ah, there's the guilty man's old question; he loves a fine mock indignation, and hugs it to his heart.

Kortes drew back a pace and bowed, as though in apology; but there was no apology in the glance he fixed on me. I would not look him in the face. I drew myself up as tall as I could, and put on my haughtiest air. If he could have seen how small I felt inside!

'Enough, Kortes,' said I, with a lordly air. 'No doubt your intentions are good, but you forget what is becoming from you to me.'

He was not awed; and I think he perceived some of the truth – not all; for he said, 'You made her love you; that does not happen unless a man's own acts help it.'

'Do girls never rush uninvited on love, then?' I sneered.

'Some perhaps, but she would not,' he answered steadily.

He said no more. I nodded to him and set forward on my way. He bowed again slightly, and stood still where he was, watching me. I felt his eyes on me after we had parted. I was in a very tumult of discomfort. The man had humiliated me to the ground. I hoped against hope that he was wrong; and again, in helpless self-contradiction, my heart cried out insisting on its shameful joy because he was right. Right or wrong, wrong or right, what did it matter? Either way now lay misery, either way now lay a struggle that I shrank from and abhorred.

I was somewhat delayed by this interview, and when I arrived at the house I found Mouraki already at breakfast. He apologised for not having awaited my coming, saying, 'I have transacted much business. Oh, I've not been in bed all the time! And I grew hungry. I have been receiving some reports on the state of the island.'

'It's quiet enough now. Your arrival has had a most calming effect.'

'Yes, they know me. They are very much afraid, for they think I shall be hard on them. They remember my last visit.'

He made no reference to Constantine, and although I wondered rather at his silence I did not venture again to question him. I wished that I knew what had happened on his last visit. A man with a mouth like Mouraki's might cause anything to happen.

'I shall keep them in suspense a little while,' he pursued, smiling. 'It's good for them. Oh, by the way, Wheatley, you may as well take this; or shall I tear it up?' And suddenly he held out to me the document which I had written and given to Phroso when I restored the island to her.

'She gave you this?' I cried.

'She?' asked Mouraki, with a smile of mockery. 'Is there, then, only one woman in the world?' he seemed to ask sneeringly.

'The Lady Euphrosyne, to whom I gave it,' I explained with what dignity I could.

'The Lady Phroso, yes,' said he. ('Hang his Phroso!' thought I.) 'I had her before me this morning and made her give it up.'

'I can only give it back to her, you know.'

'My dear Wheatley, if you like to amuse yourself in that way I can have no possible objection. Until you obtain a firman, however, you will continue to be Lord of Neopalia and this Phroso no more than a very rebellious young lady. But you'll enjoy a pleasant interview and no harm will be done. Give it back by all means.' He smiled again, shrugging his shoulders, and lit a cigarette. His manner was the perfection of polite, patient, gentlemanly contempt.

'It seems easier to get an island than to get rid of one,' said I, trying to carry off my annoyance with a laugh.

'It is the case with so many things,' agreed Mouraki: 'debts, diseases, enemies, wives, lovers.'

There was a little pause before the last word, so slight that I could not tell whether it were intentional or not; and I had learnt to expect no enlightenment from Mouraki's face or eyes. But he chose himself to solve the mystery this time.

'Do I touch delicate ground?' he asked. 'Ah, my dear lord, I find from my reports that in the account you gave me of your experiences you let modesty stand in the way of candour. It was natural perhaps. I don't blame you, since I have found out elsewhere what you omitted to tell me. Yet it was hardly a secret, since everybody in Neopalia knew it.'

I smoked my cigarette, feeling highly embarrassed and very uncomfortable.

'And I am told,' pursued Mouraki, with his malicious smile, 'that the idea of a Wheatley-Stefanopoulos dynasty is by no means unpopular. Constantine's little tricks have disgusted them with him.'

'What are you going to do with him?' I asked, risking any offence now in order to turn the topic.

'Do you really like jumping from subject to subject?' asked Mouraki plaintively. 'I am, I suppose, a slow-minded Oriental, and it fatigues me horribly.'

I could have thrown the cigarette I was smoking in his face with keen pleasure.

'It is for your Excellency to choose the topic,' said I, restraining my fury.

'Oh, don't let us have "Excellencies" when we're alone together! Indeed I congratulate you on your conquest. She is magnificent; and it was charming of her to make her declaration. That's what has pleased the islanders: they're romantic savages, after all, and the chivalry of it touches them.'

'It must touch anybody,' said I.

'Ah, I suppose so,' said Mouraki, flicking away his ash. 'I questioned her a little about it this morning.'

'You questioned her?' For all I could do there was a quiver of anger in my voice. I heard it myself and it did not escape my companion's notice. His smile grew broader.

'Precisely. I have to consider everything,' said he. 'I assure you, my dear Wheatley, that I did it in the most delicate manner possible.'

'It couldn't be done in a delicate manner.'

'I struggled,' said Mouraki, assuming his plaintive tone again, and spreading out deprecatory hands.

Was Mouraki merely amusing himself with a little 'chaff,' or had he a purpose? He seemed like a man who would have a purpose. I grew cool on the thought of it.

'And did the lady answer your questions?' I asked carelessly.

'Wouldn't it be a treachery in me to tell you what she said?' countered Mouraki.

'I think not; because there's no doubt that the whole thing was only a good-natured device of hers.'

'Ah! A very good-natured device indeed! She must be an amiable girl,' smiled the Pasha. 'Precisely the sort of girl to make a man's home happy.'

'She hasn't much chance of marriage in Neopalia,' said I.

'Heaven makes a way,' observed Mouraki piously. 'By the by, the device seems to have imposed on our acquaintance Kortes.'

'Oh, perhaps,' I shrugged. 'He's a little smitten himself, I think, and so very ready to be jealous.'

'How discriminating!' murmured Mouraki admiringly. 'As a fact, my dear Wheatley, the lady said nothing. She chose to take offence.'

'You surprise me!' I exclaimed with elaborate sarcasm.

'And wouldn't speak. But her blushes were most lovely – yes, most lovely. I envied you, upon my word I did.'

'Since it's not true – '

'Oh, a thing may be very pleasant to hear, even if it's not true. Sincerity in love is an added charm, but not, my dear fellow, a necessity.'

A pause followed this reflection of the Pasha's. Then he remarked:

'After all, we mustn't judge these people as we should judge ourselves. If Constantine hadn't already a wife – '

'What?' I cried, leaping up.

'And perhaps that difficulty is not insuperable.'

'He deserves nothing but hanging.'

'A reluctant wife is hardly better.'

'Of course you don't mean it?'

'It seems to disturb you so much.'

'It's a monstrous idea.'

Mouraki laughed in quiet enjoyment of my excitement.

'Then Kortes?' he suggested.

'He's infinitely her inferior. Besides – forgive me – why is it your concern to marry her to anyone?'

'In a single state she is evidently a danger to the peace of the island,' he answered with assumed gravity. 'Now your young friend – '

'Oh, Denny's a boy.'

'You reject everyone,' he said pathetically, and his eyes dwelt on me in amused scrutiny.

'Your suggestions, my dear Pasha, seem hardly serious,' said I in a huff. He was too many for me, and I struggled in vain against betraying my ruffled temper.

'Well then, I will make two serious suggestions; that is a handsome *amende*. And for the first – yourself!'

I waved my hand and gave an embarrassed laugh.

'You say nothing to that?'

'Oughtn't I to hear the alternative first?'

'Indeed it is only reasonable. Well, then, the alternatives.' He paused, laughed, lit another cigarette. 'The alternative is – myself,' said he.

'Still not serious!' I exclaimed, forcing a smile.

'Absolutely serious,' he asserted. 'I have the misfortune to be a widower, and for the second time; so unkind is heaven. She is most charming. I have, perhaps, a position which would atone for some want of youth and romantic attractions.'

'Of course, if she likes – '

'I don't think she would persist in refusing,' said Mouraki with a thoughtful smile; and he went on, 'Three years ago, when I came here, she struck me as a beautiful child, one likely to become a beautiful woman. You see for yourself that I am not disappointed. My wife was alive at that time, but in bad health. Still I hardly thought seriously of it then, and the idea did not recur to me till I saw Phroso again. You look surprised.'

'Well, I am surprised.'

'You don't think her attractive, then?'

'Frankly, that is not the reason for my surprise.'

'Shall I go on? You think me old? It is a young man's delusion, my dear Wheatley.'

Bear-baiting may have been excellent sport – its defenders so declare – but I do not remember that it was ever considered pleasant for the bear. I felt now much as the bear must have felt. I rose abruptly from the table.

'All these things require thought,' said Mouraki gently. 'We will talk of them again this afternoon. I have a little business to do now.'

Saying this, he rose and leisurely took his way upstairs. I was left alone in the hall so familiar to me; and my first thought was a regret that I was not again a prisoner there, with Constantine seeking my life, Phroso depending on my protection, and Mouraki administering some other portion of his district. That condition of things had been, no doubt, rather too exciting to be pleasant; but it had not made me harassed, wretched, humiliated, exasperated almost beyond endurance: and such was the mood in which the two conversations of the morning left me.

A light step sounded on the stair: the figure that of all figures I least wished to see then, that I rejoiced to see more than any in the world besides, appeared before me. Phroso came down. She reached the floor of the hall and saw me. For a long moment we each rested as we were. Then she stepped towards me, and I rose with a bow. She was very pale, but a smile came on her lips as she murmured a greeting to me and passed on. I should have done better to let her go. I rose and followed. On the marble pavement by the threshold I overtook her; there we stood again, looking on the twinkling sea in the distance, as we have looked before. I was seeking what to say.

'I must thank you,' I said; 'yet I can't. It was magnificent.'

The colour suddenly flooded her face.

'You understood?' she murmured. 'You understood why? It seemed the only way; and I think it did help a little.'

I bent down and kissed her hand.

'I don't care whether it helped,' I said. 'It was the thing itself.'

'I didn't care for them – the people – but when I thought what you would think –' She could not go on, but drew her hand, which she had left an instant in mine as though forgetful of it, suddenly away.

'I – I knew, of course, that it was only a – a stratagem,' said I. 'Oh, yes, I knew that directly.'

'Yes,' whispered she, looking over the sea.

'Yes,' said I, also looking over the sea.

'You forgive it?'

'Forgive!' My voice came low and husky. I did not see why such things should be laid on a man; I did not know if I could endure them. Yet I would not have left her then for an angel's crown.

'And you will forget it? I mean, you –' The whisper died into silence.

'So long as I live I will not forget it,' said I.

Then, by a seemingly irresistible impulse that came upon both of us, we looked in one another's eyes, a long look that lingered and was loath to end. As I looked, I saw, in joy that struggled with shame, a new light in the glowing depths of Phroso's eyes, a greeting of an undreamt happiness, a terrified delight. Then her lids dropped and she began to speak quietly and low.

'It came on me that I might help if I said it, because the islanders love me, and so, perhaps, they wouldn't hurt you. But I couldn't look at you. I only prayed you would understand, that you wouldn't think – oh, that you wouldn't think – that – of me, my lord. And I didn't know how to meet you today, but I had to.'

I stood silent beside her, curiously conscious of every detail of Nature's picture before me; for I had turned from her again, and my eyes roamed over sea and island. But at that moment there came from one of the narrow windows of the old house, directly above our heads, the sound of a low, amused, luxurious chuckle. A look of dread and shrinking spread over Phroso's face.

'Ah, that man!' she exclaimed in an agitated whisper.

'What of him?'

'He has been here before. I have seen him smile and heard him laugh like that when he sent men to death and looked on while they died. Yes, men of our own island, men who had served us and were our friends. Ah, he frightens me, that man!' She shuddered, stretching out her hand in an unconscious gesture, as though she would ward off some horrible thing. 'I have heard him laugh like that when a woman asked her son's life of him and a girl her lover's. It kills me to be near him. He has no pity. My lord, intercede with him for the islanders. They are ignorant men: they did not know.'

'Not one shall be hurt if I can help it,' said I earnestly. 'But –' I stopped; yet I would go on, and I added, 'Have you no fear of him yourself?'

'What can he do to me?' she asked. 'He talked to me this morning about – about you. I hate to talk with him. But what can he do to me?'

I was silent. Mouraki had not hinted to her the idea which he had suggested, in puzzling ambiguity between jest and earnest, to me. Her eyes questioned me; then suddenly she laid her hand on my arm and said:

'And you would protect me, my lord. While you were here, I should be safe.'

'While!' The little word struck cold on my heart: my eyes showed her the blow; in a minute she understood. She raised her hand from where it lay and pointed out towards the sea. I saw the pretty trim little yacht running home for the harbour after her morning cruise.

'Yes, while you are here, my lord,' she said, with the most pitiful of brave smiles.

'As long as you want me, I shall be here,' I assured her.

She raised her eyes to mine, the colour came again to her face,

'As long as you are in any danger,' I added in explanation.

'Ah, yes!' said she, with a sigh and drooping eyelids; and she went on in a moment, as though recollecting a civility due and not paid, 'You are very good to me, my lord; for your island has treated you unkindly, and you will be glad to sail away from it to your home.'

'It is,' said I, bending towards her, 'the most beautiful island in the world, and I would love to stay in it all my life.'

Again the pleased contented chuckle sounded from the window over our heads. It seemed to strike Phroso with a new fit of sudden fear. With a faint cry she darted out her hand and seized mine.

'Don't be afraid. He shan't hurt you,' said I.

A moment later we heard steps descending the stairs inside the house. Mouraki appeared on the threshold. Phroso had sprung away from me and stood a few paces off. Yet Mouraki knew that we had not stood thus distantly before his steps were heard. He looked at Phroso and then at me: a blush from her, a scowl from me, filled any gaps in his knowledge. He stood there smiling – I began to hate the Pasha's smiles – for a moment, and then came forward. He bowed slightly, but civilly enough, to

Phroso; then to my astonishment he took my hand and began to shake it with a great appearance of cordiality.

'Really I beg your pardon,' said I. 'What's the matter?'

'The matter?' he cried in high good humour, or what seemed such. 'The matter? Why, the matter, my dear Wheatley, is that you appear to be both a very discreet fellow and a very fortunate one.'

'I don't understand yet,' said I, trying to hide my growing irritation.

'Surely it's no secret?' he asked. 'It is generally known, isn't it?'

'What's generally known?' I fairly roared in an exasperation that mastered all self-control.

The Pasha was not in the very least disturbed. He held a bundle of letters in his left hand and he began now to sort them. He ended by choosing one, which he held up before me, with a malicious humour twinkling from under his heavy brows.

'I get behindhand in my correspondence when I'm on a voyage,' said he. 'This letter came to Rhodes about a week ago, together with a mass of public papers, and I have only this morning opened it. It concerns you.'

'Concerns me? Pray, in what way?'

'Or rather it mentions you.'

'Who is it from?' I asked. The man's face was full of triumphant spite, and I grew uneasy.

'It is,' said he, 'from our Ambassador in London. I think you know him.'

'Slightly.'

'Precisely.'

'Well?'

'He asks how you are getting on in Neopalia, or whether I have any news of you.'

'You'll be able to answer him now.'

'Yes, yes, with great satisfaction. And he will be able to answer some inquiries which he has had.'

I knew what was coming now. Mouraki beamed pleasure. I set my face. At Phroso, who stood near all this while in silence, I dared not look.

'From a certain lady who is most anxious about you.'

'Ah!'

'A Miss Hipgrave – Miss Beatrice Hipgrave.'

'Ah, yes!'

'Who is a friend of yours?'

'Certainly, my dear Pasha.'

'Who is, in fact – let me shake hands again – your future wife. A thousand congratulations!'

'Oh, thanks, you're very kind,' said I. 'Yes, she is.'

I declare that I must have played this scene – no easy one – well, for Mouraki's rapturous amusement disappeared. He seemed rather put out. He looked (and I hope felt) a trifle foolish. I kept a cool careless glance on him.

But his triumph came from elsewhere. He turned from me to Phroso, and my eyes followed his. She stood rigid, frozen, lifeless; she devoured my face with an appealing gaze. She made no sign and uttered no sound. Mouraki smiled again; and I said:

'Any London news, my dear Pasha?'

14

A Stroke in the Game

I was glad. As soon as I was alone and had time to think over Mouraki's coup I was glad. He had ended a false position into which my weakness had led me; he had rendered it possible for me to serve Phroso in friendship pure and simple; he had decided a struggle which I had failed to decide for myself. It would be easy now (so I told myself) for both of us to repose on that fiction of a good-natured device and leave our innermost feelings in decent obscurity while we countermined the scheme which the Pasha had in hand. This scheme he proceeded to forward with all the patience and ability of which he was master. For the next week or so matters seemed to stand still, but to a closer study they revealed slow, yet uninterrupted, movement. I was left almost entirely alone at the house; but I could not bring myself to abandon my position and seek the society of my friends on the yacht. Though reduced to idleness and robbed of any part in the drama, I would not forsake the stage, but lagged a superfluous spectator of an unpleasing piece. Mouraki was at work. He saw Phroso every day, and for long interviews. I hardly set my eyes on her. The affairs of the island afforded him a constant pretext for conferring with, or dictating to, its Lady; I had no excuse for forcing an intercourse which Phroso evidently was at pains to avoid. I could imagine the Pasha's progress, not in favour or willing acceptance, for I knew her fear and hatred of him, but in beating down her courage and creating a despair which would serve him as well as love. Beyond doubt he was serious in his design; his cool patience spoke settled purpose, his obvious satisfaction declared a conviction of success. He acquiesced in Phroso's seclusion, save when he sent for her; he triumphed in watching me spend weary hours in solitary pacing up and down before the house; he would look at me with a covert exultation and amuse himself by a renewal of sympathetic congratulations on my engagement. I do not think that he wished me away. I was the sauce to his dish, the garlic in the salad, the spice in the sweetmeat over which he licked appreciative lips. Thus passed eight or ten days, and I grew more out of temper, more sour, and more determined with every setting sun. Denny ceased to pray my company; I was not to be moved from the neighbourhood of the house. I waited, the Pasha waited; he paved his way, I lay in ambush by it; he was bent on conquering Phroso, I had no design, only a passionate resolve that he should try a fall with me first.

There came a dark stormy evening, when the clouds sent down a thick close rain and the wind blew in mournful gusts. Having escaped from Mouraki's talk, I had watched him go upstairs, and myself had come out to pace again my useless beat. I strayed a few hundred yards from the house, and turned to look at the light in the Governor's window. It shone bright and steady, seeming to typify his relentless unvarying purpose. A sudden oath escaped from the weary sickness of my heart; there came an unlooked for answer at my elbow.

'He acts, you talk, my lord. He works, you are content to curse him. Which will win?' said a grave voice; and Kortes' handsome figure was dimly visible in the darkness. 'He works, she weeps, you curse. Who will win?' he asked again, folding his arms.

'Your question carries its own answer, doesn't it?' I retorted angrily.

'Yes, if I have put it right,' said he; there was a touch of scorn in his voice that I did not care to hear. 'Yes, it carries its own answer, if you are content to leave it as I stated it.'

'Content! Good God!'

He drew nearer to me and whispered:

'This morning he told her his purpose; this evening again – yes, now, while we talk – he is forcing it on her. And what help has she?'

'She won't let me help her; she won't let me see her.'

'How can you help her, you who do nothing but curse?'

'Look here, Kortes,' said I, 'I know all that. I'm a fool and a worm and everything else you like to intimate; but your contempt doesn't seem much more practical than my cursing. What's in your mind?'

'You must keep faith with this lady in your own land?'

'You know of her?'

'My sister has told me – she who waits on the Lady Euphrosyne.'

'Ah! Yes, I must keep faith with her.'

'And with Mouraki?' he asked.

My mind travelled with his. I caught him eagerly by the arm. I had his idea in a moment.

'Why that?' I asked. 'Yes, Kortes, why that?'

'I thought you were so scrupulous, my lord.'

'I have no scruples in deceiving this Mouraki.'

'That's better, my lord,' he answered with a grim smile. 'By heavens, I thought we were to dance together at the wedding!'

'The wedding?' I cried. 'I think not. Kortes, do you mean – ?' I made a gesture that indicated some violence to Mouraki; but I added, 'It must be open fight though.'

'You mustn't touch a hair of his head. The island would answer bitterly for that.'

We stood in silence for a moment. Then I gave a short laugh.

'My character is my own,' said I. 'I may blacken it if I like.'

'It is only in the eyes of Mouraki Pasha,' said Kortes with a smile.

'But will she understand? There must be no more – '

'She will understand. You shall see her.'

'You can contrive that?'

'Yes, with my sister's help. Will you tell Mouraki first?'

'No – her first. She may refuse.'

'She loathes him too much to refuse anything.'

'Good. When, then?'

'Tonight. She will leave him soon.'

'But he watches her to her room.'

'Yes; but you, my lord, know that there is another way.'

'Yes, yes; by the roof. The ladder?'

'It shall be there for you in an hour.'

'And you, Kortes?'

'I'll wait at the foot of it. The Pasha himself should not mount it alive.'

'Kortes, it is trusting me much.'

'I know, my lord. If you were not a man to be trusted you would do what you are going to pretend.'

'I hope you're right. Kortes, it sets me aflame now to be near her.'

'Can't I understand that, my lord?' said he, with a sad smile.

'By heaven, you're a good fellow!'

'I am a servant of the Stefanopouloi.'

'Your sister will tell her before I come? I couldn't tell her myself.'

'Yes; she shall be told before you come,'

'In an hour, then?'

'Yes.' And without another word, he strode by me, I caught his hand as he went, and pressed it. Then I was alone in the darkness again, but with a plan in my head and a weapon in my hand, and no more empty useless cursings in my mouth. Busily rehearsing the part I was to play, I resumed my quick pacing. It was a hard part, but a good part. I would match Mouraki with his own weapons; my cynicism should beat his, my indifference to the claims of honour overtop his shameless use of terror or of force. The smiles should now be not all the Pasha's. I would have a smile too, one that would, I trusted, compel a scowl even from his smooth inscrutable face.

I was walking quickly; on a sudden I came almost in contact with a man, who leapt on one side to avoid me. 'Who's there?' I cried, standing on my defence, as I had learnt was wise in Neopalia.

'It is I, Demetri,' answered a sullen voice.

'What are you doing here, Demetri? And with your gun!'

'I walk by night, like my lord.'

'Your walks by night have had a meaning before now.'

'They mean no harm to you now.'

'Harm to any one?'

A pause followed before his gruff voice answered:

'Harm to nobody. What harm can be done when my gracious lord the Governor is on the island and watches over it?'

'True, Demetri. He has small mercy for wrongdoers and turbulent fellows such as some I know of.'

"I know him as well as you, my lord, and better,' said the fellow. His voice was charged with a passionate hate. 'Yes, there are many in Neopalia who know Mouraki.'

'So says Mouraki; and he says it as though it pleased him.'

'One day he shall have proof enough to satisfy him,' growled Demetri.

The savage rage of the fellow's tone had caught my attention, and I gazed intently into his face; not even the darkness quite hid the angry gleam of his deep-set eyes.

'Demetri, Demetri,' said I, 'aren't you on a dangerous path? I see a long knife in your belt there, and that gun – isn't it loaded? Come, go back to your home.'

He seemed influenced by my remonstrances, but he denied the suggestion I made.

'I don't seek his life,' he said sullenly. 'If we were strong enough to fight openly – well, I say nothing of that. He killed my brother, my lord.'

'I killed a brother of yours too, Demetri.'

'Yes, in honest fighting, when he sought to kill you. You didn't half-kill him with the lash, before his mother's eyes, and finish the work with a rope.'

'Mouraki did?'

'Yes, my lord. But it is nothing, my lord. I mean no harm.'

'Look here, Demetri. I don't love Mouraki myself, and you did me a good turn a little while ago; but if I find you hanging about here again with your gun and your knife I'll tell Mouraki, as sure as I'm alive. Where I come from we don't assassinate. Do you see?'

'I hear, my lord. Indeed I had no such purpose.'

'You know your purpose best; and now you know what I shall do. Come, be off with you, and don't shew yourself here again.'

He cringed before me with renewed protestations; but his invention provided no excuse for his presence. He swore to me that I wronged him. I contented myself with ordering him off, and at last he went off, striking back towards the village. 'Upon my word,' said I, 'it's a nuisance to be honourably brought up.' For it would have been marvellously convenient to let Demetri have a shot at the Pasha with that gun of his, or a stab with the long knife he had fingered so affectionately.

This encounter had passed the time of waiting, and now I strolled back to the house. It was hard on midnight. The light in Mouraki's window was extinguished. Two soldiers stood sentry by the closed door. They let me in and locked the door behind me. This watch was not kept on me; Mouraki knew very well that I had no desire to leave the island. Phroso was the prisoner and the prize that the Pasha guarded; perhaps, also, he had an inkling that he was not popular in Neopalia, and that he would not be wise to trust to the loyalty of its inhabitants.

Soon I found myself in the compound at the back of the house. The ladder was placed ready; Kortes stood beside it. There seemed to be nobody else about. The rain still fell, and the wind had risen till it whistled wildly in the wood.

'She's waiting for you,' whispered Kortes. 'She knows and she will second the plan.'

'Where is she?'

'On the roof. She's wrapped in my cloak; she will take no hurt.'

'And Mouraki?'

'He's gone to bed. She was with him two hours.'

I mounted the ladder and found myself on the flat roof, where once Phroso had stood gazing up towards the cottage on the hill. We were fighting Constantine then; Mouraki was our foe now. Constantine lay a prisoner, harmless, as it seemed, and helpless. I prayed for a like good fortune in the new enterprise. An instant later I found Phroso's hand in mine. I carried it to my lips, as I murmured my greeting in a hushed voice. The first answer was a nervous sob, but Phroso followed it with a pleading apology.

'I'm so tired,' she said, 'so tired. I have fought him for two hours tonight. Forgive me. I will be brave, my lord.'

I had determined on a cold business-like manner. I went as straight to the point as a busy man in his city office.

'You know the plan? You consent to it?' I asked.

'Yes. I think I understand it. It is good of you, my lord. For you may run great danger through me.'

That was indeed true, and in more senses than one. 'I do for you what you did not hesitate to do for me,' said I.

'Yes,' said Phroso in a very low whisper. 'You pretended; well then, now I pretend.' My voice sounded not only cold, but bitter and unpleasant. 'I think it may succeed,' I continued. 'He won't dare to take any extreme steps against me. I don't see how he can prevent our going.'

'He will let us go, you think?'

'I don't know how he can refuse. And where will you go?'

'I have some friends at Athens, people who knew my father.'

'Good. I'll take you there and –' I paused. 'I'll – I'll take you there and –' Again I paused; I could not help it. 'And leave you there in safety,' I ended at last in a gruff harsh whisper.

'Yes, my lord. And then you will go home in safety?'

'Perhaps. That doesn't matter.'

'Yes, it does matter,' said she, softly. 'For I would not be in safety unless you were.'

'Ah, Phroso, don't do that,' I groaned inwardly.

'Yes, you will go back in safety, back to your own land, back to the lady –'

'Never mind –' I began.

'Back to the lady whom my lord loves,' whispered Phroso. 'Then you will forget this troublesome island and the troublesome – the troublesome people on it.'

Her face was no more than a foot from mine – pale, with sad eyes and a smile that quivered on trembling lips; the fairest face in the world that I had seen or believed any man to have seen; and her hand rested in mine. There may live men who would have looked over her head and not in those eyes – saints or dolts; I was neither; not I. I looked. I looked as though I should never look elsewhere again, nor cared to live if I could not look. But Phroso's hand was drawn from mine and her eyes fell. I had to end the silence.

'I shall go straight to Mouraki tomorrow morning,' said I, 'and tell him you have agreed to be my wife; that you will come with me under the care of Kortes and his sister, and that we shall be married on the first opportunity.'

'But he knows about – about the lady you love.'

'It won't surprise Mouraki to hear that I am going to break my faith with – the lady I love,' said I.

'No,' said Phroso, refusing resolutely to look at me again. 'It won't surprise Mouraki.'

'Perhaps it wouldn't surprise anyone.'

Phroso made no comment on this; and the moment I had said it I heard a voice below, a voice I knew very well.

'What's the ladder here for, my friend?' it asked.

'It enables one to ascend or descend, my lord,' answered Kortes' grave voice, without the least touch of irony.

'It's Mouraki,' whispered Phroso; at the time of danger her frightened eyes came back to mine, and she drew nearer to me. 'It's Mouraki, my lord.'

'I know it is.' said I; 'So much the better.'

'That seems probable,' observed Mouraki. 'But to enable whom to ascend and descend, friend Kortes?'

'Anyone who desires, my lord,'

'Then I will ascend,' said Mouraki.

'A thousand pardons, my lord!'

'Stand aside, sir. What, you dare – '

'Run back to your room,' I whispered. 'Quick. Good night.' I caught her hand and pressed it. She turned and disappeared swiftly through the door which gave access to the inside of the house and thence to her room; and I – glad that the interview had been interrupted, for I could have borne little more of it – walked to the battlements and looked over. Kortes stood like a wall between the astonished Mouraki and the ladder.

'Kortes, Kortes,' I cried in a tone of grieved surprise, 'is it possible that you don't recognise his Excellency?'

'Why, Wheatley!' cried Mouraki.

'Who else should it be, my dear Pasha? Will you come up, or shall I come down and join you? Out of the way, Kortes.'

Kortes, who would not obey Mouraki, obeyed me. Mouraki seemed to hesitate about mounting. I solved the difficulty by descending rapidly. I was smiling, and I took the Pasha by the arm, saying with a laugh:

'Caught that time, I'm afraid, eh? Well, I meant to tell you soon.'

I had certainly succeeded in astonishing Mouraki this time. Kortes added to his wonder by springing nimbly up the ladder, and pulling it up after him.

'I thought you were in bed,' said I. 'And when the cat's away the mice will play, you know. Well, we're caught!'

'We?' asked the Pasha.

'Well, do you suppose I was alone? Is it the sort of night a man chooses to spend alone on a roof?'

'Who was with you then?' he asked, suspicion alive in his crafty eyes.

I took him by the arm and led him into the house, through the kitchen, till we reached the hall, when I said:

'Am I not a man of taste? Who should it be?'

He sat down in the great armchair, and a heavy frown gathered on his brow. I cannot quite explain why, but I was radiant. The spirit of the game had entered into me; I forgot the reality that was so full of pain; I was as merry as though what I told him had been the happy truth, instead of a tantalising impossible vision.

'Oh, don't misunderstand me,' I laughed, standing opposite to him, swaying on my feet, and burying my hands in my pockets. 'Don't wrong me, my dear Pasha. It's all just as it should be. There's nothing going on that should not go on under your Excellency's roof. It is all on the most honourable footing.'

'I don't understand your riddles or your mirth,' said Mouraki,

'Ah! Now once I didn't quite appreciate yours. The wheel goes round, my dear Pasha. Every dog has his day. Forgive me, I am naturally elated. I meant to tell you at breakfast tomorrow, but since you surprised our tender meeting, why, I'll tell you now. Congratulate me. That charming girl has owned that her avowal of love for me was nothing but bare truth, and has consented to make me happy.'

'To marry you?'

'My dear Pasha! What else could I mean?' I took my hands out of my pockets, lit a cigarette and puffed the smoke luxuriously. Mouraki sat motionless in his chair, his eyes cold and sharp on me, his brow puckered. At last he spoke.

'And Miss Hipgrave?' he asked sneeringly.

'Is there a breach of promise of marriage law in Neopalia?' said I. 'In truth, my dear Pasha, I am a little to blame there; but you mustn't be hard on me. I had a moment of conscientious qualms. I confess it. But she's too lovely, she really is. And she's so fond of me – oh, I couldn't resist it!' I was simpering like any affected young lady-killer.

Mouraki was a clever fellow, but the blow had been a sudden one. It strains the control even of clever fellows when a formidable obstacle springs up, at a moment's notice, on a path that they have carefully prepared and levelled for their steps. The Pasha's rage mastered him.

'You've changed your mind rapidly, Lord Wheatley,' said he.

'I know nothing,' I rejoined, 'that does change a man's mind so quickly as a pretty girl.'

'Yet some men hold to their promises,' said he with a savage sneer.

'Oh, a few, perhaps; very few in these days.'

'And you don't aspire to be one?'

'Oh, I aspired,' said I with a laugh; 'but my aspirations have not stood out against Phroso's charms.'

Then I took a step nearer to him, and, veiling impertinence under a thin show of sympathy, I said:

'I hope you're not really annoyed? You weren't serious in the hint you gave of your own intentions? I thought you were only joking, you know. If you were serious, believe me I am grieved. But it must be every man for himself in these little matters, mustn't it?'

He had borne as much as he could. He rose suddenly to his feet and an oath escaped from between his teeth.

'You shan't have her!' said he. 'You think you can laugh at me: men who think that find out their mistake.'

I laughed again. I did not shrink from exasperating him to the uttermost. He would be no more dangerous; he might be less discreet.

'Pardon me,' said I, 'but I don't perceive how we need your permission, glad as we should, of course, be of your felicitations.'

'I have some power in Neopalia,' he reminded me, with a threatening gleam in his eye.

'No doubt, but the power has to be carefully exercised when British subjects are in question – men, if I may add so much, of some position. I can't be considered an islander of Neopalia for all purposes, my dear Pasha.'

He seemed not to hear or not to heed what I said; but he both heard and heeded, or I mistook my man.

'I don't give up what I have resolved upon,' said he.

'You describe my own temper to a nicety,' said I. 'Now I have resolved to marry Phroso.'

'No,' said Mouraki. I greeted the word with a scornful shrug.

'You understand?' he continued. 'It shall not be.'

'We shall see,' said I.

'You don't know the risk you're running.'

'Come, come, isn't this rather near boasting?' I asked contemptuously. 'Your Excellency is a great man, no doubt, but you can't afford to carry out these dark designs against a man of my position.' Then I changed to a more friendly tone, saying, 'My dear Pasha, had you defeated me I should have taken it quietly. Won't you best consult your dignity by doing the same?'

A long silence followed. I watched his face. Very gradually his brow cleared, his lips relaxed into a smile. He, in his turn, shrugged his shoulders. He took a step towards me; he held out his hand.

'Wheatley,' said he, 'it is true, I am a fool. A man is a fool in such matters. You must make allowances for me. I was honestly in love with her. I thought myself safe from you. I allowed my temper to get the better of me. Will you shake hands?'

'Ah, now you're like yourself, my dear friend,' said I, grasping his hand.

'We'll speak again about it tomorrow. But my anger is over. Fear nothing. I will be reasonable.'

I murmured grateful thanks and appreciation of his generosity.

'Good night, good night,' said he. 'I wish I hadn't found you tonight. I should not have lost my composure like this at any other time. You're sure you forgive my hasty words?'

'From the bottom of my heart,' said I earnestly; and we pressed one another's hands. Mouraki passed on to the stairs and began to mount them slowly. He turned his head over his shoulders and said:

'How will you settle with Miss Hipgrave?'

'I must beg her forgiveness, as I must yours,' said I.

'I hope you'll be equally successful,' said he, and his smile was in working order by now. It was the last I saw of him as he disappeared up the stairs.

'Now,' said I, sitting down, 'he's gone to think how he can get my throat cut without a scandal.'

In fact, Mouraki and I were beginning to understand one another.

15

A Strange Escape

Yes, Mouraki was dangerous, very dangerous: now that he had regained his self-control, most dangerous. His designs against me would be limited only by the bounds which I had taken the opportunity of recalling to his mind. I was a known man. I could not disappear without excuse. But the fever of the island might be at the disposal of the Governor no less than of Constantine Stefanopoulos. I must avoid the infection. I congratulated myself that the best antidote I had yet found – a revolver and cartridges – was again in my possession. These, and open eyes, were the treatment for the sudden fatal disease that threatened inconvenient lives in Neopalia.

I thought that I had seen the Pasha safely and finally to bed when he left me in the hall after our interview. I myself had gone to bed almost immediately, and, tired out with the various emotions I had passed through, had slept soundly. But now, looking back, I wonder whether the Governor spent much of the night on his back. I doubt it, very much I doubt it; nay, I incline to think that he had a very active night of goings to and fro, of strange meetings, of schemes and bargainings; and I fancy he had not been back in his room long before I rose for my morning walk. However of that I knew nothing at the time, and I met him at breakfast, prepared to resume our discussion as he had promised. But, behold, he was surrounded by officers.

There was a stir in the hall. Orders were being given; romance and the affairs of love seemed forgotten.

'My dear lord,' cried Mouraki, turning towards me with every sign of discomposure and vexation on his face, 'I am terribly annoyed. These careless fellows of mine – alas, I am too good natured and they presume on it! – have let your friend Constantine slip through their fingers.'

'Constantine escaped!' I exclaimed in genuine surprise and vexation.

'Alas, yes! The sentry fell asleep. It seems that the prisoner had friends, and they got him out by the window. The news came to me at dawn, and I have been having the island scoured for him; but he's not to be found, and we think he must have had a boat in readiness.'

'Have you looked in the cottage where his wife is?'

'The very first thought that struck me, my dear friend! Yes, it has been searched. In vain! It is now so closely guarded that nobody can get in. If he ventures there we shall have him to a certainty. But go on with your breakfast; we needn't spoil that for you. I have one or two more orders to give.'

In obedience to the Pasha I sat down and began my breakfast; but as I ate, while Mouraki conferred with his officers in a corner of the hall, I became very thoughtful concerning this escape of Constantine. Sentries do sleep – sometimes; zealous friends do open windows – sometimes; fugitives do find boats ready – sometimes. It was all possible: there was nothing even exactly improbable. Yet – yet –! Whether Mouraki's account were the whole truth, or something lay below and unrevealed, at least I knew that the escape meant that another enemy, and a bitter one, was loosed against me. I had fought Constantine, I had touched Mouraki's shield in challenge the night before: was I to have them both against me? And would it be two against one, or, as boys say, all against all? If the former, the chances of my catching the fever were considerably increased; and somehow I had a presentiment that the former was nearer the truth than the latter. I had no real evidence. Mouraki's visible chagrin seemed to contradict my theory. But was not Mouraki's chagrin just a little too visible? It was such a very obvious, hearty, genuine, honest, uncontrollable chagrin; it demanded belief in itself the least bit too loudly.

The Pasha joined me over my cigarette. If Constantine were in the island, said the Pasha, with a blow of his fist on the table, he would be laid by the heels before evening came; not a mole – let alone a man – could escape the soldiers' search; not a bird could enter the cottage (he seemed to repeat this very often) unobserved, nor escape from it without a bullet in its plumage. And when Constantine was caught he should pay for this defiance. For the Pasha had delayed the punishment of his crimes too long. This insolent escape was a proper penalty on the Pasha's weak remissness. The Pasha blamed himself very much. His honour was directly engaged in the recapture; he would not sleep till it was accomplished. In a word, the Pasha's zeal beggared comparison and outran adequate description. It filled his mind; it drove out last night's topic. He waved that trifle away; it must wait, for now there was business afoot. It could be discussed only when Constantine was once more a prisoner in the hands of justice, a supplicant for the mercy of the Governor.

I escaped at length from the torrent of sincerity with which Mouraki insisted on deluging me, and went into the open air. There were no signs of Phroso. Kortes was not to be seen either. I saw the yacht in the harbour, and thought of strolling down; but Denny had, no doubt, heard the great news, and I was reluctant to be out of the way, even for an hour. Events came quick in Neopalia. People appeared and disappeared in no time, escaped and – were not recaptured. But I told myself that I would send a message to the yacht soon; for I wanted Denny and the others to know what I – what I was strangely inclined to suspect regarding this occurrence

The storm which had swept over the island the evening before was gone. It was a bright hot day; the waves danced blue in the sun, while a light breeze blew from off the side of the land on which the house stood and was carrying fishing boats merrily out of the harbour. If Constantine had found a boat, the wind was fair to carry him away to safety. But had he? I glanced up at the cottage in the woods above me. A thought struck me. I could run up there and down again in a few moments.

I made my way quickly back to the house and into the compound behind. Here, to my delight, I found Kortes. A word shewed me that he had heard the news. Phroso also had heard it. It was known to everyone.

'I'm going to see if I can get a look into the cottage,' said I.

'I'm told it is guarded, my lord.'

'Kortes, speak plainly. What do you say about this affair?'

'I don't know; I don't know what to think. If they won't let you in –'

'Yes, I meant that. How is she, Kortes?'

'Well, my sister says. I haven't seen her. Run no risks, my lord. She has only you and me.'

'And my friends. I'm going to send them word to be on the look-out for any summons from me.'

'Then send it at once,' he counselled. 'You may delay, Mouraki will not.'

I was struck with his advice; but I was also bent on carrying out my reconnaissance of the cottage.

'I'll send it directly I come back,' said I, and I ran to the angle of the wall, climbed up, and started at a quick walk through the wood. I met nobody till I was almost at the cottage. Then I came suddenly on a sentry; another I saw to the right, a third to the left. The cottage seemed ringed round with watchful figures. The man barred my way.

'But I am going to see the lady – Madame Stefanopoulos,' I protested.

'I have orders to let nobody pass,' he answered. 'I will call the officer.'

The officer came. He was full of infinite regrets, but his Excellency's orders were absolute. Nay, did I not think they were wise? This man was so desperate a criminal, and he had so many friends. He would, of course, try to communicate with his wife.

'But he can't expect his wife to help him,' I exclaimed. 'He wanted to murder her.'

'But women are forgiving. He might well persuade her to help him in his escape; or he might intimidate her.'

'So I'm not to pass?'

'I'm afraid not, my lord. If his Excellency gives you a pass it will be another matter.'

'The lady is there still?'

'Oh, I believe so. I have not myself been inside the cottage. That is not part of my duty.'

'Is anyone stationed in the cottage?'

The officer smiled and answered, with an apologetic shrug, 'Would not you ask his Excellency anything you desire to know, my lord?'

'Well, I daresay you're right,' I admitted, and I fixed a long glance on the windows of the cottage.

'Even to allow anybody to linger about here is contrary to my orders,' suggested the officer, still civil, still apologetic.

'Even to look?'

'His Excellency said to linger.'

'Is it the same thing?'

'His Excellency would answer that also, my lord.'

The barrier round the place was impregnable. That seemed plain. To loiter near the cottage was forbidden, to look at it a matter of suspicion. Yet looking at the cottage would not help the escape of Constantine,

There seemed nothing to be done. Slowly and reluctantly, with a conviction that I was turning away baffled from the heart of the mystery, that the clue lay there were I but allowed to take it in my fingers, I retraced my steps down the hill through the wood. I believed that the strict guard was to prevent my intrusion and mine alone; that the Pasha's search for Constantine was a pretence; in fine, that Constantine was at that moment in the cottage, with the knowledge of Mouraki and under his protection. But I could not prove my suspicions, and I could not unravel the plan which the Pasha was pursuing. I had a strange uneasy sense of fighting in the dark. My eyes were blindfolded, while my antagonist could make full use of his. In that case the odds were against me.

I passed through the house. All was quiet, nobody was about. It was now the middle of the afternoon, and, having accomplished my useless inspection of the cottage, I sat down and wrote a note to Denny, bidding him be on the alert day and night. He or Hogvardt must always be on watch, the yacht ready to start at a moment's notice. I begged him to ask no questions, only to be ready; for life or death might hang on a moment. Thus I paved the way for carrying out my resolution; and my resolution was no other than to make a bold dash for the yacht with Phroso and Kortes, under cover of night. If we reached it and got clear of the harbour, I believed that we could show a clean pair of heels to the gunboat. Moreover I did not think that the wary Mouraki would dare to sink us in open sea with his guns. The one point I held against him was his fear of publicity. We should be safer in the yacht than among the hidden dangers of Neopalia. I finished my note, sealed it, and strolled out in front of the house, looking for somebody to act as my messenger.

Standing there, I raised my eyes and looked down to the harbour and the sea. At what I saw, forgetting Kortes' reproof, I again uttered an oath of surprise and dismay. Smoke poured from the funnel of the yacht. See, she moved! She made for the mouth of the harbour. She set her course for the sea. Where was she going? I did not care to answer that. She must not go. It was vital that she should stay ready for me by the jetty. My scruples about leaving the house vanished before this more pressing necessity. Without an instant's delay, with hardly an instant's thought, I put my best foot foremost and ran, as a man runs for his life, along the road towards the town. As I started I thought I heard Mouraki's voice from the window above my head beginning in its polite wondering tones, 'Why in the world, my dear Wheatley–?' Ah, did he not know why? I would not stop for him. On I went. I reached the main road. I darted down the steep street. Women started in surprise at me, children scurried hastily out of my way. I was a very John Gilpin without a horse. I did not think myself able to run so far or so fast; but apprehension gave me legs, excitement breath, and love – yes, love – why deny it now? – love speed; I neither halted nor turned nor failed till I reached the jetty. But there I sank exhausted against the wooden fencing, for the yacht was hard on a mile out to sea and putting yards and yards between herself and me at every moment. Again I sprang up and waved my handkerchief. Two or three of Mouraki's soldiers who were lounging about stared at me stolidly; a fisherman laughed mockingly; the children had flocked after me down the street and made a gaping circle round me. The note to Denny was in my hand. Denny was far out of my reach. What possessed the boy? Hard were the names that I called myself for having neglected Kortes' advice. What were the cottage and the whereabouts of Constantine compared with the presence of my friends and the yacht?

A hope ran through me. Perhaps they were only passing an hour and would turn homewards soon. I strained my eager eyes after them. The yacht held on her course, straight, swift, relentless. She seemed to be carrying with her Phroso's hopes of rescue, mine of safety; her buoyant leap embodied Mouraki's triumph. I turned from watching, sick at heart, half-beaten and discouraged; and, as I turned, a boy ran up to me and thrust a letter into my hand, saying:

'The gentleman on the yacht left this for my lord. I was about to carry it up when I saw my lord run through the street, and I followed him back.'

The letter bore Denny's handwriting. I tore it open with eager fingers.

'Dear Charley,' it ran, 'I don't know what your game is, but it's pretty slow for us. So we're off fishing. Old Mouraki has been uncommon civil, and sent a fellow with us to show us the best place. If the weather is decent we shall stay out a couple of nights, so you may look for us the day after tomorrow. I knew it was no good asking you to come. Be a good boy, and don't get into mischief while I'm away. Of course Mouraki will bottle Constantine again in no time. He told us he had no doubt of it, unless the fellow had found a boat. I'll run up to the house as soon as we get back. Yours ever, DPS – As you said you didn't want Watkins up at the house, I've taken him along to cook.'

Beati innocents! Denny was very innocent, and so, I suppose, very blessed; and my friend the Pasha had got rid of him in the easiest manner possible. Indeed it was 'uncommon civil' of Mouraki! They would be back the day after tomorrow, and Denny would 'run up to the house.' The thing was almost ludicrous in the pitiful unconsciousness of it. I tore the note that I had written into small pieces, put Denny's in my pocket, and started to mount the hill again. But I turned once and looked on the face of the sea. To my anxious mind it seemed not to smile at me as was its wont. It was not now my refuge and my safety, but the prison bars that confined me – me and her whom I had to serve and save.

And he had taken Watkins along to cook; for I did not want him at the house! I would have given every farthing I had in the world for any honest brave man, Watkins or another. And I was not to 'get into mischief.' I knew very well what Denny meant by that. Well, he might be reassured. It did not appear likely that I should enjoy much leisure for dalliance of the sort he blamed.

'Really, you know, I shall have something else to do,' I said to myself.

Slowly I walked up the hill, too deep in reflection even to hasten my steps; and I started like a man roused from sleep when I heard, from the side of the street, a soft cry of 'My lord!' I looked round. I was directly opposite the door of Vlacho's inn. On the threshold stood the girl Panayiota, who was Demetri's sweetheart, and had held in her lap the head of Constantine's wife whom Demetri could not kill. She cast cautious glances up and down the street, and withdrew swiftly into the shadow of the house, beckoning to me to follow her. In a strait like mine no chance, however small, is to be missed or refused. I followed her. Her cheek glowed with colour; she was under the influence of some excitement whose cause I could not fathom.

'I have a message for you, my lord,' she whispered. 'I must tell it you quickly. We must not be seen.' She shrank back farther into the shelter of the doorway.

'As quickly as you like, Panayiota,' said I. 'I have little time to lose.'

'You have a friend more than you know of,' said she, setting her lips close to my ear.

'I'm glad to hear it,' said I. ' Is that all?'

'Yes, that's all – a friend more than you know of, my lord. Take courage, my lord.'

I bent my eyes on her face in question. She understood that I was asking for a plainer message.

'I can tell you no more,' she said. 'I was told to say that – a friend more than you know of. I have said it. Don't linger, my lord. I can say no more, and there is danger.'

'I'm much obliged to you. I hope he will prove of value.'

'He will,' she replied quickly, and she waved aside the piece of money which I had offered her, and motioned me to be gone. But again she detained me for a moment.

'The lady – the wife of the Lord Constantine – what of her?' she asked in low hurried tones.

'I know nothing of her,' said I. 'I believe she's at the cottage.'

'And he's loose again?'

'Yes.' And I added, searching her face, 'But the Governor will hunt him down.'

I had my answer: a plain explicit answer. It came not in words, but in a scornful smile, a lift of the brows, a shrug. I nodded in understanding. Panayiota whispered again, 'Courage – a friend more than you know of – courage, my lord,' and, turning, fairly ran away from me down the passage towards the yard behind the inn.

Who was this friend? By what means did he seek to help me? I could not tell. One suspicion I had, and I fought a little fight with myself as I walked back to the house. I recollected the armed man I had met in the night, whom I had rebuked and threatened. Was he the friend, and was it my duty to tell Mouraki of my suspicions? I say I had a struggle. Did I win or lose? I do not know; for even now I cannot make up my mind. But I was exasperated at the trick Mouraki had played on me, I was fearful for Phroso, I felt that I was contending against a man who would laugh at the chivalry which warned him. I hardened my heart and shut my eyes. I owed nothing, less than nothing, to Mouraki Pasha. He had, as I verily believed, loosed a desperate treacherous foe on me. He had, as I knew now, deluded my friends into forsaking me. Let him guard his own head and his own skin. I had enough to do with Phroso and myself. So I reasoned, seeking to justify my silence. I have often since thought that the question raised a nice enough point of casuistry. Men who have nothing else to do may amuse themselves with the answering of it. I answered it by the time I reached the threshold of the house. And I held my tongue.

Mouraki was waiting for me in the doorway. He was smiling as he had smiled before my bold declaration of love for Phroso had spoilt his temper.

'My dear lord,' he cried, 'I could have spared you a tiresome walk, I thought your friends would certainly have told you of their intention, or I would have mentioned it myself.'

'My dear Pasha,' I rejoined, no less cordially, 'to tell the truth, I knew their intention, but it struck me suddenly that I would go with them, and I ran down to try and catch them. Unfortunately I was too late.'

The extravagance of my lying served its turn; Mouraki understood, not that I was trying to deceive him, but that I was informing him politely that he had not succeeded in deceiving me.

'You wished to accompany them?' he asked, with a broadening smile. 'You – a lover!'

'A man can't always be making love,' said I carelessly – though truly enough.

Mouraki took a step toward me.

'It is safer not to do it at all,' said he in a lower tone.

The man had a great gift of expression. His eyes could put a world of meaning into a few simple words. In this little sentence, which sounded like a trite remark, I discovered a last offer, an invitation to surrender, a threat in case of obstinacy. I answered it after its own kind.

'Safer, perhaps, but deplorably dull,' said I.

'Ah, well, you know best,' remarked the Pasha. 'If you like to take the rough with the smooth – ' He broke off with a shrug, resuming a moment later. 'You expect to see them back the day after tomorrow, don't you?'

I was not sure whether the particular form of this question was intentional or not. In the literal meaning of his words Mouraki asked me, not whether they would be back, but whether I thought I should witness their return – possibly a different thing.

'Denny says they'll be back then,' I answered cautiously. The Pasha stroked his beard. This time he was, I think, hiding a smile at my understanding and evasion of his question.

'I hear,' he observed with a laugh, 'that you have been trying to pass my sentries and look for our runaway on your own account. You really shouldn't expose yourself to such risks. The man might kill you. I'm glad my officer obeyed his orders.'

'Then Constantine is at the cottage?' I cried quickly, for I thought he had betrayed himself into an admission. His composed air and amused smile smothered my hopes.

'At the cottage? Oh, dear, no. Of course I have searched that. I had that searched first of all.'

'And the guard – '

'Is only to prevent him from going there.'

I had not that perfect facial control which distinguished the Governor. I suppose I appeared unconvinced, for Mouraki caught me by the arm, and, giving me an affectionate squeeze, cried, 'What an unbeliever! Come, you shall go with me and see for yourself.'

If he took me, of course I should find nothing. The bird, if it had ever alighted on that stone, would be flown by now. His specious offer was worthless.

'My dear Pasha, of course I take your word for it.'

'No, I won't be trusted! I positively won't be believed! You shall come. We two will go together.' And he still clung to my arm with the pressure of friendly compulsion.

I did not see how to avoid doing what he suggested without coming to an open quarrel with him, and that I did not desire. He had every motive for wishing to force me into open enmity; a hasty word or gesture might serve him as a plausible excuse for putting me under arrest. He would have a case if he could prove me to have been disrespectful to the Governor. My only chance lay in seeming submission up to the last possible moment. And Kortes was guarding Phroso, so that I could go without uneasiness.

'Well, let's walk up the hill then,' said I carelessly. 'Though I assure you you're giving yourself needless trouble.'

He would not listen, and we turned, still arm-in-arm, to pass through the house. Mouraki had caused a ladder to be placed against the bank of rock, for he did not enjoy clambering up by the steps cut in the side of it. He set his foot now on the lowest rung of this ladder; but he paused there an instant and turned round, facing me, and asked, as though the thought had suddenly occurred to his mind:

'Have you had any conversation with our fair friend this afternoon?'

'The Lady Phroso? No. She has not made an appearance. Perhaps I wrong you, Pasha, but I fancied you were not over-anxious that I should have a conversation with her.'

'You wrong me,' he said earnestly. 'Indeed you wrong me. To prove it, you shall have a tête-à-tête with her the moment we return. Oh, I don't fight with weapons like that! I wouldn't use my authority like that. I am going to search again for this Constantine myself this evening with a strong party; then you shall be at perfect liberty to talk with her.'

'I'm infinitely obliged; you're too generous.'

'I trust we're gentlemen still, though unhappily we have become rivals,' and he let go of the ladder for an instant in order to press my hand.

Then he began to climb up and I followed him, asking of my puzzled brain, 'Now, what does he mean by that?'

For it seemed to me that a man needed cat's eyes to follow the schemes of Mouraki Pasha, eyes that darkness could not blind. This last generous offer of his was beyond the piercing of my vision. I did not know whether it were merely a bit of courtesy, safe to offer, or if it hid some new design. Well, it was little use wondering. At least I should see Phroso. Perhaps – a sudden thought seized me, and I –

'What makes you look so excited?' asked the Pasha. His eyes were on my face, his lips curved in a smile.

'I'm not excited,' said I. But the blood was leaping in my veins. I had an idea.

16

An Unfinished Letter

I have learnt on my way through the world how dangerous a thing is a conceit of a man's own cleverness; and among the most striking lessons of this truth stands one which Mouraki Pasha taught me in Neopalia. My game was against a past master in the art of intrigue; yet I made sure I had caught him napping, sure that my wits were quicker than his and that he missed what was plain to my mind. In vain, they say, is the net spread in the sight of any bird. Aye, of any bird that has eyes and knows how to use them. But if the bird has no eyes, or employs them in admiring its own plumage, there is a chance for the fowler after all.

These reflections occur to my mind when I recollect the hope and exultation in my heart as I followed the Governor's leisurely upward march through the wood to the cottage. Mouraki, I said to myself, thought that he was allaying my suspicions and lulling my watchfulness to sleep by the courtesy with which he arranged an interview between Phroso and myself. Was that what he was really doing? No, I declared triumphantly. He was putting in my way the one sovereign chance which fate hitherto had denied. He was to be away, and most of his men with him. Phroso, Kortes, and I would be alone together at the house, alone for an hour, perhaps for two. At the moment I felt that I asked no more of fortune. Had the Pasha never heard of the secret of the Stefanopouloi? It almost seemed so; but I myself had told him of it, and Denny's information had preceded mine. Yet he was leaving us alone by the hidden door. Had he remembered it? Had he stopped it? My ardour was cooled; my face fell. He knew; he could not have forgotten; and if he knew and remembered, of a surety the passage would be blocked or watched.

'By the way,' said Mouraki, turning to me, 'I want you to show me that passage you told me of some time tomorrow. I've never found time to go down there yet, and I have a taste for these medieval curiosities.'

'I shall be proud to be your guide, Pasha. You would trust yourself there with me?'

'Oh, my dear Wheatley, such things are not done now,' smiled the Pasha. 'You and I will settle our little difference another way. Have you been down since I came?'

'No. I've had about enough of the passage,' said I carelessly. 'I should be glad never to see it again; but I must strain a point and go with you.'

'Yes, you must do that,' he answered. 'How steep this hill is! Really I must be growing old, as Phroso is cruel enough to think!'

This conversation, seeming to fall in so pat with my musings, and indicating, if it did not state, that Mouraki treated the passage as a trifle of no moment, brought us to the outskirts of the wood. The cottage was close in front of us. We had passed only one sentry: the cordon was gone. This change struck me at once, and I remarked on it to Mouraki.

'Yes, I thought it safe to send most of them away; there are one or two more than you see though. But he won't venture back now.'

I smiled to myself. I was pleased again at my penetration; and in this instance, unlike the other at which I have hinted, I do not think I was wrong. The cordon had been here, then Constantine had; the cordon was gone, and I made no doubt that Constantine was gone also.

The front of the cottage was dark, and the curtains of the windows drawn, as they had been when I came before, on the night I killed Vlacho the innkeeper and fell into the hands of Kortes and Demetri. The whirligig had turned since then; for then this man Mouraki had been my far-off much-desired deliverer, Kortes and Demetri open enemies. Now Mouraki was my peril, Kortes my best friend, Demetri – well, what and whom had Panayiota meant?

'Shall we go in?' asked Mouraki, as we came to the house. 'Stay, though, I'll knock on the door with my stick. Madame Stefanopoulos is, no doubt, within. I think she will probably not have joined her husband.'

'I imagine she'll have heard of his escape with great regret,' said I.

The Pasha knocked with the gold-headed cane which he carried. He waited and then repeated the blow. No answer came.

'Well,' he said with a shrug, 'we have given her fair warning. Let us enter. She knows you, my dear Wheatley, and will not be alarmed.'

'But if Constantine's here?' I suggested, with a mocking smile. 'Your life is a valuable one. Run no risks; he's a desperate man.'

The Pasha shifted his cane to his left hand, smiled in answer to my smile, and produced a revolver.

'You're wise,' said I, and I took my revolver out of my pocket.

'We are ready for – anything – now,' said Mouraki.

I think 'anything' in that sentence was meant to include 'one another.'

The Pasha opened the door and passed in. Nothing seemed changed since my last visit. The door of the room on the right was open, the table was again spread, for two this time; the left-hand door was shut.

'You see the fugitive is not in that room,' observed the Pasha, waving his hand to the right. 'Let us try the other,' and he turned the door handle of the room on the left, and preceded me into it.

At this point I am impelled to a little confession. The murderous impulse is, perhaps, not so uncommon as we assume. I daresay many respectable men and amiable women have felt it in all its attractive simplicity once or twice in their lives. It seems at such moments hardly sinful, merely too dangerous, and to be recognised as impossible to gratify only by reason of its danger. But I perceive that I am accusing the rest of the world in the hope of excusing myself; for at that moment, when the Pasha's broad solid back was presented to me, a yard in front, I experienced a momentary but extremely strong temptation to raise my arm, move my finger and – transform the situation. I did not do it; but, on the other hand, I have never counted the desire to do it among the great sins of my life. Mouraki, I thought then and know now, deserved nothing better. Unhappily we have our own consciences to consider, and thus are often prevented from meting out to others the measure their deeds claim.

'I see nobody,' said the Pasha. 'But then the room is dark. Shall I pull back the curtain?'

'You'd better be careful,' said I, laughing. 'That's what Vlacho did.'

'Ah, but you're on the same side this time,' he answered, and stepped across the room towards the curtain.

Suddenly I became, or seemed to become, vaguely, uncomfortably, even terribly conscious of something there. Yet I could see nothing in the dark room, and I heard nothing. I can hardly think Mouraki shared my strange oppressive feeling; yet the curtain was not immediately drawn back, his figure bulked motionless just in front of me, and he repeated in tones that betrayed uneasiness:

'I suppose I'd better draw back the curtain, hadn't I?'

What was it? It must have been all fancy, born of the strain of excitement and the nervous tension in which I was living. I have had something of the feeling in the dark before and since, but never so strong, distinct and almost overpowering. I knew Constantine was not there. I had no fear of him if he were. Yet my forehead grew damp with sweat.

Mouraki's hand was on the curtain. He drew it back. The dull evening light spread sluggishly through the room. Mouraki turned and looked at me. I returned his gaze. A moment passed before either of us looked round.

'There's nobody behind the curtain,' said he, with a slight sigh which seemed to express relief. 'Do you see anyone anywhere?'

Then I pulled myself together, and looked round. The chairs near me were empty, the couch had no occupant. But away in the corner of the room, in the shadow of a projecting angle of wall, I saw a figure seated in front of a table. On the table were writing materials. The figure was a woman's. Her arms were spread on the table, and her head lay between them. I raised my hand and pointed to her. Mouraki's eyes obeyed my direction but came quickly back to me in question, and he arched his brows.

I stepped across the room towards where the woman sat. I heard the Pasha following with hesitating tread, and I waited till he overtook me. Then I called her name softly; yet I knew that it was no use to call her name; it was only the protest my horror made. She would hear her name no more. Again I pointed with my right hand, catching Mouraki's arm with my left at the same moment.

'There,' I said, 'there – between the shoulders! A knife!'

I felt his arm tremble. I must do him justice. I am convinced that he did not foresee or anticipate this among the results of the letting loose of Constantine Stefanopoulos. I heard him clear his throat, I saw him lick his lips; his lids settled low over his cunning eyes. I turned from him to the motionless figure in the chair.

She was dead, had been dead some little while, and must have died instantly on that foul stroke. Why had the brute dealt it?

Was it mere revenge and cruelty, persistently nursed wrath at her betrayal of him on St Tryphon's day? Or had some new cause evoked passion from him?

'Let us lay her here on the sofa,' I said to Mouraki; 'and you must send someone to look after her.'

He seemed reluctant to help me. I leant forward alone, and putting my arm round her, raised her from the table, and set her upright in the chair. I rejoiced to find no trace of pain or horror on her face. As I looked at her I gave a sudden short sob. I was unstrung; the thing was so wantonly cruel and horrible.

'He has made good use of his liberty,' I said in a low fierce tone, turning on Mouraki in a sudden burst of anger against the hand that had set the villain free. But the Pasha's composure wrapped him like a cloak again. He knew what I meant and read the implied taunt in my words, but he answered calmly:

'We have no proof yet that it was her husband who killed her.'

'Who else should?'

He shrugged his shoulders, remarking, 'No proof,' I said. Perhaps he did, perhaps not. 'We don't know.'

'Help me with her,' said I brusquely.

Between us we lifted her and laid her on the couch, and spread over her a fur rug that draped one of the chairs. While this was done we did not exchange a word with one another. Mouraki uttered a sigh of relief when the task was finished.

'I'll send a couple of women up as soon as we get back. Meanwhile the place is guarded and nobody can come in. Need we delay longer? It is not a pleasant place.'

'I should think we might as well go,' I answered, casting my eye again round the little room to the spot where Vlacho had fallen enveloped in the curtain which he dragged down with him, and to the writing table that had supported the dead body of Francesca. Mouraki's hand was on the door handle. He stood there, impatient to be out of the place, waiting for me to accompany him. But my last glance had seen something new, and with a sudden low exclamation I darted across the room to the table. I had perceived a sheet of paper lying just where Francesca's head had rested.

'What's the matter?' asked Mouraki.

I made him no answer. I seized the piece of paper. A pen lay between it and the inkstand. On the paper was a line or two of writing. The characters were blurred, as though the dead woman's hair had smeared them before the ink was dry. I held it up. Mouraki stepped briskly across to me.

'Give it to me,' he said, holding out his hand. 'It may be something I ought to see.'

The first hint of action, of new light or a new development, restored their cool alertness to my faculties.

'Why not something which I ought to see, my dear Pasha?' I asked, holding the paper behind my back and facing him.

'You forget the position I hold, Lord Wheatley. You have no such position.'

I did not argue that. I walked to the window, to get the best of the light. Mouraki followed me closely.

'I'll read it to you,' said I. 'There isn't much of it.'

I held it to the light. The Pasha was close by my shoulder, his pale face leaning forward towards the paper. Straining my eyes on the blurred characters I read; and I read aloud, according to my promise, hearing Mouraki's breathing which accompanied my words.

'My lord, take care. He is free. Mouraki has set – '

That was all: a blot followed the last word. At that word the pen must have fallen from her fingers as her husband's dagger stole her life. We had read her last words. The writing of that line saw the moment of her death. Did it also supply the cause? If so, not the old grudge, but rage at a fresh betrayal of a fresh villainy had impelled Constantine's arm to his foul stroke. He had caught her in the act of writing it, taken his revenge, and secured his safety.

After I had read, there was silence. The Pasha's face was still by my shoulder. I gazed, as if fascinated, on the fatal unfinished note. At last I turned and looked him in the face. His eyes met mine in unmoved steely composure.

'I think,' said I, 'that I had a right to read the note after all; for, as I guess, the writer was addressing it to me and not to you.'

For a moment Mouraki hesitated; then he shrugged his shoulders, saying:

'My dear lord, I don't know whom it is addressed to or what it means. Had the unfortunate lady been allowed to finish it –'

'We should know more than we do now,' I interrupted.

'I was about to say as much. I see she introduced my name; she can, however, have known nothing of any course I might be pursuing.'

'Unless someone who knew told her.'

'Who could?'

'Well, her husband.'

'Who was killing her?' he asked, with a scornful smile.

'He may have told her before, and she may have been trying to forward the information to me.'

'It is all the purest conjecture,' shrugged the Governor.

I looked him in the face, and I think my eyes told him pretty plainly my views of the meaning of the note. He answered my glance at first with a carefully inexpressive gaze; but presently a meaning came into his eyes. He seemed to confess to me and to challenge me to make what use I could of the confession. But the next instant the momentary candour of his regard passed, and blankness spread over his face again.

Desperately I struggled with myself, clinging to self-control. To this day I believe that, had my life and my life only been in question, I should then and there have compelled Mouraki to fight me, man to man, in the little gloomy room where the dead woman lay on the sofa. We should not have disturbed her; and I think also that Mouraki, who did not want for courage, would have caught at my challenge and cried content to a proposal that we should, there and then, put our quarrel to an issue, and that one only of us should go alive down the hill. I read such a mood in his eyes in the moment of their candour. I saw the courage to act on it in his resolute lips and his tense still attitude,

Well, we could neither of us afford the luxury. If I killed him, I should bring grave suspicion on Phroso. She and her islanders would be held accomplices; and, though this was a secondary matter to hot rage, I myself should stand in a position of great danger. And he could not kill me; for all his schemes against me were still controlled and limited by the necessities of his position. Had I been an islander, or even an unknown man concerning whom no questions would be asked, his work would have been simple, and, as I believed, would have been carried out before now. But it was not so. He would be held responsible for a satisfactory account of how I met my death. It would tax his invention to give it if he killed me himself, with his own hand, and in a secret encounter. In fact, the finding of the note left us where we were, so far as action was concerned, but it tore away the last shreds of the veil, the last pretences of good faith and friendliness which had been kept up between us. In that swift, full, open glance which we had exchanged, our undisguised quarrel, the great issue between us, was legibly written and plainly read. Yet not a word passed our lips concerning it. Mouraki and I began to need words no more than lovers do. For hate matches love in penetration.

I put the note in my pocket. Mouraki blinked eyes now utterly free from expression. I gave a final glance at the dead woman. I felt a touch of shame at having for a moment forgotten her fate for my quarrel.

'Shall we go down, Pasha?' said I.

'As soon as you please, Lord Wheatley,' he answered. This formal mode of address was perhaps an acknowledgement that the time for hypocrisy and the hollow show of friendship between us was over. The change was just in his way, slight, subtle, but sufficient.

I followed Mouraki out of the house. He walked in his usual slow deliberate manner. He beckoned to the sentry as we passed him, told him that two women, who would shortly come up, were to be admitted, but nobody else, until an officer came bearing further orders. Having made these arrangements, he resumed his way down, taking his place in front of me and maintaining absolute silence. I did not care to talk. I had enough to think about. But already, now I was out in the fresh air, the feeling of sick horror with which the little room had affected me began to pass away. I felt braced up again. I was better prepared for the great effort which loomed before me now as a present and urgent necessity. Mouraki had found an instrument. He had set Constantine free, that Constantine might do against me what Mouraki himself could not do openly. My friends were away. The hour of the stroke must even now be upon me. Well, the hour of my counterstroke was come also, the counterstroke for which my interview with Phroso and Mouraki's absence opened the way. For he thought the passage no more than a medieval curiosity.

We reached the house and entered the hall together. As we passed through the compound I had seen an alert sentinel. Looking out from the front door, I perceived two men on guard. A party of ten or a dozen more was drawn up, an officer at its head; these were the men who waited to attend Mouraki on his evening expedition. The Pasha seated himself and wrote a note. He looked up as he finished it, saying:

'I am informing the Lady Euphrosyne that you will await her here in half an hour's time, and that she is at liberty to spend what time she pleases with you. Is that what you wish?'

'Precisely, your Excellency. I am much obliged to you.'

His only answer was a dignified bow; but he turned to a sub-officer who stood by him at attention and said, 'On no account allow Lord Wheatley to be interrupted this evening. You will, of course, keep the sentries on guard behind and in front of the house, but do not let them intrude here.'

After giving his orders, the Pasha sat silent for some minutes. He had lighted his cigarette, and smoked it slowly. Then he let it out – a thing I had never seen him do before – lit another, and resumed his slow inhalings. I knew that he would speak before long, and after a few more moments he gave me the result of his meditations. We were now alone together.

'It would have been much better,' said he, 'if that poor woman – whose fate I sincerely regret – had been let alone and this girl had died instead of her,' and he nodded at me with convinced emphasis.

'If Phroso had died!' leapt from my lips in astonishment.

'Yes, if Phroso had died. We would have hanged Constantine together, wept together over her grave, and each of us gone home with a sweet memory – you to your fianceé, I to my work. And we should have forgiven one another any little causes of reproach.'

To this speculation in might-have-beens I made no answer. The feelings with which I received it shewed me, had I still needed shewing, what Phroso was to me. I had been shocked and grieved at Francesca's fate; but rather that a thousand times than the thing on which Mouraki coolly mused!

'It would have been much better, so much better,' he repeated, with a curiously regretful intonation.

'The only thing that would be better, to my thinking,' I said, 'is that you should behave as an honourable man and leave this lady free to do as she wishes.'

'And another thing, surely?' he asked, smiling now. 'That you should behave as an honourable man and go back to Miss Hipgrave?' A low laugh marked the point he had scored. Then he added, with his usual shrug, 'We are slaves, we men, slaves all.'

He rose from his chair and completed his preparations for going out, flinging a long military cloak over his shoulders. His momentary irresolution, or remorse, or what you will, had passed. His speech became terse and resolute again.

'We shall meet early tomorrow, I expect,' he said, 'and then we must settle this matter. Do I understand that you are resolved not to yield.'

'I am absolutely resolved,' said I, and at the sight of his calm sneering face my temper suddenly got the better of me. 'Yes, I'm resolved. You can do what you like. You can bribe ruffians to assassinate me, as I believe you've bribed Constantine.'

He started at that, as a man will at plain speech, even though the plain speech tells him nothing that he did not know of the speaker's mind.

'The blood of that unhappy woman is on your head,' I cried vehemently. 'Through your act she lies dead. If a like fate befalls me, the blame of that will be on your head also. It is you, and not your tool, who will be responsible.'

'Responsible!' he echoed. His voice was mocking and easy, though his face was paler even than it was wont to be. 'Responsible! What does that mean? Responsible to whom?'

'To God,' said I.

He laughed a low derisive laugh.

'Come, that's better,' he said. 'I expected you to say public opinion. Your sentiment is more respectable than that claptrap of public opinion. So be it. I shall be responsible. Where will you be?' He paused, smiling, and ended, 'And where Phroso?'

My self-restraint was exhausted. I sprang up. In another moment my hands would have been on his throat; the next, I suppose, I should have been a prisoner in the hands of his guard. But that was not his wish. He had shewn me too much now to be content with less than my life, and he was not to be turned from his scheme either by his own temper or by mine. He had moved towards the door while he had been speaking to me; as I sprang at him, a quick dexterous movement of his hand opened it, a rapid twist of his body removed him from my reach. He eluded me. The door was shut in my face. The Pasha's low laugh reached me as I sank back again in my chair, still raging that I had not got him by the throat, but in an instant glad also that my rashness had been foiled.

I heard the tramp of his party on their orderly march along the road from the house. Their steps died away, and all was very still. I looked round the hall; there was nobody but myself. I rose and looked into the kitchen; it was empty. Mouraki had kept his word: we were alone. In front there were sentries, behind there were sentries, but the house was mine. Hope rose again, strong and urgent, in my heart, as my eyes fell on the spot under the staircase, where lay the entrance to the secret passage. I looked at my watch; it was eleven o'clock. The wind blew softly, the night was fine, a crescent moon was just visible through the narrow windows. The time was come, the time left free by Mouraki's strange oversight.

It was then, and then only, that a sudden gleam of enlightenment, a sudden chilling suspicion, fell upon me, transforming my hope to fear, my triumph to doubt and misgiving. Was Mouraki Pasha the man to be guilty of an oversight, of so plain an oversight? When an enemy leaves open an obvious retreat, is it always by oversight? When he seems to indicate a way of safety, is the way safe? These disturbing thoughts crowded on me as I sat, and I looked now at the entrance to the secret passage with new eyes.

The sentries were behind the house, the sentries were in front of the house; in neither direction was there any chance of escape. One way was open – the passage – and that one way only. And I asked the question of myself, framing the words in an inarticulate low whisper, 'Is this way a trap?'

'You fool – you fool – you fool!' I cried, beating my fist on the wooden table.

For if that way were a trap, then there was no way of safety, and the last hope was gone. Had Mouraki indeed thought of the passage only as a medieval curiosity? Well, were not *oubliettes*, down which a man went and was seen no more, also a medieval curiosity?

17

In the Jaws of the Trap

I sat for some moments in stupefied despair. The fall from hope was so great and sudden, the revelation of my blind folly so cruel. But this mood did not last long. Soon I was busy thinking again. Alas, the matter gave little scope for thought! It was sadly simple. Before the yacht came back, Mouraki would have it settled once for all, if the settling of it were left to him. Therefore I could not wait. The passage might be a trap. True; but the house was a prison, and a prison whose gate I could not open. I had rather meet my fate in the struggle of hot effort than wait for it tamely here in my chair. And I did not think of myself alone; Phroso's interests also pointed to action. I could trust Mouraki to allow no harm to come to her. He prized her life no less than I did. To her, then, the passage threatened no new danger, while it offered a possible slender chance. Would she come with me? If she would, it might be that Kortes and I, or Kortes or I, might by some kind caprice of fortune bring her safe out of Mouraki's hands. On the top of these calculations came a calm, restrained, but intense anger, urging me on to try the issue, hand to hand and man to man, whispering to me that nothing was impossible, and that Mouraki bore no charmed life. For by now I was ready, aye, more than ready, to kill him, if only I could come at him, and I made nothing of the consequences of his death being laid at my door. So is prudence burnt up in the bright flame of a man's rage.

I knew where to find Kortes. He would be keeping his faithful watch outside his Lady's room. Mouraki had never raised any objection to this attendance; to forbid it would have been to throw off the mask before the moment came, and Mouraki would not be guilty of such premature disclosure. Moreover the Pasha held the men of Neopalia in no great respect, and certainly did not think that a single islander could offer any resistance to his schemes. I went to the foot of the stairs and called softly to our trusty adherent. He came down to me at once, and I asked him about Phroso.

'She is alone in her room, my lord,' he answered. 'The Governor has sent my sister away.'

'Sent her away! Where to?'

'To the cottage on the hill,' said he. 'I don't know why; the Governor spoke to her apart.'

'I know why,' said I, and I told him briefly of the crime which had been done.

'That man should not live,' said Kortes. 'I had no doubt that his escape was allowed in order that he might be dangerous to you.'

'Well, he hasn't done much yet.'

'No, not yet,' said Kortes gravely. I am bound to add that he took the news of Francesca's death with remarkable coolness. In spite of his good qualities, Kortes was a thorough Neopalian; it needed much to perturb him. Besides he was thinking of Phroso only, and the affairs of everybody else passed unheeded by him. This was very evident when I asked his opinion as to waiting where we were, or essaying the way that Mouraki's suspicious carelessness seemed to leave open to us.

'Oh, the passage, my lord! Let it be the passage. For you and me the passage is very dangerous, yet hardly more than here, and the Lady Phroso has her only chance of escape through the passage.'

'You think it very dangerous for us?'

'Possibly one of us will come through,' he said.

'And at the other end?'

'There may be a boat. If there is none, she must try (and we with her, if we are alive) to steal round to the town, and hide in one of the houses till a boat can be found.'

'Mouraki would scour the island.'

'Yes, but a clear hour or two would be enough if we could get her into a boat.'

'But he'd send the gunboat after her.'

'Yes; but, my lord, am I saying that escape is likely? It is possible only; and possibly the boat might evade pursuit.'

I had the highest regard for Kortes, but he was not a very cheering companion for an adventure. Given the same desperate circumstances, Denny would have been serenely confident of success and valiantly scornful of our opponent. I heaved a regretful sigh for him, and said to Kortes, with a little irritation:

'Hang it, we've come out right side up before now, and we may again. Hadn't we better rouse her?'

During this conversation Kortes had been standing on the lowest step of the staircase, and I facing him, on the floor of the hall, with one hand resting on the balustrade. We had talked in low tones, partly from a fear of eavesdroppers, even more, I think, from the influence which our position exerted over us. In peril men speak softly. Our voices sounded as no more than faint murmurs in the roomy hall; consequently they could not have been audible – where? In the passage!

But as I spoke to Kortes in a petulant reproachful whisper, a sound struck on my ear, a very little sound, I caught my companion's arm, imposing silence on him by a look. The sound came again. I knew the sound; I had heard it before. I stepped back a pace and looked round the balustrade to the spot where the entrance to the passage lay.

I should have been past surprise now, after my sojourn in Neopalia; but I was not. I sprang back, with a cry of wonder, almost (must I admit it?) of alarm. Small and faint as the noise had been, it had sufficed for the opening of the door, and in the opening made by the receding of the planks were the head and shoulders of a man. His face was hardly a yard from my face; and the face was the face of Constantine Stefanopoulos.

In the instant of paralysed immobility that followed, the explanation flashed like lightning through my brain. Constantine, buying his liberty and pardon from Mouraki, had stolen along the passage. He had opened the door. He hoped to find me alone – if not alone, yet off my guard – in the hall. Then a single shot would be enough. His errand would be done, his pardon won. That my explanation was right the revolver in his hand witnessed. But he also was surprised. I was closer than he thought, so close that he started back for an instant. The interval was enough; before he could raise his weapon and take aim I put my head down between my shoulders and rushed at him. I think my head knocked his arm up, his revolver went off the noise reverberating through the hall. I almost had hold of him when I was suddenly seized from behind and hurled backwards. Kortes had a mind to come first and stood on no ceremony. But in the instant that he was free, Constantine dived down, like a rabbit into a burrow. He disappeared; with a shouted oath Kortes sprang after him I heard the feet of both of them clattering down the flight of steps.

For a single moment I paused. The report had echoed loud through the hall. The sentries must have heard it – the sentries before the house, the sentries in the compound behind the house. Yet none of them rushed in: not a movement, not a word, not a challenge came from them. Mouraki Pasha kept good discipline. His orders were law, his directions held good, though shots rang loud and startling through the house. Even at that moment I gave a short sharp laugh; for I remembered that on no account was Lord Wheatley to be interrupted; no, neither Lord Wheatley nor the man who came to kill Lord Wheatley was to be interrupted. Oh, Mouraki, Mouraki, your score was mounting up! Should you ever pay the reckoning?

Shorter far than it has taken to write my thoughts was the pause during which they galloped through my palpitating brain. In a second I also was down the flight of stairs beyond. I heard still the footsteps in front of me, but I could see nothing. It was very dark that night in the passage. I ran on, yet I seemed to come no nearer to the steps in front of me. But suddenly I paused, for now there were steps behind me also, light steps, but sounding distinct in my ear. Then a voice cried, in terror and distress, 'My lord, don't leave me, my lord!'

I turned. Even in the deep gloom I saw a gleam of white: a moment later I caught Phroso by both her hands.

'The shot, the shot?' she whispered.

'Constantine. He shot at me – no, I'm not hurt. Kortes is after him.'

She swayed towards me. I caught her and passed my arm round her; without that she would have fallen on the rocky floor of the dim passage.

'I heard it and rushed down,' she panted. 'I heard it from my room.'

'Any sign of the sentries?'

'No.'

'I must go and help Kortes.'

'Not without me?'

'You must wait here.'

'Not without you.' Her arms held me now by the shoulders with a stronger grip than I had thought possible. She would not let me go. Well then, we must face it together.

'Come along, then,' said I. 'I can see nothing in this rat hole.'

Suddenly, from in front of us, a cry rang out; it was some distance off. We started towards it, for it was Kortes' voice that cried.

'Be careful, be careful,' urged Phroso. 'We're near the bridge now.'

It was true. As she spoke the walls of rock on either side receded. We had come to the opening. The dark water was below us, and before us the isolated bridge of rock that spanned the pool. We were where the Lord of the island had been wont to hurl his enemies headlong from his side to death.

What happened on the bridge, on the narrow bridge of rock which ran in front of us, we could not see; but from it came strange sounds, low oaths and mutterings, the scraping of men's limbs and the rasping of cloth on the rock, the hard breathings of struggling combatants; now a fierce low cry of triumph, a disappointed curse, a desperate groan, the silence that marked a culminating effort. Now, straining my eyes to the uttermost, and having grown a little more accustomed to the darkness, I discerned, beyond the centre of the bridge, a coiling writhing mass that seemed some one many-limbed animal, but was, in truth, two men, twisted and turned round about one another in an embrace which could have no end save death. Which was Kortes, which Constantine, I could not tell. How they came there I could not tell. I dared not fire. Phroso hung about me in a paroxysm of fear, her hands holding me motionless; I myself was awed and fascinated by the dim spectacle and the confused sounds of that mortal strife.

Backward and forward, to and fro, up and down they writhed and rolled. Now they hung, a protrusion of deeper blackness, over the black gulf on this side, now on that. Now the mass separated a little as one pressed the other downward and seemed about to hurl his enemy over and himself remain triumphant; now that one, in his turn, tottered on the edge as if to fall and leave the other panting on the bridge; again they were mixed together, so that I could not tell which was which, and the strange appearance of a single, writhing, crawling shape returned. Then suddenly, from both at once, rang out cries: there was dread and surprise in one, fierce, uncalculating, self-forgetful triumph in the other. Not even for Phroso's sake, or the band of her encircling arms, could I rest longer. Roughly I fear, at least with suddenness, I disengaged myself from her grasp.

She cried out in protest and in fear, 'Don't go, don't leave me!' I could not rest. Recollecting the peril, I yet rushed quickly on to the bridge, and moved warily along its narrow perilous way. But even as I came near the two who fought in the middle, there was a deep groan, a second wild triumphant cry, a great lurch of the mass, a moment – a short short moment – when it hung poised over the yawning vault; and then an instant of utter stillness. I waited as a boy waits to hear the stone he has thrown strike the water at the bottom of the well. The stone struck the water: there was a great resounding splash, the water moved beneath the blow; I saw its dark gleam agitated. Then all was still again; and the passage of the bridge was clear.

I walked to the spot where the struggle had been, and whence the two had fallen together. I knelt down and gazed into the chasm. Three times I called Kortes' name. No answer came up. I could discern no movement of the dark waters. They had sunk, the two together, and neither rose. Perhaps both were wounded to death, perhaps only their fatal embrace prevented all effort for life. I could see nothing and hear nothing. My heart was heavy for Kortes, a brave true man and our only friend. In the death of Constantine I saw less than his fitting punishment; yet I was glad that he was gone, and the long line of his villainies closed. This last attempt had been a bold one. Mouraki, no doubt, had forced him to it; even a craven will be bold where the penalty of cowardice is death. Yet he had not dared to stand when discovered. He had fled, and must have been flying when Kortes came up and grappled with him. For a snapshot at an unwary man he had found courage, but not for a fair fight. He was an utter coward after all. He was well dead, and his wife well avenged.

But it was fatal to linger here. Mouraki would be expecting the return of his emissary. I saw now clearly that the Pasha had prepared the way for Constantine's attempt. If no news came, he would not wait long. I put my reflections behind me and walked briskly back to where I had left Phroso. I found her lying on the ground; she seemed to be in a faint. Setting my face close to hers, I saw that her eyes were shut and her lips parted. I sat down by her in the narrow passage and supported her head on my arm. Then I took out a flask, and pouring some of the brandy and water it contained into the cup forced a little between her lips. With a heavy sigh she opened her eyes and shuddered.

'It is over,' I said. 'There's no need to be afraid; all is over now.'

'Constantine?'

'He is dead.'

'And Kortes?'

'They are both gone. They fell together into the pool and must be dead; there's no sound from it.'

A frightened sob was her answer; she put her hand up to her eyes.

'Ah, dear Kortes!' she whispered, and I heard her sob gently again.

'He was a brave man,' said I. 'God rest his soul!'

'He loved me,' she said simply, between her sobs. 'He – he and his sister were the only friends I had.'

'You have other friends,' said I, and my voice was well nigh as low as hers.

'You are very good to me, my lord,' she said, and she conquered her sobs and lay still, her head on my arm, her hair enveloping my hand in its silken masses.

'We must go on,' said I. 'We mustn't stay here. Our only chance is to go on.'

'Chance? Chance of what?' she echoed in a little despairing murmur. 'Where am I to go? Why should I struggle any more?'

'Would you fall into Mouraki's power?' I asked from between set lips.

'No; but I need not. I have my dagger.'

'God forbid!' I cried in sudden horror; and in spite of myself I felt my hand tighten and press her head among the coils of her hair. She also felt it; she raised herself on her elbow, turned to me, and sent a straining look into my eyes. What answer could I make to it? I averted my face; she dropped her head between her hands on the rocky floor.

'We must go,' said I again. 'Can you walk, Phroso?'

I hardly noticed the name I called her, nor did she appear to mark it.

'I can't go,' she moaned. 'Let me stay here. I can get back to the house, perhaps.'

'I won't leave you here. I won't leave you to Mouraki.'

'It will not be to Mouraki, it will be to – '

I caught her hand, crying in a low whisper, 'No, no.'

'What else?' she asked, again sitting up and looking at me.

'We must make a push for safety, as we meant to before.'

'Safety?' Her lips bent in a sadly derisive little smile. 'What is this safety you talk about?' she seemed to say.

'Yes, safety.'

'Ah, yes, you must be safe,' she said, appearing to awake suddenly to a consciousness of something forgotten. 'Ah, yes, my lord, you must be safe. Don't linger, my lord. Don't linger!'

'Do you suppose I'm going alone?' I asked, and, in spite of everything, I could not help smiling as I put the question. I believe she really thought that the course in question might commend itself to me.

'No,' she said. 'You wouldn't go alone. But I – I can't cross that awful bridge.'

'Oh yes, you can,' said I. 'Come along,' and I rose and held out my arms towards her.

She looked at me, the tears still on her cheeks, a doubtful smile dawning on her lips.

'My dear lord,' she said very softly, and stood while I put my arms round her and lifted her till she lay easily. Then came what I think was the hardest thing of all to bear. She let her head fall on my shoulder and lay trustfully. I could almost say luxuriously, back in my arms; a little happy sigh of relief and peace came from her lips, her eyes closed, she was content.

Well, I started; and I shall not record precisely what I thought as I started. What I ought to have thought about was picking my way over the bridge, and, if more matter for consideration were needed, I might have speculated on the best thing to do when we reached the outlet of the passage. Suppose, then, that I thought about what I ought to have thought about.

'Keep still while we're on the bridge,' said I to Phroso. 'It's not over broad, you know.'

A little movement of the head, till it rested in yet greater seeming comfort, was Phroso's only disobedience; for the rest she was absolutely still. It was fortunate; for to cross that bridge in the dark, carrying a lady, was not a job I cared much about. However we came to the other side; the walls of rock closed in again on either hand, and I felt the way begin to slope downwards under my feet.

'Does it go pretty straight now?' I asked.

'Oh, yes, quite straight. You can't miss it, my lord,' said Phroso, and another little sigh of content followed the words. I had, I suppose, little enough to laugh at, but I did laugh very gently and silently, and I did not propose that Phroso should walk.

'Are you tired?' she said presently, just opening her eyes for an instant.

'I could carry you for ever,' I answered.

Phroso smiled under lazy lids that closed again.

In spite of Phroso's assurance of its simple straightness the road had many twists and turns in it, and I had often to ask my way. Phroso gave me directions at once and without hesitation. Evidently she was thoroughly familiar with the track. When I remarked on this she said, 'Oh, yes, I often used to come this way. It leads to such a pretty cave, you know.'

'Then it doesn't come out at the same point as the way my friends took?'

'No, more than a mile away from that. We must be nearly there now. Are you tired, my lord?'

'Not a bit,' said I, and Phroso accepted the answer without demur.

There can, however, be no harm in admitting now that I was tired, not so much from carrying Phroso, though, as from the strain of the day and the night that I had passed through; and I hailed with joy a glimmer of light which danced before my eyes at the end of a long straight tunnel. We were going down rapidly now; and, hark, there was the wash of water welcoming us to the outer air and the light of the upper world; for day had just dawned as we came to the end of the way. The light that I saw ahead was ruddy with the rays of the new-risen sun.

'Ah,' sighed Phroso happily, 'I hear the sea. Oh, I smell it. And see, my lord, the light!'

I turned from the light, joyful as was the beholding of it, to the face which lay close by mine. That too I could see now for the first time plainly. I met Phroso's eyes. A slight tinge of colour dyed her cheeks, but she lay still, looking at me, and she said softly, in low rich tones.

'You look very weary. Let me walk now, my lord.'

'No, we'll go on to the end now,' I said.

The end was near. Another five minutes brought us where once again the enfolding walls spread out. The path broadened into a stony beach; above us the rocks formed an arch: we were in a little cave, and the waves rolled gently to and fro on the margin of the beach. The mouth of the cave was narrow and low, the rocks leaving only about a yard between themselves above and the water below; there was just room for a boat to pass out and in. Phroso sprang from my arms, and stretched out her hands to the light.

'Ah, if we had a boat!' I cried, running to the water's edge.

Had the luck indeed changed and fortune begun to smile? It seemed so, for I had hardly spoken when Phroso suddenly clapped her hands and cried:

'A boat! There is a boat, my lord,' and she leapt forward and caught me by the hand, her eyes sparkling.

It was true – by marvel, it was true! A good, stout, broad-bottomed little fishing boat lay beached on the shingle, with its sculls lying in it. How had it come? Well, I didn't stop to ask that. My eyes met Phroso's in delight. The joy of our happy fortune overcame us. I think that for the moment we forgot the terrible events which had happened before our eyes, the sadness of the parting which at the best lay before us. Both her hands were in mine; we were happy as two children, prosperously launched on some wonderful fairy-tale adventure – prince and princess in their cockle boat on a magic sea.

'Isn't it wonderful?' cried Phroso. 'Ah, my lord, all goes well with you. I think God loves you, my lord, as much as –'

She stopped. A rush of rich colour flooded her cheeks. Her deep eyes, which had gleamed in exultant merriment, sank to the ground. Her hands loosed mine.

' – as the lady who waits for you loves you, my lord,' she said.

I do not know how it was, but Phroso's words summoned up before my eyes a vision of Beatrice Hipgrave, pursuing her cheerful way through the gaieties of the season – or was she in the country by now? – without wasting very many thoughts on the foolish man who had gone to the horrid island. The picture of her as the lady who waited for a lover, forlorn because he tarried, struck with a bitter amusement on my sense of humour. Phroso saw me smile; her eyes asked a wondering question. I did not answer it, but turned away and walked down to where the boat lay.

'I suppose,' I said coldly, 'that this is the best chance?'

'It is the only chance, my lord,' she answered; but her eyes were still puzzled, and her tone was almost careless, as if the matter of our escape had ceased to be the thing which pressed most urgently on her mind. I could say nothing to enlighten her; not from my lips, which longed to forswear her, could come the slightest word in depreciation of 'the lady who waited.'

'Will you get in, then?' I asked,

'Yes,' said Phroso; the joy was gone out of her voice and out of her eyes.

I helped her into the boat, then I launched it; when it floated clear on the water of the cave I jumped in myself and took the sculls. Phroso sat silent and now pale-faced in the stern. I struck the water with my blades and the boat moved. A couple of strokes took us across the cave. We reached the mouth. I felt the sun on my neck with its faint early warmth: that is a good feeling and puts heart in a man,

'Ah, but the sea and the air are good,' said Phroso. 'And it is good to be free, my lord.'

I looked at her. The sun had caught her eyes now, and the gleam in them seemed to fire me. I forgot – something that I ought to have remembered. I rested for a moment on my oars, and, leaning forward, said in a low voice:

'Aye, to be free, and together, Phroso.'

Again came the flash of colour, again the sudden happy dancing of her eyes and the smile that curved in unconquerable wilfulness. I stretched out a hand, and Phroso's hand stole timidly to meet it. Well – surely the Recording Angel looked away!

Thus were we just outside the cave. There rose a straight rock on the left hand, ending in a level top some four feet above our heads. And as our hands approached and our eyes – those quicker foregatherers – met, there came from the top of the rock a laugh, a low chuckle that I knew well. I don't think I looked up. I looked still at Phroso. As I looked, her colour fled, fright leapt into her eyes, her lips quivered in horror. I knew the truth from her face.

'Very nice! But what have you done with Cousin Constantine?' asked Mouraki Pasha.

The trap, then, had double jaws, and we had escaped Constantine only to fall into the hands of his master. It was so like Mouraki. I was so much aghast and yet so little surprised, the fall was so sudden, our defeat so ludicrous, that I believed I smiled, as I turned my eyes from Phroso's and cast a glance at the Pasha.

'I might have known it, you know,' said I, aloud.

18

The Unknown Friend

The boat still moved a little from the impulse of my last stroke, and we floated slowly past Mouraki who stood, like some great sea bird on the rock. To his cynical question – for it revealed shamelessly the use he had meant to make of his tool – I returned no answer. I could smile in amused bitterness but for the moment I could not speak. Phroso sat with downcast eyes, twisting one hand round the other; the Pasha was content to answer my smile with his own. The boat drew past the rock and, as we came round its elbow, I found across our path a larger boat, manned by four of Mouraki's soldiers, who had laid down their oars and sat rifles in hand. In the coxswain's place was Demetri. It seemed strange to find him in that company. One of the soldiers took hold of the nose of our boat and turned it round, impelling it towards the beach. A moment later we grated on the shingle, where the Pasha, who had leapt down nimbly from his perch, stood awaiting us. Thoughts had been running rapidly through my brain, wild thoughts of resistance, of a sudden rush, of emptying my revolver haphazard into the other boat, aye, even of assassinating Mouraki with an unexpected shot. All that was folly. I let it go, sprang from the boat, and, giving my hand to Phroso, helped her to land, and led her to a broad smooth ledge of rock, on which she seated herself, still silent, but giving me a look of grief and despair. Then I turned to the Pasha.

'I think,' said I, 'that you'll have to wait a day or two for Cousin Constantine. I'm told that bodies don't find their way out so soon as living men.'

'Ah, I thought that must be it! You threw him down into the pool?' he asked.

'No, not I. My friend Kortes.'

'And Kortes?'

'They fell together.'

'How very dramatic,' smiled the Pasha. 'How came you to let Kortes have at him first?'

'Believe me, it was unintentional. It was without any design of disappointing you, Pasha.'

'And there's an end of both of them!' said he, smiling at my hit.

'They must both be dead. Forgive me, Pasha, but I don't understand your comedy. We were in your power at the house. Why play this farce? Why not have done then what I presume you will do now?'

'My dear lord,' said he, after a glance round to see that nobody listened, 'the conventions must be observed. Yesterday you had not committed the offences of which I regret to say you have now been guilty.'

'The offences? You amuse me, Pasha.'

'I don't grudge it you,' said Mouraki. 'Yes, the offences of aiding my prisoner – that lady – to escape, and – well, the death of Constantine is at least a matter for inquiry, isn't it? You'll admit that? The man was a rogue, of course, but we must observe the law, my dear Wheatley. Besides –' He paused, then he added, 'You mustn't grudge me my amusement either. Believe me, your joy at finding that boat, which I caused to be placed there for your convenience, and the touching little scene which I interrupted, occasioned me infinite diversion.'

I made no answer, and he continued:

'I was sure that if – well, if Constantine failed in perpetrating his last crime – you follow me, my dear lord? – you would make for the passage, so I obtained the guidance of that faithful fellow, Demetri, and he brought us round very comfortably. Indeed we've been waiting some little while for you. Of course Phroso delayed you.'

Mouraki's sneers and jocularity had no power in themselves to anger me. Indeed I felt myself cool and calm, ready to bandy retorts and banter with him. But there was another characteristic of his conversation on which my mind fastened, finding in it matter for thought: this was his barefaced frankness. Plainly he told me that he had employed Constantine to assassinate me, plainly he exposed to me the trick by which he had obtained a handle against me. Now to whom, if to any one, does a man like Mouraki Pasha reveal such things as these? Why to men, and only to men, who will tell no tales. And there is a proverb which hints that only one class of men tells no tales. That was why I attached significance to the Governor's frankness.

I believe the man followed my thoughts with his wonderfully acute intelligence and his power of penetrating the minds of others; for he smiled again as he said:

'I don't mind being frank with you, my dear Wheatley. I'm sure you won't use the little admissions I may seem to make against me. How grieved you must be for your poor friend Kortes!'

'We've both lost a friend this morning, Pasha.'

'Constantine? Ah, yes. Still – he's as well where he is, just as well where he is.'

'He won't be able to use your little admissions either?'

'How you catch my meaning, my dear lord! It's a pleasure to talk to you.' But he turned suddenly from me and called to his men. Three came up at once. 'This gentleman,' he said, indicating me, and speaking now in sharp authoritative tones, 'is in your custody for the present. Don't let him move.'

I seated myself on a rock; the three men stood round me. The Pasha bowed slightly, walked down to where Phroso sat, and began to speak with her. So, at least, I supposed, but I did not hear anything that he said. His back was towards me, and he hid Phroso from my view. I took out my flask and had a pull at my brandy and water; it was a poor breakfast, but I was offered no other.

Up to this time the fourth soldier and Demetri had remained in the boat. They now landed and hauled their boat up on to the beach; then they turned to the smaller boat which the Pasha had provided in malicious sport for our more complete mortification. The soldier laid hold of its stern and prepared to haul it also out of the water; but Demetri said something – what I could not hear – and shrugged his shoulders. The soldier nodded in apparent assent, and they left the boat where it was, merely attaching it by a rope to the other. Then they walked to the rocks and sat down at a little distance from where I was, Demetri took a hunch of bread and a large knife from his pocket, beginning to cut and munch. I looked at him, but he refused to meet my eye and glanced in every direction except at me.

Suddenly, while I was idly regarding Demetri, the three fellows sprang on me. One had me by each arm before I could so much as move. The third dashed his hand into the breast-pocket of my coat and seized my revolver. They leapt away again, caught up the rifles they had dropped, and held them levelled towards me. The thing was done in a moment, I sitting like a man paralysed. Then one of the ruffians cried:

'Your Excellency, the gentleman moved his hand to his pocket, to his pistol.'

'What?' asked Mouraki, turning round. 'Moved his hand to a pistol? Had he a pistol?'

My revolver was held up as damning evidence.

'And he tried to use it?' asked Mouraki, in mournful shocked tones.

'It looked like it,' said the fellow.

'It's a lie. I wasn't thinking of it,' said I. I was exasperated at the trick. I had made up my mind to fight it out sooner than give up the revolver.

'I'm afraid it may have been so,' said Mouraki, shaking his head. 'Give the pistol to me, my man. I'll keep it safe.' His eye shot triumph at me as he took my revolver and turned again to Phroso. I was now powerless indeed.

Demetri finished his hunch of bread, and began to clean his knife, polishing its blade leisurely and lovingly on the palm of his hand, and feeling its point with the end of his thumb. During this operation he hummed softly and contentedly to himself. I could not help smiling when I recognised the tune; it was an old friend, the chant that One-eyed Alexander wrote on the death of Stefan Stefanopoulos two hundred years ago. Demetri polished, and Demetri hummed, and Demetri looked away across the blue water with a speculative eye. I did not choose to consider what might be in the mind of Demetri as he hummed and polished and gazed over the sea that girt his native island. Demetri's thoughts were his own. Let Mouraki look to them, if they were worth his care.

There, I have made that confession as plainly as I mean to make it. I put out of my mind what Demetri might be planning as he polished his knife and hummed One-eyed Alexander's chant.

Apparently Mouraki did not think the matter worth his care. He had approached very near to Phroso now, leaning down towards her as she sat on the rock. Suddenly I heard a low cry of terror, and 'No, no,' in horrified accents; but Mouraki, raising his voice a little, answered, 'Yes, yes.'

I strained my ears to hear; nay, I half-rose from where I sat, and sank back only under the pointed hint of a soldier's bayonet. I could not hear the words, but a soft pleading murmur came from Phroso, a short relentless laugh from Mouraki, a silence, a shrug of Mouraki's shoulders. Then he turned and came across to me.

'Stand back a little,' said he to the soldiers, 'but keep your eyes on your prisoner, and if he attempts any movement –' He did not finish the sentence, which indeed was plain enough without a formal ending. Then he began to speak to me in French.

'A beautiful thing, my dear lord,' said he, 'is the devotion of women. Fortunate are you who have found two ladies to love you!'

'You've been married twice yourself, I think you told me?'

'It's not exactly the same thing – not necessarily. I am very likely to be married a third time, but I fear I should flatter myself if I thought that much love would accompany the lady's hand. However it was of you that I desired to speak. This lady here, my dear lord, is so attached to you that I believe she will marry me, purely to ensure your safety. Isn't it a touching sacrifice?'

'I hope she'll do nothing of the sort,' said I.

'Well, it's little more than a polite fiction,' he conceded; 'for she'll be compelled to marry me anyhow. But it's the sort of idea that comforts a woman.'

He fixed his eyes on me as he made this remark, enjoying the study of its effect on me.

'Well,' said I, 'I never meant to marry her. I'm bound, you know. It was only another polite fiction designed to annoy you, my dear Pasha.'

'Ah, is that so? Now, really, that's amusing,' and he chuckled. He did not appear annoyed at having been deceived. I wondered a little at that – then.

'We have really,' he continued, 'been living in an atmosphere of polite fictions. For example, Lord Wheatley, there was a polite fiction that I was grieved at Constantine's escape.'

'And another that you were anxious to recapture him.'

'And a third that you were not anxious to escape from my – hospitality.'

'And a fourth that you were so solicitous for my friends' enjoyment that you exerted yourself to find them good fishing.'

'Ah, yes, yes,' he laughed. 'And there is to be one more polite fiction, my dear lord.'

'I believe I can guess it,' said I, meeting his eye.

'You are always so acute,' he observed admiringly.

'Though the precise form of it I confess I don't understand.'

'Well, our lamented Constantine, who had much experience but rather wanted imagination, was in favour of a fever. He told me that it was the usual device in Neopalia.'

'His wife died of it, I suppose?' I believe I smiled as I put the question. Great as my peril was, I still found a pleasure in fencing with the Pasha.

'Oh, no. Now that's unworthy of you. Never have a fiction when the truth will serve! Since he's dead, he murdered his wife. If he had lived, of course –'

'Ah, then it would have been fever.'

'Precisely. We must adapt ourselves to circumstances: that is the part of wise men. Now in your case –' He bent down and looked hard in my face.

'In my case,' said I, 'you can call it what you like, Pasha.'

'Don't you think that the outraged patriotism of Neopalia –?' he suggested, with a smile. 'You bought the island – you, a stranger! It was very rash. These islanders are desperate fellows.'

'That would have served with Constantine alive; but he's dead. Your patriot is gone, Pasha.'

'Alas, yes, our good Constantine is dead. But there are others. There's a fellow whom I ought to hang.'

'Ah!' My eye wandered towards where Demetri hummed and polished.

'And who has certainly not earned his life merely by bringing me to meet you this morning, though I give him some credit for that.'

'Demetri?' I asked with a careless air. 'Well, yes, Demetri,' smiled the Pasha. 'Demetri is very open to reason.'

Across the current of our talk came Demetri's soft happy humming. The Pasha heard it.

'I hanged his brother three years ago,' he observed.

'I know you did,' said I. 'You seem to have done some characteristic things three years ago.'

'And he went to the gallows humming that tune. You know it?'

'Very well indeed, Pasha. It was one of the first things I heard in Neopalia; it's going to be one of the last, perhaps.'

'That tune lends a great plausibility to my little fiction,' said Mouraki.

'It will no doubt be a very valuable confirmation of it,' I rejoined.

The Pasha made no further remark for a moment. I looked past him and past the four soldiers – for the last had now joined his comrades – to Phroso. She was leaning against the cliff side; her head was thrown back and her face upturned, but her eyes were closed. I think she had swooned, or at least sunk into a half-unconscious state. Mouraki detected my glance.

'Look at her well, use your time,' he said in a savage tone. 'You've not long to enjoy the sight of her.'

'I have as long as it may happen to please God,' said I. 'Neither you nor I know how long.'

'I can make a guess,' observed Mouraki, a quiet smile succeeding his frown.

'Yes, you can make a guess.'

He stood looking at me a moment longer; then he turned away. As he passed the soldiers he spoke to them. I saw them smile. No doubt he had picked his men for this job and could rely on them.

The little bay in which we were was surrounded by steep and precipitous cliffs except in one place. Here there was a narrow cleft; the rocks did not rise abruptly; the ground sloped gradually upwards as it receded from the beach. Just on this spot of gently-rising ground Demetri sat, and the Pasha, having amused himself with me for as long as it pleased him, walked up to Demetri. The fellow sprang to his feet and saluted Mouraki with great respect. Mouraki beckoned to him to come nearer, and began to speak to him.

I sat still where I was, under the bayonets of the soldiers, who faced me and had their backs to their commander. My eyes were fixed steadily on the pair who stood conferring on the slope; and my mind was in a ferment. Scruples troubled me no more; Mouraki himself had made them absurd. I read my only chance of life in the choice or caprice of the wild passionate barbarian – he was little else – who stood with head meekly bowed and knife carelessly dangled in his hand. This man was he of whom Panayiota had spoken so mysteriously; he was the friend whom I had 'more than I knew of.' In his blood feud with the Pasha, in his revengeful wrath, lay my chance. It was only a chance, indeed, for the soldiers might kill me; but it was a chance, and there was no other; for if Mouraki won him over by promises or bribes, or intimidated him into doing his will, then Demetri would take the easier task, that which carried no risk and did not involve his own death, as an attack on the Pasha almost certainly would. Would he be prudent and turn his hand against the single helpless man? Or would his long-nursed rage stifle all care for himself and drive him against Mouraki? If so, if he chose that way, there was a glimmer of hope. I glanced at Phroso's motionless figure and pallid face; I glanced at the little boat that floated on the water (why had Demetri not beached it?); I glanced at the rope which bound it to the other boat; I measured the distance between the boats and myself; I thrust my hand into the pocket of my coat and contrived to open the blade of my claspknife, which was now the only weapon left to me.

Mouraki spoke and smiled. He made no gesture but there was just a movement of his eyes towards me. Demetri's eyes followed his for an instant, but would not dwell on my face. The Pasha spoke again. Demetri shook his head, and Mouraki's face assumed a persuasive good-humoured expression. Demetri glanced round apprehensively. The Pasha took him by the arm, and they went a few paces further up the slope, so as to be more private in their talk – but was that the object with both of them? Still Demetri shook his head. The Pasha's smile vanished, his mouth grew stern, his eyes cold, and he frowned. He spoke in short sharp sentences, the snap of his lips showing when his mind was spoken. Demetri seemed to plead. He looked uneasy, he shifted from foot to foot, he drew back from the imperious man, as though he shunned him and would fain escape from him. Mouraki would not let him go, but followed him in his retreat, step for step. Thus another ten yards were put between them and me. Anger and contempt blazed now on Mouraki's face. He raised his hand and brought it down clenched on the palm of the other. Demetri held out his hand as though in protest or supplication. The Pasha stamped with his foot. There were no signs of relenting in his manner.

My eyes grew weary with intent watching. I felt like a man who has been staring at a bright white light, too fascinated by its intensity to blink or turn away, even though it pains him to look longer. The figures of the two seemed to become indistinct and blurred. I rubbed my knuckles into my eyes to clear my vision, and looked again. Yes; they were a little further off, even still a little further off than when I had looked before. It could not be by chance and unwittingly that Demetri always and always and always gave back a pace, luring the Pasha to follow him. No, there was a plan in his head; and in my heart suddenly came a great beat of savage joy – of joy at the chance Heaven gave, yes, and of lust for the blood of the man against whom I had so mighty a debt of wrong. And, as I gazed now, for an instant – a single, barely perceptible instant – came the swiftest message from Demetri's eyes. I read it. I knew its meaning. I sat where I was, but every muscle of my body was tense and strung in readiness for that desperate leap, and every nerve of me quivered with a repressed excitement that seemed almost to kill. Now, now! Was it now? I was within an ace of crying 'Strike!' but I held the word in and still gazed. And the soldiers leant easily on their bayonets, exchanging a word or two now and again, yawning sometimes, weary of a dull job, wondering when his Excellency would let them get home again; of what was going on behind their backs, there on the slope of the cliff, they took no heed.

Ah, there was a change now! Demetri had ceased to protest, to deprecate and to retreat. Mouraki's frowns had vanished, he smiled again in satisfaction and approval. Demetri threw a glance at me. Mouraki spoke. Demetri answered. For an instant I looked at the soldiers: they were more weary and inattentive than ever. Back went my eyes. Now Mouraki, with suave graciousness, in condescending recognition of a good servant, stepped right close up to Demetri and, raising his hand, reached round the fellow's shoulder and patted him approvingly on the back.

'It will be now!' I thought; nay, I believe I whispered, and I drew my legs up under me and grasped the hidden knife in my pocket. 'Yes, it must be now.'

Mouraki patted, laughed, evidently praised. Demetri bowed his head. But his long, lithe, bare, brown right arm that had hung so weary a time in idle waiting by his side – the arm whose hand held the great bright blade so lovingly polished, so carefully tested – the arm began slowly and cautiously to crawl up his side. It bent at the elbow, it rested a moment after its stealthy secret climb; then, quick as lightning, it flew above Demetri's head, the blade sparkled in the sun, the hand swooped down, and the gleams of the sunlit steel were quenched in the body of Mouraki. With a sudden cry of amazement, of horror and of agony, the Pasha staggered and fell prone on the rocky ground; and Demetri cried, 'At last, my God, at last!' and laughed aloud.

19

The Armenian Dog!

The death-cry that Mouraki Pasha uttered under Demetri's avenging knife seemed to touch a spring and set us all a-moving. The sound of it turned the soldiers' idle lassitude into an amazed wonder, which again passed in an instant to fierce excitement. Phroso leapt, with a shriek, to her feet. I hurled myself across the space between me and the rope, knife in hand. The soldiers, neglecting their unarmed prisoner, turned with a shout of rage, and rushed wildly up the slope to where Demetri stood, holding his blade towards heaven. The rope parted under my impetuous assault. Phroso was by my side, in an instant we were in the boat; I pushed off. I seized the sculls; but then I hesitated. Was this man my friend, my ally, my accomplice, what you will? I looked up the slope. Demetri stood by the body of Mouraki. The four soldiers rushed towards him. I could not approve his deed; but I had suffered it to be done. I must not run away now. I pushed the sculls into Phroso's hands. But she had caught my purpose, and threw herself upon me, twining her arms about me and crying, 'No, no, my lord! My lord, no, no!' Her love gave her strength; for a moment I could not disengage myself, but stood fast bound in her embrace.

The moment was enough. It was the end, the end of that brief fierce drama on the rocky slope, the end of any power I might have had to aid Demetri; for he did not try to defend himself. He stood still as a statue where he was, holding the knife up to heaven, the smile which his loud laugh left still on his lips. Phroso's head sank on my shoulder. She would not look; but the sight drew my eyes with an irresistible attraction. The bayonets flashed in the air and buried themselves in Demetri's body. He sank with a groan. Again the blades, drawn back, were driven into him, and again and again. He was a mangled corpse, but in hot revenge for their leader they thrust and thrust. It turned me sick to look; yet I looked till at last they ceased, and stood for an instant over the two bodies, regarding them. Then I loosed Phroso's arms off me; she sank back in the stern. Again I took the sculls and laid to with a will. Where we were to go, or what help we could look for, I did not know; but a fever to be away from the place had come on me, and I pulled, thinking less of life and safety than of putting distance between me and that hideous scene.

'They don't move,' whispered Phroso, whose eyes were now turned away from me and fixed on the beach. 'They stand still. Row, my lord, row!'

A moment passed. I pulled with all my strength. She was between me and the land; I could see nothing. Her voice came again, low but urgent:

'Now they move, they're coming down to the shore. Ah, my lord, they're taking aim!'

'God help us!' said I between my teeth. 'Crouch in the boat. Low down, get right down. Lower down, Phroso, lower down!'

'Ah, one has knocked up the barrels! They're talking again. Why don't they fire?'

'Do they look like hesitating?'

'Yes. No, they're aiming again. No, they've stopped. Row, my lord, row!'

I was pulling as I had not pulled since I rowed in my college boat at Oxford nine years before. I thought of the race at that moment with a sort of amusement. But all the while Phroso kept watch for me; by design or chance she did not move from between me and the shore.

'They're running to the boat now. They're getting in. Are they coming after us, my lord?'

'Heaven knows! I suppose so.'

I was wondering why they had not used their rifles; they had evidently thought of firing at first, but something had held their hands. Perhaps they, mere humble soldiers, shrank from the responsibility. Their leader, whose protection would have held them harmless and whose favour rewarded them, lay dead. They might well hesitate to fire on a man whom they knew to be a person of some position and who had taken no part in Mouraki's death.

'They're launching the boat. They're in now,' came in Phroso's breathless whisper.

'How far off are we?'

'I don't know; two hundred yards, perhaps. They've started now.'

'Do they move well?'

'Yes, they're rowing hard. Oh, my dear lord, can you row harder?' She turned to me for an instant, clasping her hands in entreaty.

'No, I can't, Phroso,' said I, and I believe I smiled, Did the dear girl think I should choose that moment for paddling?

'They're gaining,' she cried. 'Oh, they're gaining! On, my lord, on!'

'How many are rowing?'

'Three, my lord, each with two oars.'

'Oh, the deuce! It's no good, Phroso.'

'No good, my lord? But if they catch us?'

'I wish I could answer you. How near now?'

'Half as near as they were before.'

'Look round the sea. Are there any boats anywhere? Look all round.'

'There's nothing anywhere, my lord.'

'Then the game's up,' said I; and I rested on my oars and began to pant. I was not in training for a race.

The boat containing the soldiers drew near. Our boat, now motionless, awaited their coming. Phroso sank on the seat and sat with a despairing look in her eyes. But my mood was not the same. Mouraki was dead. I knew the change his death made was great. Mouraki was dead. I did not believe that there was another man in Neopalia who would dare to take any extreme step against me. For why had they not fired? They did not fire now, when they could have shot me through the head without difficulty and without danger.

Their boat came alongside of ours, I leant forward and touched Phroso's hand; she looked up.

'Courage,' said I. 'The braver we look the better we shall come off.' Then I turned to the pursuers and regarded them steadily, waiting for them to speak. The first communication was in dumb show. The man who was steering – he appeared to be a subordinate officer – covered me with his barrel.

'I'm absolutely unarmed,' I said. 'You know that. You took my revolver away from me.'

'You're trying to escape,' said he, not shifting his aim.

'Where's your warrant for stopping me?' I demanded.

'The Pasha –'

'The Pasha's dead. Be careful what you do. I am an Englishman, and in my country I am as great a man as your Pasha was.' This assertion perhaps was on, or beyond, the confines of strict truth; it had considerable effect, however.

'You were our prisoner, my lord,' said the officer more civilly. 'We cannot allow you to escape. And this lady was a prisoner also. She is not English; she is of the island. And one of the islanders has slain the Pasha. She must answer for it.'

'What can she have had to do with it?'

'It may have been planned between her and the assassin.'

'Oh, and between me and the assassin too, perhaps?'

'Perhaps, my lord. It is not my place to inquire into that.'

I shrugged my shoulders with an appearance of mingled carelessness and impatience.

'Well, what do you want of us?' I asked.

'You must accompany us back to Neopalia.'

'Well, where did you suppose I was going? Is this a boat to go for a voyage in? Can I row a hundred miles to Rhodes? Come, you're a silly fellow!'

He was rather embarrassed by my tone. He did not know whether to believe in my sincerity or not. Phroso caught the cue well enough to keep her tongue between her pretty lips, and her lids low over her wondering eyes.

'But,' I pursued in a tone of ironical remonstrance, 'are you going to leave the Pasha there? The other is a rogue and a murderer' (it rather went to my heart to describe the useful, if unscrupulous, Demetri in these terms); 'let him be. But does it suit the dignity of Mouraki Pasha to lie untended on the shore, while his men row off to the harbour? It will look as though you had loved him little. You, four of you, allow one man to kill him, and then you leave his body as if it were the body of a dog!'

I had no definite reason for wishing them to return and take up Mouraki's body; but every moment gained was something. Neopalia had bred in me a constant hope of new chances, of fresh turns, of a smile from fortune following quick on a frown. So I urged on them anything which would give a respite. My appeal was not wasted. The officer held a hurried whispered consultation with the soldier who sat on the seat next to him. Then he said:

'It is true, my lord. It is more fitting that we should carry the body back; but you must return with us.'

'With all my heart,' said I, taking up my sculls with alacrity.

The officer responded to this move of mine by laying his rifle in readiness across his knees; both boats turned, and we set out again for the beach. As soon as we reached it three of them went up the slope. I saw them kick Demetri's body out of the way; for he had fallen so that his arm was over the breast of his victim.

Then they raised Mouraki and began to carry him down. Phroso hid her face in her hands. My eyes were on Mouraki's face; I watched him carried down to the boat, meditating on the strange toss-up which had allotted to him the fate which he had with such ruthless cunning prepared for me. Suddenly I sprang up, leapt out of the boat, and began to walk up the slope. I passed the soldiers who bore Mouraki. They paused in surprise and uneasiness. I walked briskly by, taking no notice of them, and came where Demetri's body lay. I knelt for a moment by him, and closed his eyes with my hand. Then I took off the silk scarf I was wearing and spread it over his face, and I rose to my feet again. Somehow I felt that I owed to Demetri some such small office of friendship as this that I was paying; and I found myself hoping that there had been good in the man, and that He who sees all of the heart would see good even in the wild desperate soul of Demetri of Neopalia. So I arranged the scarf carefully, and, turning, walked down the slope to the boats again, glad to be able to tell the girl Panayiota that somebody had closed her lover's eyes. Thus I left the friend that I knew not of. Looking into my own heart, I did not judge him harshly. I had let the thing be done.

When I reached the beach, the soldiers were about to lay Mouraki's body in the larger of the two boats; but having nothing to cover his body with they proceeded to remove his undress frock coat and left it lying for an instant on the shingle while they lifted him in. Seeing that they were ready, I picked up the coat and handed it to them. They took it and arranged it over the trunk and head. Two of them got into the boat in which Phroso sat and signed to me to jump in. I was about to obey when I perceived a pocket book lying on the shingle. It was not mine. Neither Demetri nor any of the soldiers was likely to carry a handsome morocco-leather case; it must have belonged to Mouraki and have fallen from his coat as I lifted it. It lay opened now, face upwards. I stooped for it, intending to give it to the officer. But an instant later it was in my pocket; and I, under the screen of a most innocent expression, was covertly watching my guards, to see whether they had detected my action. The two who rowed Mouraki had already started; the others had been taking their seats in the boat and had not perceived the swift motion with which I picked up the book. I walked past them and sat down behind them in the bows. Phroso was in the stern. One of them asked her, with a considerable show of respect, if she would steer. She assented with a nod. I crouched down low in the bows behind the backs of the soldiers; there I took out Mouraki's pocket book and opened it. My action seemed, no doubt, not far removed from theft. But as the book lay open on the shore, I had seen in it something which belonged to me, something which was inalienably mine, of which no schemes or violence could deprive me: this was nothing else than my name.

Very quietly and stealthily I drew out a slip of paper; behind that was another slip, and again a third. They were cuttings from a Greek newspaper. Neither the name of the paper, nor the dates, nor the place of publication, appeared: the extracts were merely three short paragraphs. My name headed each of them. I had not been aware that any chronicle of my somewhat unexpected fortunes had reached the outer world; and I set myself to read with much interest. Great men may become indifferent as to what the papers say about them; I had never attained to this exalted state of mind.

'Let's have a look,' said I to myself, after a cautious glance over my shoulder at the other boat, which was several yards ahead.

The first paragraph ran thus: 'We regret to hear that Lord Wheatley, the English nobleman who has recently purchased the island of Neopalia and taken up his residence there, is suffering from a severe attack of the fever which is at the present time prevalent in the island.'

'Now that's very curious,' I thought, for I had never enjoyed better health than during my sojourn in Neopalia. I turned with increased interest to the second cutting. I wanted to see what progress I had made in my serious sickness. Naturally I was interested.

'We greatly regret to announce that Lord Wheatley's condition is critical. The fever has abated, but the patient is dangerously prostrate.'

'It would be even more interesting if one had the dates,' thought I.

The last paragraph was extremely brief. 'Lord Wheatley died at seven o'clock yesterday morning.'

I lay back in the bows of the boat, holding these remarkable little slips of paper in my hand. They gave occasion for some thought. Then I replaced them in the pocket book, and I had, I regret to say, the curiosity to explore further. I lifted the outer flap of leather and looked in the inner compartment. It held only a single piece of paper. On the paper were four or five lines, not in print this time but in handwriting, and the handwriting looked very much like what I had seen over Mouraki's name.

'Report of Lord Wheatley's death unfounded. Reason to suspect intended foul play on the part of the islanders. The Governor is making inquiries. Lord Wheatley is carefully guarded, as attempts on his life are feared. Feeling in the island is much exasperated, the sale to Lord Wheatley being very unpopular.'

'There's another compartment yet,' said I to myself, and I turned to it eagerly. Alas, I was disappointed! There was a sheet of paper in it, but the paper was a blank. Yet I looked at the blank piece of paper with even greater interest; for I had little doubt that it had been intended to carry another message, a message which was true and no lie, which was to have been written this very morning by the dagger of Demetri. Something like this it would have run, would it not, in the terse style of my friend Mouraki Pasha? 'Lord Wheatley assassinated this morning. Assassin killed by Governor's guards. Governor is taking severe measures.'

Mouraki, Mouraki, in your life you loved irony, and in your death you were not divided from it! For while you lay a corpse in the stern of your boat, I lived to read those unwritten words on the blank paper in your pocket book. At first Constantine had killed me – so I interpreted the matter – by fever; but later on that story would not serve, since Denny and Hogvardt and faithful Watkins knew that it was a lie. Therefore the lie was declared a lie and you set yourself to prove again that truth is better than a lie – especially when a man can manufacture it to his own order. Yet, surely, Mouraki, if you can look now into this world, your smile will be a wry one! For, cunning as you were and full of twists, more cunning still and richer in expedients is the thing called fate; and the dagger of Demetri wrote another message to fill the blank sheet that your provident notebook carried!

Thinking thus, I put the book in my pocket, and looked round with a smile on my lips. I wished the man were alive that I might mock him. I grudged him the sudden death which fenced him from my triumphant raillery.

Suddenly, there in the bows of the boat, I laughed aloud, so that the soldiers turned startled faces over their shoulders and Phroso looked at me in wonder.

'It's nothing,' said I. 'Since I'm alive I may laugh, I suppose?' Mouraki Pasha was not alive.

My reading and my meditation had passed the time. Now we were round the point which had lain between us and the harbour, and were heading straight for the gunboat that was anchored just across the head of the jetty. Phroso's eyes met mine in an appeal. I could give her no hope of escape. There was nothing for it: we must go on, we and Mouraki together. But my heart was buoyant within me and I exulted in the favours of fortune as a lover in his mistress' smiles. Was not Mouraki lying dead in the stern of the boat and was not I alive?

We drew near to the gunboat. Now I perceived that her steam launch lay by her side and smoke poured from its funnel.

Evidently the launch was ready for a voyage. Whither? Could it be to Rhodes? And did the pocket book that I felt against my ribs by any chance contain the cargo which was to have been speeded on its way today? I laughed again as our boat came alongside, and a movement of excitement and interest rose from the deck of gunboat and launch alike.

The officer went on board the gunboat; for an hour or more we sat where we were, sheltered by the side of the vessel from the heat of the sun, for it was now noon. What was happening on board I could not tell, but there was stir and bustle. The excitement seemed to grow. Presently it spread from the vessel to the shore and groups of islanders began to collect. I saw men point at Phroso, at me, at the stiffened figure under the coat. They spoke also, and freely; more boldly than I had heard them since Mouraki had landed and his presence turned their fierce pride to meekness. It was as though a weight had been lifted off them. I knew, from my own mind, the relief that came to them by the death of the hard man and the removal of the ruthless arm. Presently a boat put off and began to pull round the promontory. The soldiers did not interfere, but watched it go in idle toleration. I guessed its errand: it went to take up the corpse of Demetri, and (I was much afraid) to give it a patriot's funeral.

At last Mouraki's body was carried on to the gunboat; then a summons came to me. With a glance of encouragement at Phroso, who sat in a sort of stupor, I rose and obeyed. I was conducted on to the deck and found myself face to face with the captain. He was a Turk, a young man of dignified and pleasant appearance. He bowed to me courteously, although slightly. I supposed that Mouraki's death left him the supreme authority in Neopalia and I made him the obeisance proper to his new position.

'This is a terrible, a startling event, my lord,' said he,

'It's the loss of a very eminent and distinguished man,' I observed.

'Ah, yes, and in a very fearful manner,' he answered. 'I am not prejudging your position, but you must see that it puts you in a rather serious situation.'

There were two or three of his officers standing near. I took a step towards him. I liked his looks; and somehow his grief at Mouraki's end did not seem intense. I determined to play the bold game.

'Nothing, I assure you, to what I should have been in if it had not occurred,' said I composedly.

A start and a murmur ran round the group. The captain looked uncomfortable.

'With his Excellency's plans we have nothing to do –' he began.

'Aye, but I have,' said I. 'And when I tell you –'

'Gentlemen,' said the captain hastily, 'leave us alone for a little while.'

I saw at once that I had made an impression. It seemed not difficult to create an impression adverse to Mouraki now that he was dead, though it had not been wise to display one when he was alive.

'I don't know,' said I, when we were left alone together, 'whether you knew the relations between the late Pasha and myself?'

'No,' said he in a steady voice, looking me full in the face.

'It was not, perhaps, within the sphere of your duty to know them?' I hazarded.

'It was not,' said he. I thought I saw the slightest of smiles glimmering between beard and moustache.

'But now that you're in command, it's different?'

'It is undoubtedly different now,' he admitted.

'Shall we talk in your cabin?'

'By all means;' and he led the way.

When we reached the cabin, I gave him a short sketch of what had happened since Mouraki's arrival. He was already informed as to the events before that date. He heard me with unmoved face. At last I came to my attempted escape with Phroso by the secret passage and to Constantine's attack.

'That fellow was a villain,' he observed. 'Yes,' said I. 'Read those.' And I handed him the printed slips, adding, 'I suppose he sent these by fishing boats to Rhodes, first to pave the way, and finally to account for my disappearance.'

'I must congratulate you on a lucky escape, my lord.'

'You have more than that to congratulate me on, captain. Your launch seems ready for a voyage.'

'Yes; but I have countermanded the orders.'

'What were they?'

'I beg your pardon, my lord, but what concern is it – ?'

'For a trip to Rhodes, perhaps?'

'I shall not deny it if you guess it.'

'By the order of the Pasha?'

'Undoubtedly.'

'On what errand?'

'His Excellency did not inform me.'

'To carry this perhaps?' I flung the paper which bore Mouraki's handwriting on the table that stood between us.

He took it up and read it; while he read, I took my pencil from my pocket and wrote on the blank slip of paper, which I had found in the pocket book, the message that Mouraki's brain had surely conceived, though his fingers had grown stiff in death before they could write it.

'What does all this mean?' asked the captain, looking up as he finished reading.

'And tomorrow,' said I, 'I think another message would have gone to Rhodes – '

'I had orders to be ready to go myself tomorrow.'

'You had?' I cried. 'And what would you have carried?'

'That I don't know.'

'Aye, but I do. There's your cargo!' And I flung down what I had written.

He read it once and again, and looked across the table at me, fingering the slip of paper.

'He did not write this?' he said.

'As you saw, I wrote it. If he had lived, then, as surely as I live, he would have written it. Captain, it was for me that dagger was meant. Else why did he take the man Demetri with him? Had Demetri cause to love him, or he cause to trust Demetri?'

The captain stood holding the paper. I walked round the table and laid my hand on his shoulder.

'You didn't know his schemes,' said I. 'They weren't schemes that he could tell to a Turkish gentleman.'

At this instant the door opened and the officer who had been with us in the morning entered.

'I have laid his Excellency's body in his cabin,' he said,

'Come,' said the captain, 'we will go and see it, my lord.'

I followed him to where Mouraki lay. The Pasha's face was composed and there was even the shadow of a smile on his pale lips.

'Do you believe what I tell you?' I asked. 'I tried to save the girl from him and in return he meant to kill me. Do you believe me? It not, hang me for his murder; if you do, why am I a prisoner? What have I done? Where is my offence?'

The captain looked down on Mouraki's face, tugged his beard, smiled, was silent an instant. Then he shrugged his shoulders, and he said – he who had not dared, a day before, to lift his voice or raise his finger unbidden in Mouraki's presence:

'Faugh, the Armenian dog!'

There was, I fear, race prejudice in that exclamation, but I did not contradict it. I stood looking down on Mouraki's face, and to my fancy, stirred by the events of the past hours and twisted from sobriety to strange excesses of delusion, the lips seemed once again to curl in their old bitter smile, as he lay still and heard himself spurned, and could not move to exact the vengeance which in his life he had never missed.

So we left him – the Armenian dog!

20

A Public Promise

On the evening of the next day I was once again with my faithful friends on board the little yacht. Furious with the trick Mouraki had played them, they rejoiced openly at his fall and mingled their congratulations to me with hearty denunciations of the dead man. In sober reality we had every reason to be glad. Our new master was of a different stamp from Mouraki. He was a proud, reserved, honest gentleman, with no personal ends to serve. He had informed me that I must remain on the island till he received instructions concerning me, but he encouraged me to hope that my troubles were at last over; indeed I gathered from a hint or two which he let fall that Mouraki's end was not likely to be received with great regret in exalted circles. In truth I have never known a death greeted with more general satisfaction. The soldiers regarded me with quiet approval. To the people of Neopalia I became a hero: everybody seemed to have learnt something at least of the story of my duel with the Pasha, and everybody had been (so it now appeared) on my side. I could not walk up the street without a shower of benedictions; the islanders fearlessly displayed their liking for me by way of declaring their hatred for Mouraki's memory and their exultation in his fitting death. In these demonstrations they were not interfered with, and the captain went so far as to shut his eyes judiciously when, under cover of night, they accorded

Demetri the tribute of a public funeral. To this function I did not go, although I was informed that my presence was confidently expected; but I sought out Panayiota and told her how her lover died. She heard the story with Spartan calm and pride; Neopalians take deaths easily.

Yet there were shadows on our newborn prosperity. Most lenient and gracious to me, the captain preserved a severe and rigorous attitude towards Phroso. He sent her to her own house – or my house, as with amiable persistence he called it – and kept her there under guard. Her case also would be considered, he said, and he had forwarded my exoneration of her together with the account of Mouraki's death; but he feared very much that she would not be allowed to remain in the island; she would be a centre of discontent there. As for my proposal to restore Neopalia to her, he assured me that it would not be listened to for a moment. If I declined to keep the island – probably a suitable and loyal lord would be selected, and Phroso would be deported.

'Where to?' I asked.

'Really I don't know,' said the captain. 'It is but a small matter, my lord, and I have not troubled my superiors with any recommendation on the subject.'

As he spoke he rose to go. He had been paying us a visit on the yacht, where, in obedience to his advice, I had taken up my abode. Denny, who was sitting near, gave a curious sort of laugh. I frowned fiercely, the captain looked from one to the other of us in bland curiosity.

'You take an interest in the girl?' he said, in a tone in which surprise struggled with civility. Again came Denny's half-smothered laugh.

'An interest in her?' said I irritably. 'Well, I suppose I do. It looked like it when I took her through that infernal passage, didn't it?'

The captain smiled apologetically and pursued his way towards the door. 'I will try to obtain lenient treatment for her,' said he, and passed out. I was left alone with Denny, who chose at this moment to begin to whistle. I glared most ill-humouredly at him, He stopped whistling and remarked:

'By this time tomorrow our friends at home will be taking off their mourning. They'll read in the papers that Lord Wheatley is not dead of fever at Neopalia, and they won't read that he has fallen a victim to the misguided patriotism of the islanders; in fact they'll be preparing to kill the fatted calf for him.'

It was all perfectly true, both what Denny said and what he implied without saying. But I found no answer to make to it.

'What a happy ending it is,' said Denny.

'Uncommonly,' I growled, lighting a cigar.

After this there was a long silence; I smoked, Denny whistled. I saw that he was determined to say nothing more explicit unless I gave him a lead, but his whole manner exuded moral disapproval. The consciousness of his feelings kept me obstinately dumb.

'Going to stay here long?' he asked at last, in a wonderfully careless tone.

'Well, there's no hurry, is there?' I retorted aggressively.

'Oh, no; only I should have thought – oh, well, nothing.'

Again silence. Then Watkins opened the door of the cabin and announced the return of the captain. I was surprised to see him again so soon. I was more surprised when he came at me with outstretched hand and a smile of mingled amusement and reproof on his face.

'My dear lord,' he exclaimed, seizing my defenceless hand, 'is this treating me quite fairly? So far as a word from you went, I was left completely in the dark. Of course I understand now, but it was an utter surprise to me.' He shook his head with playful reproach.

'If you understand now, I confess you have the advantage of me,' I returned, with some stiffness. 'Pray, sir, what has occurred? No doubt it's something remarkable. I've learnt to rely on Neopalia for that.'

'It was remarkable in my eyes, I admit, and rather startling. But of course I acquiesced. In fact, my dear lord, it materially alters the situation. As your wife, she will be in a very different – '

'Hallo!' cried Denny, leaping up from the bench where he had been sitting.

'In a very different position indeed,' pursued the captain blandly. 'We should have, if I may say so, a guarantee for her good behaviour. We should have you to look to – a great security, as I need not tell you.'

'My dear sir,' said I in exasperated pleading, 'you don't seem to think you need tell me anything. Pray inform me of what has occurred, and what this wonderful thing is that makes so much change.'

'Indeed,' said he, 'if I had surprised a secret, I would apologise; but it's evidently known to all the islanders.'

'Well, but I'm not an islander,' I cried in growing fury.

The captain sat down, lit a cigarette very deliberately, and observed:

'It was perhaps stupid of me not to have thought of it. She is, of course, a beautiful girl, but hardly, if I may say so, your equal in position, my lord.'

I jumped up and caught him by the shoulder. He might order me under arrest if he liked, but he should tell me what had happened first.

'What's happened?' I reiterated. 'Since you left us – what?'

'A deputation of the islanders, headed by their priest, came to ask my leave for the inhabitants to go up to the house and see their Lady.'

'Yes, yes. What for?'

'To offer her their congratulations on her betrothal – '

'What?'

'And their assurances of loyalty to her and to her husband for her sake. Oh, it simplifies the matter very much.'

'Oh, does it? And did you tell them they might go?'

'Was there any objection? Certainly. Certainly I told them they might go, and I added that I heard with great gratification that a marriage so – '

What the captain had said to the deputation I did not wait to hear. No doubt it was something highly dignified and appropriate, for he was evidently much pleased with himself. But before he could possibly have finished so ornate a sentence, I was on the deck of the yacht. I heard Denny push back his chair, whether merely in wonder or in order to follow me I did not know. I leapt from the yacht on to the jetty and started to run up the street nearly as quickly as I had run down it on the day when Mouraki was kind enough to send my friends a-fishing. At all costs I must stop the demonstration of delight which the inconvenient innocence of these islanders was preparing.

Alas, the street was a desert! The movements of the captain were always leisurely. The impetuous Neopalians had wasted no time: they had got a start of me, and running up the hill after them was no joke. Against my will I was at last obliged to drop into a walk, and thus pursued my way doggedly, thinking in gloomy despair how everything conspired to push me along the road which my honour and my pledged word closed to me. Was ever man so tempted? Did ever circumstances so conspire with his own wishes, or fate make duty seem more hard?

I turned the corner of the road which lead to the old house. It was here I had first heard Phroso's voice in the darkness, here where, from the window of the hall, I had seen her lithe graceful figure when she came in her boy's dress to raid my cows; a little further on was where I had said farewell to her when she went back, the grant of Neopalia in her hand, to soften the hearts of her turbulent countrymen; here where Mouraki had tried her with his guile and intimidated her with his harshness; and there was the house where I had declared to the Pasha that she should be my wife. How sweet that saying sounded in my remembering ears! Yet I swear I did not waver. Many have called me a fool for it since. I know nothing about that. Times change, and people are very wise nowadays. My father was a fool, I daresay, to give thousands to his spendthrift school-fellow, just because he happened to have said he would.

I saw them now, the bright picturesque crowd, thronging round the door of the house; and on the step of the threshold I saw her, standing there, tall and slim, with one hand resting on the arm of Kortes' sister, A loud cry rose from the people. She did not seem to speak. With set teeth I walked on. Now someone in the circle caught sight of me. There was another eager cry, a stir, shouts, gestures; then they turned and ran to me. Before I could move or speak a dozen strong hands were about me. They swung me up on their shoulders and carried me along; the rest waved their hands and cheered: they blessed me and called me their lord. The women laughed and the girls shot merry shy glances at me. Thus they bore me in triumph to Phroso's feet. Surely I was indeed a hero in Neopalia today, for they believed that through me their Lady would be left to them, and their island escape the punishment they feared. So they sang One-eyed Alexander's chant no more, but burst into a glad hymn – an epithalamium – as I knelt at Phroso's feet, and did not dare to lift my eyes to her fair face.

'Here's a mess!' I groaned, wondering what they had said to my poor Phroso.

Then a sudden silence fell on them. Looking up in wonder, I saw that Phroso had raised her hand and was about to speak. She did not look at me – nay, she did not look at them; her eyes were fixed on the sea that she loved. Then her voice came, low but clear:

'Friends – for all are friends here, and there are no strangers – once before, in the face of all of you, I have told my love for my lord. My lord did not know that what I said was true, and I have not told him that it was true till I tell him here today. But you talk foolishly when you greet me as my lord's bride; for in his country he is a great man and owns great wealth, and Neopalia is very small and poor, and I seem but a poor girl to him, though you call me your Lady.'

Here she paused an instant; then she went on, her voice sinking a little lower and growing almost dreamy, as if she let herself drift idly on the waves of fancy.

'Is it strange to speak to you – to you, my brothers and sisters of our island? I do not know; I love to speak to you all; for, poor as I am and as our island is, I think sometimes that had my lord come here a free man he would have loved me. But his heart was not his own, and the lady he loves waits for him at home, and he will go to her. So wish me joy no more on what cannot be.' And then, very suddenly, before I or any of them could move or speak, she withdrew inside the threshold, and Kortes' sister swiftly closed the door. I was on my feet as it shut, and I stood facing it, my back to the islanders.

Among them at first there was an amazed silence, but soon voices began to be heard. I turned round and met their gaze. The strong yoke of Mouraki was off them; their fear had gone, and with it their meekness. They were again in the fierce impetuous mood of St Tryphon's day: they were exasperated at their disappointment, enraged to find the plan which left Phroso to them and relieved them of the threatened advent of a Government nominee brought to nothing.

'They'll take her away,' said one.

'They'll send us a rascally Turk,' cried another.

'He shall hear the death-chant then,' menaced a third.

Then their anger, seeking an outlet, turned on me. I do not know that I had the right to consider myself an entirely innocent victim.

'He has won her love by fraud,' muttered one to another, with evil-disposed glances and ominous frowns.

I thought they were going to handle me roughly, and I felt for the revolver which the captain had been kind enough to restore to me. But a new turn was given to their thoughts by a tall fellow, with long hair and flashing eyes, who leapt out from the middle of the throng, crying loudly:

'Is not Mouraki dead? Why need we fear? Shall we wait idle while our Lady is taken from us? To the shore, islanders! Where is fear since Mouraki is dead?'

His words lit a torch that blazed up furiously. In an instant they were aflame with the mad notion of attacking the soldiers and the gunboat. No voice was raised to point out the hopelessness of such an attempt, the certain death and the heavy penalties which must wait on it. The death-chant broke out again, mingled with exhortations to turn and march against the soldiers, and with encouragements to the tall fellow – Orestes they called him – to put himself at their head. He was not loath.

'Let us go and get our guns and our knives,' he cried, 'and then to the shore!'

"And this man?' called half a dozen, pointing at me.

'When we have driven out the soldiers we will deal with him,' said Master Orestes. 'If our Lady desires him for her husband, he shall wed her.'

A shout of approval greeted this arrangement, and they drew together into a sort of rude column, the women making a fringe to it. But I could not let them march on their own destruction without a word of warning. I sprang on to the raised step where Phroso had stood, just outside the door, and cried:

'You fools! The guns of the ship will mow you down before you can touch a hair of the head of a single soldier.'

A deep derisive groan met my attempt at dissuasion.

'On, on!' they cried.

'It's certain death,' I shouted, and now I saw one or two of the women hesitate, and look first at me and then at each other with doubt and fear. But Orestes would not listen, and called again to them to take the road. Thus we were when the door behind me opened, and Phroso was again by my side. She knew how matters went. Her eyes were wild with terror and distress.

'Stop them, my lord, stop them,' she implored.

For answer, I took my revolver from my pocket, saying, 'I'll do what I can.'

'No, no, not like that! That would be your death as well as theirs.'

'Come,' cried Orestes, in the pride of his sudden elevation to leadership. 'Come, follow me, I'll lead you to victory.'

'You fools, you fools!' I groaned. 'In an hour half of you will be dead.'

No, they would not listen. Only the women now laid imploring hands on the arms of husbands and brothers, useless loving restraints, angrily flung off.

'Stop them, stop them!' prayed Phroso. 'By any means, my lord, by any means!'

'There's only one way,' said I.

'Whatever the way may be,' she urged; for now the column was facing round towards the harbour. Orestes had taken his place, swelling with importance and eager to display his prowess. In a word, Neopalia was in revolt again, and the death-chant threatened to swell out in all its barbaric simple savagery at any moment.

There was nothing else for it; I must temporise; and that word is generally, and was in this case, the equivalent of a much shorter one. I could not leave these mad fools to rush on ruin. A plan was in my head and I gave it play. I took a pace forward, raised my hand, and cried:

'Hear me before you march, Neopalians, for I am your friend.'

My voice gained me a minute's silence; the column stood still, though Orestes chafed impatiently at the delay.

'You're in haste, men of Neopalia,' said I. 'Indeed you're always in haste. You were in haste to kill me who had done you no harm. You are in haste to kill yourselves by marching into the mouth of the great gun of the ship. In truth I wonder that any of you are still alive. But here, in this matter, you are most of all in haste, for having heard what the Lady Phroso said, you have not asked nor waited to hear what I say, but have at once gone mad, all of you, and chosen the maddest among you and made him your leader.'

I do not think that they had expected quite this style of speech. They had looked for passionate reproaches or prayerful entreaties; cool scorn and chaff put them rather at a loss, and my reference to Orestes, who looked sour enough, won me a hesitating laugh.

'And then, all of you mad together, off you go, leaving me here, the only sane man in the place! For am not I sane? Aye, not mad enough to leave the fairest lady in the world when she says she loves me!' I took Phroso's hand and kissed it. It lay limp and cold in mine. 'For my home,' I went on, 'is a long way off, and it is long since I have seen the lady of whom you have heard; and a man's heart will not be denied.' Again I kissed Phroso's hand, but I dared not look her in the face.

My meaning had dawned on them now. There was an instant's silence, the last relic of doubt and puzzle; then a sudden loud shout went up from them. Orestes alone was sullen and mute, for my surrender deposed him from his brief eminence. Again and again they shouted in joy. I knew that their shouts must reach nearly to the harbour. Men and women crowded round me and seized my hand; nobody seemed to make any bones about the 'lady who waited' for me. They were single-hearted patriots, these Neopalians. I had observed that virtue in them several times before, and their behaviour now confirmed my opinion. But there was, of course, a remarkable difference in the manifestation. Before I had been the object, now I was the subject; for by announcing my intention of marrying Phroso I took rank as a Neopalian. Indeed for a minute or two I was afraid that the post of generalissimo, vacant by Orestes' deposition, would be forcibly thrust upon me.

Happily their enthusiasm took a course which was more harmless, although it was hardly less embarrassing. They made a ring round Phroso and me, and insisted on our embracing one another in the glare of publicity. Yet somehow I forgot them all for a moment – them all, and more than them all – while I held her in my arms.

Now it chanced that the captain, Denny and Hogvardt chose this moment for appearing on the road, in the course of a leisurely approach to the house; and they beheld Phroso and myself in a very sentimental attitude on the doorstep, with the islanders standing round in high delight. Denny's amazed 'Hallo!' warned me of what had happened. The islanders – their enmity towards the suzerain power allayed as quickly as it had been roused – ran to the captain to impart the joyful news. He came up to me, and bestowed his sanction by a shake of the hand.

'But why did you behave so strangely, my lord, when I wished you joy an hour ago on the boat?' he asked; and it was a very natural question.

'Oh, the truth is,' said I, 'that there was a little difficulty in the way then.'

'Oh, a lover's quarrel?' he smiled.

'Well, something like it,' I admitted.

'Everything is quite right now, I hope?' he said politely.

'Well, very nearly,' said I. Then I met Denny's eye.

'Am I also to congratulate you?' said Denny coldly.

There was no opportunity of explaining matters to him, the captain was too near.

'I shall be very glad if you will,' I said, 'and if Hogvardt will also.'

Hogvardt shrugged his shoulders, raised his brows, smiled and observed:

'I trust you're acting for the best, my lord.'

Denny made no answer at all. He kicked the ground with his foot. I knew very well what was in Denny's mind. Denny was of my family on his mother's side, and Denny's eye asked, 'Where is the word of a Wheatley?' All this I realised fully. I read his mind then more clearly than I could read my own; for had we been alone, and had he put to me the plain question, 'Do you mean to make her your wife, or are you playing another trick?' by heaven, I should not have known what to answer! I had begun a trick; the plan was to persuade the islanders into dispersing peacefully by my pretence, and then to slip away quietly by myself, trusting to their good sense – although a broken reed, yet the only resource – to make them accept an accomplished fact. But was that my mind now, since I had held Phroso in my arms, and her lips had met mine in the kiss which the islanders hailed as the pledge of our union?

I do not know. I saw Phroso turn and go into the house again. The captain spoke to Denny; I saw him point up to the window of the room which Mouraki had occupied. He went in. Denny motioned Hogvardt to his side, and they two also went into the house without asking me to accompany them. Gradually the throng of islanders dispersed. Orestes flung off in sullen disappointment; the men, those who had knives carefully hiding them, walked down the road like peaceful citizens; the women strolled away, laughing, chattering, gossiping, delighted, as women always are, with the love affair. Thus I was left alone in front of the house. It was late afternoon, and clouds had gathered over the sea. The air was very still; no sound struck my ear except the wash of the waves on the shore.

There I stood fighting the battle, for how long I do not know. The struggle within me was very sore. On either side seemed now to lie a path that it soiled my feet to tread: on the one was a broken pledge, on the other a piece of trickery and knavishness. The joy of a love that could be mine only through dishonour was imperfect joy; yet, if that love could not be mine, life seemed too empty a thing to live. The voices of the two sounded in my ear – the light merry prattle and the calmer sweeter voice. Ah, this island of mine, what things it put on a man!

At last I felt a hand laid on my shoulder. I turned, and in the quick-gathering dusk of the evening I saw Kortes' sister; she looked long and earnestly into my face.

'Well?' said I. 'What is it now?'

'She must see you, my lord,' answered the woman. 'She must see you now, at once.'

I looked again at the harbour and the sea, trying to quell the tumult of my thoughts and to resolve what I would do, I could find no course and settle on no resolution.

'Yes, she must see me,' said I at last. I could say nothing else.

The woman moved away, a strange bewilderment shewing itself in her kind eyes. Again I was left alone in my restless self-communings. I heard people moving to and fro in the house. I heard the window of Mouraki's room, where the captain was, closed with a decisive hand; and then I became aware of someone approaching me. I turned and saw Phroso's white dress gleaming through the gloom, and her face nearly as white above it.

Yes, the time had come; but I was not ready.

21

A Word of Various Meanings

She came up to me swiftly and without hesitation. I had looked for some embarrassment, but there was none in her face, She met my eyes full and square, and began to speak to me at once. 'My lord,' she said, 'I must ask one thing of you. I must lay one more burden on you. After today I dare not be here when my countrymen learn how they are deluded. I should be ashamed to face them, and I dare not trust myself to the Turks, for I don't know what they would do with me. Will you take me with you to Athens, or to some other port from which I can reach Athens? I can elude the guards here. I shall be no trouble: you need only tell me when your boat will start, and give me a corner to live in on board. Indeed I grieve to ask more of you, for you have done so much for me; but my trouble is great and – What is it, my lord?'

I had moved my hand to stop her. She had acted in the one way in which, had it been to save my life, I could not have. She put what had passed utterly out of the way, treating it as the merest trick. My part in it was to her the merest trick; of hers she said nothing. Had hers then been a trick also? My blood grew hot at the thought. I could not endure it.

'When your countrymen learn how they are deluded?' said I, repeating her words. 'Deluded in what?'

'In the trick we played on them, my lord, to – to persuade them to disperse.'

I took a step towards her, and my voice shook as I said:

'Was it all a trick, Phroso?' For at this moment I set above everything else in the world a fresh assurance of her love. I would force it from her sooner than not have it.

She answered me with questioning eyes and a sad little smile.

'Are we then betrothed?' she said, in mournful mockery.

I was close by her now. I did not touch her, but I bent a little, and my face was near hers.

'Was it a trick today, and a trick on St Tryphon's day also?' I asked.

She gave one startled glance at my face, and then her eyes dropped to the ground. She made no answer to my question.

'Was it all a trick, Phroso?' I asked in entreaty, in urgency, in the wild longing to hear her love declared once, here, to me alone, where nobody could hear, nobody impair its sweet secrecy.

Phroso's answer came now, set to the accompaniment of the saddest, softest, murmuring laugh.

'Ah, my lord, must you hear it again? Am I not twice shamed already?'

'Be shamed yet once again,' I whispered; then I saw the light of gladness master the misty sorrow in her eyes as I had seen once before; and I greeted it, whispering:

'Yes, a thousand times, a thousand times!'

'My dear lord!' she said; but then she sprang back, and the brightness was clouded again as she stood aloof, regarding me in speechless, distressed puzzle.

'But, my lord!' she murmured, so low that I scarcely heard. Then she took refuge in a return to her request. 'You won't leave me here, will you? You'll take me somewhere where I can be safe. I – I'm afraid of these men, even though the Pasha is dead.'

I took no notice of the request she repeated. I seemed unable to speak or to do anything else but look into her eyes; and I said, a touch of awe in my voice:

'You have the most wonderful eyes in all the world, Phroso.'

'My lord!' murmured Phroso, dropping envious lids. But I knew she would open them soon again, and so she did.

'Yes, in all the wide world,' said I. 'And I want to hear it again.'

As we talked we had moved little by little; now we were at the side of the house, in the deep dull shadow of it. Yet the eyes I praised pierced the gloom and shone in the darkness; and suddenly I felt arms about my neck, clasping me tightly; her breath was on my cheek, coming quick and uneven, and she whispered:

'Yes, you shall hear it again and again and again, for I am not ashamed now; for I know, yes, I know. I love you, I love you – ah, how I love you!' Her whispers found answer in mine. I held her as though against all the world: all the world was in that moment, and there was nothing else than that moment in all the world. Had a man told me then that I had felt love before, I would have laughed in his face – the fool!

But then Phroso drew back again; the brief rapture, free from all past or future, all thought or doubt, left her, and, in leaving her, forsook me also. She stood over against me murmuring:

'But, my lord – !'

I knew well what she would say, and for an instant I stood silent. The world hung for us on the cast of my next words.

'But, my lord, the lady who waits for you over the sea?' There sounded a note of fear in the softly breathed whisper that the night carried to my ear. In an instant, before I could answer, Phroso came near to me and laid one hand on my arm, speaking gently and quickly. 'Yes, I know, I see, I understand,' she said, 'and I thank you, my lord, and I thank God, my dear lord, that you told me and did not leave me without shewing me your love; for though I must be very unhappy, yet I shall be proud; and in the long nights I shall think of this dear island and of you, though you will both be far away. Yes, I thank heaven you told me, my dear lord.' She bent her head, that should have bent to no man, and kissed my hand.

But I snatched my hand hastily away, and I sprang to her and caught her again in my arms, and again kissed her lips; for my resolve was made. I would not let her go. Those who would might ask the rights of it; I could not let her go. Yet I spoke no word, and she did not understand, but thought that I kissed her in farewell; for the tears were on her face and wetted my lips, and she clung to me as though something were tearing her from me and must soon sunder us apart, so greedy was her grasp on me. But then I opened my mouth to whisper in her ear the words which would bid defiance to the thing that was rending her away and rivet her life to mine.

But hark! There was a cry, a startled exclamation, and the sound of footsteps. My name was shouted loud and eagerly. I knew Denny's voice. Phroso slid from my relaxed arms, and drew back into the deepest shadow.

'I'll be back soon,' I whispered, and with a last pressure of her hand, which was warm now and answered to my grasp, I stepped out of the shelter of the wall and stood in front of the house.

Denny was on the doorstep. The door was open. The light from the lamp in the hall flooded the night and fell full on my face as I walked up to him. On sight of me he seemed to forget his own errand and his own eagerness, for he caught me by the shoulder, and stared at me, crying:

'Heavens, man, you're as white as a sheet! Have you seen a ghost? Does Constantine walk – or Mouraki?'

'Fifty ghosts would be a joke to what I've been through. My God, I never had such a time! What do you want? What did you call me for? I can't stay. She's waiting.' For now I did not care; Denny and all Neopalia might know now.

'Yes, but she must wait a little,' he said. 'You must come into the house and come upstairs.'

I can't,' I said obstinately. 'I – I – I can't, Denny.'

'You must. Don't be a fool, Charley. It's important: the captain is waiting for you.'

His face seemed big with news. What it might be I could not tell, but the hint of it was enough to make me catch hold of him, crying, 'What is it? I'll come.'

'That's right. Come along.' He turned and ran rapidly through the old hall and up the stairs. I followed him, my mind whirling through a cloud of possibilities.

The quiet business-like aspect of the room into which Denny led the way did something to sober me. I pulled myself together, seeking to hide my feelings under a mask of carelessness. The captain sat at the table with a mass of papers surrounding him. He appeared to be examining them, and, as he read, his lips curved in surprise or contempt.

'This Mouraki was a cunning fellow,' said he; 'but if anyone had chanced to get hold of this box of his while he was alive he would not have enjoyed even so poor a post as he thought his governorship. Indeed, Lord Wheatley, had you been actually a party to his death, I think you need have feared nothing when some of these papers had found their way to the eyes of the Government. We're well rid of him, indeed! But then, as I always say, these Armenians, though they're clever dogs –'

But I had not come to hear a Turk discourse on Armenians, and I broke in, with an impatience that I could not altogether conceal:

'I beg your pardon; but is that all you wanted to say to me?'

'I should have thought that it was of some importance to you,' he observed.

'Certainly,' said I, regaining my composure a little; 'but your courtesy and kindness had already reassured me.'

He bowed his acknowledgements, and proceeded in a most leisurely tone, sorting the papers and documents before him into orderly heaps.

'On the death of the Pasha, the government of the island having devolved temporarily on me, I thought it my duty to examine his Excellency's – curse the dog! – his Excellency's despatch box, with the result that I have discovered very remarkable evidences of the schemes which he dared to entertain. With this, however, perhaps I need not trouble you.'

'I wouldn't intrude into it for the world,' I said. 'I discovered also,' he pursued, in undisturbed leisure and placidity, 'among the Pasha's papers a letter addressed to –'

'Me?' and I sprang forward.

'No, to your cousin, to this gentleman. Pursuing what I conceived to be my duty – and I must trust to Mr Swinton to forgive me –' Here the exasperating fellow paused, looked at Denny, waited for a bow from Denny, duly received it, duly and with ceremony returned it, sighed as though he were much relieved at Denny's complaisance, cleared his throat, arranged a little heap of papers on his left hand, and at last – oh, at last! – went on.

'This letter, I say, in pursuance of what I conceived to be my duty –'

'Yes, yes, your duty, of course. Clearly your duty. Yes?'

'I read. It appeared, however, to contain nothing of importance.'

'Then, why the deuce – I mean – I beg your pardon.'

'But merely matters of private concern. But I am not warranted in letting it out of my hands. It will have to be delivered to the Government with the rest of the Pasha's papers. I have, however, allowed Mr Swinton to read it. He says that it concerns you, Lord Wheatley, more than himself. I therefore propose to ask him to read it to you (I can decipher English, but not speak it with facility) in my presence.' With this he handed an envelope to Denny. We had got to it at last.

'For heaven's sake be quick about it, my dear boy!' I cried, and I seated myself on the table, swinging my leg to and fro in a fury of restless impatience. The captain eyed my agitated body with profound disapproval.

Denny took the letter from its envelope and read: 'London, May 21st;' then he paused and remarked, 'We got here on the seventh, you know.' I nodded hastily, and he went on, 'My dear Denny – Oh, how awful this is! I can hardly bear to think of it! Poor, poor fellow! Mamma is terribly grieved, and I, of course, even more. Both mamma and I feel that it makes it so much worse, somehow, that this news should come only three days after he must have got mamma's letter. Mamma says that it doesn't really make any difference, and that if her letter was *wise*, then this terrible news can't alter that. I suppose it doesn't really, but it seems to, doesn't it? Oh, do write directly and tell me that he wasn't very unhappy about it when he had that horrible fever. There's a big blot – because I'm crying! I know you thought I didn't care about him, but I did – though not (as mamma says) in one way, really. Do you think he forgave me? It would kill me if I thought he didn't. Do write soon. I suppose you will bring poor dear Charley home? Please tell me he didn't think very badly of me. Mamma joins with me in sincerest sympathy. – Yours *most* sincerely, Beatrice Kennett Hipgrave. *PS* – Mr Bennett Hamlyn has just called. He is awfully grieved about poor dear Charley. I always think of him as Charley still, you know. Do write.'

There was a long pause, then Denny observed in a satirical tone:

'To be thought of still as "Charley" is after all something.'

'But what the devil does it mean?' I cried, leaping from the table.

'"I suppose you will bring poor dear Charley home,"' repeated Denny, in a meditative tone. 'Well, it looks rather more like it than it did a few days ago, I must admit.'

'Denny, Denny, if you love me, what's it all about? I haven't had any letter from –'

'Mamma? No, we've had no letter from mamma. But then we haven't had any letters from anybody.'

'Then I'm hanged if I – ' I began in bewildered despondency.

'But, Charley,' interrupted Denny, 'perhaps mamma sent a letter to – Mouraki Pasha!'

'To Mouraki?'

'This letter of mine found its way to Mouraki.'

'All letters,' observed the captain, who was leaning back in his chair and staring at the ceiling, 'would pass through his hands, if he chose to make them.'

'Good heavens!' I cried, springing forward. The hint was enough. In an instant my busy, nervous, shaking hands were ruining the neat piles of documents which the captain had reared so carefully in front and on either side of him. I dived, tossed, fumbled, rummaged, scattered, strewed, tore. The captain, incapable of resisting my excited energy, groaned in helpless despair at the destruction of his evening's work. Denny, having watched me for a few minutes, suddenly broke out into a peal of laughter. I stopped for an instant to glare reproof of his ill-timed mirth, and turned to my wild search again.

The search seemed useless. Either Mouraki had not received a letter from Mrs Bennett Hipgrave, or he had done what I myself always did with the good lady's communications – thrown it away immediately after reading it. I examined every scrap of paper, official documents, private notes (the captain was very nervous when I insisted on looking through these for a trace of Mrs Hipgrave's name), lists of stores; in a word, the whole contents of Mouraki's despatch box.

'It's a blank!' I cried, stepping back at last in disappointment.

'Yes, it's gone; but depend upon it, he had it,' said Denny.

A sudden recollection flashed across me, the remembrance of the subtle amused smile with which Mouraki had spoken of the lady who was most anxious about me and my future wife. He must have known then; he must even then have had Mrs Hipgrave's letter in his possession. He had played a deliberate trick on me by suppressing the letter; hence his fury when I announced my intention of disregarding the ties that bound me

– a fury which had, for the moment, conquered his cool cunning and led him into violent threats. At that moment, when I realised the man's audacious knavery, when I thought of the struggle he had caused to me and the pain to Phroso, well, just then I came near to canonising Demetri, and nearer still to grudging him his exploit.

'What was in the letter, then?' I cried to Denny.

'Read mine again,' said he, and he threw it across to me.

I read it again. I was cooler now, and the meaning of it stood out plain and not to be doubted. Mrs Bennett Hipgrave's letter, her wise letter, had broken off my engagement to her daughter. The fact was plain; all that was missing, destroyed by the caution or the carelessness of Mouraki Pasha, was the reason; and the reason I could supply for myself. I reached my conclusion, and looked again at Denny.

'Allow me to congratulate you,' said Denny ironically.

Man is a curious creature. I (and other people) may have made that reflection before. I offer no apology for it. The more I see of myself and my friends the more convinced I grow of its truth. Here was the thing for which I had been hoping and praying, the one great gift that I asked of fate, the single boon which fortune enviously withheld. Here was freedom – divine freedom! Yet what I actually said to Denny, in reply to his felicitations, was:

'Hang the girl! She's jilted me!' And I said it with considerable annoyance.

The captain, who studied English in his spare moments, here interposed, asking suavely:

'Pray, my dear Lord Wheatley, what is the meaning of that word – "jilted"?'

'The meaning of "jilted"?' said Denny. 'He wants to know the meaning of "jilted," Charley.'

I looked from one to the other of them; then I said:

'I think I'll go and ask,' and I started for the door. The captain's expression accused me of rudeness. Denny caught me by the arm.

'It's not decent yet,' said he, with a twinkle in his eye.

'It happened nearly a month ago,' I pleaded. 'I've had time to get over it, Denny; a man can't wear the willow all his life.'

'You old humbug!' said Denny, but let me go. I was not long in going. I darted down the stairs. I suppose a man tricks his conscience and will find excuses for himself where others can find only matter for laughter, but I remember congratulating myself on not having spoken the decisive words to Phroso before Denny interrupted us. Well, I would speak them now. I was free to speak them now. Suddenly, in this thought, the vexation at being jilted vanished.

'It amounts,' said I to myself, as I reached the hall, 'to no more than a fortunate coincidence of opinion.' And I passed through the door and turned sharp round to the left.

She was there waiting for me, and waiting eagerly, it seemed, for, before I could speak, she ran to me, holding out her hands, and she cried in a low urgent whisper, full of entreaty:

'My lord, I have thought. I have thought while you were in the house. You must not do this, my lord. Yes, I know – now I know – that you love me, but you mustn't do this. My lord's honour shan't be stained for my sake.'

I could not resist it, and I cannot justify it. I assumed a terribly sad expression.

'You've really come to that conclusion, Phroso?' I asked.

'Yes. Ah, how difficult it is! But my lord's honour – ah, don't tempt me! You will take me to Athens, won't you? And then – '

'And then,' said I, 'you'll leave me?'

'Yes,' said Phroso, with a little catch in her voice.

'And what shall I do, left alone?'

'Go back,' murmured Phroso almost inaudibly.

'Go back – thinking of those wonderful eyes?'

'No, no. Thinking of – '

'The lady who waits for me over the sea?'

'Yes. And oh, my lord, I pray that you will find happiness!'

There was a moment's silence. Phroso did not look at me; but then I did look at Phroso.

'Then you refuse, Phroso, to have anything to say to me?'

No answer at all reached me; I came nearer, being afraid that I might not have heard her reply.

'What am I to do for a wife, Phroso?' I asked forlornly. 'Because, Phroso –'

'Ah, my lord, why do you take my hand again?'

'Did I, Phroso? Because, Phroso, the lady who waits over the sea – it's a charmingly poetic phrase, upon my word!'

'You laugh!' murmured Phroso, in aggrieved protest and wonder.

'Did I really laugh, Phroso? Well, I'm happy, so I may laugh.'

'Happy?' she whispered; then at last her eyes were drawn to mine in mingled hope and anguish of questioning.

'The lady who waited over the sea,' said I, 'waits no longer, Phroso.'

The wonderful eyes grew more wonderful in their amazed widening; and Phroso, laying a hand gently on my arm, said:

'She waits no longer? My lord, she is dead?'

This confident inference was extremely flattering. There was evidently but one thing which could end the patient waiting of the lady who waited.

'On the contrary she thinks that I am. Constantine spread news of my death.'

'Ah, yes!'

'He said that I died of fever.'

'And she believes it?'

'She does, Phroso; and she appears to be really very sorry.'

'Ah, but what joy will be hers when she learns –'

'But, Phroso, before she thought I was dead, she had made up her mind to wait no longer.'

'To wait no longer? What do you mean? Ah, my lord, tell me what you mean!'

'What has happened to me, here in Neopalia, Phroso?'

'Many strange things, my lord – some most terrible.'

'And some most – most what, Phroso? One thing that has happened to me has, I think, happened also to the lady who waited.'

Phroso's hand – the one I had not taken – was suddenly stretched out, and she spoke in a voice that sounded half-stifled:

'Tell me, my lord, tell me. I can't endure it longer.'

Then I grew grave and said:

'I am free. She has given me my freedom.'

'She has set you free?'

'She loves me no longer, I suppose, if she ever did.'

'Oh, but, my lord, it is impossible.'

'Should you think it so? Phroso, it is true – true that I can come to you now.'

She understood at last. For a moment she was silent, and I, silent also, pierced through the darkness to her wondering face. Once she stretched out her arms; then there came a little, long, low laugh, and she put her hands together, and thrust them, thus clasped, between mine that closed on them.

'My lord, my lord, my lord!' said Phroso.

Suddenly I heard a low mournful chant coming up from the harbour, the moan of mourning voices. The sound struck across the stillness which had followed her last words.

'What's that?' I asked. 'What are they doing down there?'

'Didn't you know? The bodies of my cousin and of Kortes came forth at sunset from the secret pool into which they fell: and they bring them now to bury them by the church. They mourn Kortes because they loved him; and Constantine also they feign to mourn, because he was of the house of the Stefanopouloi.'

We stood for some minutes listening to the chant that rose and fell and echoed among the hills. Its sad cadences, mingled here and there with the note of sustained hope, seemed a fitting end to the story, to the stormy days that were rounded off at last by peace and joy to us who lived, and by the embraces of the all-hiding all-pardoning earth for those who had fallen. I put my arm round Phroso, and, thus at last together, we listened till the sounds died away in low echoes, and silence fell again on the island.

'Ah, the dear island!' said Phroso softly. 'You won't take me away from it for ever? It is my lord's island now, and it will be faithful to him, even as I myself; for God has been very good, and my lord is very good.'

I looked at her. Her cheeks were again wet with tears. As I watched a drop fell from her eyes. I said to her softly:

'That shall be the last, Phroso, till we part again.' A loud cough from the front of the house interrupted us. I advanced, beckoning to Phroso to follow, and wearing, I am afraid, the apologetic look usual under such circumstances. And I found Denny and the captain.

'Are you coming down to the yacht, Charley?' asked Denny.

'Er – in a few minutes, Denny.'

'Shall I wait for you?'

'Oh, I think I can find my way.'

Denny laughed and caught me by the hand; then he passed on to Phroso. I do not, however, know what he said to her, for at this moment the captain touched my shoulder and demanded my attention.

'I beg your pardon,' said he, 'but you never told me the meaning of that word.'

'What word, my dear captain?'

'Why, the word you used of the lady's letter – of what she had done.'

'Oh, you mean "jilted"?'

'Yes; that's it.'

'It is,' said I, after a moment's reflection, 'a word of very various meanings.'

'Ah,' said the captain, with a comprehending nod.

'Yes, very various. In one sense it means to make a man miserable.'

'Yes, I see; to make him unhappy.'

'And in another to make him – to make him, captain, the luckiest beggar alive.'

'It's a strange word,' observed the captain meditatively.

'I don't know about that,' said I. 'Good night.'

22

One More Run

The next morning came bright and beautiful, with a pleasant fresh breeze. It was just the day for a run in the yacht. So I thought when I mounted on deck at eight o'clock in the morning. Watkins was there, staring meditatively at the harbour and the street beyond. Perceiving me, he touched his hat and observed:

'It's a queer little place, my lord,'

My eyes followed the direction of Watkins', and I gave a slight sigh.

'Do you think the island is going to be quiet now, Watkins?' I asked.

I do not think that he quite understood my question, for he said that the weather looked like being fine. I had not meant the weather; my sigh was paid to the ending of Neopalia's exciting caprices; for, though the end was prosperous, I was a little sorry that we had come to the end.

'The Lady Phroso will come on board about ten, and we'll go for a little run,' I said. 'Just look after some lunch.'

'Everything will be ready for your lordship and her ladyship,' said Watkins. Hitherto he had been rather doubtful about Phroso's claim to nobility, but the news of last night planted her firmly in the status of 'ladyship.' 'Has your lordship heard,' he continued, 'that the launch is to carry the Governor's body to Constantinople? There she is by the gunboat.'

'Oh, yes, I see. They seem to be giving the gunboat a rub down, Watkins.'

'Not before it was necessary, my lord. A dirtier deck I never saw.'

The gunboat was evidently enjoying a thorough cleaning; the sailors, half-naked, were scouring her decks, and some of the soldiers were assisting lazily.

'The officers have landed to explore the island, my lord. When Mouraki was alive, they were not allowed to land at all.'

'Mouraki's death makes a good many differences, eh, Watkins?'

'That it does, my lord,' rejoined Watkins, with a decorous smile.

I left him, and, having landed, strolled up to the house. The yacht was to have her steam up ready to start by the time I returned. I sauntered leisurely through the street, such of the islanders as I met saluting me in a most friendly fashion. Certainly times were changed for me in Neopalia, and I chid myself for the ingratitude expressed in my sigh. Neopalia in its new placidity was very pleasant.

Very pleasant also was Phroso, as she came to meet me from the house, radiant and shy. We wasted no time there, but at once returned to the harbour, for the dancing water tempted us: thus we found ourselves on board an hour before the appointed time, and I took Phroso down below to show her the cabin, in which, under the escort of Kortes' sister, she was to make the voyage. Denny looked in on us for a moment, announced that the fires were getting up, and that we could start in half an hour. Hogvardt appeared with his account of expenditure, and disappeared far more quickly. Meanwhile, we talked as lovers will – and ought – about things that do not need record; for, not being worth remembering, they are ever remembered, as is the way of this perverse world.

Presently, however, Denny hailed me, telling me that the captain desired to see me. I begged Phroso to stay where she was – I should be back in a moment – and went on deck. The captain was there, and he began to draw me aside. Perceiving that he had something to say, I proposed to him that we should go to the little smoking-room forward. He acquiesced, and as soon as we were seated, and Watkins had brought coffee and cigarettes, he turned to me with an aspect of sincere gratification, as he said:

'My dear Lord Wheatley, I am rejoiced to tell you that I was quite right as to the view likely to be taken of your position. I have received, by the launch, instructions telegraphed to Rhodes, and they enable me to set you free at once. In point of fact, there is no disposition in official quarters to raise any question concerning your share in recent events. You are, therefore, at liberty to suit your own convenience entirely, and I need not detain you an hour.'

'My dear captain, I'm infinitely obliged to you. I'm much indebted for your good offices.'

'Indeed, no. I merely reported what had occurred. Shall you leave today?'

'Oh, no, not for a day or two. Today, you see, I'm going for a little pleasure expedition. I wish you'd join us;' for I felt in a most friendly mood towards him.

'Indeed I wish I could,' said he, with equal friendliness; 'but I'm obliged to go up to the house at once.'

'To the house? What for?'

'To communicate to the Lady Euphrosyne my instructions concerning her.'

I was about to put a cigarette to my lips, but I stopped, suspending it in mid-air.

'I beg your pardon,' said I, 'but have you instructions concerning her?'

He smiled, and laid a hand on my arm with an apologetic air.

'I don't think that there is any cause for serious uneasiness,' said he, 'though the delay will, I fear, be somewhat irksome to you. I must say, also, that it is impossible – yes, I admit that it is impossible – altogether to ignore the serious disturbances which have occurred; and these Neopalians are old offenders. Still I'm confident that the lady will be most leniently treated, especially in view of the relation in which she now stands to you.'

'What are your instructions?' I asked shortly. 'I am instructed to bring her with me, as soon as I have made provisional arrangements for the order of the island, and to carry her to Smyrna, where I am ordered to sail. From there she will be sent home, to await the result of an inquiry. But, pray, don't be uneasy. I have no doubt at all that she will be acquitted of blame or, at least escape with a reprimand or a nominal penalty. The delay is really the only annoying matter. Annoying to you, I mean, Lord Wheatley.'

'The delay? Is it likely to be serious?'

'Well,' admitted the captain, with a candid air, 'we don't move hastily in these matters; no, our procedure is not rapid. Still I should say that a year, or, well, perhaps eighteen months, would see an end of it. Oh, yes, I really think so.'

'Eighteen months?' I cried, aghast. 'But she'll be my wife long before that – in eighteen days, I hope.'

'Oh, no, no, my dear lord,' said he, shaking his head soothingly. 'She will certainly not be allowed to marry you until these matters are settled. But don't be vexed. You're young. You can afford to wait. What, after all, is a year or eighteen months at your time of life?'

'It's a great deal worse,' said I, 'than at any other time of life.' But he only laughed gently and gulped down the remainder of his coffee. Then he went on in his quiet placid way:

'So I'm afraid I can't join your little excursion. I must go up to the house at once, and acquaint the lady with my instructions. She may have some preparations to make, and I must take her with me the day after tomorrow. As you see, my ship is undergoing some trifling repairs and cleaning, and I can't be ready to start before then.'

I sat silent for a moment or two, smoking my cigarette; and I looked at the placid captain out of the corner of my eye.

'I really hope you aren't much annoyed, my dear Lord Wheatley?' said he, after a moment or two.

'Oh, it's vexatious, of course,' I returned carelessly; 'but I suppose there's no help for it. But, captain, I don't see why you shouldn't join us today. We shall be back in the afternoon, and it will be plenty of time then to inform the Lady Phroso. She's not a fashionable woman who wants forty-eight hours to pack her gowns.'

'It's certainly a lovely morning for a little cruise,' said the captain longingly.

'And I want to point out to you the exact spot where Demetri killed the Pasha.'

'That would certainly be very interesting.'

'Then you'll come?'

'You're certain to be back in time for –?'

'Oh, you'll have plenty of time to talk to Phroso. I'll see to that. You can send a message to her now, if you like.'

'I don't think that's necessary. If I see her this afternoon –'

'I promise you that you shall.'

'But aren't you going to see her today? I thought you would spend the day with her.'

'Oh, I shall hope to see her too; you won't monopolise her, you know. Just now I'm for a cruise.'

'You're a philosophical lover,' he laughed. I laughed also, shrugging my shoulders.

'Then, if you'll excuse me – no, don't move, don't move – I'll give orders for our start, and come back for another cigarette with you.'

'You're most obliging,' said he, and sank back on the seat that ran round the little saloon.

At what particular point in the conversation which I have recorded my resolution was definitely taken, I cannot say, but it was complete and full-blown before the captain accepted my invitation. The certainty of a separation of such monstrous length from Phroso and the chance of her receiving harsh treatment were more than I could consent to contemplate. I must play for my own hand. The island meant to be true to its nature to the last; my departure from it was to be an escape, not a decorous leave-taking. I was almost glad; yet I hoped that I should not get my good friend the captain into serious trouble. Well, better the captain than Phroso, anyhow; and I laughed to myself, when I thought of how I should redeem my promise and give him plenty of time to talk to Phroso.

I ran rapidly up to the deck. Denny and Hogvardt were there.

'How soon can you have full steam up?' I asked in an urgent cautious whisper.

'In ten minutes now,' said Hogvardt, suddenly recognising my eagerness.

'Why, what's up, man?' asked Denny.

'They're going to send Phroso to Constantinople to be tried; anyhow they'd keep her there a year or more. I don't mean to stand it.'

'Why, what will you do?'

'Do? Go. The captain's on board; the gunboat can't overtake us. Besides they won't suspect anything on board of her. Denny, run and tell Phroso not to show herself till I bid her. The captain thinks she's up at the house. We'll start as soon as you're ready, Hog.'

'But, my lord – '

'Charley, old man – !'

'I tell you I won't stand it. Are you game, or aren't you?'

Denny paused for a moment, poising himself on his heels.

'What a lark!' he exclaimed then. 'All right. I'll put Phroso up to it;' and he disappeared in the direction of her cabin.

I stood for a moment looking at the gunboat, where the leisurely operations went on undisturbed, and at the harbour and street beyond. I shook my head reprovingly at Neopalia; the little island was always leading me into indiscretions. Then I turned and made my way back to where my unsuspecting victim was peacefully consuming cigarettes. Mouraki Pasha would not have been caught like this. Heaven be thanked, I was not dealing with Mouraki Pasha.

'Demetri had some good in him, after all,' I thought, as I sat down by the captain, and told him that we should be on our way in five minutes. He exhibited much satisfaction at the prospect.

The five minutes passed. Hogvardt, who acted as our skipper, gave his orders to our new and smiling crew of islanders. We began to move. The captain and I came up from below and stood on deck. He looked seaward, anticipating his excursion, I landward, reviewing mine. A few boys waved their hands, a woman or two her handkerchief. The little harbour began to recede; the old grey house on the hill faced me in its renewed tranquillity.

'Well, goodbye to Neopalia!' I had said, with a sigh, before I knew it.

'I beg your pardon, Lord Wheatley?' said the captain, wheeling round.

'For a few hours,' I added, and I went forward and began to talk with Hogvardt. I had some things to arrange with him. Presently Watkins appeared, announcing luncheon. I rejoined the captain.

'I thought,' said I, 'that we'd have a run straight out first and look at Mouraki's death-place on our way home.'

'I'm entirely in your hands,' said he most courteously, and with more truth than he was aware of.

Denny, he and I went down to our meal. I plied the captain with the best of our cheer. In the safe seclusion of the yacht, the champagne-cup, mixed as Watkins alone could mix it, overcame his religious scruples; the breach, once made, grew wider, and the captain became merry. With his coffee came placidity, and on placidity followed torpor. Meanwhile the yacht bowled merrily along.

'It's nearly two o'clock,' said I. 'We ought to be turning. I say, captain, wouldn't you like a nap? I'll wake you long before we get to Neopalia.'

Denny smiled indiscreetly at this form of promise, and I covertly nudged him into gravity.

The captain received my proposal with apologetic gratitude. We left him curled up on the seat and went on deck. Hogvardt was at the wheel; a broad smile spread over his face.

'At this rate, my lord,' said he, 'we shall make Cyprus in no time.'

'Good,' said I; and I did two things. I called Phroso and I loaded my revolver; a show of overwhelming force is, as we often hear, the surest guarantee of peace.

Denny now took a turn at the wheel; old Hogvardt went to eat his dinner. Phroso appeared, and she and I sat down in the stern, watching where Neopalia lay, now a little spot on the horizon; and then I myself told Phroso, in my own way, why I had so sorely neglected her all the morning; for Denny's explanation had been summary and confused. She was fully entitled to my excuses and had come on deck in a state of delightful resentment, too soon, alas, banished by surprise and apprehension.

An hour or two passed thus very pleasantly; for the terror of Constantinople soon reconciled Phroso to every risk; her only fear was that she would never again be allowed to land in Neopalia. For this also I tried to console her and was, I am proud to say, succeeding very tolerably, when I looked up at the sound of footsteps. They came evenly towards us: then they suddenly stopped dead. I felt for my revolver; and I observed Denny carelessly strolling up, having been relieved again by Hogvardt. The captain stood motionless, three yards from where Phroso and I sat together. I rose with an easy smile.

'I hope you've enjoyed your nap, captain,' said I; and at the same moment I covered him with my barrel.

He was astounded. Indeed, well he might be. He stared helplessly at Phroso and at me. Denny was at his elbow now and took his arm in tolerant good humour.

'You see we've played a little game on you,' said Denny. 'We couldn't let the lady go to Constantinople. It isn't at all a fit place for her, you know.'

I stepped up to the amazed man and told him briefly what had occurred.

'Now, captain,' I went on, 'resistance is quite useless. We're running for Cyprus. It belongs to you, I believe, in a sense – I'm not a student of foreign affairs – but I think we shall very likely find an English ship there. Now if you'll give your word to hold your tongue when we're at Cyprus, you may lodge as many complaints as you like directly we leave; indeed I think you'd be wise, in your own interests, to make a protest. Meanwhile we can enjoy the cruise in good fellowship.'

'And if I refuse?' he asked.

'If you refuse,' said I, 'I shall be compelled to get rid of you – oh, don't misunderstand me. I shall not imitate your Governor. But it's a fine day, we have an excellent gig, and I can spare you two hands to row you back to Neopalia or wherever else you may choose to go.'

'You would leave me in the gig?'

'With the deepest regret,' said I, bowing. 'But I am obliged to put this lady's safety above the pleasure of your society.'

The unfortunate man had no alternative and, true to the creed of his nation, he accepted the inevitable. Taking the cigarette from between his lips, he remarked, 'I give the promise you ask, but nothing more,' bowed to Phroso, and, going up to her, said very prettily, 'Madame I congratulate you on a resolute lover.'

Now hardly had this happened when our lookout man called twice in quick succession, 'Ship ahead!' At once we all ran forward, and I snatched Denny's binocular from him. There were two vessels visible, one approaching on the starboard bow, the other right ahead. They appeared to be about equally distant.

I scanned them eagerly through the glass, the others standing round and waiting my report. Nearer they came, and nearer.

'They're both ships of war,' said I, without taking the glass from my eyes. 'I shall be able to see the flags in a minute.'

A hush of excited suspense witnessed to the interest of my news. I found even the impassive captain close by my elbow, as though he were trying to get one eye on to the lens of the glass.

My next remark did nothing to lessen the excitement.

'The Turkish flag, by Jove!' I cried; and, quick as thought, followed from the captain:

'My promise didn't cover that, Lord Wheatley.'

'Shall we turn and run for it!' asked Denny in a whisper.

'They'd think that queer,' cautioned Hogvardt, 'and if she came after us, we shouldn't have a chance.'

'The English flag, by Jupiter!' I cried a second later, and I took the glass from my strained eyes. The captain caught eagerly at it and looked; then he also dropped it, saying,

'Yes, Turkish and English; both will come within hail of us.'

'It's a race, by Heaven!' cried Denny.

The two vessels were approaching us almost on the same course, for each had altered half a point, and both were now about half a point on our starboard bow. They would be very close to one another by the time they came up with us. It would be almost impossible for us by any alteration of our course to reach one before the other.

'Yes, it's a race,' said I, and I felt Phroso's arm passed through mine. She knew the meaning of the race. Possession is nine points of the law, and in a case so doubtful as hers it was very unlikely that the ship which got possession of her would surrender her to the other. Which ship was it to be?

'Are we going to cause an international complication?' asked Denny in a longing tone.

'We shall very likely run into a nautical one if we don't look out,' said I.

However the two approaching vessels seemed to become aware of this danger, for they diverged from one another, so that, if we kept a straight course, we should now pass them by, one on the port side and one on the starboard. But we should pass within a couple of hundred yards of both, and that was well in earshot on such a day. I looked at the captain, and the captain looked at me.

'Shall we take him below and smother him?' whispered Denny.

I did not feel at liberty to adopt the suggestion, much to my regret. The agreement I had made with the captain precluded any assault on his liberty. I had omitted to provide for the case which had occurred. Well, that was my fault, and I must stand the consequences of it. My word was pledged to him that he should be treated in all friendliness on one condition, and that he had satisfied. Now to act as Denny suggested would not be to treat him in all friendliness. I shook my head sadly. Hogvardt shouted for orders from the wheel.

'What am I to do, my lord?' he cried. 'Full speed ahead?'

I looked at the captain. I knew he would not pass the Turkish ship without trying to attract her attention. We were within a quarter of a mile of the vessels now.

'Stop,' I called, and I added quickly, 'Lower away the gig, Denny.'

Denny caught my purpose in a moment; he called a hand and they set to work. The pace of the yacht began to slacken. I glanced at the two ships. Men with glasses were peering at us from either deck, wondering, no doubt, what our manoeuvre meant. But the captain knew as well as Denny what it meant, and he leapt forward suddenly and hailed the Turk in his native tongue. What he said I don't know, but it caused a great pother on deck, and they ran up some signal or other; I never remember the code, and the book was not about me.

But now the gig was afloat and the yacht motionless. Looking again, I perceived that both the ships had shut off steam, and were reversing, to arrest their course the sooner. I seized Phroso by the arm. The captain turned for a moment as though to interrupt our passage.

'It's as much as your life is worth,' said I, and he gave way. Then, to my amazement, he ran to the side, and, just as he was, leapt overboard and struck out towards the Turk. One instant later I saw why: they were lowering a boat. Alas, our ship was not so eager. The captain must have shouted something very significant.

'Signal for a boat, Hog,' I cried. 'And then come along. Hi, Watkins, come on! Are you ready, Denny?' And I fairly lifted Phroso in my arms and ran with her to the side. She was breathing quickly, and a little laugh gurgled from her lips as Denny received her from my arms into his in the gig.

But we were not safe yet. The Turk had got a start, and his boat was springing merrily over the waves towards us. The captain swam powerfully and gallantly; his fez-covered head bobbed gaily up and down. Ah, now our people were moving! And when they began to move they wasted no time. We wasted none either, but bent to our oars, and, for the second time since I reached Neopalia, I had a thorough good bucketing. But for the Turk's start we should have managed it easily, as we rowed towards the English boat and the divergence which the vessels had made in their course prevented the two from approaching us side by side; but the start was enough to make matters very equal. Now the boat and the captain met. He was in in a second, with wonderful agility; picking him up hardly lost them a stroke. They were coming straight at us, the captain standing in the stern urging them on; but now I saw that the middy in the English boat had caught the idea that there was some fun afoot, for he also stood up and urged on his crew. The two great ships lay motionless on the water, and gave us all their attention.

'Pull, boys, pull!' I cried. 'It's all right, Phroso, we shall do it!'

Should we? And, if we did not, would the English captain fight for my Phroso? I would have sunk the Turk, with a laugh, for her. But I was afraid that he would not be so obliging as to do it for me.

'The Turk gains,' said Hogvardt, who was our coxswain.

'Hang him! Put your backs into it.'

On went the three boats. The two pursuers were now converging close on us.

'We shall do it by a few yards,' said Hogvardt.

'Thank God!' I muttered.

'No; we shall be beaten by a few yards,' he said, a moment later. 'They pull well, those fellows.'

But we too pulled well then – though I have no right to say it – and the good little middy and his men did their duty – oh, what a tip these bluejackets should have if they did the trick! – and the noses of all the boats seemed to be tending to one spot on the bright dancing sea. To one spot, indeed, they were tending. The Turks were no more than twenty yards off, the English perhaps thirty. The captain gave one last cry of exhortation, the middy responded with a hearty oath. We strained and tugged for dear life. They were on us now – the Turks a little first. Now they were ten yards off – now five – and the English yet ten.

But for a last stroke we pulled; and then I dropped my oars and sprang to my feet. The nose of the captain's boat was within a yard, and they were backing water so as not to run into us. The middy had given a like order. For a single instant matters seemed to stand still and we to be poised between defeat and victory. Then, even as the captain's hand was on our gunwale, I bent and caught Phroso up in the arms that she sprang to meet, and I fairly flung her across the narrow strait of water that parted us from the English boat. Six strong and eager arms received her, and a cheer rang out from the English ship, for they saw now that it had been a race, and a race for a lady; and I, seeing her safe, turned to the captain, and said:

'Fetch her back from there, if you can, and be damned to you!'

23

The Island in a Calm

We did not fight. My friend the captain proposed to rely on his British *confrère's* sense of justice and of the courtesy which should obtain between two great and friendly nations. To this end he accompanied us on board the ship and laid his case before Captain Beverley, RN. My argument, which I stated with brevity, but not without vehemence, was threefold: first, that Phroso had committed no offence; secondly, that if she had, it was a political offence; thirdly, was Captain Beverley going to hand over to a crew of dirty Turks the prettiest girl in the Mediterranean? This last point made a decided impression on the officers who were assisting their commander's deliberations, but it won from him no more than a tolerant smile and a glance through his pince-nez at Phroso, who sat at the table opposite to him, awaiting the award of justice. After I had, in the heat of discussion, called the Turks 'dirty,' I moved round to my friend the captain, apologised humbly, and congratulated him on his gallant and spirited behaviour. He received my advances with courtesy, but firmly restated his claim to Phroso. Captain Beverley appeared a little puzzled.

'And, to add to it all,' he observed to me, 'I thought you were dead;' for I had told him my name.

'Not at all,' said I, resentfully; 'I am quite alive, and I'm going to marry this lady.'

'You intend to marry her, Lord Wheatley?'

'She has done me the honour to consent and I certainly intend it; unless you're going to send her off to Constantinople – or heaven knows where.'

Beverley arched his brows, but it was not his business to express an opinion, and I heartily forgave him his hinted disapproval, when he said to the captain:

'I really don't see how I can do what you ask. If you had won the tr – I mean, if you had succeeded in taking the lady on board, I should have had no more to say. As it is, I don't think I can do anything but carry her to a British port. You can prefer your claim to extradition before the Court there, if you're so advised.'

'Bravo!' cried Denny.

'Be good enough to hold your tongue, sir,' said Captain Beverley.

'At least, you will take a note of my demand,' urged the Turk.

'With the utmost pleasure,' responded Captain Beverley, and then and there he took a note. People seem often to find some mystical comfort in having a note taken, though no other consequence appears likely to ensue. Then the captain, being comforted by his note, took his farewell. I walked with him to the side of the vessel.

'I hope you bear no malice,' said I, as I held out my hand, 'and that this affair won't get you into any trouble.'

'Oh, I don't think so,' said he. 'Your ingenuity will be my excuse.'

'You're very good. I hope you'll come and see us in Neopalia some day.'

'You expect to return to Neopalia?'

'Certainly. It's mine – or Phroso's – I don't know which.'

'There's such a thing as forfeiture in our law,' he observed, and with this Parthian shot he walked down and got into his boat. But I was not much frightened.

So, the Turk being thus disposed of, Denny and Hogvardt went back to the yacht, while Phroso, Watkins and I, took up our abode on the ship, and when Captain Beverley had heard the whole story of our adventures in Neopalia he was so overcome by Phroso's gallant conduct that he walked up and down his own deck with her all the evening, while I, making friends with the mammon of unrighteousness, pretended to look very pleased and recited my dealings with Mouraki to an attentive group of officers. And clothes were produced from somewhere for Phroso – our navy is ready for everything – and thus, in the fullness of time, we came to Malta. Here the captain had a wife, and she was as delighted as, I take leave to say, all good women ought to be at the happy ending of our story. And at Malta we waited; but nothing happened. No claim was made for Phroso's extradition; and I may as well state here that no claim ever has been made. But when we came to London, on board a P and O steamer, in charge of a benevolent but strict chaperon, I lost no time in calling on the Turkish Ambassador. I desired to put matters on a satisfactory footing at once, He received me with much courtesy, but expressed the opinion that Phroso and I alike had forfeited any claim which she or I, or either, or both of us, might have possessed to the Island of Neopalia. I was very much annoyed at this attitude; I rose and stood with my back to the fire.

'It is the death of Mouraki Pasha that has so incensed your Government?' I ventured to ask.

'He was a very distinguished man,' observed the Ambassador.

'Practically banished to a very undistinguished office – for his position,' I remarked.

'One would not call it banishment,' murmured his Excellency.

'One would,' I acquiesced, smiling, 'of course, be particularly careful not to call it banishment.'

Something like a smile greeted this speech, but the Ambassador shrugged his shoulders.

'Consider,' said he, 'the scenes of disorder and bloodshed!'

'When I consider,' I rejoined, 'the scenes of disorder and bloodshed which passed before my eyes, when I consider the anarchy, the murder, the terrible dangers to which I, who went to Neopalia under the sanction and protection of your flag, was exposed, I perceive that the whole affair is nothing less than a European scandal.'

The Ambassador shifted in his armchair.

'I shall, of course,' said I, 'prefer a claim to compensation.'

'To compensation?'

'Certainly. My island has been taken from me, and I have lost my money. Moreover your Governor tried to kill me.'

'So did your wife,' remarked the Pasha. 'At least the lady who, as I understand, is to be your wife.'

'I can forgive my wife. I do not propose to forgive your Government.'

The Ambassador stroked his beard.

'If official representations were made through the proper quarters – ' he began.

'Oh, come,' I interrupted, 'I want to spend my honeymoon there; and I'm going to be married in a fortnight.'

'The young lady is the difficulty. The manner in which you left Neopalia – '

'Is not generally known,' said I.

The Ambassador looked up.

'The tribute,' I observed, 'is due a month hence. I don't know who'll pay it you.'

'It is but a trifling sum,' said he contemptuously. 'It is, indeed, small for such a delightful island.' The Ambassador eyed me questioningly. I advanced towards him.

'Considering,' said I, 'that I have only paid half the purchase-money, and that the other half is due to nobody – or to my own wife – I should not resent a proposal to double the tribute.'

The Ambassador reflected.

'I will forward your proposal to the proper quarter,' he said at last.

I smiled, and I asked:

'Will that take more than a fortnight?'

'I venture to hope not.'

'And, of course, pardon and all that sort of thing will be included?'

'I will appeal to his Majesty's clemency,' promised the Pasha.

I had no objection to his calling it by that name, and I took my leave, very much pleased with the result of the interview. But, as luck would have it, while I was pursuing my way across Hyde Park – for Phroso was staying with a friend of Mrs Beverley's in Kensington – I ran plump into the arms of Mrs Kennett Hipgrave.

She stopped me with decision. I confess that I tried to pass by her.

'My dear Lord Wheatley,' she cried, with unbounded cordiality, 'how charming to meet you again! Your reported death really caused quite a gloom.'

'You're too good!' I murmured. 'Ah – er – I hope Miss Beatrice is well?'

Mrs Kennett Hipgrave's face grew grave and sympathetic.

'My poor child!' she sighed. 'She was terribly upset by the news, Lord Wheatley. Of course, it seemed to her peculiarly sad; for you had received my letter only a week before.'

'That must have seemed to aggravate the pathos very much,' I agreed.

'Not that, of course, it altered the real wisdom of the step I advised her to take.'

'Not in the least, really, of course,' said I.

'I do hope you agree with me now, Lord Wheatley?'

'Yes, I think I have come to see that you were right, Mrs Hipgrave.'

'Oh, that makes me so happy! And it will make my poor dear child so happy, too. I assure you she has fretted very much over it.'

'I'm sorry to hear that,' said I politely. 'Is she in town?'

'Why, no, not just now.'

'Where is she? I should like to write her a line.'

'Oh, she's staying with friends.'

'Could you oblige me with the address?'

'Well, the fact is, Lord Wheatley, Beatrice is staying with – with a Mrs Hamlyn.'

'Oh, a Mrs Hamlyn! Any relation, Mrs Hipgrave?'

'Well, yes. In fact, an aunt of our common friend.'

'Ah, an aunt of our common friend,' and I smiled. Mrs Hipgrave struggled nobly, but in the end she smiled also. After a little pause I remarked:

'I'm going to be married myself, Mrs Hipgrave.' Mrs Hipgrave grew rather grave again, and she observed:

'I did hear something about a – a lady, Lord Wheatley.'

'If you had heard it all, you'd have heard a great deal about her.'

A certain appearance of embarrassment spread over Mrs Hipgrave's face.

'We're old friends, Lord Wheatley,' she said at last. I bowed in grateful recognition. 'I'm sure you won't mind if I speak plainly to you. Now is she the sort of person whom you would be really wise to marry? Remember, your wife will be Lady Wheatley.'

'I had not forgotten that that would happen,' I said.

'I'm told,' pursued Mrs Hipgrave in a somewhat scornful tone, 'that she is very pretty.'

'But, then, that's not really of importance, is it?' I murmured.

Mrs Hipgrave looked at me with just a touch of suspicion; but she went on bravely:

'And one or two very curious things have been said.'

'Not to me,' I observed with infinite amiability.

'Her family now – '

'Her family was certainly a drawback; but there are no more of them, Mrs Hipgrave.'

'Then somebody told me that she was in the habit of wearing – '

'Dear me, Mrs Hipgrave, in these days everybody does that – more or less, you know.'

Mrs Hipgrave sighed pathetically, and added, with a slight shudder:

'They say she carried a dagger.'

'They'll say anything,' I reminded her.

'At any rate,' said Mrs Hipgrave, 'she will be quite unused to the ways of society.'

'Oh, we shall teach her, we shall teach her,' said I cheerfully. 'After all, it's only a difference of method. When people in Neopalia are annoyed, they put a knife into you –'

'Good gracious, Lord Wheatley!'

'Here,' I pursued, 'they congratulate you; but it's the same principle. Won't you wish me joy, Mrs Hipgrave?'

'If you're really bent upon it, I suppose I must.'

'And you'll tell the dear children?' I asked anxiously.

'The dear children?' she echoed; she certainly suspected me by now.

'Why, yes. Your daughter and Bennett Hamlyn, you know.'

Mrs Hipgrave surveyed me from top to toe. Her aspect was very severe; then she delivered herself of the following remark:

'I can never be sufficiently thankful,' she said, with eyes upturned towards the sky, 'that my poor dear girl found out her mistake in time.'

'I have the utmost regard for Miss Beatrice,' I rejoined, 'but I will not differ from you, Mrs Hipgrave.'

I must shift the scene again back to the island that I loved. For his Majesty's clemency justified the Ambassador's belief in it, and Neopalia was restored to Phroso and to me. Thither we went in the spring of the next year, leaving Denny inconsolable behind, but accompanied by old Hogvardt and by Watkins. This time we went straight out by sea from England, and the new crew of my yacht was more trustworthy than when Spiro and Demetri (ah, I had nearly written 'poor Demetri,' when the fellow was a murderer!) were sent by the cunning of Constantine Stefanopoulos to compose it. We landed this time to meet no threatening looks. The death-chant that One-eyed Alexander wrote was not raised when we entered the old grey house on the hill, looking over the blue waters. Ulysses is fabled by the poet to have – well, to put it plainly – to have grown bored with peaceful Ithaca, I do not know whether I shall prove an Ulysses in that and live to regret the new-born tranquillity of Neopalia. In candour, the early stormy days have a great attraction, and I love to look back to them in memory. So strong was this feeling upon me that it led me to refuse a request of my wife's – the only one of hers which I have yet met in that fashion; for when we had been two or three days in the island – I spent one, by the way, in visiting the graves of my dead friends and enemies, a most suggestive and soothing occupation – I saw, as I walked with her through the hall of our house, mason's tools and mortar lying near where the staircase led up, hard by the secret door; and Phroso said to me:

'I'm sure you'd like to have that horrible secret passage blocked up, Charley. It's full of terrible memories.'

'My dear Phroso, wall up the passage?'

'We shan't want it now,' said she, with a laugh – and something else.

'It's true,' I admitted, 'that I intend, as far as possible, to rule by constitutional means in Neopalia. Still one never knows. My dearest, have you no romance?'

'No,' said Phroso shamelessly. 'I've had enough romance. I want to live quietly; and I don't want to push anyone over into that awful pool where poor Kortes fell.'

I stood looking at the boards under the staircase. Presently I knelt down and touched the spring. The boards rolled away, the passage gaped before us, and I put my arm round Phroso as I said:

'Now heaven forbid that I should lay a modern sacrilegious hand on the secret of the Stefanopouloi! For the world makes many circles, Phroso – forward sometimes, sometimes back – and it is something to know that here, in Neopalia, we are ready, and that if any man attacks our sovereignty, why, let him look out for the secret of the Stefanopouloi! In certain moods, Phroso, I should be capable of coming back from the chasm – alone!'

So Phroso, on my entreaty, spared the passage; and even now, when the shades of middle age (a plague on 'em) are deepening, and the wild doings of the purchaser of Neopalia grow golden in distant memory, I like to walk to the end of the chasm and recall all that it has seen: the contests, the dark tricks, the sudden deaths, aye, to travel back from the fearful struggle of Kortes and Constantine on the flying bridge to that long-ago time when the Baron d'Ezonville was so lucky as to be set adrift in his shirt, while Stefan Stefanopoulos' headless trunk was dashed into the dim water and One-eyed Alexander the Bard wrote the Chant of Death. Ah me, that was two hundred years ago!

Anthony Hope

Helena's Path

The dashing and adventurous Lord Lynborough decides to give up his post in the Grenadier Guards in order to write his autobiography. And so he travels to the magnificent castle at Scarsmoor to take up residence. But little does he realise that trouble is not far away. This trouble comes in the shape of the beautiful Helena Vittoria Maria Antonia, Marchesa di San Servolo. When Lynborough learns that the volatile but charming Helena has closed his Beach Path, he is determined to retain his right of way. Passions flare as the tension between the two surly young rivals becomes all too apparent and Lord Lynborough and the Marchesa engage in a heated battle for 'Helena's Path'.

The Prisoner of Zenda

The hero of this classic swashbuckling romance, English gentleman Rudolf Rassendyll, is transported from a comfortable life in London to extraordinary adventures in Ruritania, a mythical land. Rassendyll bears an uncanny resemblance to Rudolf Elphberg, who is about to be crowned King of Ruritania; and when Elphberg's rival, the villainous Black Michael of Strelsau, attempts to seize power, Rassendyll impersonates the King to uphold the rightful sovereignty and ensure political stability. The redoubtable Rassendyll endures a trial of strength in his encounters with the infamous Rupert of Hentzau, and a quite different test as he grows to love the Princess Flavia.

Anthony Hope

Rupert of Hentzau

With the death of Black Michael of Strelsau and the restoration of King Rudolf to the throne, the troubles of Ruritania may seem to be at an end. But lasting peace cannot be secure when the notorious Rupert of Hentzau is still at large. Until now he has dared not set foot in the kingdom, but the incentives to return are impossible for Hentzau to resist – Ruritania remains under threat from this devious enemy. And trouble of a different kind exists in the hearts of Princess Flavia, now Queen, her husband, the tortured King, and the man she truly loves, Rudolf Rassendyll.

Simon Dale

England, 1647: a wise woman has predicted the birth of Simon Dale, to the very day and district. But if the rest of her ominous forecast is accurate, how can this ordinary child be predestined to love where the King loved, know what the King hid, and drink of the King's cup? For the young man, Simon Dale, only one course of action can be taken: not to seek his own path, but to leave himself in the hands of Fate.

This brilliant novel charts an absorbing period in history and the tumultuous life of an ordinary man in noble surrounds.

Anthony Hope

Sophy of Kravonia

A young, beautiful maidservant, Sophy Grouch, born into an unassuming family, spreads her wings and embarks on a life-changing journey, first to Paris and then to a Balkan principality. This poignant tale, set in the nineteenth century, is enriched with history and romance and tells of the love, courage and vivacity that stirred ordinary Sophy from her roots and transformed her into Sophy of Kravonia.

OTHER TITLES BY ANTHONY HOPE AVAILABLE DIRECT FROM HOUSE OF STRATUS

Quantity		£	$(US)	$(CAN)	€
☐	HELENA'S PATH	6.99	12.95	19.95	13.50
☐	THE PRISONER OF ZENDA	6.99	12.95	19.95	13.50
☐	RUPERT OF HENTZAU	6.99	12.95	19.95	13.50
☐	SIMON DALE	6.99	12.95	19.95	13.50
☐	SOPHY OF KRAVONIA	6.99	12.95	19.95	13.50

ALL HOUSE OF STRATUS BOOKS ARE AVAILABLE FROM GOOD BOOKSHOPS
OR DIRECT FROM THE PUBLISHER:

Internet: www.houseofstratus.com including synopses and features.

Email: sales@houseofstratus.com
info@houseofstratus.com
(please quote author, title and credit card details.)

Tel: Order Line
0800 169 1780 (UK)
1 800 724 1100 (USA)
International
+44 (0) 1845 527700 (UK)
+01   845 463 1100 (USA)

Fax: +44 (0) 1845 527711 (UK)
+01   845 463 0018 (USA)
(please quote author, title and credit card details.)

Send to: House of Stratus Sales Department   House of Stratus Inc.
Thirsk Industrial Park   2 Neptune Road
York Road, Thirsk   Poughkeepsie
North Yorkshire, YO7 3BX   NY 12601
UK   USA

PAYMENT

Please tick currency you wish to use:

☐ £ (Sterling)   ☐ $ (US)   ☐ $ (CAN)   ☐ € (Euros)

Allow for shipping costs charged per order plus an amount per book as set out in the tables below:

CURRENCY/DESTINATION

	£(Sterling)	$(US)	$(CAN)	€(Euros)
Cost per order				
UK	1.50	2.25	3.50	2.50
Europe	3.00	4.50	6.75	5.00
North America	3.00	3.50	5.25	5.00
Rest of World	3.00	4.50	6.75	5.00
Additional cost per book				
UK	0.50	0.75	1.15	0.85
Europe	1.00	1.50	2.25	1.70
North America	1.00	1.00	1.50	1.70
Rest of World	1.50	2.25	3.50	3.00

PLEASE SEND CHEQUE OR INTERNATIONAL MONEY ORDER
payable to: HOUSE OF STRATUS LTD or HOUSE OF STRATUS INC. or card payment as indicated

STERLING EXAMPLE

Cost of book(s): .... Example: 3 x books at £6.99 each: £20.97
Cost of order: .... Example: £1.50 (Delivery to UK address)
Additional cost per book: .... Example: 3 x £0.50: £1.50
Order total including shipping: .... Example: £23.97

VISA, MASTERCARD, SWITCH, AMEX:

☐☐☐☐☐☐☐☐☐☐☐☐☐☐☐☐☐☐☐☐

Issue number (Switch only):
☐☐☐

Start Date: **Expiry Date:**
☐☐/☐☐   ☐☐/☐☐

Signature: _____

NAME: _____

ADDRESS: _____

COUNTRY: _____

ZIP/POSTCODE: _____

Please allow 28 days for delivery. Despatch normally within 48 hours.

Prices subject to change without notice.
Please tick box if you do not wish to receive any additional information. ☐

House of Stratus publishes many other titles in this genre; please check our website (**www.houseofstratus.com**) for more details.